B. M. Howard is an internationally recognised and locally neglected historian and storyteller. His profound interest in the shadowy fringes of history lies in uncovering the unre-membered and obscured protagonists who fiddled unseen at the levers of power. He hides out in the Tuscan foothills while recording his characters' next foray into troubled waters.

Also by B. M. Howard

The Gracchus & Vanderville Mysteries

Blood and Fireflies
Blood on the Tiber
Blood of the Knights

B. M. HOWARD

BLOOD OF THE *Knights*

CANELO

First published in the United Kingdom in 2024 by

Canelo
Unit 9, 5th Floor
Cargo Works, 1–2 Hatfields
London SE1 9PG
United Kingdom

Copyright © B. M. Howard 2024

The moral right of B. M. Howard to be identified as the creator of this work has been asserted in accordance with the Copyright, Designs and Patents Act, 1988.

All rights reserved. No part of this publication may be reproduced or transmitted in any form or by any means, electronic or mechanical, including photocopy, recording, or any information storage and retrieval system, without permission in writing from the publisher.

A CIP catalogue record for this book is available from the British Library.

Print ISBN 978 1 80436 274 7
Ebook ISBN 978 1 80436 273 0

This book is a work of fiction. Names, characters, businesses, organizations, places and events are either the product of the author's imagination or are used fictitiously. Any resemblance to actual persons, living or dead, events or locales is entirely coincidental.

Cover design by Head Design

Look for more great books at www.canelo.co

Printed and bound in Great Britain by Clays Ltd, Elcograf S.p.A.

Dramatis Personae

In 1797 the French Republic still maintained the revolutionary terms *citoyen* and *citoyenne* as alternatives to *monsieur/madam*, or titles of nobility. In the army, and in the fledgling republics of north Italy, these terms were used simultaneously with rank or other titles, hence *Citoyen* general, or *Citoyen* Pope. The Knights of Malta addressed one another as Fra' – a contraction of Frate meaning brother. Others addressed them by their preferred distinguishing knightly title *cavaliere*.

The French

Felix Gracchus. Retired magistrate and disillusioned revolutionary.

Lieutenant Dermide Vanderville. French officer.

Lieutenant Domingo Hercule. French officer.

The Knights

Ferdinand von Hompesch. Grandmaster of the Knights of Malta.

Emmanuel von Torring. Bailli of the Bavarian *langue*.

Joseph de Rechberg. Knight of the Bavarian *langue*.

Ferdinand Haintlet. Knight of the Bavarian *langue*.

Ludwig von Seeau. Knight of the Bavarian *langue*.

The Maltese

Vassallo. Maltese Renegade in French pay.

Eva Mifsud. Public woman.

La Baida. Public woman.

Rais Murad. Ship's captain. Duccio. Leader of the *Fraternita delle Forbici*.

Granchio. Co-leader of the *Fraternita delle Forbici*.

Franca. Member of the *Fraternita delle Forbici*.

The Church

Inquisitore Carpegna. Head of the Holy Office.

Canon Gatt. Assessore of the Holy Office.

Don Stecchi. Prete of the Maddalene.

Chapter One

Mediterranean Sea, 15 Prairial, Year six of the Republic (3 June 1798)

'I have been in far worse situations,' Lieutenant Vanderville repeated to himself without conviction for the third time. The mantra was patently false and failed to provide even the barest scrap of reassurance, but the dismal repetition served to keep the full dread of his situation from further paralysing his already numb limbs.

Born in Paris, Vanderville was never a natural sailor at the best of times, so to find himself clinging in darkness to the lower yardarm that crossed the main mast of the frigate Carrère exceeded what he was comfortable with by some way. The horizontal yard pressed hard into his wavering stomach, the rope stays his feet rested on groaned and swayed alarmingly and the eyeholes in the sails above him whistled in the light wind. To increase his discomfort, from a long, long drop below him came the rushing sound of the sea slipping past the frigate's hull. Dawn was balanced on the horizon and the water was still black except far ahead of the ship where the breakers flashed white on unseen rocks below the distant fortress walls.

It had seemed a not unreasonable scheme as Vassallo had unfurled it the night before while they huddled in the captain's cabin over a bottle. Vassallo was a renegade Maltese patriot, familiar with the Maltese island kingdom of the Knights of St John, and he had claimed to know the capital city of Valletta in particular, "better than my own mother's breast." That was as well for he had undertaken to conduct Vanderville over the walls of Valletta's legendary fortifications unseen. In the exultation of his cups, he had laughed at Vanderville's trepidation and exclaimed that the leap from the ship to the bastion would be as easy as kiss my hand.

The only note of reassurance Vanderville found in his recollection of the planning was Captain Dumanoir's steady voice and clear head agreeing that yes, it might be done. If the channel permitted of the frigate being brought close enough to the foot of St Gregory's bastion, he avowed he would do it, and it was his suggestion that the stunsail booms were set, gaining a few crucial metres more.

The nautical terminology had left Vanderville all at sea, but now he appreciated that Dumanoir had extended the yards outwards a little more, leaving him further from the security of the mast, but bringing him closer to the fort. Their calculations were that the yardarm's tips would reach within mere feet of the bastion's walls, almost graze them in fact, and Vassallo had asserted that it would be nothing but a matter of stepping from the yard boom onto the parapet like a lady tripping into chapel.

Brandy had rendered them all bold in the final stages of planning, but now, in the faint dawn, there was nothing left of the fire in his own stomach but fumes, and nothing remained of his confidence except a hollow resolve seasoned with misgiving. Shivering on the boom, Vanderville wondered if Vassallo's insides felt as rotten as his own did, and if the Maltese's bravado had survived the previous evening's intoxication. He peered at the yards of the foremast ahead of him and thought that he could just dimly make out the shape of Vassallo fervently clutching onto his own peculiarly elongated yard. At least he would not be the first to jump, he reasoned.

The shadowy mass of Fort Sant' Elmo was directly ahead of them now, seen in the gathering quarter-light, its jutting angles ominous and massive against the sky and its lighthouse tower looming over all. The safe roadstead of the Grand Harbour was to the left of the fortress, but they were to pass to the right along its flanks to enter the lesser harbour of Marsamuscetto where the quarantine station would certify the frigate, and doubtless lambast them for their precipitate entry into the roads.

Vassallo had told them that in the state of heightened tension pervading the capital, Valletta would be locked down, and the gates well-guarded, rendering it impossible for intelligence agents to penetrate the knight's fortified city from landward. No, he had asserted, the best route, the safest route, was to avoid the gate sentinels' scrutiny by entering from seaward, over the parapets. There was a way to make this feasible, he had said, and he had made the necessary arrangements.

The schedule of the patrols on the walls had been obtained for a handful of scudos in Sant' Elmo's tavern; distractions had been arranged for the patrolling soldiers of the Maltese Regiment in the form of several dingy tavern drabs. All this information was brought off by Vassallo's compatriots in a fishing boat that had rendezvoused with the frigate the day before. Having stood the frigate well over Captain Dumanoir hove her to and waited for night scant leagues to the west of the Grand Harbour. Dumanoir had explained that no vessel was permitted to enter or leave the roadstead before sunrise, or after sunset. The signal of permission was a flag hoisted on the fort when a ship entered the roads, but in this dawn, he would flout the regulation to bring them in just before first light. The Maltese knew that a great French fleet was at sea, its intentions unknown, although rumour abounded. One ominous version warned that the islands of Malta were its destination and the knights who ruled the country had no intention of being caught unaware by its arrival. In these circumstances a single small ship might be allowed to slip in and out at irregular hours, mistaken for one of the despatch vessels bringing news of the armada.

Once inside the fortress of Sant' Elmo, Vanderville and Vassallo would make their way from the bastions along the winding curtain wall, and from there descend from the fortress into Valletta proper. The Convent city protected by the great fort would be breached from the seaward side. But first they had to leap from the yards of the ship onto a perpendicular face of the fortress wall. It had been done before, Vassallo had reminisced, with his eyes half closed against the reeking smoke of Dumanoir's pipe that filled the ship's cabin.

'By one of your compatriots?' Vanderville asked.

'No,' responded the renegade. 'By a Turk during the great siege of 1565.' Later, when Vassallo had been carried to his hammock, Vanderville walked with the captain on the quarterdeck. Vanderville had doubted the value of this romantic story and privately Dumanoir had concurred.

'I have heard the tale. Legend has it that the Moor made the leap from a ship moored close by the ramparts, whereas you will be leaping from the yard of a ship in motion.' He chuckled. 'In any case, the lower *enceinte* was not conceived of until long after the siege. So the story is necessarily false in that respect. However,' he had continued, stuffing his pipe with more of the curious black Indian tobacco mix he favoured, 'I know the harbour roads well enough to say that it may be just possible, and if, as I understand it, speed is of the essence, this is undoubtably the most rapid, as well as the most discrete, way of effecting an entry to the city. Besides which, the main land gate to Valletta will be heavily guarded, whereas no one will expect an infiltration from the sea.' He puffed his pipe contentedly. 'Vassallo is carrying some sort of despatch or letters for the man you are to meet in the city, I presume?' Vanderville nodded evasively, reluctant to say more.

'No, do not tell me,' said Dumanoir with a gesture of complicity, 'I don't need to know the details. But it occurred to me,' he added, 'that it might make sense for you each to carry a duplicate of your message, in case one of you becomes uh… separated from the other during the leap.'

Vanderville had turned the captain's remark over in his mind for some moments. It was a fact that Vassallo, although voluble in his cups, had proved remarkably close about; the identity of Mayflower, the mysterious agent they were assigned to meet once ashore, or the network he controlled – if he even had one. Finding neither comfort nor complicity in these recollections, he let them go out into the darkness, bade Dumanoir goodnight, and went below.

Chapter Two

Now, poised above the racing sea, Vanderville was grateful that the captain could not see him shivering apprehensively on the yard. He stared out into the darkness and tried to see where the blackness of the sea met the blackness of the night. But there was little to choose between them; the only sign of where one ended and the other began the murky white form of the fortress against the black-grey of the sky, and where the breakers flashed white as they reached the walls after their long roll across the sea.

It was cold on the yard. They had decided against wearing heavy overcoats that would impede their agility for the spring from the yard end, and anyway they wanted to be inconspicuous inside the fort. Vassallo had dressed as a plain sailor, and Vanderville wore his simple blue uniform coat from which he had removed the emblems and epaulettes that distinguished him as an officer. It was not ideal, but if he escaped close examination he might pass for a civilian. His plain black beaver hat with the revolutionary cockade removed was strapped to his back by a length of sailor's cord which cut into him as he eased his way to the end of the stunsail boom.

Dumanoir had told him to remain hunkered flat against the yard with his feet on the ratlines slung below it and his arm around the lower mainsail lift until the last moment. That way they would be taken for the ship's crew and escape notice from any curious sentries on the walls. In the final approach he was to make his way to the tip of the boom and brace his feet on the Flemish horse below it. He assessed this foothold now, bracing his foot against the thick node of rope. It creaked as it flexed, and he made the mistake of looking down. Nausea surged upwards from his stomach as he saw the surface of the sea racing past below his perch. He drew his foot back gingerly.

Dumanoir had assured him that the approach would be under an easy sail, his intent being to give any observers the impression that a careless pilot had allowed the vessel to drift just a little too close to the walls, without sparking alarm in the fort itself at the near encounter between yard and rampart. Vanderville set his jaw intently and glanced up at the walls which were streaking past to the left now as the Carrère passed the apex of the fort. The parapet top seemed a long way above them now that they were close under it, and he realised that their leap must surely bring them at best to the foot of one of the gun embrasures that pierced its battlement face like so many staring eyes. In any one of these, a sentinel more alert than his fellows might espy the two figures balanced incongruously on the boom ends. They were almost upon the last extremity of the bastion of St Gregory that was their object, and at any moment the drop below him would be not into the sea but onto the ragged tumble of blocks at the wall footing, beaten by the waves, and stained with bird droppings.

Time, which had dragged cruelly during the wait on the yard, now dashed past at a breakneck pace, and suddenly the unwelcome moment to leap was upon them. He saw Vassallo cautiously moving to the very tip of the foreyard, the horizontal yard braced behind his back looking awfully thin to bear his weight. He posed there triumphantly, his shirt tails flying out from beneath his sailor's jacket. A stupid way to position yourself, thought Vanderville, who was positioned *behind* his own yard clutching it into his heaving stomach until the last moment when he would force himself upright.

He too moved to the extremity of the yard, his thighs pressing against the boom which he clutched with one hand, the other on the rope stay above it. With his eyes intent on the tip of the bastion that was their target he did not see Vassallo take his leap from the yard, but he saw him strike the face of the bastion, his hands grasping futilely for the lip of the gun embrasure as he bounced off the wall. Arms flailing impotently, he span like a tossed rag doll down the face of the wall and was lost into the roiling foam where the waves spat at the foot of the fortress.

There was not even time to swallow his fear as the boom bore him relentlessly onwards to the angled point of the bastion. A moment later and it would be too late to jump. If he missed his opportunity, he would not suffer Vassallo's fate, but he would face something he dreaded more – an ignominious return to deck under the unforgiving eyes of the crew. Vanderville prised his frozen fingers free from the boom stay and abandoning all reason, flung himself heedlessly from the yard at the last embrasure set before the very angle of the fortress. As he sprang, he spreadeagled his body to cushion his meeting with the wall, and so the embrasure's lip struck his chest; the impact driving the breath from him as he scrambled to maintain his elbows' faint grip on the sloping floor of the gun-port. His knees met the wall equally hard, and pain surged through his legs. But his grip held.

His heart hammered wildly against his ribs, and for mere seconds he clung to the sill of the embrasure by the strength of his arms alone, feeling his knees hot, wet, and numb as he pressed them gratefully against the stone. His eyes were half closed as he rested his forehead on the cool sloping floor of the embrasure, allowing his stomach to sink back down to its accustomed place, and the frantic battering of his heart against his ribs to abate.

Then summoning his breath, while refusing the abrupt suggestion from his unruly mind to consider the perilous precariousness of his position, he minded the strength of his limbs and pushed his shoulders as far forward as possible while gently probing for the handholds that would enable him to haul himself into the embrasure's mouth. He carefully avoided the gun muzzle that loomed above his head as he edged forward precious inches and it was at that moment that a prior denizen of the embrasure made known his presence, and his rancour at Vanderville's arrival. The former was expressed by a baleful shriek and bronze eyed glare as the great black headed gull raised its wings angrily, and the latter by its red bill yawing open to spew a stream of oily fish bile and acid grit that mercifully passed over his ducked head.

'*Salut* and fraternity to you too,' Vanderville uttered through clenched teeth as he hauled his shuddering bones into the confinement of the embrasure besides the creature's nest. The sea banshee chose discretion over valour and whipped silently past him into the dawn air, leaving its rancid scent hanging behind it. The floor of the embrasure sloped downwards towards the sea, and the main part of the incision through the wall at the far end was occupied by the protruding barrel of the great gun.

The gull and his associates had deposited their debris around the barrel in sufficient density to obscure the view onto the parapet beyond and so Vanderville turned onto his back, rested his head besides the gun barrel and leaned back gratefully with his legs pulled up shy of the embrasure lip, relishing the descent from imminent heart stopping destruction to mere peril.

He looked back out at the empty sea. The *Carrère* must have passed into the bay in the moments he was suspended from the wall. She would now be gliding silently towards the quarantine service moorings, unfurling her French tricolour flag. Dumanoir had assured him that three quarters of the ships at anchor in the Marsamuscetto were merchants from Provence who flew the new French republican flag, and they would draw little notice. Well that was their problem now. He could have smiled, he felt so suddenly vividly alive now the imminent danger was past. Nonetheless it was time for him to get moving.

He rolled back over onto his stomach, flattened himself against the embrasure floor and crawled forward up the casement toward the parapet. Scraping the gull's nest out from the opening, he poked his head tentatively through to survey the guard rampart on the inner side of the wall. It was deserted! With all his senses elevated by elation at having achieved the impossible leap it was the work of a moment to wriggle furiously through the narrow embrasure port and thrust himself, sprawling, onto the rampart walk besides the gun carriage.

The pavement that served the wall was broad and stretched away in both directions. Nothing moved around him, except the weeds and grasses sprouting from the masonry that trembled in the faint salt breeze. Opposite the seawall, the internal face of the parapet was open, and the inner edge of the curtain wall tumbled away into a chasm. Beyond that yawning cleft rose a further level of fortifications where the lofty bastions of the true ancient castle abruptly jutted out of the rock itself. The fortress of Sant' Elmo was hewn from a porous sort of honey rock, faced except where occasionally its mountainous solidity rendered this unnecessary. It was a stupendous work, and beautiful where the first tentative rays of the rising sun were beginning to gild the imposing summits of its blunt towers.

Vanderville saw that as soon as he stood he would be hopelessly exposed to view from the upper fort that overlooked the whole sweep of the lower *enceinte* walls. The only cover, and that partial, was provided by the sombre guns that waited at regular intervals. Feeling uncommonly conspicuous, he crouched with thudding heart in the lee of the dilapidated gun carriage, while he assessed his next play.

In other circumstances he might have enjoyed the freedom of his situation. Its profound stillness and solitude a welcome contrast after five days at sea on a crowded and malodorous frigate. But exposed as he was, he imagined the blank eyes of a thousand guards watching him from the upper fort, and the unseen presence behind them of a thousand men preparing to arrest his progress. Yet still no cries of alarm reached him; no sound at all, apart from the faint mewling of circling gulls.

He thought bitterly of Vassallo's ill fortune – by leaping awkwardly from his position before the yardarm, instead of behind it like Vanderville, he had compromised their mission before it had properly begun. Worse, the renegade had refused to make a duplicate of the message he carried: it was not secure, he had argued, and closed the argument by invoking the bad luck attendant upon such an unnecessary precaution. Vanderville had backed down in the face of his intransigence, conscious that they needed all the luck they could muster if they were to accomplish the infiltration of the fortress in near darkness from a moving ship.

Vassallo had however unbended enough to share a scant few details of the assignation they were to effect, and although Vanderville felt helplessly exposed by the loss of a second set of eyes, and expert knowledge of the fort and city, he had been in worse scrapes, and the leap completed he felt that the worst was past. He had two vital pieces of information. He knew where he was supposed to go – to the Church of the Maddalena – and he knew that there he would be met by an agent known as Mayflower. Mayflower would be disappointed at the loss of Vassallo, but he would presumably be able to offer Vanderville shelter in a hostile city and so, with an eagerness to reach the church before the dawn woke the city of Valletta, he set out with determined stealth.

Moving crabwise down the inner face of the parapet he scuttled from gun to gun towards the juncture where the fortress walls met the curtain wall surrounding the city proper. As he went, he was startled to find hardly any gun was fixed properly on its carriage, and many of the wheels were broken or rotted away, while some of the many gun embrasures were empty entirely.

Whoever the unfortunate Vassallo had paid off to remove the sentries from the bastion wall had done their work well and, advancing from the cover of one gun carriage to the next, Vanderville found that he reached the juncture of the curtain wall overlooking the Valletta without encountering a single guard. He crouched behind the bastion wall in the lee of the rampart where it occurred to him that stealth could now be discarded. If he was being surveyed from the fort above, it was from a considerable distance, and assuming the upright posture of a sentry might serve him better under the circumstances than continuing his furtive movements. The resolution was easier to make than to follow. He felt intensely vulnerable as he uncrimped himself, and so he turned his back on the looming upper fortress to allay his sense of vulnerability. As he rose, his head cleared the parapet top and peering over the bastion wall, the city of Valletta was exposed to his gaze for the first time.

Chapter Three

The city lay on a promontory, surrounded on three sides by the sea with the main harbour on one side and the harbour of Marsamuscetto on the other. Across the isthmus that separated it from the mainland were further great fortifications, so that the whole peninsula was more like a fortified island, walled and inaccessible on all sides, except where there were landing places on the water. Even these were strongly guarded by platforms of guns.

The seawards tip of the peninsula was crowned by the rocky hill behind him, on which perched the fortress of Sant' Elmo. He occupied a position on the curtain wall that separated that fortress from the city on the landward side. The wall, protected by huge and wide counterscarps, terminated below him in a wedge-like fissure, over which were placed draw bridges. Beyond the bridges was the city, roof after flat roof of it. He would have compared it to patchwork fields seen from a mountain top, were it not for the preposterous tumble of turrets, belltowers and gates that marked its quarters.

The subdivisions of the city brought to his mind Vassallo's briefing of the night previous. Vanderville, to whom the islands of Malta were unknown, had drunk his words in with the same assiduity Vassallo and the captain applied to the brandy bottle.

'You must know that the Order governs the island, and the Convent of Valetta is their stronghold and capital, ruled by His Eminence Prince von Hompesch who is their grandmaster. The knights of the Order are composed of nobles from a plethora of nations who all bring their peculiar defects and prejudices with them to Malta. They are organised into seven *langues*, each of which recruits from the lands who speak their tongue, and they operate here much as great noble houses, in constant competition for place and advancement for their own. Besides which, many if not most of them are initiates of rival fraternal societies, and in certain aspects of their personal lives are some distance from the monastic ideal. The result is a state of permanent infighting because of pride and envy.

'Which is just as well,' he added drily. 'It suits our purpose to have them at each other's throats. Each of the *langues* is headed by a military commander, or bailli, who are answerable only to the grandmaster. That elevated office of each *langue* is constantly seeking to gain for one of its own.'

Captain Dumanoir had interjected enthusiastically at this point. 'Despite this parochial turf war, Valletta is a visionary place, a *Civitate Dei*, a City of God. The city is a marvel from a distant prospect and not less so on a nearer approach.'

Vassallo, the native, had snorted at this and expressed the antithesis – Valletta, he opined, was an earthly hell governed by an obsolete order of warrior monks who ruled the oppressed inhabitants of the islands of Malta with misplaced severity, and termed their fortress city the Convent, as if that disguised its purpose of intimidation.

Whether hell or heaven on earth, the city looked safe and peaceful enough to Vanderville. Gazing out over the bell towers, the orderly streets, and uniform ranks of fine stone houses glimmering in the dawn light, he was momentarily hard put to recall the urgency of his mission. And yet, somewhere down there was the Church of the Maddalene where he and Vassallo had been told to meet their contact, known only as Mayflower. If he could not find Mayflower, he would be alone and trapped inside the walls of a city that viewed all Frenchmen as enemies, potential spies of the Revolution to be hanged from the nearest lamp post. He cursed Vassallo's incompetence again and took stock.

The renegade had told him that the church was one of those nearest to the landward ramparts of Sant' Elmo, situated opposite the main gate of that fortress, in part of the complex of the Women's Hospital. Because the houses were two or at most three storeys high, the churches of the city were easily made out from his vantage point. They squatted beneath old fashioned bell towers, and each bore similar crinkled pediments, furbelowed cornices and turretlets, like old-fashioned clock cases bedizened with many a scroll and a flourishing fart to adorn the apartments of the Pompadour. He thought he could make out a short bell tower in the area opposite the main fortress gate away to his left. According to his bearings that ought to be the Maddalene, so he began plotting a route.

He must first descend from the bastion to the city walls, and then find a way down from there to the shanty hovels that skirted Sant' Elmo's landward ditches. By hugging the fortress walls he could arrive in the piazza before the main gate and should be able to cross that area just as the sun came up, and even reach the church without entering the maze of streets behind it. Could he pass for a local? Vanderville assessed his breeches. Though grazed and dusted white from scrambling through the embrasure, they were still respectable, and he hoped that he would attract little attention in passing through the city.

He felt in his pocket for his watch and pulled it out to find its glass face cracked. The hour hand dangled uselessly — a casualty of the rampart walls. He sighed; the rendezvous with Mayflower was scheduled for six, and that could not be far off now. He pocketed the useless timepiece and set off.

At the end of the fort's bastion, he scraped through a gun embrasure that overlooked the city, and dangling from his hands he dropped to the connected city wall. This accomplished without further damage to person or garments, he unslung his hat from the cords that held it, placed it on his head and trotted down a narrow stair leading into the city proper.

The greater part of the city slept still, though the working people were already about, and he saw them here and there in the distance silently going about their morning labours. There were few level streets because of the city's hilly situation, but there were fine pavements faced with the same honey coloured stone as the flat roofed houses. In fact, there was no wood visible at all except for the closed shutters that fronted the balconies protruding from each house over the street.

He kept winding and turning about, from street to street and from alley to alley, until he arrived at the foot of the walls of Sant' Elmo. The town petered out where it lapped the great walls of the fort and a noisy flight of starlings had just pitched on one of the fig trees in the fortress ditch. Their faint but massy chirpings were the only sounds that broke the morning stillness. No human form appeared at any of the windows around, no shout of alarm reached him, and no footsteps were audible.

A rough notice daubed on the side of a house identified the street in which he found himself as the Strada della Ficara. The serried ranks of the houses facing the fort on his right hand were elegant, but those on his left leaning against the ditch footings were squalid and downright derelict. Here there was no pavement, one walked on the bare rock, rutted, uneven, and full of holes, and before the nearest clump of huts was a wealthy dunghill, not at all offensive in the cool of the morning. A single sow was stirring there to bask in the coming sun, wending her way amiably among the wild fig saplings that sprouted from crevices in the fortress ditch and leaned out from between the shacks.

As he advanced, he saw for the first time the inhabitants of the city close-up. Two grubby shanty town children watched him pass, and although their dishevelment outmatched his own, he was aware of attracting their attention, and he read hostility in their glances. He hurried on with an affected air of nonchalance.

There was an end to the hovels as he arrived on the outskirts of the piazza before the fortress gates, and as he tentatively set foot on its pavement distant church bells started clamouring the hour. It was already six! The first chimes were picked up and repeated by others, and startled by the increasing din, Vanderville drew back into the shelter of a roofed devotional tabernacle adorning the corner of the house bordering the square. He shared this refuge with a goat who chewed disconsolately while staring aimlessly at the wall above his head, where a hand which betrayed the most casual acquaintance with letters had scrawled on a board, *Piazza dei Forbici*. A doodle of a pair of scissors had been added in case the meaning proved obscure.

From underneath the tabernacle Vanderville scanned the piazza as cautiously as he was able. It was an awkwardly shaped space composed of sweeping stone paving, studded with numerous low bollards. To his left the prows of two great ravelin bastions protruded from the fort towards the town, their sides pierced with innumerable loopholes and gun ports. The fortress gate lay between these twin scissor blades and was manned by two indolent guards. He felt that his route lay somewhere to the right, well away from the sentries, where a sodden filthy portico lined the opposite side of the piazza. Ramshackle market stalls roofed with flapping oilpaper were clustered under the littered passageway. Behind them, the few figures under the arches seemed absorbed in their business. Market traders, he thought, preparing their barrows for the day, and in confirmation the acrid smell of dried dung on cooking fires drifted across the piazza to reach him.

His stomach grumbling, Vanderville edged cautiously further into the shadow of the corner tabernacle beside the goat. Surveying the prospect carefully, his eye was drawn to a queerly authoritative figure swathed in draped cloths like an oriental passing through the market stalls. It was the pattern of the movements as much as the distinctive dress which drew his attention. The figure stopped here to resolve a problem between small boys drawing well water; there to buy green salad, before halting a young woman carrying bread in a basket on her head. He caught a flash of intense colour as the odd cloth the figure wore was swept back over one shoulder. Could it be a carpet? A shawl? He could not make it out at this distance, but as the person made their way along the arcade from one end to another, stooping occasionally to peer into the barrows and booths of the traders, he discerned that they were not one of the traders. An inspector? Police officer? No, one of the traders had just gesticulated in no uncertain terms and moved him or her on roughly.

Vanderville smiled. Despite being too distant to hear the words, the gesture was emphatically clear. Whatever, or whoever the solitary figure might be, they were not possessed of authority over the traders.

He had not anticipated so much activity in the piazza, but the bells had announced that the time of his appointment with Mayflower was nigh, and he must pass the piazza to get to the Church of Maddalena. He darted a quick glance behind him and caught a malevolent flash of bright eyes as a small dark head bobbed down behind a squalid hovel in the shadows. Seconds later, something skittered across the pavement by his feet. It was a piece of dried dung. The goat, trailing string, trotted hopefully after it.

The street urchins were stalking him. He shrugged – if thrown turds were the worst they could muster, so be it. On the other hand, it was better that they stayed silent as he crossed the piazza, so as not to attract the attention of the guards on the fort gate. He scowled at the nearest scamp who stared back unblinking. 'A fig for these kids,' he decided. They would be more scared of the guards than he was. Shards from another flung turd ricocheted from the wall above his head. 'At least this one wasn't soft,' he considered gratefully. But sooner or later one might be. A lilting voice called out, '*Franćiż mishut!*' in a dialect which passed all understanding. He did not know what that meant, but the tone indicated that it was no benediction. He smiled to himself and was struck suddenly behind the right ear by a turd in full flight. It was enough – he pulled his hat down over his eyes and strode forward boldly into the piazza.

The guards on the fort gate laughed boisterously amongst themselves as he set out and he felt their inquisitive eyes on him. With his shoulders back he allowed the bells to guide him diagonally right across the piazza, away from the fort and soldiers and towards the beckoning street corner that ought to lead him to the doors of the Maddalene, and Mayflower's help. Ten more yards, five yards, to safety, with the catcalls of the children ringing through the dawn, and the hot holes in his back where he could feel the soldiers' eyes boring into his spine. He inadvertently quickened his stride as he cut the corner fine and span smartly into the street…

In front of him, not far off, was a patrol of uniformed men marching as one in his direction. Midway between him and them lay the doors of a small church, its baroque flourishes morbid in the dawn air. He could see no other church on the street and if he were to reach the doors before the patrol, he must pick up his pace beyond anything discrete. He reached the door in an uneasy sort of a loping half run and pushed at the doors with his elbow. They did not give. With no time to spare, he tried his shoulder, but it bumped off helplessly. He dared not risk a glance at the patrol to his left, to his right he glimpsed the street children passing the corner towards him. He stepped back, pulling his hat lower and inclining his head away from the patrol, and heard the tramp of nailed boots almost upon him. And at that moment the church door swung open, and an owl-like sacristan bustled forth, clutching one withered arm to his chest. With the brusquest of nods, his face averted, Vanderville brushed him aside and passed swiftly into the church in two great strides. As he did, he pulled the door firmly closed behind him.

Once inside the church he slipped instantly into the cover of a pillar that flanked the entrance. The familiar and comforting smells of wood and wax swept over him, and he was reassured. The interior of the church was plain enough in comparison with the exterior facade, the proportions were just, and the simple arched roof was noble. What cheerfulness it had, it owed to a large window behind the altar that diffused a mild and solemn light equally over every part of the edifice.

He could see nobody in the nave, and he commenced a brisk circumnavigation of the side chapels to orientate himself, and to discover other entrances. In Mayflower's place, Vanderville would have arrived early and waited outside watching the entrance. But any vantage point in the piazza was dominated by the great scissor blades of Fort Sant' Elmo's ravelins that flanked the fort's gate. There was no secret space there, or in the street outside. Vanderville wondered if Mayflower would instead enter from the rear, where there were two low doors behind the high altar.

No tawdry ornaments, no glaring pictures, disgraced the sanctity of the place until he arrived at the last of the side chapels. It contained an altar tomb of no very remote antiquity, adorned with uncouth statues of the evangelists, supported by wreathed columns of alabaster. The altar, standing distinct from the walls, was the only object on which ornaments were lavished, with four gigantic candelabra of the stateliest shape and most delicate execution placed on its steps, which together with the inlaid floor within the sanctuary, were spread with beautiful carpets. Satisfied that he was alone in the church, Vanderville was about to settle down to wait when something awry caught his eye. A shoe had been discarded on the floor inside the chapel sanctuary. He lightly vaulted the railing and seized it up. It was an ordinary, rather good, man's shoe, with an expensive silver buckle.

Turning it in his hands he cast his eyes around the sanctuary. Where there was one shoe, there must be its fellow. But it was not a shoe, but a glimpse of a stockinged foot that he saw almost immediately, poking out from behind the altar at an unlikely angle. A step closer revealed a shapely calf encased in a laddered silk-stocking attached to the foot. He approached the altar cautiously and, placing one hand on it, peered around its extremity. There was a cavity between the altar columns and the church wall, and occupying it was the crumpled form of a body, grotesquely maintained upright by the smallness of the space in which it was confined.

The head sagged away from him, concealing the face, but he was convinced of the absence of life even before he reached out to gingerly touch the back of the not-yet-cold neck. No living person could have assumed that fantastic position, so tightly jammed in that the feet were suspended dangling above the ground. Someone must have brought him there, dislodging one shoe in the process of dragging the corpse across the sanctuary and hurriedly cramming him into the alcove.

Vanderville leant closer into the alcove and grasped the dead man's shoulder. He was clad in a smart red coat, and white breeches. The clothes were those of a gentleman, and he saw a bundled mantle and discarded sack wig on the ground beneath those naked feet. He tried to wrench the body towards him but succeeded only in dislodging it so that the head slumped towards him, provoking him to recoil in disgust. The cheeks were purpled, the tongue protruding, and he saw dark marks buried in the ample folds of the neck. Whoever he was, he had evidently been strangled by powerful hands.

Regaining his grip on the shoulders, he braced himself awkwardly against the altar and attempted to heave the obstruction free. Where his arm pressed against the coat of the body it caught on something sharp – an enamel cross attached to the breast. He remembered that Vassallo had told him that in Malta, the knights, and only the knights, wore the cross. 'Mayflower, I presume,' he grunted, and forced himself into the alcove to exert more pressure. Just as he grasped the further arm the church door banged ominously, the echo ringing around the empty church – and Vanderville knew he was no longer alone!

He froze, his stomach revolving peculiarly as he craned an ear to the sound. Someone was advancing with a faint clicking noise up the nave. Someone who was walking softly, but quickly. Someone who had also now paused to listen. With a shudder of distaste, Vanderville forced himself fully into the channel behind the altar, shoving the body further into the alcove as he did so. Crouching enabled him to reach the coat pockets, and he swiftly rifled them.

He knew that Mayflower's value lay in the information he had gathered regarding those French knights who had agreed to betray the Order, as well as those who intended to remain neutral in any conflict. Vassallo had hinted at intelligence of secret bays where landings could be made, a network of saboteurs ready to spoil powder magazines, deflect patrols and detachments from their posts, and assure that the weaker unsteady militia were diverted to the points marked for the French assault. Surely, Mayflower must have been carrying documents and bona fides? But there was nothing except a watch and a pocket wallet. The first he palmed, and the second he fumbled and dropped out of reach under the altar. He abandoned the search.

Wonderful, he thought, I am a lone Frenchman on a tiny island that knows a great and hostile French fleet is just over the horizon. Not a good time to be flying the tricolour. Even the street children can tell that I do not belong here. Now my only ally on the island is dead, murdered in a church. And here I am jammed into an anchorite's refuge in close communion with his none-too-pleasant corpse. My situation is grave enough without being caught in the embrace of a dead spy. The situation was curiously elating – he never felt so alive without the immediate prospect of imminent danger.

He pushed one of the flopping dead hands away from his face, observing that the fingernails were bitten and none too clean. There was no chance of further examination of his companion in confinement, and he began frantically to recall the parts of the chapel he had seen from his reconnaissance, to assess his route of escape. Surely, those doorways beyond the sanctuary rails led to a vestry with a route to the outside.

His deliberations were interrupted by the faint clicking of hobnailed shoes approaching. The footsteps paused before the chapel in which he was concealed. He raised himself from his crouch and risked a glance out from the gap between two baroque flourishes on the altar piece that might partially conceal his face. The intruder wore the same white coat with red facings as the guards on the gate of the fort, and Vanderville realised with regret that this man was perhaps the advance guard of the patrol he had encountered come to investigate his refuge.

In a curious nod to the sacred space, the soldier clutched his hat in one hand, but the musket cradled in his other arm gave his assumed sanctity the lie. Vanderville inched back down into cover, cursing his luck. The awkward mass of the traitor knight's corpse impeded his exit from the far side of the alcove, and though he had no intention of being caught in close company with Mayflower, he could see no option but to remain crouched where he was. Then with a jolt he remembered that the dead man's shoe was still before the altar, and simultaneously with that realisation there came the creaking of the sanctuary gate being pushed open. Realising he had been holding his breath, Vanderville breathed out softly, in an attempt to ease the pounding of his heart, which sounded so loudly that he could not believe the soldier on the other side of the altar could not hear it as clearly as himself.

The momentary silence was excruciatingly tense. Take the shoe, and move on, he prayed, mutely urging the soldier to depart. Just move on! He raised his crouch into a fighting stance as best he was able in the cramped space. Every muscle in his body tingled with anticipation as he prepared to move. The adjustment brought him closer to Mayflower whose cold lifeless eyes seemed to regard him accusingly. He averted his gaze abruptly, bumping his forehead on the rear of the altar, and it was then that he heard a slap of leather on marble as if the incriminating shoe had been tossed aside. It was succeeded by the familiar precise metallic snap that signalled the cocking of a musket for action.

Chapter Four

As the muzzle end of a musket hove into view Vanderville stood, grasped the barrel, and pushed hard upwards. There was a deafening report, as an unseen finger jerked at the trigger, and Vanderville was half blinded by the flash of the musket detonation. So much for stealth! Honed instinct carried him from his hiding place, still clutching the hot barrel, and he sprang forward, driving his left fist towards the blur of the soldier's startled face. His wrist jarred with the connection, which was as sweet as he could have wished, and staggering forward he followed through, swinging wildly against the expected riposte. The first blow had been true however, and as the shapes of his vision coalesced into something more proximate to reality, and the ringing in his ears receded, he saw the soldier stretched on the chapel floor. He leapt the obstruction, ran for the high altar, and vaulted the low railings. There were the expected doors to each side of the sanctuary, and with no time to choose he made for the nearest.

Behind him he heard the slap of the church doors being flung open and the clatter of boots as the rest of the patrol arrived, drawn by the discharge of the musket. He grasped the door handle desperately and gratefully found it turned in his hand. Unlocked! He wrenched it open and flung himself heedlessly through it. He was instantly brought up short by the barrel of a spiral stair. This was no vestry, he had chosen wrong, but without time for second thoughts he crashed up the stair as fast as he was able. He had only moments until the patrol was on his tail and he grimly prepared himself to sell himself dearly should they corner him.

Clattering up the stair he threw himself at the first door in the sidewall – locked! He heard jostling below. One of the patrol must have seen him traverse the nave, and headed straight after him, rather than investigating their fallen comrade. At least they would be delayed by caution and hampered by their unwieldy muskets on the tight staircase, he might still break free. He started up again.

The stair reached its conclusion in the blank face of another sturdy door, but thankfully it was not secured by a lock, and thrusting through it he found himself on the flat roof of the church, blinking against the sudden light whose rosy beginnings promised another fine June day. All around him the roofs of Valletta were laid out, rising and falling in honey-coloured troughs, and his flight urged him onwards to the low parapet at the very edge of the roof, where he wavered on the brink of a deep channel plunging to the streets far below. The tumble-down roofs of the adjacent monastic buildings were close enough for a hurried leap and he took it at a run, landing hard and barking his knees on the coarse surface. He scrambled precariously across the adjoining terraces, selecting each new route by convenience rather than design. His presence created some confusion among the roof tops' no doubt seldom-molested inmates; and fowls, cats and kittens flew out in all directions, as he plunged and leapt, the loose matted surfaces skittering beneath his feet.

Shouts and barked orders broke out behind him, as the soldiers reached the church pinnacle and spied his progress. Would they hazard a musket shot? He dared not risk a glance behind, the awkward planes of the complex roof tops and the perilously shifting surfaces required all his concentration. A coping stone shifted beneath his feet as he prepared to leap another gulf and threw his balance awry. He floundered for a moment on the crest and then his foothold gave way completely and he was flying through the air, flailing for a grip as he bounced from the face of the next house. His scrambling hands seized some guttering on the edge of the roof. For a moment he thought he had a handhold, but with a sickening lurch of the stomach he felt the gutter detach itself from its anchoring. In a flash he was clutching nothing but thin air and tumbling off the edge of the roof.

As he plummeted backwards, he was vaguely aware of the fast-approaching corner of another roof top below whose arrival was no sooner heralded than announced by a jarring impact that propelled him over the edge of another precipice. Powerlessly revolving, he caught a glimpse of approaching flagstones and then something terribly solid struck his head and knocked all the sense from him and that was the last he knew.

—

Vanderville was suffering a strange sort of nightmare dream. Three agitated, disjointed heads were babbling over him in a strange harsh demonic language. His vision was utterly blurred, and he understood their meaning more by intuition than by reason. One voice was female and had an air of authority over the other two younger voices. Finally she spoke in familiar Italian, blended with other peculiar guttural words.

'He is wanted. The guard were chasing him. He will bring them to us here.'

'There may be a reward,' said another voice pitched high like a child. 'If the guard seek him there will be money or favours for us.'

'They will do nothing for us. When have they ever? They will even use it against us and ask questions about why we rescued him in the first place.'

A third voice broke in, shushing the others. 'Be quiet, I am trying to think like Rais Murad. What would he do?'

'He would clap him in irons and sell him to the Barbary pirates.'

'No, that is for infants,' said the female voice. 'He would not sell him. He is too old, and not beautiful and smooth like me. Look at his ugly red face, disfigured with hair all over his lip. And he is damaged.'

'You are mistaken. The rais would take him for ransom. Look at his clothes, he is French and probably a spy. He would hide him and then ransom him to the Sultan Hompesch, to Carpegna, to the highest bidder. Then with his fortune, he would buy us all free of this rock, and I should sail at last and see Africa and the Barbary coast, and the world.'

'The rais will not take you. Look at yourself, you are not able to pull an oar. He would leave you crying on the beach. No one comes to rescue us, most of all, not you. You were born slow and awkward.'

'Yet every morning I am thankful that I am not as you, whose mother sold herself for little cream cakes.'

'And are you so content that the knight who left your mother crying by the window was a great red-headed Russian pig?'

The female voice spoke again, 'If Donna Eva could hear you two, she would regret ever feeding you. For shame, to speak of your mothers so. You must both report to Steak-eye for confession immediately after matins.'

Then he felt the tugging of many hands trying to move him, and the pain was so great that the voices fell back into blackness blotted out by an all-engulfing agony and for a while there was nothing more.

—

It was some time before the battered Vanderville came to his senses, and when he did surface, it was to find himself horizontal in a small room with a whitewashed ceiling made indistinct by a mosquito net half furled above his head. He became aware that a white damask bedspread covered him, and at the foot of the bed were iron pillars topped by latticed gold bed knobs in the shape of animal heads. Facing the bed was an effigy of Our Lady of Sorrows. With his eyes half closed, Vanderville waited for the flashes in his head to settle down and the incoherence of his thoughts to settle into a useful pattern. He could remember swinging over the roof terraces between tethered goats, and coops of pigeons and chickens shattering at his progress. After that – nothing.

His thoughts were interrupted by the sounds of voices raised nearby and he resolved to investigate. Trying to hold his tender head, he found that his left arm was in a sling, and that shoulder hurt abominably. When he rose, he realized that he was clad only in his threadbare shirt and the remainder of his clothes were nowhere to be seen. Also missing was the linen belt he always wore against his belly that contained his papers and his money.

There was a small window high on one wall and he peered out to check the sun's position but this initiative was rewarded only by a blinding pain in his eyes that drove him backwards. His legs at least seemed sound, but there was a pounding in his head like the whole of the siege batteries before Mantua discharging in rhythmic sequence. Eventually he remembered his arrival on Malta and some of the subsequent events and concluded that it must be late morning, and here he was wasting time abed. He hobbled angrily out of the room, feet slapping on the tiled floor, and made towards the sound of voices.

The door from which the sounds hailed was open, and bracing himself against the unexpected, Vanderville stalked into the room purposefully. Or rather, to stalk purposefully was his intention. What he accomplished was closer to the limp of one of those goats who perpetually wander the circumference of a hill in the same direction, their legs growing inevitably shorter on the one side than the other.

The room he entered was larger than the bed chamber and scented with something like jasmine. Around the walls were a plethora of small tables bearing cages filled with little Brazilian doves, parroquets, and canary birds. In a deep recess of a balcony window shielded by a closed wooden lattice was a chaise, and on it waited a woman, whose gesticulating conversation ceased abruptly on his entry.

She was of middling height and rather above than below a slender build, simply clothed with her dark hair confined by a blue handkerchief with white stripes. This contrasted with the pride of her poised chin that hinted at something beyond her thirty-odd years. Her seated lap was covered by scattered papers, and she held a closed fan in one hand with which she pointed at a very young woman seated on the floor before her.

Her companion was possessed of an abundantly exuberant mass of unconfined black hair, and she was accompanied by a swarthy young boy of about eight years old whose hair she was caressing fondly. Both looked as if they had been suckled on olive oil instead of milk and were so sparsely clothed as to be almost barelegged. In distinction to the suppressed smile of the seated woman both regarded Vanderville with frankly baleful eyes.

Vanderville covered the handful of strides to the chaise with wincing brevity and drew himself up in the manner of an officer of cavalry addressing his social equal as best he could under the circumstances, being in his underthings and lacking a hat to remove. 'A good day to you, *Signora*,' he began, in his Italian, which was passable. His bow brought sharp regret from his ribs, and a reminder of his travails that brought a temporary cessation to his speech.

The woman arranged her hands gracefully in her lap and Vanderville surveyed the papers resting there and frowned. The documents consisted of his identity credentials and passports. He met her expectant eyes with less confidence, his credentials were all in French, the language of Malta's enemy, and she had obviously perused them while he was unconscious. He shifted his weight and his shoulder complained ferociously. 'I believe you have the advantage of me. It appears you are in possession of something rightfully mine,' he stated bluntly. Her expectant half smile disappeared abruptly, but Vanderville blundered on. 'Something that you took from me, whilst I was not disposed to defend it,' he continued. 'A purse containing my bona fides and some personal papers.'

'Donna,' she suggested, deftly supplying the words he lacked. 'We say Donna here. You may address me as Donna Mifsud.' Her voice had something remarkable in it, melodiously purring and authoritative at the same time. She tapped the fan in her hands impatiently and continued, 'And you have something that should by rights be mine.'

'What is that pray? What do I owe to a stranger who robs a prostrate man?'

She snapped her fan shut scornfully and tossed it onto the chaise beside her. A glimmering light shone in her eyes, as she said sternly, 'Your gratitude, young man. I take some pleasure in beholding my Lazarus risen,' she said evenly. 'Whom, if he had not the appearance of a man who had passed through a pergola roof at full pelt would cut a bravura figure. I could wish that your manners had recovered with the same velocity. Perhaps now would be the moment for you to introduce yourself, and explain your business and extraordinary means of arriving in my courtyard?'

Vanderville was a little dumbfounded, and while he gathered his thoughts a pregnant pause developed and hung in the air between them. The three pairs of eyes viewing him with varying degrees of contemptuous hostility did not contribute to his composure. It certainly did not seem that she was instantly going to turn him over to the authorities, he reasoned furiously, but he did not have a cover story pat to hand that would adequately cover the circumstances.

He was spared further contemplation as she broke the silence. 'Let me help untie your tongue. These,' she indicated his papers with a vague wave, 'indicate that you are an officer in the French service, and that your name is Vanderville, which doesn't sound very French, but that is by the bye. They are scarcely necessary anyway to confirm the evidence of my eyes, which deduce from your outlandish garb, your republican credentials.'

Vanderville nodded in agreement despite himself. 'The street children this morning, they pursued me because they thought me French,' he mused aloud.

'They learn it from the townspeople, who learn it from hating the knights, who are dominated by the French faction. French knights they detest, but the agents of the Revolution might get a different reception,' she said. 'I daresay we might find out before too long.'

She turned her head to the figure at her feet, 'Franca, my dearest, would you bring the lieutenant's clothes as soon as you have finished with them, please, and then run to fetch Don Stecchi to set our guest's arm.'

As the girl complied, there was a silvery tinkling of small bells and an unintelligible shout from the street without, and the boy jumped up and ran to the window behind his mistress, '*Il signor mungitore!*' he called with eager anticipation.

Donna Mifsud had not taken her eyes from Vanderville. 'We have begun with incivility,' she stated. 'Would you care to recommence?' Vanderville nodded hangdog agreement and took the seat she indicated, opposite her own.

'Will you take milk with coffee?' she asked, and when he nodded again, 'Duccio, fetch some milk please.' The boy appeared unwilling to leave his mistress alone with Vanderville and glared at him as he departed. She ignored this and summoned Vanderville, 'Come and watch the transaction, you may find it picturesque.'

She stood, and entered the small, enclosed balcony behind her. It was one of those that projected from the stone exterior of the house over the street, paned with glass on three sides, and made private by louvred shutters that concealed the occupants from the passers-by below. She adjusted one of the shutters and invited him to watch a scene at her doorstep.

A man dressed in short white trousers was herding goats further up the street, his dark waistcoat and blue cap were worn and tired. As the boy Duccio emerged onto the doorstep, he was alerted by the opening of the door. Taking a goat by the ear, he brought it to the child, who handed him a cup. Vanderville watched as he began milking the goat into the cup.

The shutter next to Vanderville's head sprang open, and his rescuer stuck her elegant head out of the window.

'Be sure to see that he does not dilute the milk, Duccio,' she called, speaking in a curious Italian with some words of dialect. The goat herd smiled ruefully and waved a dismissive hand without looking up, to which Donna Mifsud responded cheerfully. 'What is being said in the piazza, Antonio?'

The goatherd removed his cap and ran his fingers through a thick black mop of hair. 'Grave tidings Donna Eva. The *Cavaliere* von Seeau has been murdered at the foot of the altar of the Black Madonna in the Maddalena.'

'God grant him rest,' she said. Then after the briefest pause, 'By the patriots?'

'By a renegade French spy. The patrol caught him bloody stiletto in hand, but he escaped across the roof tops.' He replaced his cap and squinted up at the balcony, causing Vanderville to recoil before remembering that the shutters shielded him from view. 'There is a hue and cry afoot, the patriots say they will drag all of the French knights from their *auberges* and wreak bloody revenge.'

'So, life goes on as before?'

'All goes on as before,' he confirmed, shrugging, 'They say anybody harbouring the spy will be hauled before the grand-master and forfeit all of their property on the island, and patrols are doubled.'

Vanderville drew his head a little further back into the shade of the room and glanced sideways at his host. A fine earring sparkled against the golden skin of her long neck, but her face was concealed from him by the shutter held in graceful fingers.

She dismissed the goat herd and came back into the room, conducting Vanderville to a seat at a table laid with breakfast things. She considered him carefully from under long dark eyelashes as she poured coffee, and they both remained mute until the boy, Duccio, had brought the milk and at her sign, sulkily departed, leaving them alone.

After pouring in silence, she took up her cup and watched him as he drank. The uneasy bonhomie established at the window had apparently evaporated, and she carefully assessed him.

'It appears that you have not been entirely honest with me, *M'sieur*,' she began. 'Naturally, I shall not believe the innocent explanation of how you came to arrive in my house you are about to offer,' she waved away his burgeoning protest. 'I was expecting a glib excuse to perhaps cover the traces of some misguided escapade. One of those gallantries to which your sort is so addicted. Perhaps you had an assignation that miscarried, and were forced to take to the roof tops to make good your retreat? I am inclined to take a lenient view of such matters, but murder, and murder of a knight is another thing altogether. You must realise that here in Valletta, we are strangers to such extravagances.'

He opened his mouth to object, but she waved away his protest before he could begin.

'Oh, the knights kill each other, and more often us, over trifles of honour, and the life of a Maltese is of little consequence to our bold *cavalieri*, accustomed as they have become over the centuries to treat us as their servants, or as animals lower even than the Turkish slaves who carry their parasols for them. But the murder of a knight by a Maltese, or worse, an interloper from outside Malta is a matter as close to a blasphemy as they know, and it will not go unavenged.'

Vanderville opened his mouth once more, but again she cut him short. 'They will turn over every stone in the city to get to the miscreant. There is no safe place for you on this rock now.

Not even here, in the house of a woman under the protection of the bailli of the Anglo-Bavarian *langue*. It can only be a matter of time before the quarter is searched, your route traced, and His Eminence's guard appear at my door baying for blood.'

'If I have not yet been candid, Donna Mifsud,' began Vanderville, 'it was from a desire to spare your house the unfortunate complications that have nevertheless ensued attendant on my precipitate descent into your property. I can assure you, however, that whomsoever assaulted the knight this morning, it was not I.'

'Regardless, your journey here over the roof tops brought you through the properties of at least one of my rivals, La Baida, and she would fain report your progress to inconvenience me, even if you were just a common adventurer.'

'Your rival, Donna Mifsud?'

'I am what is popularly known here in Valletta as a public woman. That is, my company is available to the highest bidder. Which in Valletta means the knights.' She drained her cup and set it down. 'Oh, do not be shocked young man. The rewards of my position can be substantial, and where there is money, there is competition. There is no honour among our kind.'

As Vanderville digested these piquant details the scruffy haired girl re-entered the room carrying Vanderville's things. Watching her studied grace he realised that that awkward age between child and woman was almost beyond her, and that despite her humble clothes she promised to become a startlingly attractive young woman. Slightly discomforted under the steady gaze of her large black eyes, he received his clothes from her with a bow. His stockings and breeches had been expertly mended and his coat and hat well brushed.

'Don Steak-eye is coming up, Donna Eva,' she announced.

'Don *Stecchi* to you, my dear,' said Eva primly.

'It is extraordinarily good of you to succour me,' Vanderville said, standing with difficulty. 'But I regret that my presence here may be an embarrassment to you, and I am resolved to depart immediately.'

She sighed patiently. 'You are French, and the French battle fleet is nigh. The situation here for a Frenchman alone in the streets would be impossible. Normally to insult a knight is unthinkable, but in recent days, even the French knights have ventured abroad at their peril. The patriots believe that they have sold out the Convent, as we term Valletta, and all is upheaval and danger. If the French come – or rather *when* the French come, we will have a resolution. But perhaps you are in a better position to inform me of General Bonaparte's intentions than anyone else on this misbegotten rock?'

'I regret Madame, that as the merest imp of the republican devil, I am not able to enlighten you as to the General's intent. I can only tell you that he has ambition beyond Malta. The full scope of that ambition will be revealed only with the passage of time.'

'And only time will tell how many bones he will grind up in his progress.' She looked down at her lap and shuddered. Then raising her eyes again, she said, 'You have met him, then, this little master of Europe?'

Vanderville's mind was drawn back to those desperate days passed at Mombello the previous summer, in company with the intractable but marvellously clever Felix Gracchus. 'I have the honour of knowing the General's family better than the General himself,' he prevaricated.

'I have a bargain for you then, heaven-sent one,' she said slowly. 'You shall tell me frankly your business here, and if I discover that you mean our people no harm, then I may aid you in your endeavours here, or at least see you safely to your next port of call.'

Vanderville shook his head wryly, 'Even if I wanted tell you what brought me here, I could not,' he said sadly. 'I know only that I was to meet an agent sympathetic to the republican cause in the Church of La Maddalene, and with him dead I suppose my mission is a lost cause, and I have to think of a way to get off this island or lie low until Bonaparte arrives.'

'He *is* coming, then?' she asked breathlessly, and when Vanderville assumed a blank face in reply she snorted pertly, 'Lost causes often have feline vitality, and like a cat with its many lives, your time here may yet not be wasted. I have an idea, let us betake you to the *Auberge* de Bavaria. It is from there that the dead knight hailed, and he was the confidant of my protector, Bailli von Torring, who is head of the Bavarian *langue* here.'

Vanderville considered this. It was possible that if Mayflower had consigned his intelligence to paper, some traces of it might be found in his chambers. 'What about your servants?' he asked, 'won't they talk?'

'My servants?' she laughed, and the sound was delightful. 'You mean Duccio and Eva? They are street children; not my servants, but they are loyal to me, and anyway, they have an interest in you now. It was they who discovered and recovered you after you fell and transported you safely here. You owe them your life I daresay, and that creates a bond of interest between you and them. I think you can rely on the *Fraternita delle Forbici*. Anyway, the knights, and the militia are no friends of theirs. Now go and dress yourself, we are expecting company.'

—

'It was very good of you to come, Don Stecchi, I hope you have not been too inconvenienced?' said Vanderville through gritted teeth. The priest was a well-fleshed man, almost as tall as Vanderville and possessed of curious heavily lidded eyes from which his nickname evidently derived. The two men were alone in the room in which Vanderville had awoken, and Stecchi was massaging his tender shoulder as he lay on the bed, his arm painfully extended above and behind his head.

'You suggest that a priest in the house of a woman of fragile morality occupies an ambiguous position, perhaps?' said Stecchi, his fingers gently rotating Vanderville's arm as he grunted that he had meant no such thing. 'There is something in what you say but understand that Donna Eva's occupation is not designated as a profession here, but as a woman's craft much like hairdressing, or glove making. Her husband was a sailor and was taken or killed by the Turk many years ago, a not uncommon occurrence for our seagoing men, and after that she was forced to live on her own resources. Long use has made the Maltese accustomed to these irregularities, in Valletta at least, and a public woman is not necessarily excluded from society, especially when she endows the Maddalene hospital complex in the generous way that Donna Eva has.'

He carefully pulled Vanderville's damaged arm towards the other shoulder. A nauseating popping sound announced its return to nature's intended position, drawing an agonised yelp of pain from the patient.

'Arm in a sling for a few days,' announced Stecchi, nodding his head contentedly, and wiping his hands on a cloth. 'You may have found Donna Eva a little brusque, but there is no better heart on the island. She is a person who is confessed on a regular basis, a devout churchgoer and very charitable, especially with wayward girls abandoned by their lovers, who lack dowries, and the foundlings who live wild in the Piazza Forbici. You are in good hands here, young man, however unorthodox her business.'

'I regret the disruption in your church this morning, Father,' said Vanderville. 'Even if my part in it was purely incidental. I can assure you that I was not the means of the knight meeting his end.'

Stecchi considered Vanderville's arm and deftly tested the rotation movement with practised fingers a long time before answering carefully. 'Every death is to be regretted,' he said eventually, not meeting Vanderville's eye. 'But some, perhaps, less than others.'

Before Vanderville could ask him what he meant by this, Donna Eva re-joined them, and ignoring Vanderville, communicated rapidly with Stecchi in a flurry of words of the local language that he could not follow. Vanderville considered his position as he waited for the waves of pain in his shoulder to recede. He had been proud to be considered for this mission. Success meant promotion, which was what he wanted most in the world. The sky was the limit for a good republican soldier. But if he had considered his mission difficult to complete when Vassallo had died, it had seemed impossible with the death of the knight he presumed was Mayflower. He knew very little of the substance of it in any case – only that Mayflower was to help him establish contact with agents favourable to the Republic. But now his hopes began to revive.

His priority must now be to stay alive on this rocky island until Bonaparte should arrive with the fleet. But mere survival would not be enough. It would mean that his mission had concluded in failure, and failures did not lead to promotion in the republican army. If, though, he could contact Mayflower's network, his mission could still be a success, and he might accomplish more, much more. While Donna Eva and Don Stecchi conversed in their barbarous tongue, he gave himself up to pipe dreams for precious minutes. Imagine Bonaparte arriving in person in two or three days, to find Lieutenant Vanderville happily able to offer him the keys to the city of Valletta.

This agreeable daydream was interrupted by the return of the boy Duccio, who entered a fervent discussion with Donna Eva and the priest. She appeared worried, and explained to Vanderville quickly, 'Duccio says that all Piazza Forbici is ablaze with the news of the hunt for the murderer. We must get you to the *Auberge* of Bavaria immediately to see Bailli von Torring. Don Stecchi has suggested we disguise you in a woman's *faldetta*, but on foot you may be stopped. Instead, we shall travel by a *kalesh* carriage I have the use of. Duccio will lead the mule, and if we keep the curtains closed, the patrols may not hinder us.' She turned to the priest. 'Don Stecchi, is he fit to travel?'

'I would fain keep him abed for a few days, but the arm is set, as long as he keeps it in a sling, no further harm should result.'

The *kalesh* carriage that waited at the door was an uncouth-looking dark blue cabin made to carry four persons and slung upon a pair of clumsy shafts between which loitered a single mule displaying the misanthropy of his race. Vanderville allowed himself to be settled inside, his back to the mule, and Eva took her perch on the facing seat. The interior was well upholstered and there were curtains at the windows to afford privacy to the occupants and protect them from the sun. He soon found that the two wooden wheels were shod with iron rims, and since the cabin did not have any spring suspension, but was slung on leather thongs, the ride was rough, and the jerk and sway of the cabin reduced his equanimity profoundly as they proceeded at the pace set by the boy walking at the mule's head.

Chapter Five

Valletta had awoken to bustling morning life in the time Vanderville had lain unconscious in Eva's house. As the stolid mule powerfully negotiated the steep ascents of Valletta, some of which were mere flights of steps, without even stumbling, Vanderville peered out of the veiled windows. As they rattled and bounced along with the boy trotting ahead of them, Donna Mifsud indulged Vanderville's curiosity and answered the questions that his snatched glimpses of the city provoked.

All the women of quality abroad in the streets wore the hooded cloak that Donna Mifsud had donned to leave the house. The garment, called a *faldetta*, enveloped the whole body with a curious rigid hood that framed the face rather than hiding it. He saw it deployed in a variety of ways, coquettishly left open by tripping young women, and gravely drawn closed by others. But whereas Donna Mifsud's was a green silk so dark as to appear almost black, many of those he saw worn in the streets were of coarser stuff, and the women of the people left it off altogether, wearing a simple shawl that covered the shoulders as well as the head.

So while the women were all more or less shrouded, by contrast the men of the lower orders were distinctly underdressed. They were without coats, instead sporting sleeveless waistcoats, supplemented with colourful sashes and caps. There were few nobles abroad at this hour, but one or two merchants paraded in the fashionable style favoured in France before the Revolution. He also saw the efficient representatives of the Regiment of Malta in their now-familiar white coats, and the smart *Cacciatori* in their green – the various militiamen scattered about impressed him less, being distinguished only by their armament, which looked current and serviceable enough.

There were also men whose heads were completely shaved except for a top knot, and others with skin as black as could be. Eva informed him that these were seafarers taken by the galleys of the Knights as slaves. He expressed surprise at their number, and she shrugged. 'It is the custom of the sea, you will find an equal number of Europeans so employed in any town south of the sea.' To Vanderville's raised eyebrow she added, 'A contrast drawn between these people and the slaves imported from Africa to work on the farms and plantations of the New World will not be wholly to the disadvantage of the Knights. Or even the Turks come to that.'

Vanderville set his jaw against this. The idea that one man could be the property of another went against everything the Revolution stood for. Refraining from further comment he politely admired the well-ordered and solid buildings, all more or less alike, and constructed entirely of stone. To reduce the risk of fire? Vanderville wondered aloud. She shook her head, telling him it was because timber was so scarce on the islands. The uniformity of design was owing to the city being conceived and constructed by the knights as a model city. Every house had an underground cistern filled by rainwater from the roof, but the fountains and urban reservoirs were supplied and replenished by an aqueduct built and maintained by the knights. The Order also built great warehouses for trade, and there were many foreign merchants invited to trade there. Enormous granaries were excavated along the ramparts and under the streets, each holding masses of grain.

She had waxed lyrical, and when she paused for breath Vanderville observed politely, 'Donna Mifsud, your city is as impressive as I had heard. It makes the Paris I was born in look like a pigsty.'

'Perhaps you had better call me Donna Eva if we are to become friends,' she said, smiling at his wonder. 'It's not my city anyway,' she added, 'I was born a barefooted country girl. The townspeople and we country people are worlds apart and heartily despise each other. Those who work on the land are mostly illiterate, fanatically pious, and bigotedly devoted to their priests. Barefooted and featherbrained, they pay their rents in dried goat dung for the city folk to burn in their winter stoves, and the city dwellers for their part think that shovelling that dung is all we are good for. In the country the life is work from sun-up to down sustained by barley bread, onions, radishes, and an occasional sardine on Fridays if you are fortunate. We married early, and close to home. I was luckier – I got away.'

The mutual contempt between city and country was a refrain familiar to Vanderville, who had travelled widely in the service of the Republic's proselytising armies. He twitched the curtain aside again to observe the now-crowded streets. He found the colourful signs on the taverns and workshops endlessly entertaining. They paused momentarily outside a workshop that read, 'Here is a broombinder's house, where brooms are bound to whiten houses and redden behinds. Praised be the broombinders, who correct behaviour and clean floors.'

Eva tapped him on the knee with her fan bringing his attention back inside the carriage. 'You had better know where we are headed and why,' she said. 'I presume you know that the Knights are divided into *langues*. That of Bavarian is a recent addition; their leader, Count and Commander Emmanuel von Torring is a particular friend of mine. He will be keen to hear any details of this morning's events from a near witness.'

'Will he not imprison me? A French republican agent involved with the murder of a knight may not meet with universal favour during this time of alarm.'

'You must understand that although His Eminence the grandmaster rules here, each *langue* operates almost as an independent power, and like any petty princelings they feud, and thrive on petty power games. As a representative of the threatening power of France you are not without value or interest to the Bavarians, and as a warrior you will experience fraternal courtesy. Then the Bailli von Torring is a masonic adherent and keenly interested in the ideals of that movement, so if you are inclined the same way be sure to let him know, it may help. Do you have it all?' she asked, rapping his knuckles sharply with her fan.

'I believe so,' he answered attentively, privately considering that although he had already had much of the background from Vassallo during their voyage from Italy, it was always useful to hear an insider's view. Like so many of his regiment, he had taken the vows of Freemasonry more from boredom than through conviction. The society's only charm for Vanderville was that the tedium of the rituals was generally followed by a wine-ridden debauch of generous proportions. It was generally accepted that the fraternal societies constituted a supra-national bond that could be of benefit to young officers taken by the enemy. Thankfully, until now, that had remained an entirely hypothetical situation for him, and he fervently tried to recall the formulaic phrases that would identify him as an acolyte of the rite.

Eva interrupted his thoughts. 'Here we are, they are not expecting us so we will have to descend outside, but the warden will admit me instantly, so we need not tarry in the street to be gaped at.'

The *Auberge* de Bavaria was a large two-storey block of monotonous masonry. Its austere facade was embellished by an open stone balcony, the length of the facade, and pierced in the centre by the main doors. They were hustled inside by liveried attendants and mounted a staircase overlooking the central courtyard before entering an antechamber. Before long, the communicating doors to the bailli's set of private saloons were opened to them and they found themselves in a snug abode, its low roof surmounted by a depiction of a saint surrounded by a malicious set of imps and leering devillesses.

Bailli von Torring was simply dressed in the knight's uniform and his face was weather-beaten like old sun-stained driftwood.

He was attended by a single young man dressed in the uniform of the knights, his face extremely attractive although he had a slightly vulnerable nose, unexpectantly pink like that of a rat. The bailli greeted Donna Eva courteously before turning to Vanderville and inviting him to be comfortable in the ample armchairs and couches which furnished the room.

Von Torring listened carefully as Eva explained their predicament. She appeared to have the bailli's complete confidence, and he nodded avidly as she recounted Vanderville's adventures. When she introduced Vanderville, he conspired to pronounce the accepted forms of identification for the fraternal society to which he belonged, although the bailli showed no outward sign of having understood him. His eyes rested constantly on Vanderville as she spoke, and he remained silent until she had finished.

'Do not despair young man,' he told Vanderville. 'Perhaps I may be able to offer you some small assistance. I was expecting an approach from your principals. I am certain to within a cat's hair of the purport of your mission despite the unfortunate loss of your companion with his bona fides.' He stood and walked to his window to gaze out thoughtfully.

'I suspect that Vassallo's task was to deliver a proposal to the knights of Bavaria to join with those French knights who will support the republican forces should they land here. I must tell you that we are not entirely unsympathetic to some of the ideals of the Republic, although they have no place here in the Convent of Valletta. Sadly, although I consider your intentions sound, I must inevitably warn you to prepare yourself for disappointment.'

He turned back to Vanderville. 'The *langue* of which I am the head will refuse to reach an accommodation with the French Republic. They prefer to fight and if necessary, die, protecting the Order's independence. But they will protect you as an honourable envoy, and as a fellow warrior. You have nothing to fear from being exposed by us, we are bound by fraternal interest.'

Eva smiled encouragingly at Vanderville, and the bailli continued. 'Now. You had better go from here to wait on His Eminence the grandmaster of the Order.'

'Is that really necessary?' asked Vanderville hesitantly, loath to explain the means of his arrival on the rock to its master.

'Absolutely necessary I'm afraid. One must wait on His Eminence to announce one's presence in the Convent.' He turned away from Vanderville to the window again. 'Without which one cannot claim his protection should that become necessary.'

'His protection?' asked Vanderville. 'Surely it is better that I remain incognito. Donna Mifsud has told me the penalty for homicide is death.'

'Under some circumstances, yes. You will have to see that the grandmaster is persuaded, as I am, that you are innocent of any involvement in the murder of our compatriot.'

'You are?' said Vanderville, bewildered. 'Why?'

'You will find that news travels quickly in the Convent, we gossip like a pack of old nuns. The sacristan did not see the face of the man who entered the Maddalena as he was leaving, although he describes his coat as blue. He says that the street children were shouting, "accursed Frenchman" at the stranger. In fact the sacristan was a better *ear witness* as opposed to an eyewitness.'

Von Torring paused for Vanderville to join him in an appreciative chuckle at this example of Bavarian wit and, disappointed it was not forthcoming, he fixed a glaucous eye on him as he continued. 'We do not have many strange Frenchmen visiting us at present, and you will naturally be connected with the events at the Maddalene whether you wish it or not.' Vanderville examined the ceiling frescos with an air of unconcern. 'Be that as it may,' continued the bailli, 'Von Seeau, God grant him rest, was the second member of our *auberge* to meet an untimely end in the last three weeks, as well as a whole string of other unexplained events.'

He tailed off and looked troubled for a moment, the first slip in his composure Vanderville had witnessed. He coughed into a spectacularly large laced handkerchief and resumed, 'Since you had no plausible reason to batter to death the only friend you can have hoped to find in the Convent, I am inclined to think that von Seeau's fate is linked to that of his colleague, and not to you.'

'Hopefully, the grandmaster will be likewise convinced,' muttered Vanderville.

'In any case,' said the bailli, 'the *auberges* of the Order are sacred and cannot be violated at will. According to our law, only a judge is empowered to authorise the search or seizure of such persons as shelter under the protection of a bailli and only in the case of a state crime. The grandmaster has no such right. I have been in the Order since my youth and have no recollection of having ever seen such an event. So, while you are in Valletta you will stay here safely. As my guest.'

'I had heard that Grandmaster von Hompesch is no friend to the French Republic,' began Vanderville cautiously.

Von Torring steepled his fingers, and rested his chin on them, 'His Most Eminent Highness Prince von Hompesch was only elected last year. He is the first grandmaster to be selected from the German *langues* and his election reflected the Order turning away from France, which country's revolution has near mortally wounded it, towards Russia and the East.

'The election of von Hompesch was strongly championed by our Anglo-Bavarian *langue*. They felt some renewed vigour was needed; after a remarkably successful tenure as grandmaster, the previous incumbent, de Rohan suffered a stroke, after which his utility to the Order was extremely limited. In fact, each year that he lingered after that, he was a drag on the Order much as seaweed, constantly growing, slows the passage of a ship through the water.'

Vanderville scratched his head thoughtfully. 'You support the increase of Russian influence in the Order, then?'

'Since the total loss of the French commanderies, the Order lacks a financial powerbase. After the Revolution the Order started to look towards Russia as its protector. Russia, not France, is now our diplomatic orient, and from her comes the light. A faint light it is true, and false in some ways, but seeing that it has lit up the horizon, we must follow where it leads. We adapt or we fall.'

He turned away to the window silently, his hands clasped behind his back, and Vanderville became aware that the interview was over. You will fall when General Bonaparte arrives with the grand fleet, he thought, but he did not say it.

Eva indicated that she would join him downstairs shortly, and as he bowed his way out of the room, he reflected that the courtly soldier von Torring's deep affection for the Order had touched his sympathy. He regretted the necessity of disrupting this chivalric relic's peace for the security of France, but, he shrugged, General Bonaparte knew what he was about. He made for the staircase.

'Wait a moment!' came a voice as he began his descent.

Vanderville lifted his head to see a slender well-formed young man with very light hair clattering down the passage towards the stairs, his sword bouncing on the floor with each step. He recognised him as the bailli's pink-nosed attendant. 'I wanted to take a good look at a Frenchman of the Republic while I had the chance,' said the newcomer.

Without stopping, Vanderville said over his shoulder, 'Are French men in Malta so rare as to be a public curiosity? I thought most of the knights, your brethren, are French?'

'Ah, but you are one of the French devils we shoot at, not one of those we fight alongside,' said the young knight cheerfully.

'Well, you are seeing the back of one, make the most of it, for you will be facing our fronts soon enough.' Vanderville reached the landing of the staircase and halted. He held up his arms and revolved slowly on the spot. 'Take a good look. Note that I have no tail nor horns.'

The young man covered the last steps to close with him and broke into an unexpected smile and a chuckle. He was about Vanderville's own age, and wore his uniform well, while the long sword he bore was so old as to be an antique. His eyes twinkled merrily, and he said, 'It would be a shame to shoot any man so bold as to make Sant' Elmo's leap from a moving vessel.' He swept off his hat and bowed. 'I regret that I have the advantage of you. My name is De Rechberg, will you breakfast with me, *m'sieur*? A quick cup only, but there is time. Your escort Donna Mifsud will tarry some time above with the bailli, you can be assured of that.'

Without waiting for Vanderville's assent he led the way to a terrace overlooking the internal courtyard, and summoned coffee and cups of chocolate from a servant.

'I cannot tell you what a pleasure it is to see a new face,' said de Rechberg companionably. 'I arrived here myself only recently after a long sojourn ashore, but already I am sadly reminded how tedious much of the company here on our rocky Convent can be. I can assure you that an addiction to loose women and strong drink is very common among my fellows – I fear you will find our manners very low, nowhere grace or education. The Order is, I'm afraid, in this respect very much decayed.'

To Vanderville's startled look, he laughed lightly and said, 'You think I am running down the Order to a – I shall not say enemy, but to an adversary. It is true we are not what we were, there is no state secret betrayed in telling you *that*. And I believe I am right in saying that it is too late now for any intelligence you may glean to be ferried out to our adversaries. The traitor Possuelgieu and his fellow spies accomplished all that could be done in that direction months ago.'

De Rechberg sighed and downed another coffee, 'But there are enough of us of the right spirit to man our walls when called upon. Even if we have failed to keep you out!' He laughed again, and patted Vanderville's hand companionably. 'And the

Order still has much besides our walls to boast of. Have you seen the hospital?'

He waved at another knight who was crossing the galleries above, peering at them over the balustrade. The man frowned darkly as his eyes rested on Vanderville and he appeared to hurry his way towards the grand staircase.

'Here comes one of those I told you about now,' said de Rechberg. 'Nothing of religion about him. This is what I mean by corruption. Persons who are blinded by their rude habits might find a certain wellbeing and commodity here. Their laziness will never be disturbed. One wakes up late, passes the day in idleness until the arrival of supper, followed by another round of gaming. Finally, one goes to sleep at four in the morning after a night of playing cards and indulgence. For many of these idle fellows that is the most desirable life they can imagine.'

'In this matter of the Republic, maybe you are on the wrong side after all?' offered Vanderville mischievously.

'Perhaps you are right,' agreed de Rechberg. 'But it is too late to rearrange the ranks now.' He half rose and picked up his hat from the table. 'And speaking of late, I had better get to my duties. I have a fort to secure, and powder magazines to inspect. Will I walk down with you?'

As they arrived at the stair, de Rechberg spoke again.

'Do not commit the error of believing that because their lives are dissolute and ill focussed on religion the knights cannot fight. That disgusting creature coming down the stair now, for instance, whom I am almost ashamed to admit is one of our own brothers, is one of the most accomplished swordsmen on the island. The hours he does not spend in dissipation he sweats out in the *salle d'exercise*. More than one of the new knights have made the error of believing that because he is a foul drunk, he is not deadly. And as for the poor Maltese, the number he has prinked or slain is indeed legion. The art of violence is no respecter of conviction.'

Vanderville reflected that the individual skill of a swordsman was insignificant weighed in the balance against the science of war as practised by the Republic. Their engineers, massed battalions of seasoned veterans and numerous well-served artillery would sweep away these brave relics of the feudal past if they could not modernise themselves. It had been true on the continent, and here on the Convent rock, time had run out for the medieval adherents of the Order.

The knight descending the stair was shaped much the same as de Rechberg, but fuller in the body, and with an oddly narrow head that appeared to have been transposed from another smaller person. Whereas de Rechberg was fair, what hair the newcomer still possessed was dark like his face and eyes. He greeted de Rechberg affably enough and the two knights loped down the wide stone stair on either side of Vanderville. They both moved like soldiers, and he sensed that these two, at least, were not mere sinecure hunters.

Vanderville was setting a fair pace, and they bobbed along with him like two eager thoroughbred puppies. The new arrival was bubbling over with something he wanted to say, and after several awkward false starts, he adjusted the hang of his sword self-consciously before blurting out abruptly, 'Is it true that you came over the parapet of St Gregory's bastion?'

Vanderville frowned without checking his pace, and de Rechberg blushed. 'I am sure Fra' Haintlet does not mean to imply any... elaboration on your part,' he said, tailing off abruptly. His eyes sought confirmation from his peer, who was knitting his dark brow.

'It's quite incredible,' said the dark-faced knight. 'I would scarcely have believed it possible, had the bailli not a confirmation.'

Vanderville looked sideways at him, and Haintlet nodded thoughtfully as he continued, 'A fisherman observed what the grandmaster's sentries failed to – a ship passing too close to the bastion. Its unusual proximity to his little tub caused him some handling problems distracting him from his tunny gazing. He could not credit it himself when the first man jumped, he thought it was a trick of the light. He was not convinced he had seen straight until he saw the second man leap.'

'I was given to understand that the leap has been made before,' began Vanderville cautiously.

'Oh, there are legends,' said de Rechberg waving a hand airily.

'Don Loqui is said to have made the leap in full steel harness during the time of the Great Siege three hundred years ago,' added the other knight. 'But we have always thought the tale so much feudal braggadocio.'

'I don't think it would have done had I been wearing armour,' said Vanderville thoughtfully. 'It was a damn near-run thing as it was.'

'Then it is true,' sighed de Rechberg. 'I would have given anything to have been there.'

'To hurl me from the ramparts?' answered Vanderville wryly.

'I don't think I could have quite brought myself to that,' mused de Rechberg seriously. 'Naturally you would have been arrested on reaching the parapet itself; we must cleave to duty.'

'Of course,' added Haintlet, 'I myself would have run you through, but it was damnably well done all the same.'

'Truly it was a bold leap,' sighed De Rechberg. 'You must promise to tell us everything. Under the discretion of the fraternity of arms of course.' He winked. 'We may be enemies, but we are brothers I believe.' He traced a pyramidal sign on the pommel of his sword.

They paused a moment in the cool vestibule at the bottom of the stairs. The door of the *auberge* was open and hot sun flooded through it to dapple the floor at their feet. Vanderville started towards the street, but De Rechberg placed a hand gently on his arm.

'After you have seen the grandmaster, will you sup here with us and relate the full history of the exploit to us?'

At his hesitation, Haintlet laughed scornfully and added, 'No state secrets – just the jump.'

'Just the jump,' assented Vanderville, relieved. 'I shall return then, this evening should I still be at liberty.' The two knights stood back nodding with satisfaction. Vanderville returned their courteous bows and stepped out into the light.

He emerged blinking into the sunshine. There was no sign of Eva, her *kalesh* or the boy Duccio, and he squinted unsuccessfully up and down the street to see where they rested. With a sigh he straightened his aching bones and hobbled to the nearest corner to see if they were waiting there in the shade. Around the corner it was cooler, better for his aching head, but then out of the sun's beating heat he was reminded that his shoulder still hurt him considerably. Chiding himself at his cavilling like an old man, he mastered his impatience and settled down to wait for Eva, using his good shoulder to lean on the palace wall.

On the wall of the house opposite there were painted a number of small red crosses and stooping down to examine them he saw a name and date on each. The last and lowest cross was fresh, the paint still tacky. He peered closer to make out the name, and at that moment he sensed a rapid movement from the shadows behind him. As he responded to it, two arms were flung forcefully about him from behind, pinning his good arm to the slung one.

He struggled furiously, but a second pair of hands thrust a sack over his head, tugging it down, and tying it around him. The sack stank like a stable, and blinded, confused and confined, he was bodily lifted from the ground and hurled down onto something that was hard, at the height of his waist. He kicked out backwards and had the satisfaction of hearing a grunt as his heel connected, but the respite gained was lost, as his head and shoulders were pummelled under a rain of clumsy but rapid blows. The surface under him lurched to one side, and he realised it was a cart or carriage that had pulled away. Then in darkness to the sound of trotting hoofbeats he was carried away to God knew where.

Chapter Six

After the jolting progress had continued for some time, unseen hands dragged Vanderville up and pushed him into a seat and the sack was removed from over his head. It was a relief to have the use of his arms again, but on trying them he was rewarded with a renewal of the morning's agony in the damaged shoulder. He clutched it impulsively and the other arm griped where the sack's cords had cut into it. He resigned himself to the seat for the moment.

He was inside a sombre *kalesh* facing forward, and opposite him was a man in a black cassock who was peering out through a gap in the drawn curtains. The priest was not a pleasant-looking man. He was of middle age and had the purple bloated face of the perpetually self-indulgent. His flesh was gross, and he inhabited it uncomfortably, as if the essence of the man himself was a diseased and blackened kernel revealed by a bite into an overripe plum. One of his hands rested carelessly on a large evil-looking knife in his ample cassocked lap.

After the violence of his abduction, the contrast of this plump priest opposite him in the relative comfort of the *kalesh* was stark to Vanderville. It was a peculiar and uneasy feeling that he resented doubly while feeling temporarily unequal to contest it. He glared at the side of the priest's head and tried the handle of the door, but it appeared to be locked. He looked up at the leather roof of the carriage, creaking above their heads. It was boldly embossed and gilded with a scene of a thirsty hunter and his thirsty dog sprawled besides a brook, sipping the water.

Drawing his head back into the interior the priest met his eyes and announced, 'I am Assessore Gatt.' He spoke in an ugly graceless croak which did nothing to modify Vanderville's initial appraisal of his person, and from his breath there came a sickly-sweet smell of rotten meat. 'You will hand me your papers now,' added the priest, carefully covering the knife hilt with one hand.

'The only papers I have are for wiping my behind,' replied Vanderville with scorn. 'When I have finished you are welcome to them.'

The priest Gatt did not even bother shrugging. He drew back the curtain and leaned against the open window's sill to nod to someone outside. Vanderville leant forward to observe. They were proceeding through a quiet street at a lope, and a second vehicle drew up alongside them.

The vehicle trotting alongside them was a small one, little more than a wheeled chair with a leather hood, drawn by a powerfully muscled mastiff dog. It was somewhat below the level of the window and Vanderville had to crane his neck to see its occupant who was both passenger and driver. He was an unwieldy and meagre man, not ill-clad in a gentleman's dark suit of clothes, and he held the dog's reins with his knobbled knees. The poor animal puffed and panted, Monsignor smoked, and gaped around himself with the most blessed indifference. He possessed a not-unpleasant face, waxy in texture, mottled cream and grey, much like a cod's belly. Above it his hair rose to a carefully coiffured and powdered summit.

The effect was whimsical, but the eyes of the man were anything but when presently those pale objects were turned up to regard Vanderville whom he greeted affably, through a gust of exhaled smoke.

'Good morning to you. You will forgive the unorthodox way I have contrived our meeting. My name is Carpegna. Monsignor Giulio dei Conti Carpegna. Do not fret young man, I mean you no harm, but it was essential that I speak with you at the earliest opportunity.'

'Could you not have accomplished that without this charade?' asked Vanderville, glancing and scowling at the smug ham-beast opposite him who covered him warily with the knife, his red face redolent of malevolent intent.

The man in the dog cart considered this, his eyes flicking from the road before him and back to Vanderville as he continued, 'I have found that the nature of my position – I am the head inquisitor of the Holy Office on Malta – is often misunderstood by foreigners. Labouring under misconceptions about the nature of our business, they are loath to accede promptly to the prospect of an interview with the functionaries of the Holy Office.' He paused to navigate a narrow arch under which both vehicles clattered and swayed.

'A desecration of a church, especially of the mortal kind, merits the involvement of our organisation,' he said, tugging his reins. 'Our palace, what the locals call the Palazz tal-Inkwizitur, is in Vittoriosa, the ancient headquarters of the knights, but we maintain facilities here in Valletta, the new city. It's all a bit sub-rosa, you understand, because we of the Church must not be seen to encroach on the civil power's prerogatives – which here in Malta means His Eminence the grandmaster of the Order.'

'Doubtless I will meet Pilate in due course,' answered Vanderville with careless defiance, recovering his battered hat from the carriage floor.

The man raised his eyebrows and emitted a strange vibrant titter, which jarred equally the ears and eyes, but then said gravely, 'You are pleased to be facetious, my dear young man, but this is very far from being a laughing matter. You would be better advised to direct your humour towards explaining the circumstances in which you came to be seen in company with a dead man behind an altar in the Maddalene.'

Vanderville considered. It appeared that he was not immediately to be charged by this clerical relic with murder, which was much a better state of affairs than he expected. He was vaguely aware that his brain had been neatly making connections while they sparred and had arrived at a conclusion and was waiting for his mouth to catch up. Whether it was the beating heat of the sun on the leather roof of the *kalesh* or the after-effects of his fall that morning, he had the impression that he was being slow. It seemed the other man was in possession of certain elusive facts that evaded his own understanding and was corralling them long before Vanderville became aware of them, before releasing them tamed and harnessed to his will. His experience with commanding officers had equipped him to stand interrogations with patience, if not with equanimity, and he decided to hold his peace as far as possible and let the interrogator make the running.

While they discoursed and Vanderville asserted his innocence, the corpulent priest Gatt had hung his head from the opposite window of the *kalesh* and settling his bulk back into the rearward-facing seat addressed his superior. 'We are being followed, *Monsignor*.'

Carpegna too glanced behind his cart's hood, and hunching over his reins, drove the dog chair into a faster trot that was matched instantly by the *kalesh*.

'It appears that you have friends who wish to recover your person. I propose to escort you to Vittoriosa where we will have leisure to talk, but should that not prove possible, we must come quickly to an understanding here and now.' He glanced behind his dog cart and spoke more quickly now.

'There are two great powers on this island, the Order, and the Church, and you must needs be under the power of one or the other. My purpose is to make you aware of this and offer you a choice. As inquisitor I also serve as Apostolic delegate, the Pope's voice, and right-hand man on the island. If you consider the Grandmaster von Hompesch as the Pope's lay administrator, this naturally gives rise to room for much confusion and antagonism. I have tried to recast this relationship, and His Eminence is not closed to these overtures, although he is suspicious.'

He had gradually been increasing the pace of his dog cart while they spoke. It was apparent that they were in a race, and the *kalesh* lurched alarmingly as one of its speeding wheels glanced against a kerbstone. Vanderville became aware of hostile shouts from close behind them; their pursuers were closing the gap. Carpegna's face was tense, and he had to raise his voice to a shout to impart his last words of advice.

'The grandmaster and his inquisitor live physically in two opposite wings of the Grand Harbour urban node. The grandmaster here in the new convent city, and I in the old, but still important Vittoriosa. The two cities are interconnected and separated by the harbour itself. Be aware that those who exist under the protection of one authority can walk as per their whim against the will of the other authority. If you find the patronage of the grandmaster not to your taste, and find yourself in need of my protection, cross the harbour by boat, and come to me or Canon Gatt.' He glanced again over his shoulder. 'I am in need of your help,' he said urgently, 'if I am to get to the bottom of the events at the Maddalena. If you are removed from my custody, beware of everyone, there is sinister work afoot here. And young man, keep your eyes and ears open.'

Carpegna's voice tailed off as all his concentration turned to the handling of his cart, which he was swinging into a sharp loop as he pulled up on the reins, forcing the panting dog to a halt. The *kalesh* accomplished the same manoeuvre with less grace, and Gatt manipulated some hidden lever behind his head and kicked open the door deftly. He bundled Vanderville sharply out of the carriage, whipping his knife into the capacious sleeve of his cassock as they emerged right onto the edge of a deserted dock. The harbour water lapped at the wall below them, and a small boat bobbed at the dock's stair with two boatmen waiting at the oars.

'At your service,' said Carpegna, rising nimbly from the dog chair and bowing to Vanderville. 'And we have no time to lose if we are to prevent a tragedy. I can tell you already that the *Cavaliere* von Seeau was quite possibly murdered by the knights of his own *langue* and there will most likely follow another death within days.'

He was interrupted by a second *kalesh* that thundered into the narrow dock's edge, both doors bursting open before it stopped, and two figures, swords in hand, rushed towards them. Gatt presented himself between the person of the inquisitor and the new arrivals, in whose persons Vanderville recognised the knights Haintlet and de Rechberg.

The Bavarians sprinted forward, fanning out as they came like experienced swordsmen. Haintlet covered Canon Gatt with his weapon, separating him from his master and fixing him to the spot, while de Rechberg tucked his blade under one arm, and eluding the mastiff's reach, halted before Carpegna and Vanderville.

De Rechberg bowed briskly and addressed Carpegna. 'I thought we could have a conversation about the illegal rendering of suspects.'

They were interrupted as Gatt lurched towards de Rechberg, he was surprisingly quick on his feet for a large man, and Haintlet, who was quicker still, growled ominously and interposed himself between them, closing the distance on the canon, and forcing him away from the others at sword point. Gatt's knife hand was inside his other sleeve. Stepping away from the combatants De Rechberg cleared his throat and muttered from the side of his mouth, 'Can we make this simpler, Fra' Haintlet?'

Pouncing forward, Haintlet punched Gatt twice in the face, hard, with his off hand. His movements were so swift that Vanderville's eyes could hardly catch them. Neither, it appeared, could Gatt, and he staggered backwards two steps before toppling off the wharf into the water. Carpegna began to intervene, but De Rechberg held up a hand politely to intercept his protest. The two burly boatmen rose as one to mount the quay, but Haintlet's sword was now covering the steps that led from the quay to the boat. Its occupants decided wisely against interference and instead busied themselves retrieving Gatt from the water.

'Now,' said de Rechberg brightly. 'Where were we?'

Carpegna ignored him, inclining his head politely to Vanderville. 'I'm sure we will have the opportunity to speak again shortly. When you discover that not all is as it seems here in the Convent you may find the need of friends in the Church. You know where to find me.'

With that he tripped neatly down to the waiting boat where a sullen Gatt had been retrieved and was crouched dripping in the bows, his hate-filled gaze intent on Vanderville and the Bavarians. It was the inscrutable eyes of Carpegna that stayed with Vanderville though, and he met them for a long time as the boat slid off into the Grand Harbour, the inquisitor standing boldly in the prow and staring evenly back at the figures conferring on the wharf.

Haintlet had a hand inside his coat holding his chest and he winced now. When he drew his hand out, it was sticky with blood. In response to de Rechberg's enquiry he indicated the boat with a wave and said in something between a cough and a smile, 'He liked the knife. I doubted not he liked the knife, but he still gave me a sting.' Vanderville and de Rechberg helped him into the waiting *kalesh*, and the liveried muleteer led them from the docks at a more sedate pace than that with which they had arrived.

While the *kalesh* lumbered away, de Rechberg occupied himself in opening Haintlet's coat to ascertain that the wound was of no great consequence, though bloody enough until bound with a handkerchief. As he worked, he explained to Vanderville how the two knights had witnessed his abduction by the inquisitor from a window of the *Auberge* de Bavaria before following at a desperate pace.

'The worst of it,' said Haintlet, grunting as de Rechberg helped him back into his coat, 'is that the inquisitor's little devil I slapped is my confessor. God only knows what penance I shall receive from him next time he has me in his box. Normally he rather enjoys my renditions, especially those about persuading reluctant girls with the back of my hand, but a man and his confessor should not strike one another if they can help it.'

'One must follow the conventions,' agreed de Rechberg, grimacing at Vanderville, to whom he said, 'What did they want with you, anyway?'

Loath to relate his near-involvement with von Seeau's death, Vanderville prevaricated. 'They wanted to know if I had heard the Good News, and to check I was not a Moor.' Even Haintlet chuckled at this, although the effort cost him no uncommon pain.

Vanderville was still expressing his thanks to the Bavarian knights when the *kalesh* arrived at the residence of the grandmaster of the Order, which was another of those honey-coloured self-effacing palaces. It was well that the stones were imbued with a shade of rose from the stark noon light, as the repetitive facade more resembled a prison than the residence of a petty monarch. It consisted of four immense stark walls with windows cut in at irregular intervals. Even the balconies were irregularly constructed without symmetry, planning or taste.

At the door he was handed over by the porter into the custody of the grandmaster's guards, a development that promised anything but good. Bidding farewell to de Rechberg and Haintlet he surrendered himself into the escort's custody and they led him into the depths of the vast structure. In the lower part of the palace reigned the most deathly calm, and no sound reached his ears as his escort strayed through winding passages and intricate galleries of the immense edifice before fetching up at the foot of an absurdly grand staircase. It was of such dimensions that two carriages could pass abreast without touching.

They were stairs built to imbue the lowly with a feeling of inferiority, and Vanderville recalled Dante's perpetual lament of the exile, 'It is bitter to climb the stairs in other people's houses.' It must be bitter indeed for those stairs to be scaled by people who have never known power, he thought, and for some reason the Maltese vagrant children came to mind – what would the boy Duccio make of this symbol of his island's subjugation?

At the top, the majestic stairs divided into two stately branches, one, he was told, leading to the library, the other to the armoury and picture gallery. They took the latter and arrived in an antechamber thronged with a courtly bewigged masculine flock sufficiently numerous to compensate for the previous deserted rooms. Here were bishops daubed over with lace, stern baillis of *langues*, bustling secretaries of state, self-important generals, fine lords of the bedchamber and prelates of all denominations, as conspicuous as embroidered uniforms, stars, crosses, and gold keys could make them. A multitude of bows and salutations were going forward with refined pomposity, and to a man they swayed instinctively away from Vanderville as he entered, surrounded by his armed escort.

They were greeted by a liveried palace chamberlain who was plump, fair, and doughy with large unblinking eyes. He struck Vanderville as something between an underdone bread roll and an owl, alarmingly human, in the way that owls are. With a portentous airy manner, he divested Vanderville of his escort and jostled him along to the portal of the presence chamber. The ceremonial for entering was almost royal; there was a clash of halberds, and a thumping of rods of office appropriate to the dignity of His Eminence Ferdinand Joseph Hermann Anton von Hompesch zu Bolheim, the first German grandmaster of the Knights Hospitaller, formally the Order of St John of Jerusalem, now better known as the Knights of Malta.

The presence chamber he was admitted to looked much as Vanderville would have imagined the throne room of a medieval fortress. The walls were bare but for colossal Gobelin tapestries that hung from the beamed roof to the floor, which was of the same pale gold stone as the walls. The sparse solid furniture was garishly adorned with painted armorial bearings. Behind a vast table, seated in a neo-gothic armchair, was perched the sovereign of Malta attended by a circular enclosure of fine clothes and smirking faces. The grandmaster called to Vanderville's mind nothing so much as a cobbler in carnival dress. His magnificent robes dominated his shrivelled frame and instead of being made more imposing by the folds of brocade the man was reduced to a mere coat hook, and a coat hook composed of ill-looking grey meat at that. He was reading from an elaborate scroll and the moment he had finished, twenty long necks were poked forth, and it was a glorious struggle amongst some of the most decorated who should kiss his hand first.

Along one wall under tall windows hovered a further string of footsore counsellors and supernumerary knights, exuding haughtiness and anxiety in disharmonious measure. The old knights were like tortoises, stretching out their thin-skinned necks and blinking rheumy eyes for favours. Their younger brethren bustled and bobbed like arrogant inflamed hares, eager for insult, an excuse to bounce their honour's fragile probity against some passing functionary. They affected to ignore Vanderville, while their bristling ears betrayed their assumed insouciance.

With his hair and face still singed from the discharge of the musket in the Maddalena church, his worn and dirty second-best coat, and scuffed boots, Vanderville was acutely aware of the poor figure he cut. So, he drew himself up just a little straighter to compensate, suppressing the muted murmur of protest from his still-strained limbs with an effort of will, and tucked his battered hat smartly under his slung arm.

The chamberlain marched him to a point in the centre of the frightful room and halted him there before the grandmaster. 'The *gentleman* you requested your guard to apprehend, Your Most Eminent Highness,' he announced. Vanderville was unsure of the etiquette; he knew the grandmaster was equivalent to a sovereign prince, but did a prisoner bow? He settled for a defiant lift of his chin and rested his gaze above the grey wig of the shambles sitting inside the over-large throne.

As Vanderville was announced the councillors surrounding the grandmaster raised their heads sharply to assess him. The grandmaster himself seemed oblivious to his presence and continued his examination of the scroll. As he waited to be noticed, Vanderville's thoughts strayed back to Carpegna's last words. He had insisted that Mayflower, if von Seeau was indeed Mayflower, might have been murdered by the knights of his own *langue*. Were then von Rechberg and Haintlet the friends to him that they appeared? He could certainly see the deadly and uncouth Haintlet as an assassin, and, after all, they had delivered him up here to the grandmaster's mercy despite their fraternal protestations.

Not that it mattered now. Vanderville had lasted less than a day in his new covert occupation before being arraigned here as a prisoner of the knights. He assumed that by dusk he would find himself in a dungeon as barbarically antiquated as this chamber, with nothing to look forward to but beatings, and a last glimpse of the sea before they hanged him from the walls of the Great Harbour.

While he was intent on these dismal preoccupations, a little door in the exterior wall between two windows flew open and, from a place where nothing would have been suspected except a broom cupboard, out popped a figure whose head and shoulders were swathed in a curious oriental robe. It was the man of the marketplace in Piazza Forbici who Vanderville had dismissed as unimportant, and as he shuffled haplessly across the chamber in capacious carpet slippers, the ranks of councillors parted deferentially, and even the grandmaster looked up expectantly.

There was something about the way this self-possessed bundle of old clothes moved that was familiar, and as the figure approached the grandmaster to make his obeisance, he shrugged off his hood, displaying his ponderous greying profile and Vanderville gasped, knowing him instantly. It was Felix Gracchus: the hero of Mombello, the villain of Rome, and his own most accomplished and devious former companion in intrigue. Vanderville blinked in astonishment and dropped his hat.

As he rose from his deep bow Gracchus turned his head slyly to Vanderville and blinked twice like an owl, and when Vanderville merely goggled at him in consternation he repeated the gesture with calm impatience, and slowly Vanderville recalled the system of signals they had developed together for private and silent communication in public. Oh Christ! Here we go again, he thought.

'Say nothing' was the message conveyed by Gracchus. Say nothing to the grandmaster? Say nothing to indicate you have recognised me? Say nothing and follow my lead? Terms half remembered and perhaps never fully understood jostled in his mind. Not for the first time he resented the ridiculous silent language invention of Gracchus that had served them so ill at the papal embassy in Rome.

'But my dear Tirdflingen! Here you are at last!' exclaimed Gracchus suddenly, performing a theatrical doubletake, and both Vanderville and the grandmaster regarded him with baffled surprise. 'But there has been some mistake Your Most Eminent Highness,' Gracchus continued, addressing the grandmaster. 'This young man is neither a Frenchman, nor, to the best of my knowledge, a spy.'

'He is known to you, Baron?' asked the grandmaster, turning his head to survey Vanderville's sorry figure better. Vanderville saw Gracchus repeat the signal for silence, and he turned his eyes modestly to the ground under the combined gazes of the two older men.

'Why certainly,' continued Gracchus glibly. 'He is Dermide Tirdflingen, a young Fleming who has been in my service as a private secretary for... Oh, some three years now. We became separated during the unpleasantness I mentioned to you at Naples, and now I suppose, he has made his way onwards by some merchant ship to join me here.' He bowled his eyes back to Vanderville. 'I am delighted to see you again Tirdflingen, I hope you are prepared to resume your duties immediately?'

Vanderville bent low in a sweeping bow that served to conceal his astonishment. By the time his head returned to its usual posture his composure was also substantially recovered, and he managed a brave smile and uttered, 'I am equally pleased to be able to place myself at your service again, sir.'

The grandmaster looked slowly from one to the other of them. 'Well that appears to clear up this mystery,' he mused distrustfully. And then more sternly he advised Vanderville, 'It would have saved considerable trouble if you had simply presented your papers and passport on landing at the docks, young man.'

'I greatly regret having inconvenienced your guardsmen, Your Highness,' said Vanderville, repeating his bow. 'The fact is that my papers were mislaid as a consequence of the unfortunate incident my master has described, and finding myself landed here, I thought it best to discover him before presenting myself at the *questura* for the purpose of having new papers issued.'

'Well perhaps you were right,' frowned the grandmaster. He shrugged. 'Since you vouch for this young man, Baron Pellegrew, I will release him into your custody until such time as a proper investigation can be conducted into his antecedents, and his situation regularised according to the proper procedure.'

His head nodded down again under the momentous weight of his royal wig, and he regarded the foot of his throne gravely. The matter appeared to be closed, and Vanderville was wondering how to take his leave when the antiquated hairpiece flicked up again and the grandmaster addressed Gracchus, who had withdrawn towards his broom cupboard.

'One moment, Pellegrew. I believe you are practising a subterfuge on me.'

The councillors leaned in with the smug sureness of sharks scenting blood. Gracchus had frozen, motionless, halfway to the windows and a tremor ran up Vanderville's spine and lodged icily in his wounded shoulder.

'What did you say the name of this secretary of yours is? Dermide Tirdflingen? Your secretary is the *poet* Tirdflingen then?' Vanderville saw the frozen tension evaporate from Gracchus's frame as the grandmaster continued, addressing him now,

'I am no less delighted to have you here, young man, than I am in the company of your master.' Gracchus bowed extravagantly once more. 'Your fame, as well as your eccentri— that is to say, your peculiar and vivid approach to life, are not unknown to us here.'

He was interrupted by a crash, as Gracchus upset a tray of refreshments which had been placed on an elegant antique half pillar besides the window.

'Forgive me my clumsiness Your Eminence,' he said, stepping aside from the pillar as a page of the grandmaster rushed in to attend to the debris. 'Perhaps we had better reconvene at a more propitious moment. I have remembered also that I am engaged to dine at the *Auberge* de Bavaria, and I fear we do not have long to make Tirdflingen presentable. Repairing the ardours of a long journey and the loss of all his luggage will doubtless wreak havoc both on my purse, and the demands of the Convent's tailors.'

The grandmaster appeared doubtful, but he confined himself to a shake of his white head. 'You are quite right, Baron Pellegrew, although I feel sure your renowned purse will stand the strain of your charge's new equipage. We must all be packing our wardrobes soon unless I attend to the grave matters threatening our peaceful moments here. No matter, when this storm has passed over the rock, we will have leisure again to enjoy more cultured moments.' He stroked his chin thoughtfully. 'But stay, need we wait so long? A poetry evening can be arranged even in these strained times. At my residence of San Antonio shall we say? No – perhaps it is too far from the seat of things in these perilous times. The people are restless, and I must maintain my seat here in the Convent for now. No matter, the details will be arranged. Shall we say the evening three days hence? I will send word. In the meantime, Pellegrew, I positively forbid you to let this young man leave us before those moments arrive, do you hear me?'

He appeared to be joking, but Vanderville caught the merest hint of steel beneath the grandmaster's urbane manner as he added, 'Please young Tirdflingen, give your parole to the captain of the Guard and make yourself free of the byways and peaks of our convent city. When you have gratified the first impulses of curiosity, return here and I will be honoured to have time to hear your thoughts.'

Gracchus inclined his head with a slight bow, which Vanderville mirrored, and under the merciless and unconvinced stare of the Captain of the Guard the two purveyors of deceit passed out of the audience chamber side by side.

As a chamberlain ushered them through the antechamber doors Vanderville opened his mouth eagerly to ask the first of a hundred questions, but Gracchus silenced him with an impatient hiss, 'Later!' Despite his earlier words, he seemed anything but pleased to see Vanderville, and he strode ahead, leaving Vanderville, who had belatedly realised his hat was still on the audience room floor, to trip after him through the meandering halls and antechambers that led from the audience room to the palace gates.

Vanderville was concerned to see that Gracchus appeared still to be in an ill humour at the gates, and he even snapped at the porter as he handed him a stick. A guardsman caught up with them there and imposed on them both to sign a document releasing Vanderville into Gracchus's custody. This paper he rolled up and carried away, depositing Vanderville's hat on the table as he left. This article was the worse for wear and did little to shield Vanderville's eyes from the flare of scorching sun that greeted them as they stepped out into the piazza before the grandmaster's palace.

Gracchus removed a pair of green-tinted spectacles from some hidden place in his shawl and waved away the young boys advancing on them with parasols. 'I suppose you did not eat anything in there?' he asked with a nod at the building they had just left.

'If there are kitchens in there, I saw nothing of them,' concurred Vanderville, suddenly aware of an appetite stimulated by the rapid and unsettling oscillations of fortune he had been subjected to over the preceding twenty-four hours. 'Very well,' said Gracchus. 'Let us address your stomach while you tell me what on earth you are doing here, apart from upsetting the progress of long-deliberated plans with your ill-considered gallantries and disreputable appearance.'

Vanderville opened his mouth to quibble, but finding his indignation directed only at the rapidly disappearing back of Gracchus's head as he hobbled off down one of the vertiginously steep stepped streets, he thought better of protest and set off after him.

Chapter Seven

Despite Gracchus leaning resolutely on his stick, they made short work of the dusty pavements, and after countless twists and turns that left Vanderville at a loss to recover his bearings, the older man pulled up at a dirty brown door set in the wall of a crumbling palazzo. After an extraordinary set of contortions and delving, one of Gracchus's myriad coat pockets disgorged a heavy iron key that was partner to the lock, and with a furtive glance up and down the street, he pushed the door open. 'They will have followed us of course,' he explained, and ushered Vanderville through the door which he locked behind them. They passed into an enclosed garden that was miserably untended.

Where the tall palms that soared overhead had been colonised by climbing plants a trellised canopy had been created that provided shade and seclusion. Gracchus led the way under this to a central fountain whose basin was clogged with fallen leaves. The unkempt undergrowth had been cleared to expose a bench of the same stone as the high walls that enclosed the courtyard. The garden was small, no more than thirty feet on each side and Vanderville observed other open doors that led into the palazzo.

Vanderville was unsure how to begin. The relations between the two men had been sundered in Rome and they had parted company with a determination to pursue different paths, yet here they were, and worse, he was in Gracchus's debt. 'You appear to have bagged yourself good quarters,' he said brightly to Gracchus, who merely grunted and eased himself carefully down onto the bench, indicating to Vanderville to do the same.

'The trees, as well as shading us from the sun, offer some degree of privacy from prying eyes and ears,' he announced. 'The grandmaster has placed this palazzo at my disposal, but unfortunately all of the servants are his creatures, and I cannot so much as roll over in bed without them reporting it to His Most Eminent Highness.'

'Are you here in some official capacity, then?' questioned Vanderville, looking around carefully. The dilapidated palazzo was grander than it had appeared from the street, and four storeys of serried windows opened onto the garden, the upper ones quite obscured by the unfettered profusion of advancing vegetation. The lower windows were barred and shuttered.

Gracchus ignored his question. 'This is a prison of a different sort from the one from with which you have recently been threatened,' he began. 'Although I am ostensibly an honoured guest of Grandmaster von Hompesch, I am convinced that he is not altogether happy about my bona fides, and I owe my reception here to his covetousness and curiosity as much as the dignity of my name.' He stretched out his leg and rubbed it thoughtfully. 'By the way, I go here by Baron Pellegrew – please be careful to use it at all times. The slightest misstep will be observed and reported, and besides having the direst consequences for both of us, will also have repercussions for many, many others of the most serious nature. There is a deep game at play on this misbegotten rock.

'I wish I could take you fully into my confidence, but it would be highly dangerous for us both, so for now you must be content with half-truths, and in any case, instead of indulging your curiosity you must immediately familiarise yourself with the cover identity I have improvised for you.' He fumbled under the bench and pulled out a dirty bell that may once have been bright brass. At its sound, an aged retainer emerged from the palazzo, and Gracchus ordered refreshment in precise terms.

As the retainer departed Gracchus tuned to Vanderville and, removing his spectacles, contemplated him with a penetrating eye. 'And now, perhaps you will tell me what *you* are doing here in Valletta? I can only presume that your business is of the kind to complicate matters.'

Vanderville began to recount his adventures since they had parted so unceremoniously at Rome, but Gracchus cut him short. 'As long journeys, however interesting their incidents and pleasant the prospects that may present themselves to the traveller, merely weary the listener, you shall confine myself to an account of your movements since arriving at this singular rock, and I shall do the same.'

'I regret that I am unable to reveal my mission. Confidential orders.'

'I see. Yet it requires no great leap to imagine why a French staff officer is here incognito. So the rumours are true, and the great fleet is on its way.'

'Don't you dare try to squeeze me for information,' said Vanderville, cutting in, 'unless you are prepared to tell me your own business. If I am to pass as your personal secretary, I must at least know what we are about and where we are supposed to have been.'

'If I am evasive with you, I assure you that it is merely through an unwillingness to expose you to unwelcome attention. It may be that some danger accrues to my activities here in the Convent, and I am loath to expose you to the consequences of my quixotical enterprise. However, as you point out, your new position as my secretary demands that you must be familiar with my cover, my legend of deceit.'

Gracchus paused his digression as a servant brought a tray bearing small glasses of white-coloured liquid and little silver dishes of oysters with hot pepper sauce. He shucked two oysters in quick succession and consumed them as if he was inhaling air and then began again as the servant departed.

'I called my purpose here quixotical, and it is,' he said, his eyes shining with a strange enthusiasm that might have been partially owing to the piquant sauce. 'But if it is a ridiculously over-ambitious attempt to achieve sublime results, it is at least a noble cause. I cannot be more specific than that at that moment, and I must crave your indulgence in not being more forthright. You must allow me the utmost discretion, until I can enlighten you, which I hope will happen naturally in the fullness of time and may eventually require some slight exertions on your part,' he added with a sly, hopeful look at Vanderville.

'That's quite alright,' said Vanderville, sampling an oyster, and wondering when Gracchus might arrive at the point. 'I am a spy too, you see, although I have the good fortune to be travelling under my own name. I was advised to give myself superior rank to increase my authority, but it didn't seem quite right, to gain position by the sinister side of the blanket, in a left-handed sort of trick.' He suddenly remembered that he was addressing *Baron* Pellegrew, and added a hasty addendum about necessary stratagems, and not implying any hierarchy of deception, but he had already lost Gracchus, who was demolishing more oysters as he waited for him to finish meandering. As Vanderville trailed to a halt, Gracchus belched contentedly and resumed.

'Now let me tell you how the Baron Pellegrew came to be. Or rather, how I came to be the Baron Pellegrew.' He stood and moved towards a shaft of sunlight, placed himself astride it, with his posterior directed at the light, as if it were a lit fire and he was warming his nether regions. Vanderville cautiously removed his handkerchief from his pocket, wiped his face and listened intently.

'It all began at a coaching inn on the road to Naples, near Caserta, which is the last stop on the road through Campania. In travelling I had fallen in with one Baron Pellegrew who was proceeding in the same direction as myself and, finding one another's company convivial, we voyaged together until the Baron was overtaken by a virulent fever and expired at that place, while belabouring himself atop a chambermaid.'

Gracchus handed him a glass, and clinking his own against it, hurled the liquid down his throat.

'As a result of fears that the fever may have proved contagious, the inn keeper was compelled to remove all the Baron's belongings, and myself, who had shared his table, into a post-chaise that was required to be driven immediately to the *lazaretto* outside Naples to enter quarantine without stopping. The mute who conducted the chaise being accustomed to this task, which required discretion and skill, proceeded at some despatch. Unfortunately, his desire for velocity outweighed his discretion on this occasion, and being singlehanded, he took the descent from Monte Balbir at a fair old clip and upset the coach, breaking the traces and his own neck in one mismanaged piece of driving. I myself was unhurt, though grievously jarred, and so I found myself deserted and alone on the road.'

He picked up the little glass of aqua forte that Vanderville had abandoned after a sip and threw it off before replacing the glass carelessly on the tray.

'In gathering the dismounted luggage belonging to the Baron, I discovered one trunk sufficiently damaged to admit of a spillage of its contents. Imagine my surprise when I discovered among the wreckage a considerable quantity of gold coin in neat rolls, bound up in what I suspected to be a servant girl's under things! It occurred to me then, that with some application I might evade the rigours of quarantine which would have proved a great inconvenience to me. What to do with Pellegrew's wantonly laded luggage? It seemed wastefully improper to abandon it to common thieves, and it occurred to me that if I took it with me I might, by examining its contents, find in his papers some idea of where his family resided, so that I could inform them of his unfortunate demise. Naturally, I would also take the opportunity to despatch them his possessions for their relief.

'So, with the help of a passing carter, I found myself translated to a superior inn on the Strada di Toledo in Naples. That evening I dined extravagantly well for only the second time since leaving Rome. Fortified after this welcome and so necessary repast I repaired to my room with an extra candle to survey the contents of my late companion's valises. His open-handed ways and generosity on our mutual journey had been a comfort to me, and I had previously wondered in idle moments about the source of his beneficence, so strange in a man travelling alone by post-chaise. His easy way with money, if not the actual expenditure, was more on the level of a great prince, or milord, and yet he was travelling by himself, discreetly. And then, although I had found him a most welcome companion, affable and charming, our conversation had somehow always failed to touch on the purpose of his voyage.

'The reason for this reticence was now laid out in splendid abundance. Inside his travelling desk, the application of a particular gadget of my own invention enabled me to discover a secret drawer, and within I discovered a cache of letters of credit. A sensible way to transport large sums of money, requiring only a few documents and a signature to translate into cash, or to transfer sums too large to be safely entrusted to a courier. The sum of credit revealed was astronomical. There was also plenty of cash for ready expenses.'

Gracchus paused to recharge his glass, casting his eyes around the garden for eavesdroppers as he did so.

'As for a clue to the poor Baron's family or relatives, there was none. The only information I gained by my investigations was that he was travelling to Malta at the express invitation of the grandmaster himself to deliver certain information and items, and that he travelled on the business of none other than Tsar Paul of Russia. My duty was clear. I decided to carry his effects on to Malta where they could be forwarded to the correct authorities. And yet, as you can imagine Vanderville, using a little of his splash cash to ease the ardour of the voyage and finding the effect of being taken for a rich man not unpleasant, slowly, carefully, a plan began to hatch.'

'The plan you are not about to reveal to me?' observed Vanderville sourly.

Gracchus removed his spectacles and polished them on a dirty napkin. 'It appears that fate has determined that we are to rely on one another again. Despite my quite considerable reservations, I see no alternative, but I must enjoin you to follow my instructions – we have no room for your intrepid forays into sentimentality here.'

Vanderville bit his lip angrily. None of his own objections to Gracchus had diminished in the least since his return to the army. The military life suited him, he slept better knowing that the moral ambivalences of Gracchus's milieu were behind him. But he needed help to establish himself in security in Valletta, and as the ex-magistrate obviously knew, peering at him from behind his sun spectacles, he had little alternative but to surrender himself to the yoke, at least temporarily.

'And what possessed you to announce me as a poet, Gracchus?'

'A happy inspiration, was it not? I admit it was a fortunate concatenation of ideas entirely unpremeditated. I must have seen the name somewhere, perhaps in the grandmaster's own library, and it came to me most suddenly. I observe that your precipitate appearance, no less than your crimes, left me no time to ponder.'

'Alleged crimes. I imagine that the grandmaster would consider your imposture of a Russian agent a no less serious matter if you care to practise the splitting of hairs.'

'No matter. It was the lyre or the rack. The sonnet or the strappado for you, until I saved your neck.'

There was no time to endure more of his friend's verbosity, because Vanderville had to brush himself down before joining de Rechberg and Haintlet for the promised dinner. Gracchus revealed that he, too, would impose himself on the *Auberge* de Bavaria to dine, and so it was in one of the borrowed voluminous shirts of the deceased Baron Pellegrew, and in the company of the live, ambulant though ersatz, version that Vanderville set out for the *Auberge* de Bavaria.

Gracchus went to pay his compliments to the bailli immediately on arriving at the *auberge* of the knights of Bavaria and Vanderville was scooped up into the company of the junior knights. De Rechberg monopolised Vanderville from the moment he appeared and led him proudly to his chambers in the knightly accommodation, followed by a half-dressed Haintlet. De Rechberg explained as they went that the rooms were allocated according to grade, single chambers for the junior knights, and suites in increasing order of grandeur for the adepts.

'So the late von Seeau for instance, occupied a suite?' asked Vanderville.

'Precisely,' continued de Rechberg. 'The better apartments are reserved for the Grand Crosses. A GC gets four or five rooms, and even have bathroom facilities – I only get two and a chamber pot. Doubtless in due course von Seeau's quarters will be reallocated. They occupy that prime position overlooking the Marsamuscetto harbour.'

'I should like his apartment, his Grand cross, and above all else his mistresses,' leered Haintlet, indicating a door that Vanderville took careful note of. It was his intention to gain access to the dead knight's rooms as soon as possible. The more he knew of his character the better, and there was the chance of discovering some traces of his clandestine activity.

'Because we are a military order, the accommodation is robust without being as austere as that of a purely monastic order,' said de Rechberg, leading Vanderville to his own door. 'We must create a bit of a splash, because we are the youngest of the seven *langues*, so Bailli von Torring makes sure the *auberge* is not embarrassed by her larders. And because most of our members' blazoned shoulders groan beneath the accumulated burden of three hundred years of nobility, we have a reasonable table to sustain their sense of self-importance and to assuage their sybaritic instincts.'

Haintlet trailed after them into de Rechberg's quarters, which comprised a small chamber spartanly furnished, and immediately mounted on a chair, from which height he commenced trying to carve his name into a cherub's face amid the ceiling frescoes.

'The disadvantage of being nominally a monastic order is the lack of privacy,' observed de Rechberg. 'We leave our chambers unlocked, which encourages overfamiliarity.'

Haintlet chose to accept this without churlishness, and heedlessly continued his vandalism unperturbed, having apparently decided on supplying the cherub with the generously proportioned generative organs that the artist had omitted, so de Rechberg commenced dressing himself and Vanderville for dinner. He laid out some clothes for Vanderville, and after inviting him to try them for size, indicated a sword panoply hung from a hook on the back of the door.

'It's as well to wear this here,' he told Vanderville as he tied his cravat at a mirror. 'You need the sword to distinguish yourself from a merchant. You would not want to embarrass yourself, or a knight, by allowing him to inadvertently insult you. And then this coat, though a little tired, is not so obviously republican as that you arrived in. Such precautions are especially necessary now. Because of the imminent arrival of your fleet, anti-French feeling is running high. Some of the merchants with French sympathies were lynched just last week.'

'Indeed,' interjected Vanderville wryly. 'I have had the honour of being pelted with turds by street children who suspected my dress of being subversive.'

'Oh, really?' said De Rechberg brightly. 'That's interesting. I did not realise the common people had become so invested in the defence of the island. It is normally we knights who suffer their greasy missiles,' he explained.

'He stood out in his coat,' observed Haintlet, 'because he was roaming the Convent at an hour too early for a noble, never mind a bourgeois. Only the common people and servants occupy the streets in the morning.'

De Rechberg reluctantly concurred the value of this observation. 'You might also consider wearing this mantle at night,' he added, proffering a capacious hooded garment. 'If you don't have one, you would prove conspicuous. Without a mantle, you are a knight or a foreigner.'

Another black mark against Vassallo's so-called precautions, thought Vanderville. He was starting to regret trusting so profoundly in the dead spy's capabilities. He buckled on the sword belt and unsheathed the blade to examine it.

'Try not to fight a knight if you can avoid it,' said Haintlet from his perch, examining a cut he had contrived to make in his own thumb. 'Normally you would be expelled from the island for crossing swords, as I know to my cost. But with the Order moving to siege preparations as soon as His Eminence wakes up and smells the wind, you will just be arbitrarily imprisoned or hanged from the walls of Sant' Elmo, since you are, after all, a mere French spy. Fighting the Maltese is a blameless enterprise, it's considered no worse than the killing of a goat.'

'Haven't you bled enough for one day?' asked de Rechberg, irritably. 'Vanderville, the Maltese nobility and merchants don't fight, yet all the Maltese common people wear a knife in their belt sash. But beware, a true ruffian might also carry a stiletto concealed in his cap.'

'I anticipate getting through the next days without having to kill anyone,' said Vanderville. 'Thank you for the sword and clothes all the same,' he continued, 'I appreciate both your discretion and your courtesy more than I can express.'

De Rechberg answered him with a smile. 'It is nothing. In two months, the French will come, and we will all be dead at our posts, or triumphant. And in either case we will never need to meet our tailor's bills.'

'Silver linings and all that,' said Haintlet, dropping lightly from his chair, and helping himself to Vanderville's sword for inspection. 'Here we favour the Italian school of fencing, rather than the French. If you are not familiar with it, we might go through a few of the differences in the salle tomorrow?'

Vanderville absentmindedly nodded assent before noticing de Rechberg's frantic negative semaphoring behind Haintlet's back. 'I must ease myself before we eat,' he said, with simulated embarrassment. 'An oyster, you understand...'

'Of course,' said de Rechberg, 'You could use the chamber of ease in the vacant Grand Cross's quarters. Do you remember the way?'

Haintlet rested his eyes on Vanderville for a second and was it only in his imagination that he saw a dark flicker of suspicion harboured there before Haintlet suggested the use of his own chamber pot, which was much more convenient being located in the cell next door to that in which they were at present. Vanderville complied with Haintlet's unwelcome suggestion with the best grace he could muster, being equally burdened with de Rechberg's unsolicited advice on the dangers of eating summer oysters. He regretted the over-confidence that might have alerted Haintlet's misgivings, and reminded himself to proceed more cautiously in what was after all, despite the apparent bonhomie, the headquarters of a military opponent.

As they made their way downstairs to the refectory de Rechberg announced, 'We had an unexpected guest this afternoon – His Eminence the Grandmaster von Hompesch was here, and no one knows why.'

'I saw his *kalesh* clogging up the street,' grumbled Haintlet. 'You would think he had better things to do, like preparing our defences, rather than interrupting us and turning the *auberge* upside down.'

'Perhaps *you* know why he has honoured us Vanderville?' asked de Rechberg. 'Or should I call you Tirdflingen?'

'Ah,' said Vanderville. 'News travels fast.'

'Don't worry,' soothed de Rechberg, 'your secret is safe with us. You were well advised to choose an incognito. But why did you choose such a well-known poet? The painter and antiquarian Tirdflingen is hardly unheard of, even here.'

'Is he so notorious?' Vanderville asked tentatively. He had never heard of the man.

'Not at all,' reassured Haintlet. 'Never heard of him.'

'He is a very minor poet, but he is *the* favourite of Grandmaster von Hompesch,' added de Rechberg, barely containing his glee at Vanderville's discomfiture. 'I hope you can quote a good thing.'

'I am fair skewered,' observed Vanderville, inwardly cursing Gracchus. He imagined himself quailing under the grandmaster's eye at their next audience, expected to perform and render horrible poetic flights at every opportunity and shuddered. It was not the first time that he had been sacrificed by Gracchus in order that his friend might surmount the peak of deception, pass through the saddle of suspicion, and enter onto glorious sun dappled uplands of trust where he could repose and pursue his own peculiar and impractical endeavours.

'It serves you right if you end up in the palace dungeons,' said Haintlet, feinting at a pillar with his small sword. 'A soldier's business is fighting for his honour or his sovereign, not going around in mufti under false names.'

'I thought it might be the case that you were unfamiliar with Tirdflingen's oeuvre,' said de Rechberg dryly, ignoring Haintlet's glower. 'So I took the liberty of calling on the Prete of the Maddalene, Don Stecchi. He has a library of moderns – and guess what?' He produced a small unbound volume from his coat tail pocket. Evading Vanderville's grasping hands with a nimble skip, he opened the book.

'We have here a copy of Tirdflingen's *Night and Valley Meditations*. Unfortunately, Don Stecchi has never perused it, the pages are still uncut. We can conclude that the meaty prose proved a little strong for his priestly sensibilities, the analogies a little rich, and the emotion too putrid.'

He tossed the virgin copy to Vanderville, who found it indeed still closed after the first few pages. Haintlet pulled a knife from the rear waistband of his breeches and handed it to him. Vanderville selected a sample page and sliced it open. 'Reflections on dawn at St Justinian's,' he read aloud. 'Never do I view a celebrated sight for the first time save at dawn in case

I should forever mar my perception with a view too vivid. No, the dusky twilight of dawn is the only way for a soul of sense to view new sights.'

De Rechberg was right – this was rotten stuff. He leant against the wall, flipping the pages despondently, and the other two lounged on the stairs while he committed the style, and a purple passage or two, to memory as fast as he could. There was no time for anything more before a functionary ushered them in to dine.

The *Auberge* de Bavaria, being modern in outlook, supped fashionably late, although their silverware was veritably antique, and had apparently only recently added mismatched forks to the arsenal. The dinner was laid in a suite of saloons with low arched roofs, glittering with arabesques in azure and gold. Heroic medallions poked out from amongst the wreaths of painted foliage, they bore representations of sea battles and of jaded ocean-going men in armour, their salt-encrusted hair and clothes coated in dust. Beneath these reminders of the gallant past, half a dozen Bavarian knights were present, along with the lay brothers and priests who formed the bulk of the *langue*'s numbers.

That evening was not one of the interminable fast days that were a hangover from the Order's less secular past, and the refectory table groaned with boiled and roasted meat, small meatballs, soup, dry and wet sausages, and other rare victuals. Gracchus in his role as Baron Pellegrew was seated in the place of honour next to the bailli. Looking at their host's salt-weathered face, Vanderville was reminded again of the porous loam of a thrice circumnavigated ancient sea bough. He found that even the puppyish enthusiasm of de Rechberg, and the absurd profanity of Haintlet were tempered in the presence of the bailli of the *langue*. Vanderville was pleased to be almost unnoticed by the bailli, having acquired such a doubtful and unwelcome alias since their morning meeting. Von Torring talked mainly to Gracchus, of the agriculture of the island, which was apparently in need of improvement.

'I admit,' Gracchus, was saying, as he savoured a dish of rabbit cooked with olives, 'I had not expected to eat so well on what is, if you will pardon me, a small island.'

'Islands,' corrected von Torring. 'We have two, there is Gozo of course, then three if you count Comino, and twenty more mere rocks that are nothing to speak of. Some things we import of course, but the local produce is not insignificant. If you come on Friday, I can offer you a dolphin fish marinated in honey.'

At the other end of the table the knights talked of the women of the island of whom they were in favour, of the dubious loyalty of the newly modernised militia regiments, and of the number of knights fit for active duty. Vanderville admired the fortifications he had seen, as he was expected to do, but offered a cautious enquiry as to whether the small standing army was sufficiently large to staff all the beautiful forts, even with the addition of a large militia.

'It is enough,' said Haintlet, spearing a sausage with his knifepoint. 'It's my opinion that you don't want too many men inside a besieged city anyway. The more there are, the faster your rations diminish.'

'You must consider,' said de Rechberg, his eyes lighting up, 'that any siege of the Convent cannot be prolonged, because the island's reserves of food will be soon exhausted. Whereas for their part the besiegers supplies must come by sea, and the French do not control that element. The Order has powerful friends like the Baron Pellegrew's Russian master,' he waved a spoon in the direction of Gracchus. 'Whereas the French Republic has numerous enemies with great fleets at sea.'

He slapped Haintlet, who was choking on a sausage, vigorously on the back. 'No my friend, the Knights will fight, the Maltese will fight, and your General Bonaparte will not swallow this morsel whole.'

Vanderville toyed with his beef, it was tough. He remembered the dilapidated state of the gun carriages he had seen in Sant' Elmo. 'What about the Knight's fleet?' he asked.

Haintlet finally coughed up his obstruction, and glowered darkly at Vanderville. He started to say something about spies, but de Rechberg intervened by calling for more wine, and said with a smile, 'Peace Fra' Haintlet. This is nothing the Directoire does not know. The French knights write home…'

'The fleet is on caravan, which is how we term our marauding expeditions,' he explained to Vanderville. 'It is due to return any day now, but even so,' he added brightly, 'the fleet is our offensive arm, they are not absolutely necessary for repelling any invader, and even without their intervention, would you enter the Grand Harbour in the face of our defences, and affect contempt for the Order?'

Vanderville considered, he had seen rank upon rank of great guns arrayed in and over the walls and forts around Valletta. Even if some had been in poor order, General Bonaparte did not know that yet. He conceded that, no, he would not expect to enter unscathed.

Privately he thought of Toulon, where Bonaparte had been the besieger, and achieved in days with one battery of guns what the other generals of the Revolution had failed to do in months. By grasping instantly that a slight pressure on the essential pivot could accomplish what siege work and digging had failed to do, the General had forced the English fleet from the harbour. Without that naval support the British troops and their allies had been forced to quit their toehold on the republican soil and France had been saved. But he held his peace and made shop talk about gunnery and wondered if the Order's artillery were up to date. Haintlet predictably took the bait and the conversation mellowed as he boasted vociferously about their arsenals.

After the covers had been drawn, de Rechberg apologised for the dull fare and conversation, and insisted that the following evening would prove more lively, as the bailli would be on a tour of inspection of fortifications, and a mess dinner was planned for the remaining knights whose duties kept them confined in Valletta. The bailli withdrew for coffee, drawing Gracchus after him. Vanderville was about to slope off to smoke with his companions when a message was passed to him by a flunkey to wait on the bailli in his solar.

—

The entrance to the bailli's solar was guarded by twin pilasters, delicately carved in trophies and clusters of ancient armour, and surmounted by fine antique busts, standing on each side of the entrance. Within, Vanderville uncovered Gracchus and von Torring deep in conversation at a table before a magnificent solar window. They stood expectantly to greet him, and von Torring addressed him, spreading his arms in conciliating abundance to include both men in his remarks.

'I was just saying to the Baron that it seems to me, that under the circumstances, it would be wise for *both* of you to accept the hospitality of our *auberge* for now. This will have several advantages. It will make it certain that I can extend my protection to you. The umbrella of a knight commander and bailli is not an insignificant matter in Valletta. In fact, I would go as far as to say it gives you virtual immunity from prosecution for all but the most serious crimes. The alternative is that you find yourself alone in the Convent surrounded by many hostile enemies. Since arriving here you have each separately managed to acquire a bewildering and imposing set of ill-wishers, and I would regret not being able to afford you sanctuary. I applaud your courage and determination, but to enumerate further, this is a rock of spies, and it may come as a surprise to both of you that I am aware of your real identities and purposes here.'

Vanderville swallowed nervously, and Gracchus jutted his chin out a little further. Von Torring stood and regarded the view from the window before resuming.

'You, Baron Pellegrew, are here ostensibly as a private traveller, a tourist if you like, entitled to the hospitality of the order. But your real and secret purpose here is as an ambassador of the

Tsar Paul, who covets the Order, the island, and this wondrous Convent crouched on it. The extensive letters of credit you bear are to be used for the purpose of subverting the will of the grandmaster and the council in this matter.'

Gracchus leant back in his chair and stretched unconcernedly. Vanderville was afraid that he would break wind, so heavily had he eaten, and so relaxed did he look. But, undeterred by his nonchalance, the bailli continued without pausing.

'Besides that, you have aroused the envy that always accrues to those possessed of vast wealth. This becomes more dangerous when you travel alone, the act of a fool or madman! Whichever you are it is of little consequence. It may be that you do not wish to tell me why you are so unattended?' He paused expectantly, but Gracchus maintained his silence, and shrugging, the bailli resumed.

'You are a target for evil men and the jealous. The ambitious, and the merely depraved, alike covet your scalp. Your private interests here are more artfully concealed, but you have been observed to meet so regularly with Rais Murad, a slaver and corsair captain, that it must be presumed there is business between you.'

'Wasn't it the last grandmaster who said that as long as we don't sell weapons to the Turk, we can trade with him?' asked Gracchus, admiring the twin busts of Hadrian and Antoninous that flanked the portal. 'As for cultivating the acquaintance of the local people, it appeals to my curiosity, which I admit is as insatiable as it is regrettable.'

The bailli nodded sympathetically. 'You are wise in this, Baron. I am of the opinion that the Order must resign their stewardship of Malta if they cannot forge a better relationship with the indigenous inhabitants of the island. It is true that I have myself come to meet and know many Maltese of quality. And for this revelation do you know what I have to thank? Regular intercourse with a local woman.'

Gracchus examined the floor and blinked thoughtfully as he considered this statement. Vanderville's attention had abruptly reverted to the conversation, and as he appeared about to utter an endorsement, Gracchus interjected with scarcely a pause. 'I have heard it is beneficial, and even considered the same course myself upon occasion. The ancients were not silent on the matter, either.'

Von Torring knitted his brows and turned his attention instead to Vanderville. 'You, Lieutenant Vanderville, are here as the envoy of another great power with designs on the Order. What you, or your masters, do not realise in their hurry to pluck the fruits of the tree we have cultivated here is that we are not finished. We have weathered worse than your Revolution, and we will see this too, pass.'

'I regret,' said Vanderville carefully, 'that I am not privy to the councils of either the Directoire, or General Bonaparte.'

Von Torring picked up a sheaf of paper from the table, and peering at one page continued, 'Your secret endeavours are of a more mundane sort to those of Pellegrew, you were promoted to the personal bodyguard of your Caliph Bonaparte, and then curiously dismissed from that service, all within the space of a humid week's work in the palace of Mombello at Milan. Since then you have entered, and left, the service of General Bonaparte's brother. Not a stellar record. Presumably, you are willing to accept tasks of an outré, not to say dubious legality to regain the favour of your Prince.'

He looked up at Vanderville, who shrugged the insult off. He was nonetheless perturbed to find the bailli so well informed. Not only were his antecedents reasonably well described, but apparently the Order had known of his coming before he had even set sail.

'And as to why you are posing as Pellegrew's secretary, or why he has allowed you to do so, I have no idea. Yet…'

Gracchus stared out the window as the bailli's monologue droned on. He sighed inwardly with relief. So long as the knight was not aware of his true identity, he maintained a slim chance of bringing off his coup. He was perilously close to discovery though. How could the bailli know of Vanderville's presence at Mombello, and yet have missed his own part in that tragic series of events? It was clear enough. Although the bailli might have become aware of the presence of one Felix Gracchus at Mombello, he had not made the connection yet between that man and the Baron Pellegrew. But when he did, Gracchus would be enclosed in von Torring's great mailed fist as surely as a baby hawk, and he had a feeling that being in his power would not be a pleasant place to be.

A hand rested lightly on his shoulder, and he turned to face the bailli, who said, 'I have a quid pro quo for you, Pellegrew. I know that you have performed as an investigatory agent for the Tsar before. Oh, do not trouble to deny it. My sources are profound. Our organisation has tendrils everywhere. You are both initiates of the fraternal order of masons, so I know your discretion can be trusted. Well, I have need of an investigatory agent here. Someone is killing members of my *langue*, and I must know who that person is. I appeal to you in the fraternal capacity.'

'It is some time since I was initiated,' said Gracchus. 'Remind me of the obligations owed between brothers under the set-square.'

'A formal request from a *philosophe* of the highest grade must be fulfilled on pain of disgrace and expulsion.'

Gracchus nodded sagely. The substance of von Torring's proposal was clear – work to find the murderer of the Bavarian knights, or the bailli would expose Vanderville and himself to the grandmaster as spies. For the moment, his own flimsy cover as Baron Pellegrew held, but for how long? The irony of the extinct Baron being an investigator did not escape him. In cover, or under his own name he seemed destined to be employed in clearing up unfortunate messes.

Vanderville was regarding the tapestries with meagre delight and considering his own position. He had been inculcated into the cult of Freemasonry in a misguided moment while bored in cavalry cantonment lines. He had expected it to be merely a drinking club, and the source of some carousing moments to leaven the hard bread of siege work. But ever since he had found himself prevailed upon by losers and scoundrels to supplement their purses, ease their passages, and conceal their petty misdeeds, all in the name of fraternity. Fraternity, go hang, he muttered to himself, sure that some fresh imposition was afoot.

Then he became aware that Von Torring had addressed him again, and that the attention of Gracchus and the bailli were upon him. Expectation hung in the air, clearly some question of considerable import had been raised and he was considered negligent in having let his attention stray. An answer was required of him. What had they been discussing?

'I will be happy to do everything in my power,' he ventured cautiously, and the knight nodded contentedly. Gracchus sighed heavily in exasperation, yet whatever it was appeared to be settled.

Von Torring considered Vanderville carefully from those piercing eyes lurking under his rheumy grey brow. 'You have been sheltered in the house of Donna Mifsud, a notorious public woman. No, do not bother denying it, she is reliable, and her name is not one from which it is necessary to preserve the whiff of scandal. Let us for the sake of brevity confine ourselves to the truth momentarily. Whatever the kernel of the matter might be, it appears that she has taken an interest in your fortunes, and she can be extraordinarily useful to you in the investigation I have proposed.'

Gracchus was pondering what it must be to have a bonny carapace like that of Vanderville, that every woman he met might want to mother or love him. He had observed this phenomenon several times now and was at a loss to account for it. Gracchus's own face was of the type people generally term homely. His features were misshapen and downright uneven. It was a common kindness to say that a face such as his was enlivened by insightful eyes, fine hair, or even a stubborn chin, but his, he was aware, was not so redeemed.

It would be pleasantly troublesome, he thought, to arouse such intense interest from so many of the women with whom you came into contact. It was impossible to dislike Vanderville for it, as he was genuinely unaware of his gifts. Nor did he take undue advantage, quite the opposite in fact. He preferred to squander his affections on an unattainable and unworthy object – General Bonaparte's sister. Yes, he did not resent his companions' peculiar fortune in this field, but he would be very content to emulate the effect to a minor, a very minor degree.

Von Torring, his proposals made and accepted, dismissed them cordially, and they descended to the *kalesh* the bailli had provided for them, while Gracchus expressed himself with his habitual lack of reserve.

'It will serve our purposes better if you retain freedom of movement,' he complained. 'By agreeing to accept the Bavarian *langue*'s protection you have placed yourself in the bailli's debt and exposed yourself to constant invigilation. What is more, if Carpegna is right about some blood feud within the *Langue* of Bavaria, you have placed yourself in the lion's den. Better you had not agreed so readily to the bailli's proposal. We could at least have made some better bargain for your liberty.'

'In the same vein you might have refrained from casting me as a bad poet,' observed Vanderville. 'God knows I have few enough talents in that direction.'

'Perhaps you are in the right of it,' mused Gracchus. 'But fear not, there will be work for your sword arm too before we are through here. On further acquaintance, do you trust any of the knights in this *auberge*?'

'I believe de Rechberg is sound. Haintlet is erratic and murderous, and the others belong to the bailli bound hand

and foot. They intend to fight the French but are prepared to tolerate my presence. They believe the French knights will join them in resisting Bonaparte and are more worried that the Maltese subjects fancy a change of regime. On the other hand, the Inquisitor Carpegna suggested that the Bavarian knights were involved in the assassination of Mayflower, one of their own, who was an agent of the Revolution.'

'There is no love lost between the Bavarian *langue* – Freemasons to a man – and the Holy Office. The Inquisition views Freemasonry and its freethinking offshoots as a threat to the Church,' said Gracchus thoughtfully. 'But where does the grandmaster fit into this? We must find out. First I think I should meet this Donna Mifsud of yours and her bunch of merry urchins tomorrow. Go to bed now, you look as if your head is twisted in knots to match your shoulder.'

Gracchus watched as Vanderville allowed one of the servants with which the *auberge* was amply provided to conduct him back inside towards his quarters, which were a modest set of rooms continuous to those of de Rechberg and Haintlet. He knew, however, that Vanderville had no intention of turning in early as he had suggested. For as soon as the *auberge* slept he would be afoot in his stockings, padding his way to the Grand Cross chambers where he would avail himself of the dark to ransack the murdered knight von Seeau's possessions. He shrugged, it could not hurt to have Vanderville's attention diverted in this way, and some good might even come of it.

—

The sun was sunk, and the whole balmy ether was aglow as Gracchus's *kalesh* rattled him home down hidden alleys spanned by citron-scented arches, followed at a discrete distance by the usual spies of the grandmaster. His indignation at Vanderville's complaisant acceptance of quarters in the *Auberge* de Bavaria had been genuine – he was worried for the safety of his too-trusting companion. Yet it was not without advantages, for he had his own game to play, and Vanderville's proximity would have rendered that more difficult.

Unable to decide whether the young lieutenant's presence in Valletta would prove a liability or a boon, he shelved his thoughts on the matter as a distraction. He had enough to do without the inconvenience of the murder investigation von Torring had forced on them, and he would be compelled to rise early to accomplish all the new day would encompass.

Chapter Eight

At daybreak Vanderville made his way to the Piazza dei Forbici, where he had arranged to meet Gracchus to discuss the beginning of their inquiry into the dead knight's murder over breakfast. He had hoped to have something useful to lay before the wily old fox, having succeeded in gaining access to von Seeau's cell during the night. The sad reality was that his reconnaissance had yielded scant results – revealing nothing that seemed to have a bearing on the inquiry.

He knew now that von Seeau had a low taste in literature, his sparse library being composed of works in German whose corrupting theme was revealed to Vanderville only by the provocative nature of the accompanying illustrations, several of which were quite startlingly novel to him. Of letters and personal papers there had been no trace, and further, his effects revealed an entire absence of interest in the religious life, to the extent that the dignity of the crucifix affixed above the bed had been subjected to the addition of a fencing practise mask and gloves.

Worse, the ensuing sequel to Vanderville's nocturnal predations had been a sleepless night. When he had finally drifted off it was merely to wake sweating moments later, afflicted by a bad dream of the corpus that had almost ceased to plague him in the last months, so busy had he been kept by the preparations for equipping the expeditionary force embarked under General Bonaparte. These sombre reflections were dispelled by his arrival in the Piazza Forbici, however.

He was relieved to find the place busier than when he first saw it, but as oppressed by the looming mass of Fort Sant' Elmo bastions as on his first encounter. How this bulwark of nature wrought formidable by artifice could be taken by storm surpassed Vanderville's credit – fifty men could hold its blank staring gunports against a whole division. He shrugged and turned away, that would be a problem for the army when they arrived, and there was little he could do about it now. From the vantage of the fort's narrow gates, the piazza flowed towards the town broadening like a fan. As the piazza widened, its inhabitants and their clutter multiplied where the market had begun to overrun the perimeter of its arcades.

The paving was sporadically pitted with bulbous-domed stone caps that announced the presence of subterranean granaries. They erupted from the rough paving like so many petrified fungi, punctuating the market stalls around the piazza's lower end, and serving as display benches and bargain rails for the traders. There was a pillory too, near the first houses. It was placed to one side of the broad end of the piazza where the market ended, like a shameful afterthought, and there it perched apologetically on an octagonal platform raised on stone steps, its wooden arms sinister against the sun.

The topmost of the pillory steps were littered with twisted bundles of old rags, clustered around sticks as though the rejected wardrobe of a slopshop had been emptied there. As he drew closer, Vanderville saw that the sticks were not sticks, but the meagre legs of undernourished children, posed awkwardly where sleep had overcome their owners, and the rags were the inadequate swaddling that had averted the chill morning air from their limbs. Alone above these still-slumbering forms, on the top step leaning back against the pillory post with his knees brought up to his chin, was a child more alert than the rest. It was the boy Duccio, who had bought milk at Donna Eva's bidding.

Vanderville mounted the pillory steps, stepping carefully over the sleepers. Placing one booted foot on the summit, he nodded companionably to the boy, who, for his part ignored Vanderville. His head rested on the knees brought up to his chin while his glance swept constantly over his domain, the sad brown eyes encompassing the scenes and life of the Piazza without judgement. After a while, feeling that grass was growing beneath his feet, Vanderville offered a noble greeting and observed, 'I imagine that not much that passes hereabouts escapes your eye.'

Duccio did not remove his gaze from a turbulent band of squabbling pigs who were encroaching on his territory as he restrained a heavy sigh. The long passage of his eight or so years had rendered him immune to clumsy flattery and he appeared content to wait calmly before acknowledging Vanderville's graceless approach to acquaintance.

'Yesterday, for instance,' tried Vanderville gamely again. 'I imagine you or one of the *Fraternita delle Forbici* was *en vedette* in the early morning.'

Duccio's dark eyes flicked slantways at Vanderville, and quickly away. It appeared that the military analogy had piqued his vanity, but he was not about to let this interloper know that. His face betrayed his conviction that if they were both soldiers, then they were equals at the least. In fact, Vanderville, whatever he was off the rock, was without a command here, whereas he, Duccio, had the services of a great many children to call upon. He was virtually the general of the *Fraternita* and was evidently inclined to consider the other a supplicant.

While Vanderville fumbled to breach this divide of authority, rather at a loss to understand how it had developed, the other children began to stir, and the bolder ones raised themselves on one arm to look at their visitor. Gradually they formed a semi-circle below Duccio and Vanderville on the steps.

The children wore a dilapidated version of the dress of the Maltese market people. A loose cotton shirt tucked into variously ragged pantaloons, and over the shirt, a waistcoat without sleeves – on which not one of them had buttons. They regarded him with mute curiosity, and the only one who approached them on the pinnacle was a sinewy boy with globulous eyes and malformed hands. He climbed the steps sideways with some difficulty, and Vanderville saw that his deformities extended to his legs, which supported him with difficulty. Settling down a discreet distance from Vanderville, and resting his head against Duccio's legs, the new arrival blinked the sleep crust lazily away from his watery eyes and opined to Duccio, 'He is about to ask us if we saw the knight's murderer. See if he isn't.'

'Everyone knows who killed the knight in the Maddalene, Granchio,' sighed Duccio. 'It was the Demon Haintlet. They quarrelled over Donna Eva, whose affections they both covet, as all knights do, and Demon stabbed him through the eye.'

Vanderville saw his sap opened for him at last, and exploited the opening, 'You saw *Cavaliere* Haintlet that morning?'

'Donna Eva set eyes on him leaving the fort under a thunderous dark brow and told us to hide from him,' said the deformed boy Duccio had called Granchio, and then he clammed up as his companion bestowed a scornful look on him.

'She too was abroad then?' probed Vanderville, but Duccio's commanding glance had inhibited Granchio, and he stayed his mouth this time.

Duccio frowned and stood, sending one of the smaller boys to drive away the pigs who were encroaching on their territory with a commanding gesture. It seemed that he was not inclined to pursue their conversation further, and Vanderville, defeated, rose to leave. But as he dusted off his hat, the boy spoke again.

'Donna Eva was at her devotions. She does not attend private squabbles on the ramparts, nor conduct her affairs outside churches like a common drab.'

He smoothed down his clothes and adjusted his cloth waist girdle self-consciously. Alone among them, Duccio sported this exceedingly long sash, artfully twisted where it passed around the waist. The carved wooden hilt of a knife protruded there, and he adjusted it now, determinedly. Taking his cue, Vanderville admired the ostentatiously displayed knife.

Granchio snorted. 'It is not real,' he muttered enviously to Vanderville. 'His knife is just a piece of carved wood.'

'I have a knife,' exclaimed Duccio, his pride outraged. He jutted his chin out pugnaciously. 'When I need one, I have one.'

'You are quite right,' said Granchio judiciously, rolling his eyes at Vanderville. 'It is not just for a man who lives under a stone to cast aspersions on his comrade's poverty. My apologies to you.'

Duccio rested his chin back on his chest. 'There are no such words necessary among comrades,' he muttered graciously, permitting Granchio to mollify him by adjusting his girdle into a manner more elegant. The two had quite forgotten Vanderville and he maintained his peace, unwilling to speak in case he should break the spell, disturb their world of barefoot courtesy, and prove himself a trespasser.

Granchio's twisted hands worked busily tidying the torn scraps of Duccio's shirt which fell away over his belly, which alone among his fellows carried a little padding. He sniffed as he did so. 'Never mind this great ugly Frenchman's mystery. The puzzle is how an urchin attains such a gross carcass on meagre scraps. We all eat seldom enough. How you accomplish it is beyond my understanding.'

'Here we go again,' said Duccio wearily, regaining his perch on the steps.

'Perhaps his position as courier and *maggiordomo* for Donna Eva allows him to harvest a private store of victuals,' said Granchio sourly, addressing his remarks to the air.

Now it was Duccio who rolled his eyes for Vanderville's benefit, it was clearly a familiar refrain. Granchio held up one claw-like hand magisterially. 'I aver no mischief,' he stated. 'But all the same, it seems somehow dishonest to attain such a bulk on leftovers and stolen market-stall scraps.' He regarded his own scant frame and malformed limbs sadly as he sat down again. 'Myself, I am unable to grow my limbs straight on what we scavenge, let alone see my belly become a gross encumbrance to me.'

Granchio squatted and rested his head on the lap of his friend. Slowly the arm of Duccio inched protectively around his skinny form and presently he commenced a soothing employment in delivering his companion's jetty black locks of too abundant a population, discarding the crushed fleas inconsiderately close to Vanderville's boots. The boy Granchio's wandering eyes finally came to rest on Vanderville again. 'Are you still here, Frenchman? I wonder, will your Bonaparte feed us when he comes?' he asked hopefully.

Vanderville gazed out across the piazza. There were a few rough chairs laid out near the market stalls where people were taking coffee from a battered urn, and he saw Gracchus there, watching them. He waved one indolent arm in their direction and Vanderville nodded back. 'The General feeds those who work,' he answered.

'I heard,' said Duccio, 'that these *carmagnoles* eat children, plump or not.'

'Yes, and crunch them like apples too,' agreed Vanderville absently. He had just spotted the elegant figure of Donna Eva wending her way through the market. Her ward Franca was obediently behind her, wearing a *faldetta* like that of her patron, but overlong, and she had gathered its length in her hands to keep it from dragging on the ground. A few tentative curls of her raven black hair had escaped the hood, and the effect charmed him.

The boys' eyes followed his, and Granchio shook his head dejectedly. 'Franca must soon cease to accompany the *Fraternita* on foraging expeditions.'

'Whyever would she do that?' said Duccio, applying himself to a discarded orange rind. 'She is, by the providence of God, the best and boldest at what we do, and anyway our combinations wouldn't work without her.'

'Heroic she may be, yet it's not safe for her out there. Donna Eva is right; she needs to stay indoors now.'

The other child rubbed his head as he ruefully considered this revelation and at that moment a passing market dray piled high with produce obscured the ambling duo of Eva and Franca from Vanderville's view. He turned his attention back to the boys who were squabbling as their reluctantly awakened companions began gathering up their scant bundles of possessions.

'If Donna Eva is so concerned for our safety, why did she let the knight take you in his *kalesh*?' Duccio was asking Granchio.

Granchio adjusted his bony posterior on the steps. 'She has warned me that it is dangerous, but I have nothing, so there is nothing for me to lose. She would never let Franca go though, she said she was the only one of us who had something worth stealing.'

The last of the orange rind disappeared into Duccio's mouth and he wiped his hands on his dirty knees. 'Her innocence?' he asked through his bulging cheeks.

Granchio snorted. 'She has visited the farms with Donna Mifsud you half-wit changeling. She knows what the knights want. Eva said their attentions would destroy her beauty too soon and she couldn't bear it.'

Gracchus was beckoning Vanderville again, impatiently now, and it seemed a just moment to take his leave. He bowed with careful precision to the leaders of the *Fraternita* and from his coat tails he produced a napkin full of pastries which he presented as a parting offering. Mollified by this display of courtesy, Duccio accepted the bundle with a rapacity leavened with dignity. He unfolded the napkin at the foot of the pillory and his supporters clustered around him like a flight of squawking sea gulls.

Duccio waited for Granchio to take the first morsel before summoning the rest of the children to eat. As he consumed the last portion he pointed past Vanderville to Gracchus while addressing him through a mouthful of crumbs.

'If your fat friend has any more questions for you to ask us, you may tell him the *Fraternita* sees everything that passes in this quarter.'

Vanderville acquiesced sagely, indicating that he would pass on the message, and they parted with cordial nods. As

Vanderville tripped down the steps Granchio took post beside him, and whispered to him aside, 'When your general lands, we will see what he can do for us.' He gave Vanderville one of his pathetic claws to clasp. 'Until then I grant you our protection. You may call on us when in need.'

As Vanderville crossed the piazza he noticed de Rechberg wending his way amongst the market stalls. Falling in besides him with his habitual good cheer, he freely admitted to having stalked him to the marketplace.

'Actually, the bailli gave Fra' Haintlet the duty of following you, but he is incapable of rising so early as you manage. By the way, the bailli wants you to sup with us where we can keep an eye on you this evening. Unless you have a better offer?' He raised one eyebrow quizzically.

Unable to muster a refusal, Vanderville accepted gracefully as their progress culminated at the café tables. Gracchus removed his feet from a stool and invited them to join him for coffee and a pipe. Greetings accomplished; they sipped a brew brought to them from an urn. The coffee was thin, made with twice-rinsed grains, and sweetened with hot goat's milk, and de Rechberg winced as he tasted it.

'An acquired taste no doubt,' he observed, setting down his cracked cup. 'But a cup is always welcome. Chocolate we unfortunately do not see a great deal of here, except when the Order's caravans bring in a capture. When that happens, the whole Convent turns out to celebrate, and the fortunate galley enters the Grand Harbour with flags flying and the oarsmen whipped into a frenzied double time!'

'That must be a great joy to the galley slaves,' muttered Gracchus.

'You rather despise the Order, don't you Baron?' asked de Rechberg equably.

'I am at a loss to understand in what way this organised brigandage fulfils the vows and purpose of your monastic calling, I confess,' responded Gracchus.

'Consider the position of the knights,' said de Rechberg, spreading his hands expansively. 'Expelled from Rhodes, a verdant and rich island, no earthly paradise perhaps, except when compared with its sequel. Malta is an isolated bare island, devoid of resources, except those we have carefully cultivated. We have worked wonders with the cotton and mulberry trees, and with the people, though they do not always appreciate it. One day the Maltese will be fit to govern themselves, but until then, we have our duty of stewardship to minister to them. In the meantime, the Order must find sources of subsistence and income.'

'My heartstrings quiver at your benevolent plucking,' murmured Gracchus, draining his coffee.

'Well, I must be off,' said de Rechberg, pushing back his chair. 'We will see you tonight then, Vanderville. Do try not to be arrested before then.' He bowed to Gracchus with a grace that would have shamed a less recalcitrant acquaintance and took his leave.

'You handled him roughly,' observed Vanderville, pulling out a pipe, which had been among the donations made by the Bavarians to his comfort.

'I abhor slavery of all kinds,' said Gracchus, 'and here it is rife in one form or another.'

Vanderville grunted and squinted at the sky. 'No doubt. Do you not find the bright light of this sunburnt promontory, glorious as it is, a little blinding?'

Gracchus smiled lazily from behind the comfort of his green tinged spectacles. 'It did not take me long to get used to it. The sea breeze restores me to vigour; I set the heat of mid-day at defiance, and no longer credit the horrors of the scirocco. What news from the *auberge*?'

Vanderville related the failure of his nocturnal exploration, suffered detailed questioning with patience, and for his part, enquired after Gracchus's own efforts.

'Earlier, I spoke to the priest at the Maddalena.'

Vanderville signalled for more coffee, 'Oh, yes? Father Steak-eye?'

'Steak-eye? He told me his name was Stecchi. He is a Maltese.'

'Sorry, it is what the *Fraternita delle Forbici* call him,' explained Vanderville.

Gracchus nodded, peering towards the pillory. 'Don Stecchi uses those street children for errands. The priest is reliable, by the way. There are witnesses to place him under alibi for the morning of the murder, and he asserts his absolute trust in the custodian of the church.'

'The man was leaving a little abruptly when I arrived.'

'He had finished sounding the chapel bells for matins, and was in a hurry to finish his rounds and get home for his breakfast. You may have noticed his withered arm; he is an adequate bellringer but an unlikely strangler. On a calm day the Moorish clock bells on the grandmaster's palace can be heard throughout the city. They are used to regulate the others including those in the hospital complex.'

Vanderville nodded and drew on his pipe. 'What do you mean by the hospital complex? Those roofs I passed over?'

Gracchus waved away his smoke. 'The very same. The monastic buildings of the Maddalena are dominated by the hospital for women. It is distinct from the main knights hospital, which is superb, by the way. Anyway, the knights in principle are obliged to minister to women but prefer not to. Their hospital is one place at least, where they avoid temptation, although many of them seem rather to seek it out.' He laid his pipe on the table. 'The grandmaster insisted on sending me on tours of all the most important buildings soon after I arrived, and they are justifiably proud of their facilities.'

Vanderville poked at his pipe intently. He wondered if the hospitals could do anything for Granchio. He became aware that Gracchus was observing him.

'Can I meet this *Fraternita* of yours?'

Vanderville looked at the sky and breathed out at length. 'I don't know,' he said. 'Perhaps better not. They are wary of anything like authority. I may make some progress with them, given time. But surely you do not need to interview them for the investigation? None of them has the build of a killer.'

Gracchus grunted, 'I agree. By all accounts von Seeau was a powerfully built man, I cannot see one of your urchins overcoming him in a struggle.'

'The *Fraternita* have enough of a battle just getting enough to eat. Their sorry situation convinces me that this place is ripe for revolution.'

'You think so? Is revolution your infallible remedy for all ills? Admittedly the Maltese labour under an almost oriental fatalism and a sense of inferiority and dependence cultivated by the knights. But would their lot be improved by adding the double yoke of unscrupulous lawyers and thirsty imperialists of liberty?'

'You have never approved of the Revolution,' sniffed Vanderville.

'I?' responded Gracchus, 'I adored the Revolution. But she was a deceiver and robbed me and everyone else just as thoroughly as the King and his bishops did, but without their grace, and with a great deal of hypocrisy and lies thrown into the bargain.' He took a sip of coffee and winced. 'France suffers revolution in the same way that a cow's stomach revolves constantly, grinding with grit and gravel until there is nothing left but effluent waste and stifling malodorous air.'

This was conversational ground they had traversed together so often before as to find it a comfortable balm to accompany coffee, and both were contented enough to lay discussion aside as a cumbersome obstacle on the road to a high ground which was yet to be reached, if not unobtainable. So instead, they sat back and watched the life of the piazza unfold. Donna Eva was still moving through the market and Vanderville pointed her out to Gracchus and restated her role in his deliverance.

'Who is the extraordinarily pretty young woman accompanying her?'

'Her protégé, Franca,' said Vanderville with an appreciative sigh. 'Has she not the most radiant glance? I would trade one of her smiles even for the sight of the charge of mounted men boot to boot.'

Gracchus appeared content to let this accolade pass under a diplomatic pondering silence, prompting Vanderville to consider privately that this was not the first time he had inflicted such an observation on his friend.

'So this Donna Eva lives close to the Maddalena? If you get the opportunity of asking your friends in the *Fraternita delle Forbici* about their mistress's doings early yesterday morning, I would be grateful. Discretion please, Vanderville.'

'Donna Eva? They let slip that she was abroad. What has she to do with this?'

Gracchus took his time answering. Among Baron Pellegrew's belongings he had discovered expensive sketching equipment and he had started to carry the things around with him and to affect the habits of an amateur artist. He doodled on his pad as he unfolded his thoughts.

'From the moment that you arrived here, various interested parties have taken some pains to collate an account of not only your movements, but those of others. Thankfully, they have been only partially successful in your case, but their record of all those seen abroad in the vicinity of the Maddalene complex that morning is more complete. It did not require much outlay for me to obtain copies of their reports, then to follow up on those rather obvious loose ends they had left unexplored. The church custodian is remarkably inobservant on the whole, capable of recalling only exceptional events – faces he sees every day do not register with him at all. For instance, he described the person who barged into the church past him as a poorly dressed foreign gentleman, which I presume was you.'

Vanderville wrinkled his nose. 'Perhaps you could exploit your position as the new Croesus to have a tailor pass a tape over my shoulders?'

Gracchus disregarded this request as an unreasonable imposition and continued, 'Apart from that, he saw no one and heard nothing until the soldiers started a commotion. Yet as you made your progress across the roofs you outraged several householders with your clumsiness, and they too described you.'

Vanderville opened his mouth, but Gracchus cut his protest short with a dismissive gesture. 'These things are contained in the official reports to the *Cancellaria*, which is where I accessed them. Naturally, you are the focus of their limited attention, and as a result they too, like the custodian, overlook all the people who are commonly abroad at that time, assuming that they were simply going about their usual business. Since there is no substitute for traversing the ground oneself, I did so, and then I went to sample the wares of each bakery in the neighbourhood.'

He sighed serenely, 'It is a maxim of mine that the baker is the investigator's best friend. He rises early, before even the goatherds, he works in silent contemplation, and he departs his employment at hours separate from the rest of the world. He is a creature apart from mankind.'

Vanderville sat back, shaded his eyes with his hat diplomatically, and began to examine the meagre battered threads of his shirt cuffs, which were in a parlous condition.

Gracchus was in full spate. 'The *fornaio* of Forno Corni is an indifferent baker but an excellent witness. He states that he saw who he termed *the Public Woman of Strada delle Ficara* passing away from the Maddalene at just the time when you were entering Piazza dei Forbici. She was covered of course, as all woman on the rock are when in public, but he recognised her *faldetta* by the brocade, which is of a particularly superior quality.' He paused for breath and patted his pockets down for his pencil knife.

'It is often the case that a witness will impugn a woman in such a position from an invidious motive of spite. But in this case the *fornaio* is not prejudiced against prostitutes.'

'Well quite,' said Vanderville, adjusting his necktie with embarrassment. He tapped his pipe out on the table, spilling stale tobacco over its surface and drawing disapproving looks from the café proprietor. He sucked on its cracked tip speculatively to see if it still drew.

'His wife is one in fact – though entertaining an entirely different and less elevated clientele to that of your Donna Eva.'

Vanderville shifted his buttocks awkwardly on the seat – he had just spotted Eva making her way towards them between the market stalls. She smiled at him and seemed inclined to approach their table. He was keen for Gracchus to conclude his line of repartee before she did so.

'This he told me entirely of his own accord,' added Gracchus contentedly. 'Although it required me to perjure myself by offering his pastries an homage to which they were not in the slightest entitled.'

'It is a lead,' admitted Vanderville, hurriedly, 'and she certainly knows the knights of the Bavarian *langue* and could have arranged an assignation with one of them in the church. But why would she murder one of her benefactors? Her metier is to soothe rather than savage those feudal relics.'

'I do not know,' admitted Gracchus. 'But I shall spend the afternoon going through the reports of the first murder, and I shall want to know her whereabouts at the time that occurred. The *Langue* of Bavaria has few enough knights here that they can afford to squander more of their blood at a time when the Convent may soon make its own demands of that precious commodity. They could prove very awkward for us if we cannot deliver a bound murderer to them promptly.'

Donna Eva concluded her progress through the market before their table, and they rose to greet her. Vanderville made the introductions, remembering just in time to name Gracchus as Baron Pellegrew. He noticed that his companion was exerting all his limited repertoire of courtesy as he offered a chair to Eva. Franca remained standing dutifully behind her, where Vanderville unfortunately could not observe her without turning his head.

Eva expressed much genuine pleasure at finally meeting the Croesus-like Baron Pellegrew of whom she had heard so much, and Vanderville found himself compelled to explain his new dual identity as Pellegrew's secretary. It passed off not too badly, and he was grateful to her for the questions she left unasked.

'Welcome news,' Eva whispered to Vanderville when Gracchus rose to call for more coffee. 'A corpse washed up this morning in the Marsamuscetto harbour. It has been presumed to be the man a fisherman observed jumping from the ship. His body serves remarkably conveniently to mask your presence in Valletta. The frigate captain denied all knowledge of the operation, but naturally the watering of his ship was unceremoniously ceased. The ship was given her sailing orders and she has presumably returned to her station off the island of Gozo.'

Vanderville nodded. It was unfortunate that the *Carrère* had been compelled to depart, removing his last vestige of safety, but even with that potential refuge removed he felt that his position was made more secure. It was better than he had hoped for, and it was even possible that his dead accomplice Vassallo might be bruited abroad as the murderer from the Maddalene. Events were combining to add verisimilitude to his impersonation of Tirdflingen, and God knew, he needed all the help he could get in that direction.

Gracchus arrived bearing a tray of fresh provisions and narrowly avoiding being engulfed by a disturbance in the marketplace. To the delight of the market bravos and the disgust of the stallholders, one of the market women was going hammer and tongs at a customer – a remarkably well-dressed woman. The former was flourishing a fish wildly, and having considerably the worst of it, her hair being clutched by the customer who was lambasting her with a long cane which she applied with one hand. As the combatants clattered towards their table Eva sighed demonstratively and gathered her *faldetta* ostentatiously out of their way, and wound a protective arm around Franca. This provoked the notice of the fish bearer, who addressed her spitefully. 'No need to put your nose in the air. You were one of us, before you earnt a cross with your—'

Vanderville began to rise, but Franca's hand went to his shoulder, pressing him back into his seat. He glanced up and saw her eyes shining as she watched.

'I traded nothing that you would not sell if you were able to find a buyer,' retorted Eva calmly. She nodded her head to the other woman, whose *faldetta* had been wrenched from her shoulders. 'Good day to you, Donna Baida, I hear the fish in the market is very fresh today.'

Parting with heaving breasts and panting breaths, the two miscreants eyed Vanderville and Gracchus cautiously, before they thought better of further discussion and stalked off in various directions. Vanderville swallowed uncomfortably. Gracchus picked his teeth with a pencil, and it was Eva who broke the ensuing silence.

'It is no disgrace to be what she accused me of – every respectable family that wants to get on has a patron knight to whom some sacrifice has been made. Sometimes more than once. That tall woman, La Baida, is of a family that has disposed of three daughters in this way, and as you can see, she is still of the market people she pretends to despise.'

'Indeed...' began Gracchus before trailing off. He tried again, 'I have noticed this unusual relationship between the Order and the Maltese people. The knights claim that the beauty of the fair Maltese is too great a provocation. So naturally...'

Eva smiled at him. 'You are correct in fact, that we are bound to a social contract: one that those traded by their relations for social advantage do not always benefit from. Having found themselves excluded from the society they were born to, what are they to do? The truth is, some find life outside of social convention to their liking, and the price, if disagreeable, worth paying for their liberty.'

'Liberty is expensive,' agreed Gracchus, 'as I have found out.'

'You can afford it!' exclaimed Vanderville. 'Here you find yourself with all of the wealth of Golconda at your disposal.' Gracchus made a sign for him to discontinue the conversation, but Eva had already picked it up.

'It is curious, is it not? Everyone speculates on his wealth. Some say he is here to buy the Order on behalf of the Tsar of Russia, and that's why the grandmaster is so well disposed towards him. Others allege he plans to acquire the entire island *from* the Order and install himself here as our Sultan.'

'Which would be a boon to your profession, *Zia* Eva,' chimed in Franca.

Eva shushed her. 'A seraglio is not necessarily a retirement home for time-served baggages, my treasure. Except for that of His Eminence the grandmaster, of course,' she added archly, after a moment's thought.

Gracchus smiled enigmatically. 'Speaking of that worthy, I have an audience with His Eminence imminently, so if you will forgive me...' He rose and bowed, 'I hope I may allow myself the pleasure of calling on you, Donna Mifsud?'

She nodded. 'I should be delighted. Come this afternoon to dine if you are at liberty. The priest of the Maddalene Don Stecchi is expected and would take a pleasure in your company equal to mine.'

Gracchus acquiesced and after informing Vanderville he would be all day engaged, and early to bed, he left them.

'Is your friend always so sphinx-like?' asked Eva, as they watched Gracchus hobble off through the market stalls. Vanderville, who sometimes found himself at sea with classical allusions shrugged impatiently.

'If a *spinks* is some sort of smug toad, then yes.'

Chapter Nine

Such cursed ups and downs thought Gracchus cantankerously. Such shelving descents and sudden rises, as occur at every step! Why, when building this exquisite city, did the knights not think to level it off first? He had taken a roundabout route to evade his habitual tailing rogue, and fifty times he imagined himself on the point of being overturned into the gutter by sedan chairs and mule-drawn *kaleshes*. As he eventually tottered his ponderous way down Strada della Ficara, reasonably sure of having lost his pursuer, he heard the raised voice of Donna Eva before he arrived at her house. She was berating a street boy on her doorstep, and had a firm grip on his ear.

'*Ruffiano*, Duccio! You have destroyed your breeches, playing in the dirt with the neighbour's cat. What have you done with your silver knee buckles?'

'Granchio said they are not silver, but tin,' replied the boy pugnaciously. 'He exchanged them with Borucchio the rabbit-seller.'

'That misbegotten thief? What did he get?'

'What do you think?' said the boy wiping his nose on his sleeve. 'A rabbit.'

'Which you ate, I suppose.'

'No, he gave it to Franca to make broth for the *Fraternita*.'

Eva spotted the footsore Gracchus arriving and turned to greet him, releasing the boy who cast a baleful look at the new arrival.

'Don Stecchi is already above, so we can begin at once,' she said, with her charming smile, ushering Duccio aside. 'The boy is afraid the priest will beat him,' she explained. 'He is so slow; he can't learn even two verses of the creed. Much good it will do him. Inside, *ciacciarone*,' she ordered the boy. As they mounted her doorstep a sporadic distant crackling caused Eva to flinch and crane her head towards the sea. 'What is that? Are the French here already?' she asked in dismay.

'I believe not,' said Gracchus. 'It is just the militia practising their gunplay. His Eminence has called them out as a precaution. Unfortunately, the master at arms says that with their limited training the militia are a bigger danger to the people than the French republicans for now.'

'Duccio believes that the French will all be like your secretary, and therefore they will enter Malta as easily as he did, hurl the knights from the battlements, and throw a party where we all eat until we burst.'

'Well, that is entirely possible. Not many armies could resist a French one with General Bonaparte leading them, and from what I have seen of the knights, however brave they may be individually, they do not have a single head, the necessary single will, animating them. So yes, Bonaparte will have them for his breakfast.'

'You have no doubt that the knights days are over?' asked Eva.

'Not much. Of course, water is not the General's element, so anything could happen if he is caught at sea.'

The boy Duccio had been listening avidly, and now he thought about this for a bit. Cradling his ear in his grubby hand he said, 'They say that the French are going to liberate us from the knights.'

'Hmm,' replied Gracchus.

'What will our life be like after the French free us?' he asked.

'I don't know,' said Gracchus bluntly.

'You believe then, that if they remove the knights, the French will stay?' Eva asked, opening the house with a key attached to her long waist girdle and ushering the boy towards the staircase.

'It appears to have been the invariable policy elsewhere,' said Gracchus following them, 'and it may even be that it is preferable to their immediate departure.'

'You think we Maltese are not capable of governing ourselves?' rallied Eva over her shoulder as she led the way upwards, pausing on a landing to remove her *faldetta* and hang it on a hook.

'Where the French have not remained to support the new republics, the counter-revolution has been swift and brutal,' observed Gracchus. 'Do you think the islanders would take to a change of regime?'

'Do they have a choice?' she said, as they emerged from the second flight of stairs onto the roof terrace and into the sun blazing in a cobalt sky.

'After three hundred years of the Order's benevolence they are used to the yoke. It is possible that the French will rule well, but they are talking of liberty, of freedom, and of equality. That is well and good if the lives of the people see an improvement. If not, talk of liberty may be the French's undoing. The Maltese may just decide that liberty means ruling themselves rather than submitting to another set of foreign overlords.'

Her eyes shone. 'That would be something worth seeing.'

The generous shape and booming welcome of Don Stecchi awaited them on the terrace. While Eva supervised Duccio and Franca to adjust a canopy on poles that shaded the simple table, he conducted Gracchus to the utmost reach of the terrace to admire the view. Gracchus tripped over a rank of large wooden tubs in which plants spotted with vivid yellow flowers were growing. 'Why, these are charming,' he observed, rubbing his shin. Don Stecchi wrinkled his brow with displeasure and moved the offending tub out of the way.

'Never mind those. Donna Eva, I have told you a hundred times not to keep these flowers here. You risk another visit from Canon Gatt. Come and look at this,' he said to Gracchus.

The view from the terrace was indeed worth the climb up the stairs. The great harbour was just visible, and the warm tremulous light beating upon the sapphire waters illuminated the sails of the ships that packed it, their different flags mingling in cheerful communion. Between their viewpoint and the water were the creamy yellow sloping walls of the great forts, and the hills of Valletta crowned with castles, convents, and churches, while immediately below was the agreeable babbling confusion of the marketplace in Piazza Forbici. The lights and shadows, the cries of the stallholders, and the mingled crowd of soldiers in white and scarlet, women in coloured *faldettas*, seafarers, and jostling children all added to the impression of a thriving metropolis.

Don Stecchi leaned his full priestly bulk upon the parapet, and pointed out a church some distance away. 'That is the Maddalena complex, where I work. It extends between here and the church tower,' he said in his rich, fruity voice.

'It was there that you were working the morning that von Seeau was murdered,' pondered Gracchus, 'Your movements...'

'Can be confirmed by the nursing sisters at the hospital complex.'

'As can those of your church's custodian,' concluded Gracchus, 'whose infirmity renders him an unlikely assassin. The account of your interview with the grandmaster's police – those inefficient and spiteful fellows, the *sbirri*, says that Donna Eva was with you. Yet a witness places her near the Maddalene church and not in the nursing halls as you asserted. Whereas she herself pled that she had not left this house at that hour.' He watched as Don Stecchi's unruffled demeanour unravelled. 'Which of these three reports is true, I wonder?'

'Witnesses can easily be mistaken in their recollections as to the time,' suggested the priest.

'I have observed that here the bells of the Convent regulate the days of the people precisely,' said Gracchus. 'Donna Eva says that she did not leave the house. Can anyone confirm that?'

'No one that counts. The girl Franca confirms this, but her evidence would be inadmissible in a court of law, since she is an enslaved person.' He glanced over his shoulder at the young woman who was playfully chastising Duccio as they set the table.

It was Gracchus's turn to be discombobulated, and Don Stecchi clearly enjoyed the reversal of positions. 'She should have been manumitted long since, it is nothing but an oversight on Donna Eva's part. None the less it affects her testimony.'

'I put it to you, as a court might, that you would say anything to clear Donna Mifsud of suspicion. The court might construe that as the product of infatuation.'

'The insinuation would be as unnecessary as it is unjust,' said Don Stecchi calmly. 'No one who knows Donna Eva even half as well as I do, could do other than admire her devotion to good works, and her character in the face of injustice.'

'That very character, so strongly concerned with charity, gives her a powerful motive for removing those who oppress her and threaten the children she takes such a worthy interest in.'

Don Stecchi shook his head ruefully and laughed. 'You are wasted as a diplomatic agent, Baron. You should have gone in for Carpegna the inquisitor's line of work.'

Gracchus was no great admirer of the church, but he knew a good priest when he encountered one, and it would take extraordinarily strong evidence to convince him that Stecchi was malignly involved in the murders. He sighed glumly as he considered the prospect of a protracted investigation, and finding the table not yet ready, peered out again over the roof tops towards the Maddalene.

It was extraordinary that Vanderville had come so far by that means. Although one could trace a path across the roofs, there were places where the gaps were bridged only by washing lines and pigeon cages, incapable of supporting a man's weight, even a stripling flyweight like Vanderville.

'The complex of the women's hospital is remarkably extensive,' he commented. 'It must be satisfying to do so much good in the face of the world. Do you also minister to the homeless children?'

Don Stecchi leaned forward on the parapet, his face suddenly troubled. 'We do what we can,' he said. 'That is little enough. And we have failures too – just this year there was a child whose spine was crushed under the wheels of a *kalesh*. We could not save him, and I still wonder whether we could not have done better if he had been taken up sooner.' His face became wretched with recollection. 'Despite that, the hospital is a beacon for the downtrodden. Not least for the *Fraternita delle Forbici*. They have a furious longing to have the child they call Granchio admitted, believing he could be cured in some way. It is useless I suppose, but the hope it represents binds them together.'

'Can he really be known just as Granchio?' asked Gracchus, recalling Vanderville's description of the boy. 'It is a meagre moniker for so great a spirit.'

'The surname usually given to foundlings is Spiteri, a corruption of Ospitalieri, the original name of the knights. When foundlings are deposited at the *ruota* in our infirmary we try to rear them in the country at the Order's expense, but these children in Forbici have evaded that destiny, and so they have only the names they give themselves.'

Franca called Don Stecchi to the table to carve, and as he obliged, she took his place at the parapet. Gracchus polished his spectacles on his waistcoat and cast a speculative eye over her. She had regular and pretty features, green eyes, and a pale complexion. Inside the house, with her *faldetta* discarded, her hair was of a very dark colour and hung in a profusion of braided tresses over her shoulders, scarcely constrained by a house bonnet.

Immune to his scrutiny she hung heedlessly out over the rail and drew his attention to two knights promenading in the piazza.

'Aren't they fine? With their little white windmills on their coats they always look so smart.'

Gracchus agreed that they were indeed marvellous, but that he preferred the simple dress of the boatmen in this heat. She waved at an acquaintance below. 'Duccio would agree with you. He wants to become a sailor because they get plenty to eat. Dry biscuits, and on a Friday stockfish fried in batter and beer. The Order feels compelled to feed them, whereas they let us go without.'

'Franca,' called Eva. 'Stop tattling to the baron. Go and find that lost key and close the front door. We are ready to eat.'

-

'How I love a pigeon, roasted in sweet oil,' sighed Gracchus, helping himself to his second bird. He offered the tray of birds to Franca, who declined, helping herself instead to more bread.

'I don't know how Don Stecchi can bear to eat them after raising them so tenderly,' she said with an embarrassed shake of her head.

'It is my passion,' said Don Stecchi, who was on his third pigeon. 'Not the eating of them so much, but the breeding. The exercise of my profession forbids me the art of procreation, except in this vicarious form, and I flatter myself I have gained some proficiency. I keep them on the roof of the hospital complex, and the children help me with them whenever they can get away.'

'From the roofs you must see a great deal that passes below?' suggested Gracchus.

'So, the *sbirri* must believe,' concurred Don Stecchi. 'For they have questioned me three times now about the death of *Cavaliere* von Seeau. I am starting to think, that rather than investigate the Bavarian *langue*, which no doubt is at the heart of the mystery, they will try to pin the murder on one of the locals.'

'Does the Church not insulate you from harassment by the *sbirri*?' enquired Gracchus through a mouthful.

'Carpegna of the Holy Office is worse than the *sbirri*,' replied Stecchi, moving the carcass of his bird around his plate soulfully. 'Almost as persistent as yourself, Baron. Because the first knightly victim was an ordained knight, and the second died in the Maddalene, Carpegna is convinced that the Bavarians are improperly using the churches for secret rites. The pursuit of the sin of Freemasonry is a sort of mania of his.'

Eva nodded. 'Not I suspect, from moral conviction, but because a successful prosecution of the Minerves, or Illumines, or whatever they are calling themselves this week, would enhance his position in Rome.'

Gracchus toyed with his fork. 'The Church's rabid opposition to the cult of Freemasonry seems at odds with what appears to me just one more way for idle nobles to be parted from the revenues of their estates. Unlike the mania for gaming, which is a true social evil, part of the money spent by the lodge-goers goes towards beneficial acts to assist the needy. They do not cause harm or offence to anyone. Membership in a lodge is about being in the centre of the intellectual avant-garde, and aimless meandering in philosophy or sociological theorising.'

'To a certain extent I agree with you,' said Stecchi. 'The Freemasons' so-called rituals are fundamentally absurd, so there is no reason to cry blue murder or categorise them as dangerous or evil acts. At worst one may see them as gentle fools. They do not harm the Order or our religion. Unfortunately, Inquisitor Carpegna does not take that view.'

Don Stecchi fastened one great hand to Gracchus's arm for emphasis, 'It may surprise you, Baron, that despite what I say, I am convinced that Inquisitor Carpegna is a good man.' He flapped his arms theatrically. 'Although he sits like some eternally moping condemned bird of darkness on the blank rafters of the Palazz tal-Inkwizitur, since his arrival here the Holy Office has showed restraint. He arrests, warns, and shames malefactors, but no one has been whipped, exiled, or sent to the galleys for hard labour or worse.'

'His creature, Canon Gatt, on the other hand...' said Eva with a shudder, and Don Stecchi nodded vigorous agreement.

'You mentioned the first victim was also a knight,' said Gracchus, mollifying with a napkin some gravy-wrought destruction to his waistcoat.

'A knight *and* a priest,' mused Stecchi. 'Two weeks before von Seeau met his Maker in the Maddalene, Abbe Alois von Schilternberg, also of the Bavarian *langue*, died under unfortunate circumstances in a house of assignation. The details of that were not made public by the *langue* for obvious reasons, but it would appear from what the pall bearers put abroad afterwards that he died of asphyxiation. There were no witnesses, and no culprit was identified.'

'Von Seeau was also strangled,' stated Gracchus bluntly. 'So, there is a pattern of knights of the Bavarian *langue* ceasing to breath abruptly. Carpegna thinks that someone in the Bavarian *auberge* is cleaning house, and the solution is to be found inside its walls. The only one of the knights who cannot account for his movements is the one they call Haintlet. He has refused to collaborate with the *sbirri*.'

'Deacon von Schilternberg was a bad man,' said Eva. 'It was commonplace to say so among the public women. Not content with their attentions he turned his eye towards those too young to defend themselves. But he is not the only one. There is a sickness in the *Auberge* of Bavaria. What the bailli does not know, or will not admit, is that it involves a level of depravity, organised depravity beyond that commonly encountered. He refuses to countenance this.'

'The *langue* has that reputation for deep engagement in fraternal societies...' began Gracchus.

Eva poured more wine. 'Half of them are members of the so-called Minerves, a secret society within the Freemasons. That may be part of it, but all the knights play at these games. However, in the *Langue* of Bavaria it has passed the usual stage of being a diversion for bored knights with too much time on their hands. There is something worse.'

'There must be a list of members of these societies. Perhaps with the inquisitor,' said Gracchus, spearing a vegetable. 'If there is a link between the murders and the membership of a particular sect, the grandmaster or the bailli will have to act.'

'So, what will you do?' asked Eva, placing figs and barley bread beside him.

'Obtain the lists, and watch the knights,' said Gracchus simply.

'And what can we do to help?' asked Don Stecchi.

'Co-operate with the *sbirri* in their investigations,' said Gracchus, chewing methodically. 'Both of you were in the Maddalene or nearby when von Seeau was killed and will fall under suspicion. And perhaps you can start to think about motive before our phantom choker strikes again. Who were the enemies of these two Bavarians and what linked them?'

Eva looked down at the tablecloth. 'For my part, I feel helpless,' she said. 'I shall protect the children and Franca, I can do no more.'

Gracchus inclined his head. 'You could also oblige with a very few more of those preserved apricots.'

-

Haintlet was waiting for Vanderville at the *auberge* and conducted him to the *salle d'armes* which was in a cellar gallery that doubled as the armoury of the *langue*. As they proceeded down the stairs, he teased Vanderville about his forthcoming poetry bout with the grandmaster.

'It will be at His Eminence's country house at Sant Antonio I expect. I went there once.'

'I have heard the countryside is more verdant than this sun-baked rock and look forward to seeing it. Is it far from Valletta?' asked Vanderville.

'Not much distant. A nice little place, with a pretty bridge and many prettier country girls. I left it more fertile than before my passing.' He laughed roughly, 'Time for the *salle d'armes*! Let us see what the French fencing masters have forgotten to teach you.'

The walls of the practice room armoury were lined with antique arms and armour, but there were also ranks of modern French muskets. Haintlet unfurled some small swords and proficiently added protective tips to their points.

'You have been observed frequenting a certain house in Strada della Ficara. A word of advice to you Tirdflingen – though there are no longer witches at sea to raise a tempest and untie the wind, there are vixens on this island, potent in raising storms within it. From such, not even a bachelor's good fortune can always secure him.'

Vanderville tested his weapon, 'We are not unacquainted with the temptations of the fair sex, even in the French army.'

Haintlet chuckled, but his face was serious. 'A friendly warning, which is all. The French ballet dancers at the opera also caught my eye, but it is all a trap; you have to stay on the lookout, or you will be a purse or two short, or worse, end up like poor von Seeau.'

Vanderville nodded vaguely, the man bored him as soon as he strayed from imparting useful information, and he was ready to exercise. His shoulder felt much recovered, and he stretched his arm speculatively. 'Was von Seeau a Francophile then?'

'Von Seeau a French sympathiser?' He chuckled. 'No, that is ridiculous. He hated the French. Even if he had not contracted a social disease after a sojourn in the Palais Royale and contrived a lifelong distaste for Paris as a result, he was passionately addicted to the Order. He lived for it.'

—

He soon found that Haintlet's style of sword practice was unorthodox. Vanderville had seen the rules of the salle posted on the back of the door, and Haintlet showed a casual disregard for these, breaking all those about safety, blaspheming and low talk with a bewildering rapidity. He shunned masks or quilted jackets, which was common among experienced fencers, but even more unnerving was his ability to conduct conversation throughout their bout.

Although the substance of this monologue was gossipy drivel of the most uninspiring sort, the combined effect of hard exercise and responding to a parallel though entirely separate exchange of nonsense, unsettled Vanderville. When he paused, sweating, to remonstrate, Haintlet insisted that by forcing Vanderville's mind to concentrate on his words, he was freeing his heart to communicate with his sword arm without the conscious mind getting in between them. Was that the secret to his diabolically skilled swordplay, wondered Vanderville?

They recommenced, and Vanderville knuckled down, but he had no tricks that Haintlet was not privy to, and his one vain attempt at novelty ended in humiliation and disarmament.

'You have potential, but you need to work. Your posture is too settled,' explained Haintlet, as Vanderville retrieved his blade. 'Against an opponent who needs time to think, it may serve, but allowing your man time to form an opinion is a mistake. Never rest in any single guard, you will be broken. Motion is all.'

They set to again, and Haintlet picked up his chattering, harping on a now familiar theme. 'Once in a fit of enthusiasm, I took an apartment for one of these Maltese enchantresses, whose mother proved most tractable. It was an expensive way of taking pleasure, but at least she was so young that there was no risk of disease. I have no desire to ruin my health for a poppet.'

Fluidity, always fluidity, remembered Vanderville; attack and parry are not sequential, but interchangeable and transferrable. His regimental fencing instructor had taught him that the ability to move and alter without thought was paramount against a master. Although the man Haintlet was an idiot, and a gross one at that, Vanderville was learning more than he thought possible to digest. He resolved to begin his studies in the martial arts anew at the first opportunity.

'One day she confessed that she loved me, and that I could ask for her hand in marriage. I told her that the thought had never crossed my mind. She assured me that I had pleased her best of all the knights of other *langues* who her family had introduced her to, and she enumerated their number and various qualities. Remarkable in a girl of her tender years. I had to turn her out of course.'

Vanderville chose that moment to unleash his best combinations, and with some fortunate improvisations made up a deal of ground. He still failed to touch Haintlet, but at least the knight too was panting hard now, and less composed. His monologue dried up as a result.

Vanderville meanwhile, was thinking of Granchio. 'I grant you our protection,' Granchio had said to him earnestly. It was pathetic and touching. The child had nothing, he would never have anything, and was condemned to a life of servitude and hard knocks, and yet what he had, his knowledge of the streets and hard-earnt tricks of survival, he had placed freely at Vanderville's disposal. His loyalty and affection to Duccio touched Vanderville deeply too, and absurdly he found himself vowing to be worthy of Granchio's trust. Forced back against the wall again by a low trick, he kicked Haintlet hard between the legs, and the knight staggered back panting and snorting like a donkey.

Vanderville slumped down against the wall to catch his breath. 'Listen,' he said. 'Baron Pellegrew says that you were at the Maddalene complex when von Seeau died but have refused to cooperate with the *sbirri*'s investigations.'

Haintlet snorted as he massaged his damaged portion. 'I see no need to account for my movements to you or anyone else.'

'That leaves you in a weak position. Even Donna Mifsud has someone prepared to vouch for her movements. A priest no less.'

'Don Stecchi?' sneered Haintlet. 'He knows that when she dies, half her property will go to the Maddalene. It is the law

– dead whores pay for the hospital. Should she die convicted, the state takes everything, and the hospital is left high and dry.'

Vanderville gazed aimlessly at the monstrous Gobelin tapestries that swathed the cellar walls. Amid the kings and courtiers depicted there, he saw a court dwarf, cavorting for his liege lord's amusement, and he tried to imagine the life of the deformed Granchio, reduced to the role of curiosity and jester. It was a hard road, he thought, and his thoughts continued in this earnest vein until an unwelcome lascivious vision of Franca at her toilette dispelled them and he found himself comparing her with Paolette Bonaparte, whose person had occupied the vastest part of his affections over the previous months, and whose place in his regard no one had seriously threatened until now. He called himself back to the present with a stern and disproving admonition to put both women from his mind. He went to slap himself and was conscious suddenly of Haintlet clambering to his feet and calling out.

'Had enough? Good. Me too.' He laid aside his small sword and took down another from the wall, 'Now – sabre!'

In sabre Vanderville tended to lead with his wrist too much, exposing it to counters, and Haintlet exploited this ruthlessly, warning, 'You are exposing your wrist to a cut!' the first time, and in the second bout he hit him hard with the flat of the blade, and shrugged apologetically. But his eyes were wolvish. Haintlet started at a low pace and waited for the first exhaustion to hit, before accelerating the energy of his movements enormously. This reflected his supreme fitness and his cunning equally, thought Vanderville, and they soon abandoned the game.

'How much training do you think is necessary?' said Vanderville as he recovered.

'Three or four hours a day, I suppose. More when needed to learn a new weapon or technique.'

Vanderville blinked, 'It doesn't leave much time for anything else,' he suggested.

Haintlet stared at him, his gaze level, 'You need to decide if you are going to earn your place as a lion. Or become prey.'

His small pin-shaped head made him look like a visitor from another species, and Vanderville was so busy considering this, that they were off and into a bucket bath before he knew where he was.

—

The *Auberge* of Bavaria was a substantial handsome-looking building; but so full of dusty state rooms and malodorous offices that, for both privacy and the benefit of the air, the knights assembled for the evening were obliged to lay their mess table on its very summit, on a lofty terrace open to all the winds. This terrace commanded half the roofs of Valletta, and all lay below them, except where here and there a bell tower shot up from among the roofs, rivalling their own elevated peak. The velvet azure of the sky, the cages of carrier pigeons gently cooing, and the softness of the air inclined Vanderville to think of some magical city of Persia.

The company was composed of a train of high-spirited young knights, rapping out the broadest oaths, as they quaffed their flowing cups of iced lemonade heightened with rum, and playing off each other in not exactly the most decorous specimens of practical wit. But everyone was magnificent in regimentals for the occasion, and pregnant with anticipation for the feast. Before long, their faces were glistening with sweat, so overdressed were they all despite the warm evening.

The mess table sparkled with silverware under a blaze of candlelight, and the fish dishes, especially, were splendid. Vanderville regretted Gracchus's absence. He would have dearly liked to carry his friend something of the fruits of the sea, but Gracchus had been adamant that he would retire early, so as to meet Vanderville early the next morning at the grandmaster's palace for an interview with that worthy.

Probably as well, thought Vanderville. Gracchus had never quite grasped that soldiers' bacchanals represented a communion, and had even been dismissive of them upon occasion, suggesting that excessive consumption of wine blunted the faculty of taste.

Vanderville had explained before that wine was merely the sacrament chosen when the members of the mess remembered and emphasised the past glories of their peers. In doing so they affirmed their commitment to communal values and identity. Gracchus had wondered aloud what sacrament was represented by officers crawling under the table to vomit, and since then, by mutual assent, Vanderville had ceased to issue invitations to his heretical companion.

The presidency of the mess was rotated among the knights, and this evening it fell to Haintlet who seated de Rechberg and Vanderville on his flanks.

'I am the mess knight of the mess night,' he announced proudly to Vanderville.

'How very democratic that you take turns.'

'Nonsense,' said Haintlet, who had already drunk deeply from his silver cup. 'Democracy would be letting the servants preside. Here we operate on merit, which is easily adjudged.' He poured more wine for them all. 'You see, the thing is, there are two sorts of young officers: intelligent ones, and the stupid. They can be further subdivided into hard workers, and the lazy. So, there are only five types, and no more.'

Much of the evening passed in this fashion of amiable nonsense, and gradually there was introduced a pseudo-masonic air to some of the proceedings, consisting of the usual tired allusions, hints at secret knowledge and plain gibberish. Vanderville was alert to any hint of irregular rites, or mention of the Minerves, but found none in the formality that reigned as long as relative sobriety endured. The sole advantage of this fraternal window dressing was that the whole table was *sub rosa*, even to the extent that an actual drab garland of roses was in place above the president's chair. As such Vanderville was implored to dispense with his alias as Tirdflingen and relate once more how he leapt from the Carrère to assail the bastion of Fort Sant' Elmo.

'How camest thou here?' intoned de Rechberg in the approved fraternal masonic formula, and the table listened gravely as Vanderville recounted yet again his stirring story.

'You will not live long in this manner,' said one of the visiting knights approvingly.

'A light cavalryman should aspire like our good Lord not to live past thirty-three,' responded Vanderville. A tired republican trope, but one which provoked a general riot of cheers and raising of glasses. As the warm bonds of drunkenness enveloped the company, their tongues loosened with the easing of cravats and buttons.

'I thought I saw one of Carpegna's men in the courtyard earlier,' Vanderville mentioned to his neighbour at the table.

De Rechberg shrugged off his coat. 'It could be,' he said. 'The priest known as Canon Gatt who took a ducking at the docks haunts this place. Some of the brethren actually allow him to confess them, although one suspects he has more to be forgiven than most.'

'But not you?' asked Vanderville.

'That oaf?' sneered Haintlet, picking his nose industriously with a corner of his napkin. 'He is from I forget which university; I hope not Bologna. He told me that one of the nuns of the Convent of the Maddalene, having intrigued horizontally with old Beelzebub in *propria persona*, had been sent to the inquisition, and the window through which his infernal majesty had entered upon this gallant exploit, walled up and painted over with red crosses. The same precautionary decoration, he explained, has been bestowed upon every opening in the nun's façade, so that no demon, however sharp set, can get in again.'

'A man who enjoys his work,' said de Rechberg.

'He seems keen on exposing the fraternal societies,' opined Vanderville.

De Rechberg filled Vanderville's glass and his own inexpertly. 'We have been guilty of playing up the whole Minerves thing to annoy Carpegna, because for some reason, he has a grudge against the *Langue* of Bavaria. It is so much nonsense, the brotherhood was effectively dissolved years ago.'

'So, there is nothing in it?' pressed Vanderville.

De Rechberg leaned in closer. 'A few still promote the secret societies as a cover for debauchery,' he whispered. 'The worst of the knights in some *auberges* abuse women too young even to be married. I cannot tell you how foul they are to the people here.'

'Are you talking the Order down again?' belched Haintlet, whose movements and judgement were becoming increasingly erratic with wine taken. He leaned forward across the table to address Vanderville, his face just a little too close for comfort.

'The fact is, that the Maltese are cattle. Their so-called nobles are nothing of the sort, they would not even enter society back home. They are corrupt and offer their daughters up to us as concubines, so how can we be expected to extend them courtesy when they contaminate themselves in this filthy way?'

De Rechberg averted his eyes, but Haintlet, whose own eyeballs were glassy now, continued. 'The merchants are what they are everywhere, so we take what we want from them, and they are grateful that we notice them. As for the Public Women and street children, you may choose to contaminate yourself by associating with them, but they live as beasts, and like beasts they are hunted for sport, or culled to keep down a nuisance. They are not worth a dot of your misplaced compassion, and you lower the fraternity of this sacred table by pleading for them.'

'Peace Fra' Haintlet,' muttered de Rechberg. 'Remember you may not insult a guest or brother at the mess table.'

Any offence was curtailed by another round of toasts, and Vanderville hazily contemplated the magnificent antique silver centrepiece that dominated the table. It represented a walled height where an armoured knight stood astride a breach, clasping the head of a Turk in one hand, and brandishing a sword in the other. Two dead turks were sprawled at his feet, their pallid argent faces turned to the sky. The glister of the silver was reflected in the perspiration of the faces around the table.

'Why do you suffer Haintlet?' Vanderville whispered to de Rechberg.

'He is coarse it is true,' he whispered back. 'But you must understand – we are bound to each other by the Order. It is forbidden to us to betray a brother knight. Loyalty to one's *auberge*, to the Order itself is everything; it overmasters all other considerations – including those of creed, lodge, language, or nation.'

One of the younger knights had been recalling the tale of the Great Siege to Vanderville, who listened with one ear as he observed his fellows. He felt sure that he would be required by Gracchus to describe their various qualities in the morning, with particular reference to Minervan tendencies. But the softness of the evening breeze had emboldened him to quaff too freely in pace with the brethren, and he found himself enveloped in the gossamer threads of drunkenness that were settling their web over the heads bowed at their trencher work. As the endless details of the siege continued to be recounted to him, he realised that in performing the acts of inebriate communion, by toasting their predecessors and their exploits, those present expressed their wish to achieve something good and great in common with the past. They wanted a magnificent event to be part of. Their wish for a siege comparable to the Great Siege might soon be granted, he reflected. Although he hoped it would find him outside the walls looking in rather than confined here under the hail of fire.

His speculation was unexpectedly mirrored by Haintlet, who addressed the table in general. 'What if the French do not come and we are deprived of our moment of immortality?'

The younger knights pled with Vanderville, who reassured them through the wine fumes that the French would come, and that right soon.

'My only dread,' Haintlet whispered to Vanderville confidentially, his breath reeking of brandy, 'is that I shall be killed by an ignominious cannon ball, and not die hand-to-hand in combat. I seek only to kill very many Frenchmen before being cut down.'

'Beware Bonaparte's gunnery then,' said Vanderville. 'It is his branch, and we ply the great guns pretty hot.'

'We have a capable battery or two emplaced in my post,' boasted de Rechberg. 'We must contrive to have you exchanged by parlay before the ball opens. I hope you survive the first exchanges of fire. It would be a shame to preserve you from the inquisition merely to see you cut in two by a ball a few days later.'

Haintlet nodded. 'You must have your chance to take an honourable part in events, Vanderville. Rest assured; we shall not let you be imprisoned as a spy or massacred.' He clapped him on the back too hard, and Vanderville spluttered.

'Not at all, I shall save my sword for you,' said Vanderville. As the company acclaimed this sentiment he stood abruptly, swaying a little. De Rechberg supported his elbow to steady him and helped him stagger to the low parapet. As he eased himself over the rooftop, a profound calm descended upon him, and for a few blissful moonlit moments all his troubles were absent.

He shook his head to clear the wine fumes, and with increasing clarity came a vague sense of shame. The purpose of his mission was to help deliver the Order to the French Republic by subterfuge. By fulfilling it he would deprive the knights of their moment of glory and extinguish the glory of the Order – the one thing that justified their feudal existence on this rock, as the last outpost of an anachronistic order.

Was it treachery, he asked himself? Not on his part, he decided; he was, after all, doing his duty, but he was doubtless prepared to encourage treachery in others. His concern was not for Haintlet and the other oafs, but for de Rechberg, who desperately required a reason to exist, to earn a right to deserve his parasitic existence. A bibulous cheer broke out behind him, and he shook his head again. It was later than he thought, he had taken overmuch wine, and become maudlin as a result. He began to think of his bed.

'A steeplechase then,' someone roared drunkenly behind him, 'and we shall see how the Frenchman runs!'

Vanderville gradually collected that some of the less impaired knights had proposed a steeplechase race to ring the bells of a church. This course agreed upon, discussion now focussed, if that word was appropriate, considering the inordinate quantity of ardent spirits that had been consumed, on the church to be targeted.

De Rechberg proposed the bells of Saint Roch, patron saint of bachelors, to great approval. Haintlet countered with the bells of the Maddalene, and his champions roared assent. Whether agreement was reached or not, Vanderville never found out, as they all set off on a harum-scarum race through the streets, and he found himself carried along without knowing where they went.

He knew only that they found the doors of St Roch securely barred against intruders. One of the knights suggested that the scaffold erected for repairs on the facade of Saint Ursula made it a more feasible target, and they departed pell-mell for that place, where, somehow, they scaled the heights. The scaffolding was on three levels, and it was on achieving the second of these that disaster almost overtook them. Haintlet and Vanderville reached it together, climbing hand over hand at breakneck pace, but in his haste to join those already mounted, the knight misjudged his hold and began to teeter on the very edge of the planks.

It was the hand of de Rechberg that reached out to grasp him, preventing by a cat's whisper his plummet to the ground. Vanderville, passing Haintlet as he was pulled to safety heard him mutter to himself.

'Saved by a Minerve,' grunted Haintlet. 'There's something to write home about.'

For a moment Vanderville felt de Rechberg's eyes on him, his pale face unreadable in the darkness, but the moment passed as the spirit of competition bore them on upwards in a mass of cheerful elbowing and jostling for pre-eminence. Although among the first and boldest climbers, Vanderville never reached the bells, for as he reached the utmost platform of the scaffolding, an unexpected event below arrested his attention.

Two men swathed in dark mantles were passing silently below, their persons utterly indistinct from above, and yet one of them moved in a familiar manner that he recognised. They appeared anxious to avoid the drunken knights, drawing into the shadows as they passed down in the direction of the harbour, but as they turned the corner Vanderville clearly saw the telltale stick of the limping man. De Rechberg was lying flat on the scaffold giggling haplessly at some private reverie, and Vanderville tugged at his sleeve and pointed to the route the furtive shadows had taken. 'What lies in that direction?' he asked.

De Rechberg shrugged, 'Nothing. It goes up to the Maddalene, and downwards there is nothing. Nothing but the *bagnio* – the slave prison,' he said, and promptly vomited over Vanderville's hand.

Chapter Ten

A rod of stippled light reached from between the slats in the shutters, across the rosy flags of the floor and dipped onto Vanderville's bed, finally alighting on his pillow. Bells filled the air with their bronze clamour, jostling and contradicting one another in their morning altercation. Now and then a stronger deeper bass growl broke like a fateful stride into their confusion, imposing its rhythm, rebuking the din.

Vanderville woke with a start. The mess night had left him liverish and pale, with a trembling head. His shoulder, so skilfully set by Don Stecchi, now felt like a pulsing sea of pain, and tidal waves of nausea lapped at his stomach. Oh Christ! He remembered with a lurch, the bell towers! He must have wrenched the arm in the assault on the bell towers. As a flood of better-forgotten moments surged into his recollection he lay back and groaned. He had allowed himself to become overfamiliar with the knights, been privy to things better left unsaid, and said things better left unheard. He remembered embracing that gross creature Haintlet with an inebriate's ardour and shuddered with shame. He whimpered and then remembered his appointment with Gracchus at the palace, and realising he would probably be late, began reluctantly to dress.

—

Gracchus was at the wharves before breakfast, searching among the sailor's booths for an acquaintance. The eternal lounging at rude tables and sipping of coffee agreed well with the merchants of the Ottoman empire, who stalked about in their proper dresses, and smoked their exotic pipes without being stared and wondered at. The booth he chose was composed of a small cavity hewn from the rockface that formed the inner limit of the quay. Inside this cave, an old woman laboured at a smoking stove, dispensing coffee through a railing that separated her from the rough tables outside at which sailors and porters were noisily consuming their morning *merenda*.

Just outside the railings, seated in luxurious ease was a raven-haired, black-whiskered man, with wide springing eyebrows of sooty black, attired in the full excess of the East.

'Baron Pellegrew! What an unexpected pleasure,' he grinned toothily as Gracchus neared him. 'I was about to take another cup of this poor hovel's coffee; will you honour me with your company?'

As he drew up a ramshackle chair, Gracchus considered him more closely. His dark skin, heavily beaten by the rays of the sun, was almost the true African ebony shade now. Some of that even sun had been absorbed into his face and sparkled in his eyes, which were merry and filled with good humour. The hair on the crown of his head was absent, and the polished dome was surrounded by a bushy black growth flecked with grey that continued into his beard. With his sparkling gold earrings competing with the flash of his ready smile, he could have stepped from the stage in the role of the Corsair King.

'I am glad to have found you, Rais Murad,' said Gracchus. He moved his feet aside as two women swept by, their noses in the air, and their *faldettas* tastefully drawn around the head, throwing additional expression into their contemptuous dark eyes. Murad leapt to his feet and bowed deeply, but they ignored his gesture, and he sat back down resignedly at the table.

'Have you noticed the beautiful feet of these island women?' sighed Murad, neither expecting nor waiting for a reply. 'Truly peerless ankles. It is a great shame though, that they sometimes squint, owing to their always looking out of the same eye; half of the face being covered with those ridiculous veils.'

Gracchus, to whom the subject of fashion was of scant interest at that moment contented himself with collecting his coffee and regarded it dubiously. Murad took a swig from his own cup.

'One cannot however help admire exceedingly the graceful twisting way they arrange it about themselves. They appear also extremely fond of gold and silver trinkets. Perhaps that is the way to command their attention.' He fingered his own earrings speculatively, as if he was about to wrench one out and run after the sources of his concern to proffer it as an offering.

'Yes, I have noticed that they wear both clothes, and upon occasion, jewellery too,' observed Gracchus, who was wondering when the conversation might take a more productive direction.

'Unfortunately, in all my time visiting at this port it has proved impossible for me to meet them socially. The barriers are too great.'

'Indeed,' said Gracchus, whose tolerance of the baroque meanderings of polite oriental negotiating practice was inclined to evaporate quickly. 'Whatever you say. I daresay there are women on the wharves. I myself observed a very rack rent specimen entertaining company behind drying fish nets on the way here. Now, about the ships…'

Murad was still locked onto his rail of thought. He adjusted his clothing and asserted, 'The women of the common sailors could never interest a man like me. Look at the stair behind you where the mule is kicking up. Tripping lightly down the steps behind is a Maltese lady, enveloped in her elegant black silk gown. What did you call it? A *faldetta*? So grave, and yet so coquettish, are its rustling folds that the piquant costume renders even the ugly attractive, while the pretty become positively irresistible!'

Gracchus smiled, spotting an opening. 'I may be able to help you assay a few steps into Maltese society. But first I have a question for you. It might be that you sometimes come across the ships carrying mail to the island?'

'Not so much. Owing to harsh weather and little problems like the French army being in Italy, sometimes no post ship arrives here for twenty or even thirty days.'

'That is well, it serves my purposes that the mail should be even later this season. And speaking of ships – Will there be enough of them?' asked Gracchus.

'The use of the knight's ships is licensed to me,' said Murad with a proud toss of his head. 'They will be sufficient.'

Gracchus frowned, 'If there are complications afterwards, won't the knights miss their vessels?'

'Do not worry about that, it is a problem of mine. You do not need to know.' He spat on the floor. 'We have other concerns. Every sailor who can find a ship is leaving Malta. Keeping the crew I have already retained is a labour to exhaust the Prophet, peace be upon him, although I flog a score of them nightly. As a consequence, I regret the cost of hiring crew has doubled, there is nothing to be done about it.'

—

When Vanderville, his head still pounding, arrived at the palace he found an impatient Gracchus waiting for him in the salon outside the grandmaster's audience chamber. As they waited to be summoned Gracchus introduced to him a headache of a different order. They whispered furiously between themselves, 'Don't you know *any* poetry?' hissed Gracchus.

'From school, yes. They beat a little into us as small boys. And I picked up a bit in the Palais Royale. A friend of mine thought himself a versifier, and some of it was pretty fine, so I committed one or two passages to memory. I thought it might be useful in impressing women. There is one called *The Curve that Yields*. It begins, "O downy milky white curve pres't, going by the name of downy breast..."'

Gracchus cut in, 'Yes, yes, very well.' He scratched his head thoughtfully. 'Tell me, did it serve its purpose with the Parisiennes?'

Vanderville cast his mind back and replied dolefully, 'I can't say it did exactly, there is a knack to bringing these things off well, and I suspect somehow my pronunciation was awry.'

Gracchus sighed. 'I will see if I can find something more in the knights' library, but I do not think they go in much for moderns. Can you at least quote from Tirdflingen's book?'

'It will not stick,' said Vanderville shaking his head regretfully. 'This whole poet disguise seems like to prove a damnable disaster, Gracchus.'

Gracchus nodded po-faced and tried but failed to persuade his face to assume a more confidant mien. 'The burden of the lyre is often underestimated, my dear Vanderville. Still, I have faith that you will labour under it with equanimity. I too have my cross to shoulder; my disguise to render efficacious.'

'You are posing as an eccentric dilettante possessed of crass wealth, Gracchus. The first part of this combination is no great stretch for your acting talents, whereas the second is an improvement on your customary situation. Any few difficulties you encounter in sustaining this illusion are alleviated by the showers of gold that emit from your squeaking pockets every time you so much as bend down to adjust your shoe buckle.'

'Oh, come, come, it is not so bad as all that,' said Gracchus, fetching him a hearty and unwelcome slap across the shoulders. 'You pose as a celebrated man of letters, with all the prestige and opportunities that accrue to that status. Best of all the grandmaster adores your poetry, so we shall derive advantage from that fortuitous happenstance.'

'I cannot do it. I lack the poetic bent.'

Gracchus drummed his fingers on the chair arm impatiently, 'There is no alternative. If you wish to maintain your liberty – and mine, now that I have given parole for you, you must drain this cup. You must be perfect, you understand me? This is not a game. Von Hompesch is a weak sort of a spider, every string he spins flaps flabbily, but nonetheless, we are in his web at his mercy. The *sbirri* are rounding up suspected French sympathisers every night, and when they have finished with the common people they will begin on the nobles, which class I now have the misfortune to belong to. If the grandmaster penetrates your disguise, then mine will not stand long. If we are discovered, we may not leave this rock alive.'

The chamberlain arrived at that moment to usher them into the presence. The grandmaster was waiting for them in his throne room and once they had entered with due ceremony the chamberlains departed, and a relative informality reigned. They stood before the throne respectfully and listened to a preoccupied von Hompesch lament.

'This palace is woefully situated. It is too close to the restless people who frisk and dance and tinkle their guitars, from sundown to sun rise. What with the bellowing of litanies by parochial processions, perpetually setting off in honour of some member or other of the celestial hierarchy and dogs too, yelping and howling without intermission, Valletta is insufferable. Last night the squabbles of my bullying rake-hell knights scouring the streets in search of adventures, stole from me the merest wink of sleep. I should leave for Sant Antonio tomorrow if I had any sense.'

Gracchus inclined his head diplomatically. 'You are wise to do so at the first opportunity, I have no doubt, Your Eminence. I very much look forward to accepting your kind invitation in company with my dear Tirdflingen.'

The grandmaster peered at Vanderville from his throne. 'Ah. I knew there was something this morning. Tirdflingen, welcome back. You will find we have many good things here, and I have longed for an artist such as you to arrive to describe them. To see things as they were meant to be seen, I mean. Surely this is a heaven-sent opportunity that you come to me at this time when we are in all the path of the approaching maelstrom of history.'

He cleared his throat with a sound like the raking of gravel. 'Although the Greeks said that poetry is finer and more philosophical than history; for poetry expresses the universal, and history only the particular.'

Vanderville coughed. 'My muse has lately spurned the well-trod path of Greek allusion, I think that sort of thing is rather a hog's patch nowadays.'

The grandmaster looked startled. 'You are with the avant-garde now then? You favour the Etruscan allusions?'

'I have turned away from the bosky bower of Etruscan mythology also. You must understand, Your Eminence,' ventured Vanderville warming to his theme, 'I abhor the beaten grass where other feet have passed. I recoil from the fell boar's scrape as the barefooted nymph does from the serpent disturbed in his sun bower.'

'If not Rome, if not the Hellenes, if you turn your back upon, heaven help us, the Etruscans, then to what genius do you hark, what ancient wisdom is your lode stone?' He was leaning forward in his throne, baffled, and frowning.

'The Gallic bards, Your Eminence,' said Vanderville proudly, his head throbbing. He swallowed with difficulty. 'The phlegm-flecked prose of far flung Galles is the tongue of my muse.'

Gracchus, who had been gazing out of the window, his face turned aside from the two scholars, turned his head abruptly, and flicked his eyes worriedly from one man to the other. Vanderville had veered wildly off script, and although von Hompesch was tentatively following him up the garden path, the grandmaster was no fool, and Vanderville's arse was showing where he had tucked his poet's tunic under his girdle of lyricism. Any minute now, Gracchus feared, he would begin banging his metaphorical lyre with even further abandon and blow the whole game out of the water.

'Orpheus was not even Greek, I believe,' the grandmaster started gamely. 'Yet he managed some good things…'

Vanderville bestowed a benign smile on the grandmaster and turning moistened eyes upwards suggested, 'Your Eminence, let us embrace this moment of discovery together in song.'

Von Hompesch grunted happily, his frail white head bobbing up and down enthusiastically. Gracchus sighed with relief and lowered himself back into the window seat. But at that moment a chamberlain approached and whispered in the grandmaster's ear. A cloud passed over von Hompesch's brow. 'Very well, show Monsignor Carpegna in,' he ordered the chamberlain abruptly.

'You shall forgive me, Tirdflingen,' he grunted to Vanderville. 'Matters of state must take precedence over the lyre in these troubled times. You have not forgotten I am holding a party at my country house in two days. We will hear your song then.'

To Gracchus he added, 'Baron Pellegrew, stay here a while with me, I seek your counsel.'

Gracchus flicked his fingers impatiently at the lingering Vanderville, who bowed his way out of the audience chamber. Once clear of the doors he bounded from the adjoining salon heedless of the chamberlain's offended gaze, and upon regaining sanctuary outside the palace shook himself, like a wet spaniel fresh from a dripping copse.

—

The grandmaster beckoned Gracchus closer. 'You will enjoy this little pantomime,' he croaked conspiratorially. 'Observe Monsignor Carpegna's face as he passes into this chamber. He is prevailed upon to follow precedence issues laid down by the great Grandmaster la Valette and deeply resents it.'

He sighed contentedly, and then frowned. 'Now I find myself sat in the chair I have inherited from de Valette. It is, as you see, too big for me, yet who could sit in the greatest grandmaster's chair, without being diminished?'

As Gracchus pondered this pettiness, through the portal he glimpsed the inquisitor and his retinue arriving in the antechamber. Palace officials swarmed around them, isolating Carpegna from his retinue. When he stepped across the threshold into the audience chamber, Carpegna was in no doubt that he was entering as a subordinate guest of the Order's sovereign. Gracchus respectfully withdrew into the shadows behind the throne and watched as the representatives of church and state greeted each other with a precisely regulated degree of courtesy.

Their conversation began in the same formulaic manner as their greeting but did not stay that way for long. Gracchus had observed the pair duelling courteously before over minor points, but with a start he realised this was different. The grandmaster was displaying unhabitual energy. He had displayed passion occasionally before – now he was out of his chair, and striding about the room in fitful little jumps and starts. The inquisitor occupied the centre of the chamber, but his attempt to assert dominance of that space was put in doubt by the constant adjustments he had to make to maintain his front respectfully to the grandmaster. The consequent fidgeting of his feet deprived him of gravitas, and his discomfiture was sufficient to tip the balance of authority in favour of the reinvigorated sovereign. Their discord centred around the licentious behaviour of some of the knights, and the Church's inability to focus the knight's devotions in useful directions.

'I will not have the knights going around wantonly destroying the families of the people. It is bad enough that they steal, shall we say, the mature fruit from the trees with impunity, and offer open insult to the people when challenged, but to wantonly damage the trees before the fruit ripen?! It is excessive.'

Carpegna, whose sleek black head and sallow countenance was overshadowed by an enormous pair of green spectacles, removed these, and folded them carefully. He inclined his head gracefully and nodded with the appearance of great agreement. 'You have penetrated to the heart of the matter, Your Eminence. These depredations are deplorable, and the Church shall render you the utmost support.'

'The behaviour of the knights has been reprehensible, and at a time when they should be setting an example of steadiness to the people. The clergy should be reprimanding them, and instead they are in many cases as corrupt as the Bavarians.'

Carpegna nodded assent, and suggested, 'Some of the people too, do not protest as hard as they should. They hope by their compliance to curry favour with the knights.'

'You are saying they actually conspire to provide the knights with an opportunity for this infamous behaviour? They are complicit in the extortion of their own daughters' virtue?'

'I am afraid, with the greatest will, Your Eminence, I can put no other construction on their actions. Undoubtably it is easier to tip a nod and a wink than to bring an action against a knight. I need not remind you of the case against the Bavarian Schilternberg. And then, if your orchard is to be ransacked anyway, why not make sure that you gain something in exchange from the plunderer too?'

Carpegna had achieved the varnish of hypocrisy in abundance and with distinction, thought Gracchus. 'Infamous!' he grunted, almost unheard.

The grandmaster whirled around, his eyebrows wiggling furiously. 'Exactly! Infamous. And the baillis connive at this too. Why are they not protecting the people?'

'Ah, I believe you have arrived at the crux of the matter Your Most Eminent Highness. If the baillis restrained the knights of their respective *auberges* with a fraction of the rigor they apply to the cases where a priest is caught embarrassed in his cups, we would not be here lamenting the moral decline so evident in the Convent.' He shook his head mournfully. 'Is it your wish that the *auberges* should be subject to an inquiry into their conduct and malpractice?'

Gracchus was awestruck at the audacious checkmate, and grudgingly acknowledged the true courtier's peerless touch. Thus was the ire of the grandmaster skilfully misdirected away from the evil done by the knights and onto the baillis who were already powerless to enforce the rule of the Order.

'There may be something in that,' grunted the grandmaster. He summoned Gracchus forward. 'Now let us hear what Baron

Pellegrew has discovered about the unfortunate business in the Maddalene. With my approval he has initiated an investigation.'

Gracchus bowed respectfully. 'There are certain persons known to have been in the vicinity of the Maddalene complex at the pertinent hour. Those who have failed satisfactorily to account for their whereabouts include *Cavaliere* Haintlet of the Bavarian *langue*, the priest Don Stecchi, and the *meretrice* Donna Eva Mifsud.'

'An infamous trio. And all known to my office,' breathed Carpegna. 'It will not surprise you, Your Highness, to know that I have conducted my own investigation. Don Stecchi, I must reluctantly admit, is free of any taint – in this respect at least,' he added smoothly. 'He claims to have been engaged at the women's hospital that morning and attended by the sisters there throughout. He is not reliable, but they are.'

'Does that tally with your own enquiries Pellegrew?' asked von Hompesch, and Gracchus nodded cautiously.

'*Cavaliere* Haintlet, I believe we can also clear,' resumed Carpegna. 'He was meeting my assessor, Canon Gatt, that morning for the regular review of his spiritual wellbeing, which although it continues lamentably, at least excludes him from the list of those whose movements cannot be accounted for.'

The grandmaster sat down, his face grave. 'So, we must conclude, gentlemen, the public woman is indicated as our murderer?'

'I agree that Don Stecchi is in the clear,' began Gracchus carefully. 'However, I am not altogether happy about the nature of Haintlet's alibi.'

'Naturally. I would not expect you to have my faith in my assistant's integrity,' said Carpegna glibly. 'But he is outside, I can call him in immediately if that will reassure you?' The grandmaster nodded and summoned one of his chamberlains who brought in Carpegna's pet.

Canon Gatt's physical appearance was even more against him than usual, his face bearing the marks recently inflicted upon him at the docks. He wore the crow-black robes of a canon of the Order, with its cross on his cape, and his uncovered hair was scraped back and powdered for the occasion. His mouth was wet lipped and his face greasy as he compliantly confirmed the inquisitor's account. The grandmaster heard his evidence in truly short order.

'You may go,' said von Hompesch, and then, as the assessor scuttled towards the door, 'Wait!' Gatt turned and stood attentively with hands clasped. 'You are the spiritual advisor of Fra' Haintlet. Do you find his condition much improved?' asked the grandmaster.

Gatt hesitated and wrinkled his prying nose. His face, thought Gracchus, seemed incapable of any expression but a sneer. 'Despite his reprehensible propensity for violence, Your Eminence, I find him the best of the Bavarian *langue*,' Gatt said.

'Hmm? How so? Let us dismiss the pretence that he is preoccupied with his honour. He is a common assassin.'

'Yet alone among his fellows,' Gatt drawled placidly, 'he has avoided the taint of Freemasonry.' His eyes flicked to Carpegna for reassurance and the inquisitor nodded imperceptibly. Gracchus saw malice flicker in his eyes. Gatt licked his lips and continued, 'You may or may not know that Sabbat meetings have been taking place for quite some time at a garden in Floriana. Several times a week, more than fifty damned souls, all members of the Order, without shame or regret, spend entire days committing God knows what crimes and profanations. Among them one can even find two priests.'

Gracchus interjected, 'This is extraordinary, one can hardly credit it, grandmaster. But allow me to make one observation to Canon Gatt: these gentlemen are not Jewish, why do they observe the sabbath? Are you not being misled by whoever is telling you this?'

'The word makes no difference, Monsignor Baron,' replied Gatt. 'Be it Sabbat, hell, or a Freemason's lodge, they all mean the same thing. The fact is that there are underground ritualistic mysteries, obscure initiation ceremonies in sinister robes, bones and skulls, blood, yellow candles, and horrific blasphemies.'

Gracchus's mind strayed unwonted to the reliquaries and baroque magnificence of the chapels of St John's cathedral, and he watched fascinated as a little spume of froth gathered at one extremity of Gatt's mouth as he ranted on.

'And, to cap all this, an orgy with torches, in the middle of the day! Where they drank coffee and wine, sang obscene chants, and performed all kinds of libertine acts. In short Monsignor, what they do is worse than the prostitution of the ancient pagans. And,' he added, as if it sealed the matter, 'there were crocodiles present at this debauch.'

'Oh,' said Gracchus, calmly. 'This is too much. I cannot believe it.'

'And yet it happened, Your Eminence,' said Gatt, appealing to the grandmaster now. 'Just as surely as you and I are standing here.'

'That will do!' said von Hompesch sharply. 'You are dismissed. I will treat your caution, and your advice with the gravity they deserve.'

'But Your Eminence, be careful of what you say and of what you do, these people have their spies everywhere, even here in the palace.' He glared at Gracchus.

'I do what I have to do, Canon Gatt,' said the grandmaster curtly, 'and you can go and do the other thing.' Having spoken, the grandmaster turned his back on him. The canon left, confused and angry. He was in such a fit of temper that he did not return Gracchus's grin.

'Admittedly his manner is not lucid,' began Carpegna. 'But the substance of his account is verifiable. Minervism is flourishing unhindered among the members of the...' but the grandmaster halted him.

'I have heard enough for one afternoon. Your man is not an inspiring witness. We cannot proceed yet against the public woman while the matter is unresolved. Bring me some evidence, either of you, but do it soon. This matter is dragging, and I have other concerns to attend to.'

On the stair as they left, Carpegna excused his assistant to Gracchus and gracefully changed the subject. 'You have access to all the councils of state now, Baron Pellegrew?'

'My position opens all the portals of government to me. I could grow accustomed to it, I must admit. Everyone wants to smooth my feathers and see where I intend to lay my golden egg. Rumour on the subject abounds around every corner.'

'There is something in that,' said Carpegna measuredly. 'It is well called a Convent; they gossip like a pack of desiccated nuns. Yet it *is* true that the infection of Freemasonry is well established here. What they call vulgarly 'high philosophy' is nothing else than the sect of Minerves, which the Holy Father has pronounced high folly. These mystery-shrouded societies are far too inclined to resort to abuse to seek gain. They proselytise amongst the brethren and find adherents even among the baillis, some of whom are obsessed with all the latest ideas which they believe will broaden the minds and fulfil the spirit of mankind. The grandmaster is also an initiate of course, although I believe he is merely foolish in this rather than demonic.'

Gracchus protested politely, 'My experience of the matter is that it consists of lively fraternal banquets and japes. If only this brought chivalry back to the Order and if it served to spread the word of moral values, physics, science, and industry. It would represent progress.'

'I hope you are right,' said Carpegna, 'and I am all in favour of progress. But in this I am guided by our Holy Father in Rome, and although Freemasonry may appear a harmless diversion to the salons, he has decreed that it may serve as a gateway to worse errors and serious spiritual and temporal harm.'

'And crocodiles too,' said Gracchus to himself under his breath, and then aloud. 'I don't see what this has to do with the murder of the Bavarian knight?'

'You will,' replied Carpegna parting from him at the palace gates as his dog cart was brought round.

Whipping out his tinted spectacles, Gracchus peered across the palace piazza. His view was obscured by a fountain in full squirt, but he believed he could make out Vanderville's noble figure near the barber stalls opposite the palace entrance.

—

Vanderville gazed about himself curiously. The figures moving around him seemed strange ghosts inspiring fear and wonder. The barbers were all men, of every shade of colour, alike dressed in dark Levantine robes. All the hair on their heads had been shaved, save a forelock, and as well as their strange appearance they conversed among themselves in a strange tongue, more guttural even than Maltese. Even their razors were of an unaccustomed shape and watching them wield these strange tools he was not altogether sure he wanted a shave after all.

'They are slaves,' explained Gracchus, arriving beside him, and greeting the nearest barber by name. Settling himself into a chair, he indicated the vacant one next to it for Vanderville. 'Among themselves they speak Arabic, but they have also *lingua franca* – the slave language. An amalgam of Spanish and Italian, innocent of tenses, inflexions, or grammatical form. I have picked up a little of it myself,' he announced contentedly.

'I thought the slaves all rowed in the Order's galleys,' said Vanderville, surrendering himself to the chair with misgiving, and flinching as napkin and lather were applied.

'The few galleys left are manned by volunteers and criminals on the whole,' said Gracchus through his lather. 'Slavery is not some novel vice of the knights. Maltese sailors and corsairs were as infamous as the Arab version even before the knights came to Malta. On the shores of the Mediterranean Sea, the culture of hostile maritime descent on coastal villages is so ancient as to defy any attempt to aver culpability to any single race or creed. The fruits of the sea have always included human bounty, and the line between a trader and a pirate has since time immemorial been defined more by opportunity than by any stiff principle.

A salt-rimed tumescence of brigandage lurks in every seagoing man.'

There was a pause while his barber proficiently flicked his oddly shaped razor swiftly over Gracchus's chin and cheeks. When he had finished, Gracchus took his napkin and wiped his face of the last traces of lather. 'The Order's slaves are used in construction and repair of fortifications, the manufacture of sails, and at the dockyards. The fortunate ones work here or for merchants. Regardless, they all sleep in the slave prison at night.'

Vanderville opened his mouth to form the question that had dominated his thoughts all morning, but at that instant the doors of the palace opposite them opened, and out flaunted a hubbub of knights, with ladies, and priests and puppy dogs, gabbling and flirting. They both averted their eyes to the spectacle, and the moment passed.

Gracchus flicked his towel playfully at Vanderville. 'That's the male slave's life, of course. The enslaved women are effectively domestic servants – like your beautiful friend Franca.'

Vanderville spluttered, and sitting up too swiftly narrowly avoided a precipitate end to his career. 'Franca isn't, I mean, she *can't* be a slave!'

'Ask Donna Eva who holds her papers,' said Gracchus.

Chapter Eleven

Vanderville decided to call on Eva on his way to the Maddalene that morning, but he was intercepted by Franca outside her house. She told him that Donna Eva was engaged and suggested that instead she show him the sights of Valletta. They agreed to meet at the Maddalene church after she had finished her chores.

As a boy reared by nuns, Vanderville had learned to loathe churches but somehow, perversely, he now found there was peaceful nostalgia in the scents of a sacred space: wax, incense, and cold stone mingled in comfortable combination. He was early, and the church was empty, and so he made himself comfortable in a pew and contemplated the altar as he enjoyed the airy solitude. Deep in thought, he stretched his feet out extravagantly and put his hands behind his head to rest. Was it just like this for Mayflower, he wondered? Relaxing in a pew before a noose was thrown about his neck – the thought was immediately succeeded by the impulsive urge to glance over his shoulder in trepidation.

He was still alone, the church behind him empty, and he smiled wistfully at his foolish imagination and allowed his eyes to wander. They came to rest eventually on a feature of the church of which he had been previously unaware. Above the chancel was a fretwork grill that followed the curve along the back wall. It must have been one of those trellises that allowed persons of quality to attend church without being exposed to the gaze of the congregation. But how was it accessed?

It was then that he remembered the first locked door he had encountered during his precipitate flight from the church after discovering Mayflower. Perhaps... It was the work of a moment to find himself again in the spiral turret staircase, and this time he found the door yielded to his pressure. It gave onto a short stone-clad passage that terminated, as he had suspected, in a narrow, curved space behind the trellis containing three rows of pews. At the far end was another door that was locked. He took a seat on one of the wooden benches that allowed the occupants to observe the church below through the grill, and as he did so one of his feet encountered some resistance under the pew. Bending to explore the obstruction, he found a girdle snagged on his foot. It was made of knotted silk brocade and as he extracted it, he discovered that attached to one end was a cumbersome iron key.

He tugged it free and turned it thoughtfully in his hands. A thought was on the verge of crystallising when he became aware of the sound of a key turning in the far door, and hurriedly he bundled the girdle up and placed it guiltily in his pocket. This was barely accomplished before the door opened, and his curious gaze was confronted by the bony pate and hooded eyes of the Inquisitor Carpegna, who cordially wished him a good morning as he entered. After some light-hearted remarks about the unlikeliness of finding a republican poet at prayer Carpegna went to move on past him.

Vanderville gratefully resumed his seat with a wince of agony as he twisted his damaged shoulder. Carpegna paused before him. 'You are in much discomfort?' he asked. 'You are no doubt damaged from a fall. You have wrenched the muscles of the neck, where they are attached to your shoulder joint. My manservant has a sovereign remedy for these dislocations, allow me to show you.'

Prior to Vanderville becoming quite aware of what was happening, and before he could form words of protest, the inquisitor had taken post behind the pew he occupied, his tall frame bowed over Vanderville's head like a mantling hawk. Carpegna's hands were already on his shoulders, massaging them with a strange prickling motion.

He began to protest this unorthodox manhandling, but as he spoke Carpegna shushed him. 'You must empty your head of thoughts to allow the fibres to relax properly. Do not speak, do not move. Be as a pinned mouse and suffer the ministrations. Now, you feel discomfort, but release is inevitable as you submit.' His bony fingers were strumming furiously now on Vanderville's shoulders.

'It is a curious thing,' said the inquisitor, 'I should deeply love to have you in my tribunal. We have many French knights on this island, but none of them has decayed as far as to embrace the republican infection.' He laughed, an odd sort of familiar tittering that set Vanderville's teeth on edge. 'I wish you no malice young man – quite the opposite, I assure you. It is only that I have so little opportunity of examining the truly republican conscience, and for me, it is a fascinating conundrum. After all, the hostility of the republicans towards the Church can have at its root, none other than the detestable creed of the Freemasons.'

'But *monsignore*,' protested Vanderville. 'There is nothing antithetical to the Church in Freemasonry, far from it! I can assure you, trowel botherers and baby dunkers go hand in hand in this.'

'Holy Father! Are you an initiate too!' cackled Carpegna with delight, and he began easing Vanderville's coat from his shoulders, 'I may have to revise my earlier promise and have you conducted to my dungeons after all. A republican Freemason! I may not have such a chance again to unpeel the layers of heresy accumulated around such a soul. Tell me poet,' he said, his lithe hands flicking to and fro across Vanderville's shoulders. 'Where were you inducted into the ranks of the Church's adversary?'

Although the man's touch was repellent, Vanderville reluctantly admitted that the impact of the flickering fingers on his strained ligaments was efficacious, and he breathed in deeply. 'Paris – but Freemasonry is no enemy of the Church. It is just a talking and drinking shop. For real anticlerical chops you need to go to the dark root secret societies. The Illumines or Minerves, for instance...'

Carpegna's hands froze. He swallowed like a stork processing a generously proportioned frog, and emitted a few hoarse words in a strangely stifled voice. 'You have encountered them, then?'

'Hmm?' said Vanderville. 'The Minerves?' he shook his head vigorously and a further twinge of pain went down his neck.

As his muscles spasmed, Carpegna's hands responded deftly and recommenced their insistent tattoo upon the sides of his neck. 'Have you perchance met with them here?' His voice dropped another half octave. 'In the Convent itself?'

'I can't say I really know anything about them,' said Vanderville, to whom Carpegna's utterings were of secondary interest to the explosions of white heat inside his head as the man worked his aching bones with a studied ease. 'But there was a sort of craze for secret societies in the army, after we all got bored of Freemasonry, and some of the lads went in for it in quite a big way. Their enthusiasm wore off when they saw the reading list. It was intolerably dry stuff, I promise you. Wont to put off all but the most ardent philosophicist.'

'But of course, you are staying in the *Auberge* de Bavaria,' muttered Carpegna to himself. He brought his hands down to clasp Vanderville's head, and with adept movements, turned it first one way and then the other, causing his vertebrae to click sequentially. 'How does that feel now?'

Vanderville eased his shoulder up and down tentatively. 'Extraordinary. Your manservant certainly taught you a thing or two about bone waggling.'

'He studied it in Constantinople when he was held there as a slave. They have a school of medicine that teaches these arts.' Carpegna's voice trailed off as he walked back round the pew and sat himself down uncomfortably close to Vanderville, forcing him to move up.

'Is your master the baron also a heretic?' he asked suddenly, pulling out a small black notebook from his cassock.

Vanderville frowned, it had never occurred to him to question Gracchus on the matter of religious orthodoxy. He could not remember the matter ever having come up.

'As Catholic as the day is long,' Vanderville said. 'Unless… Is gluttony still a big problem for the Church?' he hedged cautiously.

Carpegna considered. 'We do not really go in for that sort of thing anymore,' he said regretfully. 'If you got so fat it obstructed your devotions or conjugal duties we might have to take notice, but that sort of sin would be left to the parish priest.' He looked up, and his face brightened as a thought tracked across it. 'If you used witchcraft in the kitchen, then *that* would be a matter of concern to the Holy Office.'

'I'm sure he would if he knew how,' pondered Vanderville.

Carpegna pulled out a pencil and used it to scratch himself behind the ear, then scribbled, 'Pellegrew – seeker after arcane knowledge' on his pad and covered it discreetly with his hand.

Vanderville shifted uncomfortably further down the pew away from the inquisitor. Carpegna seemed not to notice and, his pencil poised, asked brightly, 'You have also had intercourse here with the enchantress Eva Mifsud?'

'Enchantress? She is not a witch, if that is what you mean. I have become acquainted with her,' said Vanderville uncomfortably. There reigned a silence for a while, as Carpegna scribbled, and Vanderville asked, 'Pray, is there much witchcraft on the island?'

'I know what you are thinking, Tirdflingen. You have heard the silly stories about the Holy Office. Most of our business nowadays is beyond reproach. We root out confessors who try to have carnal knowledge of their penitents, and deal with friars who dally dishonestly with one another. Overall, my staff deal with the sordid business of enforcing public morality on the unwilling. I dedicate myself to the more serious errors, which are thankfully rare here, or at least, so well-concealed as to pass unnoticed.' He sighed. 'What time do we have now for superstitions and ghouls that bump in the night?'

Vanderville stood up and resumed his coat. 'I am glad to hear that you don't torture people anymore,' he said. 'The Inquisition – sorry, Holy Office, has such a bad name in France.'

'Yes, it is unfortunate, but even in these times when renewed danger to the Church arises not from heretical forms of our own religion, but from atheistical movements, we will surely not be forced to revert to the bad old ways. It is generally recognised by our institution, as by most enlightened states, that the rigorous examination, what you call torture, is an insufficient way to elicit the truth. I myself have only seen it applied once in forty years, and on that occasion, it was ineffectual. The prisoner, sustained by the devil, could withstand the pain right up until the point where she passed away laughing at the examiner's efforts.'

Vanderville shuddered and was pleased to be spared further conversation by the arrival of Franca in the church below. Both men looked down through the grill at her. She halted uncertainly in the nave when she saw the church empty and drew the edge of her green *faldetta* over her face as she perched gracefully on a pew. Smiling mysteriously to himself, Carpegna bid Vanderville good day, and returned through the door from which he had come.

—

Out of the chill of the church Franca thawed a little, and Vanderville found himself describing the inquisitor's remarks to her as they strolled towards Piazza dei Forbici.

'By all accounts, Carpegna is some way from the hideous creatures of the Holy Office that inhabit the gothic novel,' he told her. 'He says that the days of torture and the rack are past.'

'He told you that?' she laughed dryly. 'Is it not torture then to confine men, women in dungeons, away from their families?

To keep them for years under durance vile with no means of redress or repeal? Even when they are released, broken and cowed, to crawl to church every Sunday with worms gnawing at their hearts, the threat of further duress is held over them. An unguarded comment, a neighbour's envy, a malicious merchant, any of these is sufficient to send them back into the granite purgatory under the Vittoriosa Holy Office.'

She led the way through the market along the edge of the piazza and paused to exchange greetings with a stallholder.

'The faults you mention are common to the institutions of unenlightened states,' said Vanderville, who found himself preaching and disliked himself for it. 'Evils addressed in some part by the revolution in France,' he continued, sidestepping a shouting hawker, and ducking under a market stall. 'In states where the French liberators find the Holy office still functioning, they empty its cells, and send the old devils packing.'

'Then they can't come quickly enough,' said Franca, nimbly avoiding the hot stream of a urinating goat. 'The sooner they release the Holy Office's prisoners here, the better.'

'Where do they keep them locked up?' asked Vanderville.

'In the cellars underneath the Holy Office, where they eat little, fast completely often, and are compelled to pray day and night. That is the sentence for those women deemed guilty of a little knowledge of herbs or plants. The men are consigned to row in the Order's galleys. They call that punishment spanking sardines, which diminishes its terrible reputation. Sometimes the prisoners go mad or mutilate themselves so as not to be condemned to the galleys. Sometimes they simply destroy themselves.'

'The Republic will eliminate these evils when it arrives,' stated Vanderville confidently.

'Donna Eva says where the church leads, the state will surely follow. And then they too will be able to lock up indefinitely anyone who does not agree with them.'

They had arrived at the limit of the market, and she paused by a grill in the ground, and frowned at animal viscera discarded around the drain, wrinkling her nose. 'Scraps for the *Fraternita*,' she said sadly. 'If they are lucky, the stallholders leave out buckets of water for them too. On a good day, there is enough to bath Granchio's sores. They could receive water from the Maddalene hospital, but Duccio is too proud to ask. So they use the drains.'

'Don't the Knights, or the *sbirri* have anything to say to you?'

'The *sbirri* tolerate us,' she said. 'Because we collect the market rubbish, so it does not foul the fortress ditch. Then we carry, tidy and scrape for the market people. But mainly we look out for each other.' She shrugged. 'It's a *Fraternita*, we are brothers and look after one another.'

'And sisters.'

'Yes, that too,' she frowned. 'Although its more complicated. We girls don't live here with them, so we can't really be part of the fraternity. It's not safe for us on the streets.'

Vanderville regarded the motley band of boys hiding behind the pillory and reflected that it hardly seemed to be safe for them either, but he held his council while she stared at the heavens disconsolately.

'*Squadra delle Forbici, Fraternita delle Forbici, Banda delle Forbici*: we were all these grand things in succession. Duccio and Granchio are great ones for building palaces in the sky.'

'You have a limited belief in the utility of the *Fraternita*, then?' inquired Vanderville.

'Not at all. It is useful. It kept us alive. But we will never be anything more than they are. That's what Granchio doesn't conceive – maybe he can't. I suppose without the tissue of illusion he would be quite naked.'

'That is the least of his problems. He is already in rags – he does not even have a proper name.'

As they walked back through the market past the stalls they continued talking. She was unflagging in questioning him about the wider world. Her appetite for novelty was relentless, and she was desperately amused to hear that Eva had proposed giving Vanderville dancing lessons.

'She tried to teach me a little – she said it would be useful, but I struggle to remember the steps, and then both Duccio and Don Stecchi make wretched partners in a quadrille. Now she is teaching me my letters, you would be amazed to hear me read.'

She nodded at a haughty woman with a beautiful aquiline profile in an expensive *faldetta*, who regarded both of them with disdain before averting her eyes ostentatiously. Franca giggled.

'That is Baida. She is Donna Eva's rival. Sometimes she makes up the fourth in our dancing, but she struggles to keep her nose in the air while she dances, and then she does so resent taking instruction from Eva. She is always nosing around when Eva leaves the room, so brazenly that she must not suspect that Duccio and I tell Eva everything that she does. I think she believes Eva must be a witch and is trying to find evidence of her powers.'

Vanderville smiled. 'A witch? Why would she think that?'

'Eva moves in circles she cannot dream of and is invited to every *auberge*. She even meets the grandmaster in church. That makes Donna Baida jealous. Because she is resentful of Eva's success, she hopes to interest the inquisition in Eva's proficiency with plant medicine. She studies herbs and flowers with Don Stecchi. They use them in the women's hospital, which is where I shall take you now.'

'It seems to me,' said Vanderville, 'that Eva is intent on helping everybody. She certainly wants to improve both of us.'

Franca frowned, and drew her *faldetta* across her face, as they passed a group of idle workmen. 'She means well. I have always wanted to travel and she offered to take me to Rome with her.'

'You must go! What a wonderful opportunity,' said Vanderville. Then he caught her eyes and saw the expression there. 'But surely you are not going to refuse? Do not be scared of the voyage or the sea sickness – it is nothing and soon over.'

'It is not that. I want to leave Malta for good. I wish most eagerly to see the world. I'm just not sure that I want it to be in her path that I follow.'

She paused. They were on a part of the walls where the people promenaded, and she leant out over the parapet to look at the sea below.

'When I first arrived here, I was very small, and I couldn't speak a word. Donna Eva said it was because of the way I had been treated on the voyage. She cured me with her herbs eventually, but before that we used to walk besides the sea every day. I don't think I have ever been so happy as I was then. She was so strong and certain about everything – I idolised her!

'But even then, in those happy days, following behind her and stepping in the footprints she left in the sand besides the water, I knew I still didn't belong. Just as I don't belong with the *Fraternita*. She sees so many men in her way of life. I can't imagine it for myself. She says I am not old enough, and I will understand the work when I meet someone I like – but what if she is wrong? What if it's not inside me?'

These were deep waters indeed for Vanderville, and his consternation must have shown on his face, for she pulled him away from the parapet by the arm. 'Do not mind me,' she said, smiling up at him. 'I shall stop talking about myself now, and show you the rest of our cage.'

After they had walked a circuit of the town taking in the promenades on the walls and the piazza before the grandmaster's palace, they returned down the steps towards the Maddalene, where she showed him part of the hospital complex. Vanderville was not permitted to enter the women's wards, but he admired the dispensary in the apothecium, the well-ordered laundry and above all the refectory. This last was graced by a vast fresco of fallen women brought back to grace that was remarkable more for the artist's loving depiction of the half-naked penitents' charms than for their apparent return to piety. Normally Vanderville would have lingered ardently before this depiction, but inhibited by Franca's gaze, he truncated his appreciative admiration.

'You said Granchio doesn't have a real name, which is sad,' she said presently. 'But neither do you. The baron calls you

Vanderville, and everyone else calls you Tirdflingen. Which should I use?'

'Dermide,' said Vanderville. 'That is my given name, but everyone calls me Vanderville.'

She suddenly blurted out, 'Would you like to see where I live, Dermide Vanderville?'

Vanderville considered whether this was quite proper. His contemplations were coloured by consideration that the tour of Valletta was proving to include rather more churches and institutions than he had expected, whereas he was keen to see more of the fortifications, so he acquiesced politely and allowed her to guide him back into the maze of shelving alleys until they fetched up at a pokey door let into the side of a tabernacle. Draping her *faldetta* around her face as they approached, she let them into a narrow corridor that appeared to have been crammed into the gap between two larger houses.

They mounted a little staircase and Vanderville found himself inside a narrow triangular apartment, simply formed by the shape of the roof, which being again entirely composed of glistening stone, cast that comfortable yellow glow which he so admired. Bright tiles composed the floor; straw dollies, neatly plaited, covered the walls, and a drab curtain half covered a sleeping alcove. Franca drew the curtain back from a small window that looked out over the Maddalene complex, hooking it behind a small terracotta flowerpot perched precariously on the window ledge.

'This was a place used by Donna Eva,' she said. 'She rarely comes here now, but she preserves it as a place for memories and also to hide – herself or other people needing discretion.'

Her eyes were shining, and Vanderville reflected that Eva had not screened Franca from her world of assignations as effectively as she might have hoped. As she moved around the room, rearranging the sparse contents to her satisfaction, Vanderville stood awkwardly on a small carpet and watched her.

She took a small mirror out of a cupboard and hung it on a nail in the wall. 'Baron Pellegrew does not appear to be making much progress in finding the knight's murderer, does he?'

Vanderville shook his head. 'There isn't really a great deal to go on. He thinks von Seeau might have been part of a secret society that made him a target.'

'Von Seeau a member of a society! I can't see why. Nobody liked him. Even Eva forbade him the house. He was a bore. Even the other knights barely suffered him. Your master doesn't seem very active. I don't even understand why the grandmaster appointed him to look into it. The inquiry appears to have been turned into the plaything of bored nobles, when the *sbirri* should be in charge. They at least would be conducting a more vigorous approach.'

Vanderville agreed, 'Yes, his investigatory technique seems quite indolent from the outside. He once described it to me as shaking the apple tree and watching where the apples fall. But I don't see the *sbirri* have accomplished anything much either.'

'I think dozing in the apple tree's shade while waiting for the wind to blow the fruit down might be more apt,' suggested Franca. She removed her green *faldetta* and draped it over a chair under a devotional niche. Aware that Gracchus would not approve of him discussing the case, Vanderville took the opportunity to admire the quality of the fabric, and she held it up for his approving inspection.

'Those of merchant's wives are sometimes trimmed with lace, but that is vulgar. This is much better. It was a gift of Donna Eva of course.'

Vanderville nodded. 'It's a shame that they obscure the hair,' he observed. 'At a distance one could hardly recognise the particular *faldetta* of an acquaintance. They are so similar that anyone could be inside.'

Franca shook out her own hair, which was of a very dark black, contrasting with her pale creamy skin. She arranged it with pins in the mirror. 'Donna Eva wears her hair up in the

Greek way, and she has earrings, chains and bangles – how could she be mistaken for anyone else?' said asked in awed contemplation.

'Of course,' she said simply, 'if you want to have good things, you must attract the attention of a knight. But Donna Eva does not want me to do that yet. She says that the Maltese cannot stay respectable unless they keep their wives, sisters, even their mothers and children away from the knights. So, I must leave Valletta, perhaps even the islands themselves now I have come of age. Before I attract attention, you understand.'

Vanderville cast a judicious eye over the bare-footed young woman with a strained but necessary impartiality and looking away from her profile with difficulty, he reflected that Eva was cutting things a bit dammed fine.

'Couldn't you marry a local man?' he suggested. 'I understand there are Maltese of very good standing here in Valletta, and they have money too – enough to buy a hundred bangles.'

She sighed extravagantly and turned the full force of her gaze upon him, 'The lowliest knight is a more important person than the highest Maltese. The knight's legal system excludes anyone born in Malta from nobility, no matter how old or important their family.' She turned back to the mirror, and pinned an unruly strand of hair into place. 'I must leave this island, even if I am to follow Donna Eva into the craft of *meretrice*.'

'That would be a terrible waste,' said Vanderville, swallowing nervously. This is ridiculous, he thought, she is barely more than a girl, and yet here I am stuttering as if she was Eva herself. He thought that it was high time they continued their tour, and steeled himself to suggest that, but she interrupted him.

'Sit down,' she said. 'You are in the way.' She placed a hand on his chest gently to guide him and his protest was stifled by the unfamiliar sensation of her touch. He sat obediently on the edge of the bed behind him. She bustled back and forth completing her toilette, while he looked about himself uncomfortably. She finished and turned so that he could admire her. 'What do you think?' she asked. 'Am I like one of the women you admired so thoroughly in the fresco of the Maddalene?'

Vanderville's throat was a little dry. It had been a mistake to follow her up the stairs, he thought, but he did not leave his seat on the bed. He swallowed, remembering the fallen women so lovingly depicted by the artist. 'Yes,' he said, 'very like.'

She nodded agreement. 'Of course,' she said, 'and I am part of it.'

'One of the young women?'

'All of them.' She stood a little distance from him and revolved, enjoying showing him the beauty of her shape. Then she took a tentative step towards him, and his mind cleared of everything, as he instinctively half rose to meet her. In the moment before she reached him, she glanced through the window, and catching her breath, she froze. 'Donna Eva!' she breathed. 'Her *kalesh* is arriving below! I have forgotten my writing lesson.'

Eva sat back in the seat of her *kalesh* and surveyed Vanderville, who felt vaguely discomforted under her gaze. 'I am glad to have found you,' she said. 'The Baron Pellegrew called looking for you. He confessed himself astonished that you were passing the morning gallivanting around the ramparts with my protégé.'

Vanderville squinted out of the carriage window. They were moving at a considerable pace, and Eva seemed in some hurry to deliver him. He studied her *faldetta*, which was down about her shoulders in the privacy of the vehicle. He was sure that the girdle in his pocket was a match for the brocade of her garment. She caught him looking and smiled, then leaned forward and pulled the curtains shut, obscuring the view, so that he had no choice but to concentrate on her.

'Yes, I can imagine you were also concerned to know where your property was,' he said spitefully. She returned his stare, waiting patiently until courtesy obliged him to look away.

'Did I tell you the story of how I came by the child?'

He winced at the word, but assumed the complacent attentive mask he reserved for superior officers when they were divesting themselves of wisdom.

'She was brought in by a nautical caravan as part of the booty. As luck would have it, the master of that caravan was Bailli von Torring. Normally such a beautiful woman, even a child, enslaved by the laws of the sea, would have been fair prey for the knights. But von Torring's tastes do not lie in that direction, and I begged him to allow me to purchase her. He refused, saying she would be safer with him, but she did not find the *Auberge* of Bavaria to her taste either, and ran away to find her home with the street children.

'There she would have stayed until one of the knights discovered her refuge and groomed her to become his mistress, but one evening she turned up on my doorstep and begged my protection. I granted it of course, despite knowing that evil tongues would assert that I was training her to take up my position. But I have better things in mind for her than marrying a farmer or becoming the plaything of some knightly seigneur.

'Her age is problematic. Slaves are required to have their age recorded, but that merely means an estimation in this case. Often the guess is incorrect, being based on physical development, which is late in the undernourished. Let us say that she has passed into womanhood physically and mentally. She does not have the habit of casting backwards glances at her infancy perhaps since there was no shelter there, no childhood worth speaking of. She is immersed in the present and intent on the future.

'I say this to you,' she continued, 'because I can see, let us not toy with words, that you appeal to her, and I think, despite your better intentions, she attracts you too.' She leaned forward and tapped his knee with her fan for emphasis. 'She is not for you. You know that do you not? I appeal to you that Franca needs a protector at this stage in her life, and not a lover, or at least she needs a protector more.'

'Are the two roles mutually exclusive?' asked Vanderville more boldly than he felt.

'If you are referring to yourself as the potential ambivalent, I say without impugning your strength or honour, yes. Not here. Not now. This is not your world, nor do you have the allies necessary in the Convent to prevent evil befalling her.

'No, my dear Vanderville. I shall not move on this. I have a different proposition for you. You are a good-looking young man, but you lack polish and want confidence, and when you return to Paris, you will need it to make your mark with the *grandes dames* of the salons. This is something I can help you with. I can teach you how to make conquests in society. In exchange, I want to learn everything about the new France. You teach me whether this Republic is worth it, and I will take your education in hand.'

Vanderville was attempting to digest this when the *kalesh* gave a sudden lurch. He swivelled in his seat and slapped open the visor that gave a view of the street ahead. There was no sign of Duccio at the mule's head, instead Canon Gatt held the mule's bridle. He snapped the visor shut and his hand went to his sword hilt, but Eva pushed him back into his seat and put a finger to her lips. She drew back just enough of the curtain to expose her own face, and Vandeville heard the honeyed tones of Inquisitor Carpegna address her from his dog cart.

'You will forgive me for accosting you in this way, Donna Mifsud. The truth is that I needed to speak to you, and you can appreciate that I cannot be seen entering the dwelling of a Public Woman.'

'You were not always so shy,' she answered defiantly.

There was another lurch and rough sound as the wheel of Carpegna's dogcart struck the *kalesh*'s door and Vanderville fumbled at his sword again. It was awkward in the confined interior which gave Eva time to restrain him again with a gentle touch on his leg. Her face was intent on Carpegna, who appeared as yet unaware of Vanderville's presence.

'As I was saying, you are remarkably elusive nowadays, and so have forced this distressing compulsion upon me,' he said. 'It is time, Donna Mifsud, that the creatures under your protection are brought into the arms of the Church.'

'This again,' she said resignedly.

'Besides anything else,' drawled Carpegna, 'the *sbirri* are unlike to tolerate the state of the Piazza Forbici much longer. It resembles a squalling brattery, and words have been passed on the matter from His Eminence himself, as well as the captain of the fort.'

'Who surely has nothing better to worry about just now,' offered Eva.

Vanderville was inclined to agree that these concerns, petty at any time, were occupying the grandmaster's thoughts while the island lay under threat of invasion and subjugation by the forces of the Republic. He moved closer to the curtain, which was sufficiently gauzy and worn to permit him a hazy view of Carpegna trotting alongside.

Eva spoke again, 'If they were to attend church would you stop referring to them as creatures – as though they were beasts? They are children.'

Carpegna blinked twice, unaccustomed to being gainsaid by anyone, let alone a woman. He swallowed and mastered himself. 'The terminology is correct, I'm afraid. The teaching of the Church is quite clear on the matter: stillborn and unbaptised creatures are technically in the same position as the progeny of infidels, pagans, or Jews. If you find this distressing, you should admit the unfortunates to the sacrament of catechism, and the grace of God will elevate their status. The escaped young slave woman you are harbouring, for reasons known only to yourself, can be released from her state of imperfection by baptism. Just think! Then she can be married to a Christian, and you will no longer have to conceal her in this ridiculous fashion.'

'And the God-touched child? Will baptism cure his afflictions?'

'The cripple?' mulled Carpegna. 'His case is more complicated, being a physical, as well as a spiritual imperfection. Baptism can only improve his condition though; I assure you of that.

'Donna Mifsud,' he continued smoothly, 'do not think I am insensible to your point of view. Your instinct of care for these unfortunates is commendable.' He paused and licked his thin lips. 'Remember that although you have seen the humanity inside them waiting to flower, not everyone is possessed of your Christian virtue or charitable instincts. While there are those who would prey upon them, their exclusion from the community leaves them vulnerable. Consider that your small part in maintaining their impure state does them no favours. I shall expect them to be presented for their catechism at St Christopher's school in Vittoriosa before Holy day.'

He whipped up his dog, and Vanderville noticed that Gatt had appeared behind Carpegna and was jogging sweatily at the heels of his master.

'I have completed my catechism,' called Eva, drawing Carpegna back. 'Much good it did me. And in any case Vittoriosa is out of the question. They will not cross the water, your holiness,' she said flatly.

'At St Frederick's then. That is their parish church after all,' he said, with a blithe gesture of graceful concession, and Vanderville heard him allowing his dog to bear him away again.

'At the Maddalene.' Eva spoke through clenched teeth now, as she leaned over the sill. 'They will attend at the Maddalene, Saturday week.' Vanderville saw a hand appear under the curtain, groping at her.

'There are problems with Don Stecchi...' Carpegna barked, over his shoulder, and then with suppressed irritation, 'Oh very well then.'

Vanderville heard him whip up his dog, and then the curtains parted, and the leering face of Gatt appeared suspended there, licking his already wet lips. With his damaged nose he seemed like some pudgy clay gargoyle. 'Make sure *all* of your charges attend, Donna Mifsud,' he sneered as she drew back from his questing hand, covering her face with her *faldetta*. His already protruding eyes widened as he suddenly took in Vanderville's presence in the litter, and his mouth flapped open wetly.

'Take your eyes. Off the lady,' Vanderville said, punctuating his words with a smarting punch roundly in the centre of his face. With a compressed yelp Gatt's face disappeared. Through the gauzy covering they saw his shadowy figure swaying as he was left in their wake. Worth a few new bruises, thought Vanderville, rubbing his sore knuckles contentedly.

Chapter Twelve

Von Torring and Gracchus settled down together amiably on the cushions in the window of the bailli's solar. Even on an overcast afternoon, the prospect from the window was extraordinary. The tête-à-tête began with some commonplace observations, and Gracchus agreed in succession that the weather was not all it might be, that children continued to show an unruly disposition to grow, and to disrespect their elders increasingly as they did so, and finally they reached agreement on the scarcity of beef having reached outrageous proportions.

These subjects dispensed with, von Torring poured their second cups of coffee, and fixed Gracchus with that stare from under lowered brows that indicated the preliminaries had been dispensed with, and his assault was about to be opened in earnest. He unveiled his guns as he added the sugar, of which they were both uncommonly fond. Without his eyes leaving the sugar tongs, he suggested that Gracchus's business on the rock must, in the nature of things, be drawing to a close. It was a statement rather than a question, but Gracchus was equal to the stratagem, and swatted it aside with ease, without giving an appearance of casualness that might offend. He was not prepared to concede ground until the inevitable ultimatum showed its head above the assault parapet. It was not long in coming.

'The council meets soon, and your proposal will be decided upon there. I anticipate that my endorsement will be sufficient to pass the motion. I confess though that I am baffled to learn that your investigation into the death of von Seeau has not yet reached its conclusion. I confess I have reached the limit of my patience in this matter. Since one matter being resolved will necessarily lead to my support in the conclusion of the other, I hoped you might have some news for me today.'

Gracchus took a cautious sip from his cup. 'I am happy to inform you that a resolution is imminent, bailli,' he lied. 'I anticipate that today I shall apprehend the person involved, but you must allow me to draw a veil over their identity for just a little longer. In the meantime, I have a further request; will you be good enough to furnish me with a list of your knights in order of seniority?'

'That is well, then,' said the bailli with satisfaction. 'My secretary will draw up the list for you at once. I may also be able to render you further assistance in your other endeavour.' He crossed to a cabinet behind his desk which he opened with a small key and withdrew a red silk envelope. 'Your acquaintance Rais Murad is not what he seems. He has an extensive history as a corsair.'

Gracchus shrugged. 'It appears to me that the line between merchant and pirate is a fine one, better observed in principle than in practice.'

Von Torring came back to Gracchus, unwrapping a pale silver ribbon around the envelope as he sat. 'Oh, he is a merchant, that much is true – when it suits him. But he is a merchant in human flesh.'

At Gracchus's raised eyebrows, the knight raised one hand in exculpation. 'I do not pretend that the Order are innocents in this matter. It has long been the custom in these waters to reduce those enemies captured in battle to the status of enslaved people, but that is the fortune of war, accepted and endured by the combatants as a hazard of occupation. The Arabs have a phrase for it. "Today you – tomorrow me," which is an apt attitude. But the trafficking of people taken by deceit and through malice or greed is another matter.'

A fine distinction thought Gracchus to himself, but he set his cup down and waited for the bailli to continue.

'That Rais Murad is a pirate and a slaver there is no doubt; the sources are all in agreement on that point. Or rather, he was. Recently his dealings here have become strangely impeccable. The apparent moment of this Damascene volte-face came when he was seized by the caravan and underwent a fleeting period of slavery himself before buying his release with a ransom that reduced his fleet of merchant ships to a single xebec. His conversion into a simple merchant was so profound and dramatic it could scarce have been expected to endure, and yet, three years later, here we are, with his good faith intact and demonstrated constantly. So much is he trusted that he now leases some of his old ships back from the Order to transact a merchant trade on the Barbary coast.'

'If he is now considered reliable,' observed Gracchus, 'why are you warning me?'

Von Torring turned the envelope he still grasped over in his hands. 'Can he be trusted indefinitely? That is the question.' He leant back in his chair. 'Will you indulge me if I tell you a story?'

Gracchus nodded, his eyes not leaving the red envelope that the bailli clutched so proudly.

'Not so very long ago a corsair force was involved in the attempted capture and accidental sinking of a ship carrying one of the Ottoman Sultan's favourites. So furious was the Sultan that he issued a warrant against the captain of the corsair ships, that should the perpetrator be identified would prove of the most fatal kind, for him and his family.'

He slid the envelope across the table to Gracchus, who read it with avid interest, as the bailli continued.

'It happens that since Rais Murad began leasing ships from the Order, I have had the most urgent investigations made into his antecedents, and astute observers have also observed and traced all his dealings among the merchant wharves. There came into my hands incontrovertible evidence that Murad was in personal command of the vessels whose violence so outraged the Sultan. Ever since I have had sole possession of that evidence, ready to serve should he ever take liberties with the property of the Order.'

Gracchus finished reading. It was apparent that should Rais Murad ever be exposed the Mediterranean and all its shores would become deadly to him. The Turks were notorious for the inventive forms of judicial execution inflicted on those who had incurred the Sultan's wrath.

'As long as you hold this document,' said Gracchus, waving it in his hand, 'You hold a veritable sword of Damocles over his head.'

'Just so,' said von Torring with a touch of vanity. 'This is the key to his loyalty. To the Order, and to me personally.'

Gracchus picked up the envelope from the table and folded the document back inside carefully before handing it back to the bailli. 'Was it expensive to obtain?'

'Very,' nodded the bailli, 'though the Order, and others, have found it useful to recompense me for the use of the information it contains. It is an infallible insurance policy that keeps the venerable captain on the leash. I would not do business with Murad without it.

'Now,' he said, draining his cup and putting it down. 'Let us be clear. Come to me with a murderer, and you may dispose of this document in your dealings with Rais Murad for a suitable renumeration. Do not bring me the murderer, and I will expose you to the grandmaster for the charlatan you are.'

'I see,' said Gracchus carefully, reflecting again on the line between merchants and pirates. He put down his cup on the saucer with infinite precision. 'May I trouble you for another cup of this excellent coffee? I have one or two questions about von Seeau to put to you.'

—

Vanderville was lying on the cot in his quarters, resting his limbs and recalling a delightful morning labouring under Eva's social instruction that had utterly put present danger from his mind, and left him in the mood for building castles in the air. When Gracchus came to inform him of developments, he met him with equanimity.

'It seems straightforward enough to me, Gracchus. The bailli and the grandmaster want the murder solved, and so do we. Now we know there is a corridor linking the Maddalene church to the convent, it ought to be simple enough for you to pin a suspect. I suggest you start by questioning the staff at the hospital to see who might have slipped away to use the passage. We just find our man, hand him over to the grandmaster, the bailli or Carpegna, it doesn't matter which, we can let them sort it out themselves. Then we hole up somewhere and try to stay alive 'til Bonaparte arrives and captures the island, at which point we can pop up and rejoin the army.'

He stretched his legs out, and worked his damaged shoulder speculatively. 'At least we will be comfortable with all the wealth of Golconda at your disposal.'

He wondered if he could borrow a hundred scudos from his friend's wallet to buy Franca some clothes that weren't Eva's cast-offs. Better make it two hundred, he considered. Then he could refit his own wardrobe with something comfortable in cotton for Egypt, or wherever they were going, and possibly a new full-dress coat and hat too. Was there a decent sword cutler in Valletta he wondered? And what about real gold epaulettes? He was sure Gracchus's purse would run to that, but would the local trade be equal to such a luxury?

He poured himself a glass of wine and summarized. 'If we can do a few virtuous deeds along the way, like looking after the *Fraternita* and so on, all the better. Yes, maintaining our cover is difficult, but if the poetry party passes off well, we should be home and clear – it's only a few more days.'

'You are too sanguine by far, Vanderville. I have been listening to people talk about von Schiltenberg, the other Bavarian knight who died here in squalid circumstances. I am convinced that he met his end at the hands of the same person as von Seeau. That rather rules against a crime of passion and indicates a buried plot. Something links the two knights beyond their kinship in the *Auberge* de Bavaria. Nothing is simple, and I lack that single piece of evidence that points to the hands of the murderer.'

'Speaking of good deeds,' said Vanderville, blithely passing over Gracchus's summary of their difficulties, 'did I see you last night at the slave *bagnio*?'

'I have inspected many of the facilities here. Is that so peculiar to an inquiring mind and a curious nature? We cannot all spend our leisure in frequenting brothels and wine shops.' He prodded Vanderville in the chest. 'For instance, last week I saw the *lazaretto* where quarantine is imposed on vessels coming from the Levant, or in times of plague.'

Vanderville sighed inwardly. He knew Gracchus well enough to understand that the question unanswered would not be addressed until the fullness of time revealed his motives. Drawing a veil over his business and keeping to the shadows had long since become second nature to his companion, and an insistence would merely provoke him to withdraw further. He let Gracchus continue his waffling.

'On your arrival you escaped the necessity of performing quarantine. Did you know that while incarcerated the *lazaret* attendants never approach you? Visitors are kept at a distance of six feet, separated by barriers. A guard places your cutlery on the floor and immediately backs away. All your possessions are opened and disinfected, even letters. That simple question, "How are you?" develops sinister overtones in such a situation.'

'Everything on this rock is sinister,' said Vanderville, yawning. 'I can't wait to leave and get back to the army. Lieutenant Hercule is almost certain he can get me a berth in Bonaparte's Guides. I should like that above all things.' He swung himself from the cot and commenced rooting around under the bed. 'Have you moved my belt clips, Gracchus?'

Gracchus's face betrayed his familiarity with the entire spirit of this species of inquiry: its petulant beginning, rambling circular process and eventual conclusion, and he ignored Vanderville, apparently lost deep in his own thoughts. As Vanderville proceeded to invert the contents of his portmanteau all over his cot, Gracchus rubbed his chin thoughtfully, and apropos of nothing, asked, 'Do you not find it curious to be surrounded by dark faces, as we were at the barber stalls?'

Vanderville answered without raising his head or abandoning his methodic and fruitless search. 'I know what you mean. When I first shared quarters with Hercule I sometimes found myself staring at his face. It was so different to my own and those to which I was accustomed that I found it beautiful and fearsome at the same time. It was more like looking at a painting or a sculpture than a man. Once he caught me staring and smiled rather sadly and I realised I must have cut a very poor figure with my gawking. And then the next time I thought on the matter it had already become irrelevant, and when I looked at him, I saw only the man. A man like any other. Only rather taller of course.'

He paused and opened his sword case, from which he seized upon two small metal clips and brandished them at Gracchus triumphantly, as if to say, 'Am I not a clever boy?' Then he frowned and lifted something else from the case. It was the key and girdle he had discovered in the Maddalene. Between avoiding any entanglement with Franca, and the excitement of Eva's interview with Carpegna, he had forgotten to return it to either of them. He tossed it carelessly onto his cot, where Gracchus picked it up, and turned it through his fingers thoughtfully.

'And then I have served under Dumas of course,' continued Vanderville. 'Although he is too much a prodigy to be considered on the same plane as other men. His vanity alone is the equal of a platoon of everyday fellows. The thought never occurred to me with him. He made nothing of his blackness, so it passed me by unnoticed too. Epaulettes and authority have that effect on you. Have you noticed it?'

Gracchus was frowning at the key and clasping it in both hands. 'Do not the common soldiers resent being commanded by a negro?' He essayed cautiously, 'I have heard them speak ill of Dumas.'

Vanderville adjusted his sword belt and admired the effect in the mirror. 'I'm sure they have ripe words for all of us on the staff. That's what they hatch while they scratch their ignorant arses in the bivouac waiting for orders. You would have to be a pretty mean sort of person to seize upon someone's skin colour to denigrate them. You may as well condemn a man for his hair or knock knees.'

Gracchus, whose own hair was unremarkable and whose knees reasonably sound, nodded and smoothed his waistcoat over his belly, which was perhaps the most generous part of him, his spirit apart. 'Vanderville,' said Gracchus blithely, holding up the girdle. 'Where did you find this?'

'That? It was at the Maddalene, someone must have dropped it under a pew. Is it important?'

'I am taking it. You may just have enabled me to keep a promise to the bailli. Now listen, I need your help.'

'Of course,' said Vanderville. 'Anything. If it is a button come loose on your coat, put it there on the chair. I'll do it later.'

'You remember the magnificent solar of Bailli von Torring?' asked Gracchus.

'Hmm?' said Vanderville, swigging at his glass. 'Lots of dodgy antiques, big round window, statues of sodomites. I think so, why?'

'Yesterday afternoon the bailli showed me a document he keeps there inside his private cabinet. It is easily recognized, being in a red silk velvet portfolio envelope bound with pale silver ribbon.'

'Like the collar on a surgeon's uniform coat?' asked Vanderville.

'Yes, exactly like that, if you say so,' said Gracchus patiently. 'Tonight, I would like you to break into the private cabinet and remove that document.'

Vanderville found himself temporarily embarrassed by a mouthful of wine, which had attempted the wrong route down. He sat down abruptly on the bed. Once he had hawked the wine up onto the floor, he spluttered, 'Have you lost your head, Gracchus?'

'I need it most urgently,' said Gracchus conclusively.

Vanderville goggled at Gracchus. 'I thought we wanted to earn the bailli's trust, not rob him. And anyway,' he shook his hands in exasperation. 'I am a watched man at the *auberge*. They think I am a spy. I *am* a spy in fact, not a safe-cracker. Not much of a spy, either when it comes to it,' he added regretfully.

'Tonight,' said Gracchus evenly, 'the bailli will depart Valletta to inspect the fortifications under his bailiwick. He may not return before the party at San Antonio where he will wait on the grandmaster for what is ostensibly a social call, but which will actually comprise the meeting of the Council of War for the defence of the island. The bailli being away, it should be easy enough for you to abstract the document without anyone noticing.'

'I should rather like to be in the vicinity when the Council of War happens,' protested Vanderville, 'I might learn something useful.'

'You are not listening,' said Gracchus impatiently. 'Tonight, you go to the bailli's solar. Don't come back without that document. Now I must pay a visit myself. Will you meet me at Donna Eva's house in one hour? Bring that thing.' He pointed at Vanderville's sword. 'I expect you promptly, be sure of your watch.'

—

Gracchus reflected carefully as he passed through the streets towards Eva's house. His own plans were rather more complicated than even his summary for Vanderville indicated. He had to satisfy the Bailli von Torring and Inquisitor Carpegna's opposing requirements to ensure their support in the council.

The bailli wanted the murderer apprehended and no more dead knights. Carpegna wanted evidence of the Minerves, and also wanted the knights kept alive for trial, or to give evidence at trial. The grandmaster would appreciate the *shirri* being able to apprehend the murderer, rather than either of his two lieutenants, and Gracchus needed the grandmaster's favour even more than the other two. He would have to play them all along until his carefully laid plans reached fruition.

A further complication with the bailli was that he had concluded he also needed the use of the bailli's warrant to ensure Rais Murad's obedience, which would be expensive, and impossible without also exposing the murderer, which would surely be von Torring's price. Murad was a problem. He could not trust him an inch without the means of enforcing his compliance. He glared at a goat who seemed inclined to block his progress, it returned his gaze amicably, utterly absorbed in the business of masticating mindlessly, and he thought suddenly of Vanderville, who was probably lying on a couch drinking wine, lost in some reverie about that young woman Franca. He dismissed the sour reflection and hurried on down the street. First things first, he decided.

—

'I believe this is the key to your house,' Gracchus said to Eva immediately he had entered her apartment.

Eva considered the object he held up without touching it. 'The girdle is mine I think,' she said. 'So, yes. Where did you come by it?'

Gracchus pursed his lips. He walked up to her bureau where a marble bust of a young man was in pride of place between two bird cages. Lifting it carefully, he carried it over to the low table beside her chaise-longue and placed it there.

'Investigator, Croesus, patron of poets; do your talents extend also to interior decoration, Baron?' she asked archly.

Gracchus held the girdle up for her inspection again. The strip of cloth had been knotted to form a loop at one end and he placed his hand inside the loop end and braced it, swinging the heavy key on the other end speculatively.

Eva stood motionless in the balcony window and watched him impatiently as he rearranged the bust to face her. 'Be careful with that please,' she said. 'It is worth more than the house.'

Gracchus moved behind the bust, his eyes searching hers as he swung the key to and fro in his hands. 'Oup-là!' he cried dramatically, bending his knees, and swinging the key around the front of the bust. As it arrived, he grasped it with his other hand and pulled the girdle taut against the marble neck. The bust toppled from the table into his arms and the unexpected impact carried him back onto the couch where he reposed like a startled owl, the bust nestling in his lap.

'Bravo,' said Eva. 'I take it that this impromptu theatrical display is supposed to convey something of significance?'

Gracchus placed the bust beside him and removed the girdle. 'The Bailli von Torring told me a few things this morning. It appears that the murdered knight, von Seaau had designs on your protégé. Improper designs.'

'That comes as no surprise to me,' said Eva in measured tones. 'He was one of the foremost libertines in the *Auberge de Bavaria*, which is notorious for such behaviour. Under the cover of their secret society, the Minerves, they systematically debauch unprotected children.'

'I know it was not news to you,' said Gracchus. 'Because the bailli himself warned you of von Seaau's malign intentions. While that knight waited in a pew in the Maddalene on that unfortunate morning someone entered the church via the passage that leads from the Maddalene, slipped into the pew behind him and strangled him with this girdle. Taken by surprise from behind, handicapped by his constricted position in the pew, he was ruthlessly assassinated. It would not have required much strength to exert the necessary force. Even a woman could manage it. And this,' he held up the girdle, 'is a woman's weapon.'

'And so, you are convinced that because the murderer *could* have been a woman, it *must* have been a woman?'

'You were at the Maddalene that morning, you tried to conceal the fact. You admit you had motive. Although their bailli is your protector, you despise the Bavarians.'

'Bailli von Torring is a good man, unlike his *cavalieri*. The Minerves deserve what they are reaping. Would you expose me as a murderer to the grandmaster, even knowing what the knights have done? Or to the tender embrace of the inquisitor?'

Gracchus spread his hands equably, as if daring her to continue. She stared out of the window a long time, her erect back turned to him. He watched her patiently, and he saw her bite her lip uncertainly as she turned to face him. Yet he met not uncertainty nor resignation in her eyes, but pride and fire.

'And yet you will not expose me, Pellegrew. Shall I tell you why?'

He indicated assent, and she invited him, 'Make yourself comfortable, you are quite safe for now, with my garotte safely in your lap. Let me tell you a story – do you have time, or must you summon the *sbirri* this moment?'

'How else do we pass on wisdom if not through stories?'

'I have reached the summit of my profession, or craft rather, as we say here. My protectors have included some of the most influential men on the island. Three years ago, I agreed against my better instincts to accompany one of those friends on a visit to Rome. I have rarely left the island before, and it was an exciting time for me.

'While in Rome I was badly treated by my knight, who soon tired of me and who turned me out into the street. I was saved from destitution by a most kindly man, with whom I embarked on a tour of his estates in the south, before he courteously bid me farewell and sent me back to Malta with my most urgent expenses met. He was even kind enough to promise to visit me here one day, a commonplace meaningless courtesy that I did not take at face value.

So you can imagine how delighted I was to hear recently that my benefactor had arrived on the island, and I hastened to his palazzo to catch a glimpse of him, and perhaps to make myself known. A few years having passed, and the unforgiving sun of the Convent having darkened my skin, I was anxious that he would find me changed. I decided to approach him cautiously, a little at a time, and not to force myself on him and make myself ridiculous. Imagine my surprise to find it was not I, but he who was very much altered in appearance. More so, in fact, than even the passage of years could render feasible.

'The name of my benefactor, as you may have surmised, was Baron Pellegrew. So let us put aside fairy stories, Baron Imposter. We have spoken of the petty distinctions that divide people, the Maltese, the Knights, the Minerves. Yet ultimately there are solely two classes of people – the honourable and the malicious. Which are you, and what is your business in the Convent?'

Gracchus placed his head in his hands and reflected deeply. He stared long at himself in the mirror. Its milky cataracts and hazy flaws reflected as they pleased, and he found no answer there. At length he met her still constant gaze.

'If I tell you the nature of my business here you will hold a secret that renders me in mortal peril if known.'

'We have an equal interest in maintaining our silence then,' she said simply.

'The bailli is afraid that the Minerves are to be eradicated one by one,' said Gracchus, 'I cannot allow that to continue.'

'I repeat that there is nothing about this business that I will reveal to you, even if I could. The knights could best preserve themselves by ceasing their predatory behaviour. I fear that as long as the society of Minerves continues its depredations a danger exists to its members. I cannot undertake to protect the knights; it is not in my power.'

'And you will not undertake to desist?'

'Would that not be an admission of guilt? In any case, even had I done the things you say, what further could I accomplish with you watching my every step?'

Gracchus found himself at an impasse. 'Donna Mifsud,' he said tentatively.

'Eva, please. Now that we understand one another better.'

'Donna Eva then. I have a delicate request to make of you. I must submit this as part of the bargain you suggest.'

'I wondered when you would get round to that.' She stood, removed her head scarf so that her hair tumbled about her shoulders, and approached him more nearly.

'No, no,' said Gracchus hurriedly. 'Nothing like that.'

She stopped and stared at him curiously. 'You are an unusual man,' she stated as she pinned her hair back up. 'Are you one of those rare truly married men?'

'No,' he answered. 'I had a woman once yes. A wife if you like. And children. They gave me all that a man could need. I left them because I could not give them anything in return.'

'You could go back.'

He shook his head, 'She died. Before we could be reconciled – in the Revolution. It is a matter of intense regret to me, and I prefer not to discuss it. And besides,' he continued hurriedly, before she could express sympathy, 'unlike yourself, I am not of a form to please, unclothed. My request is of a less personal nature. May I enquire if the Bailli von Torring will call on you this afternoon?' he asked, knowing the answer already because the bailli had boasted of the regularity of his visits.

'Perhaps yes, perhaps no,' she countered.

'My request is a mundane one. The Bailli von Torring keeps a small key in his waistcoat pocket...'

'The one to the cabinet in his solar where he keeps his erotic engravings?'

'Just so. I need to borrow it for a few hours, it occurred to me that you might find it easy to accomplish that task.'

She frowned. 'It will not be so simple. The bailli has forbidden me the *auberge*. Our former close acquaintance is at an end. Or suspended at least. Whether it is the finger of suspicion you appear to have laid upon me, or the whisperings of La Baida and the inquisitor's man, I do not know. It does not really matter, whether witch or murderess, I am finding doors formerly open to me, now closed in my face. I will send a note to demand an explanation of von Torring – it may be possible that I can approach him in his *kalesh* as he leaves the *auberge*. Joining him there and taking what you want will be difficult. I will try for you, nonetheless, because he has offered me, an old friend, discourtesy. These knights would not behave in so cavalier a fashion if they knew what secrets of theirs I could tell. Yes, I will fetch your key: if only you tell me why you want it.'

Gracchus considered. In a way they were allies now. Of everyone on the rock, she was now perhaps the only one he could trust with his secret, 'Very well,' he concluded, 'listen carefully...'

Chapter Thirteen

Vanderville was in the cool of the Bavarian armoury exhausted after an intense session of sabre practice with de Rechberg and several of the junior knights. He had come there directly from Donna Eva's house where he had attended as instructed by Gracchus, nervous at what he would discover within. He had been admitted by Duccio, who darted out past him without saying a word. The boy had lacked all of his usual composure, and Vanderville had mounted the stairs in some trepidation at what awaited him within.

His surprise at finding Gracchus and Eva with arms entwined had been only partially ameliorated by the discovery that they were not embracing but dancing. Apparently, Eva had embarked Gracchus on his own course of instruction. It appeared to Vanderville that it would take some years for Gracchus to arrive at proficiency so, finding the spectacle grotesque and his presence apparently superfluous, he had descended the stairs as baffled as when he arrived.

After the other knights had left them alone in the *salle d'armes*, de Rechberg had promised to explain to Vanderville his secret fencing gambit, but despite an hour of sweat drenched practice Vanderville was no closer to mastering it. The secret involved a perilous switch of weapon from the dominant hand to the other, and a simultaneous change of leading foot. The sequel was a darting lunge combined with a seizure of the opponent's blade that seemed to Vanderville designed to cost the aggressor fingers.

'Only if you get it wrong,' explained de Rechberg. 'Performed correctly there is scant risk.'

'Wouldn't it be easier to use the offhand to deflect the opponent's blade?' suggested Vanderville.

De Rechberg held up his left hand, and displayed two fingers that were missing the upper portion. 'Doesn't work,' he said grimly.

'Are there truly so many duels fought on the island as to render this continual practice and development of gambits necessary?' asked Vanderville as they hung up their practice weapons.

De Rechberg pushed his mask back onto the top of his head and considered a moment. 'We have a lot of over-privileged young men confined together here. A strange mixture of badly spoiled scions, and unwanted third sons, all of them prickly and proud.' He shrugged, 'And then it's a boring life here on this rock. What else is there to do? Duelling is the Homeric ideal of combat, is it not?'

'Your opinion of your fellow knights is uniformly bad?' suggested Vanderville, removing his mask.

'Too much money, too much spunk, too little character,' shrugged de Rechberg. 'Schooled just enough to give them a lifelong but spurious sense of the superiority of their breeding. Speaking of which,' he said, nodding at the door to the armoury antechamber Vanderville was approaching, 'don't go in there, Demon is in his cups.'

Vanderville went in anyway to replace the sabres, studiously taking no note of Haintlet who sat alone at one table, cup in hand, a bottle beside him. He was staring glumly at a knife which he had been polishing. When de Rechberg traipsed warily in after Vanderville, Haintlet bellowed a none-too-cordial greeting and flung the knife in his direction. Whether the intent was to shock by a near miss or to wound, the throw was a poor one, and the knife clanged off an antique iron corselet and span harmlessly away into a corner.

'Some good news at last!' roared Haintlet, whose boozy face suited his nickname Demon more than ever. 'The personal effects of our dear von Seeau have been returned by the *sbirri*. And guess what? Among them was a scrap of scented paper with a scribbled reference to a certain house in a certain street! Curiously enough, it does not fit any of the known whore's houses. So, the bailli gave it to me and asked me to find out just whose door it might lead to.'

He leaned on the table with some difficulty, belched, and beckoned Vanderville closer. In a hoarse whisper he confided, 'Now, many of the knights have a little suite of apartments in some out-of-the-way corner, of which their peers are totally ignorant. To these they repair in the dark and revel unobserved with the companions of their pleasures.' He belched again for emphasis. 'Jealousy itself cannot discover the alleys, the winding passages, the unsuspected doors, by which these retreats are accessible. When a gallant has a mind to pursue his adventures, he meets his goddess in the crowd and vanishes from all beholders.'

He jabbed de Rechberg in the chest with one finger. 'I had an inkling that von Seeau's scrap of a note might unlock the mystery of just one such as these, and I was right. On questioning his valet, I discovered that von Seeau had boasted that he had been approached by that beggar girl protégé of Donna Mifsud who had promised him a means to uncover her rathole. He told his man that she had promised him such a thing, for the girl is on heat to bag herself a knight. The dog must have been visiting her there!'

Haintlet's eyes glowed. 'It's an ill wind that blows no good,' he grinned. 'And von Seeau's loss shall be my gain. As soon as I have raised a band of like-minded bawds, I shall discover her hiding place and pay her a visit.'

Seeing Vanderville's frown he waved his hands in exasperation and added angrily, 'It is what von Seeau would have wanted.' Vanderville controlled himself with some effort, while

Haintlet regarded him coolly across the table, enjoying the effect of his words. Their eyes locked and held, and there passed between them a thing primeval, bestial, a mutual recognition of mortal antipathy.

'Our friend does not approve, Fra' de Rechberg!' jeered Haintlet, breaking the spell.

'I confess, neither do I,' said de Rechberg.

'You two have allowed this rock to weaken your spirits,' said Haintlet. 'Weakness of the spirit leads to weakness in the body. Me, I train my body and like it, my essence remains hard. You detest me, de Rechberg, but I will demonstrate the difference between us.' He laboured to his feet drunkenly. 'Strike me with your fist as hard as you can,' he challenged the other knight.

'I have no wish to do so,' said de Rechberg, but he too drew back his chair and stood.

'I give you my word of honour that I will not retaliate,' said Haintlet.

De Rechberg wavered, and then irresolutely took half a step forwards, punching him half-heartedly in the stomach. Haintlet's response came like lightning, and the blow almost felled de Rechberg, who doubled over, winded and panting.

'You swore you would not retaliate,' he coughed, gasping for breath.

'I gave you one because you stroked me like a kitten,' announced Haintlet. 'Do it again but put all your strength into it. Strike me here,' he indicated his skinny little belly. 'With all of your force.'

Before the words were finished De Rechberg struck him. It was powerful this time, with full intent to harm, but he simultaneously found himself hopelessly enveloped by Haintlet's arms. They wrestled, staggering for a moment, before Haintlet dropped a hip and threw his opponent to the floor. Prostrate on the floor, de Rechberg was powerless to prevent Haintlet from inflicting real damage.

Vanderville was on his feet and between them in a flash, but Haintlet gripped his arm with fingers as strong and crushing as a horse's bite and forced him backwards, leering into his face. He disengaged as they encountered the table and eased himself back into his chair. Sitting back in his chair complacently, he surveyed them with contempt.

'You two will never get better without training,' he said, addressing the ceiling.

Vanderville rubbed his arm, but it was no balm for the seething loathing inside him. The brute shape of Haintlet's naked narrow cranium was slick with perspiration, and the ridiculously over groomed hair struck Vanderville again with its jarring inappropriateness. Haintlet glanced at de Rechberg and grunted with satisfaction. Then he turned abruptly and meeting Vanderville's gaze hot on him, he held it until there was no mistaking that they understood one another completely. Haintlet shrugged. 'You are a novice. If you are a clever novice, you will stay in your place.'

'Come away,' said de Rechberg, getting to his feet. 'You can do nothing with him in this state.' As they went back up the stairs to the courtyard, he shook his head with frustration. 'I shall have to challenge him of course,' he said. 'Will you act for me?'

Vanderville bobbed his head, but his spirits sank at the news. He had seen his fair share of bouts. The practice of fighting over insult given or taken was endemic in the light cavalry, despite being officially forbidden. In his first years of service, he had seen seven officers killed in duels, while others had suffered the bitter ignominy of being unable to accompany the regiment on campaign as a result of incapacitating duelling wounds.

Later, in his quarters, de Rechberg wrote out his challenge and read it aloud for Vanderville's approval.

'How does this sound to you — The behaviour you have shown towards me ill fits the dignity of an officer and compels me to demand satisfaction. I shall await you in Strada San

Frederico tomorrow. Come to me at five in the morning and I will correct you by the sword.'

Vanderville took the paper without a word, folded it, and put it in his breast pocket.

'*Che palle!*' swore de Rechberg. 'It is ridiculous that I, detesting the stupid prejudice which makes it impossible to refuse a duel, am now dragged into one myself. The fear of appearing a coward really is reprehensible nonsense and is a proof of a want of courage rather than the reverse. Does surviving a duel make a skilful bully respectable? Is an honest man who falls beneath the sword contemptible?'

'Why Strada San Frederico?' asked Vanderville.

'Tradition dictates it,' said de Rechberg. 'It is a narrow street where we shall not be disturbed at that hour, and the ground is level. In this place alone, penalties are suspended. You may have seen the crosses which are always painted on the wall opposite to the spot where a knight has been killed.'

'I saw some the day of my arrival,' said Vanderville. 'And counted more than twenty. Are the duels here so often invariably deadly?'

'The seconds usually prevent any interruption where the offence has been grave,' murmured de Rechberg, putting his pen away. 'It is obligatory to desist when ordered to do so by a fellow knight, a woman, or a priest, but that rarely happens.'

'*Epées* I suppose?' asked Vanderville. They fell to discussing the merits of various weapons and agreed that small swords offered a slight advantage in the circumstances as well as being more decorous and easier to explain on the streets should they encounter a patrol. De Rechberg felt that his secret combination might be employed successfully to exploit Demon's speed against him. It offered a chance that de Rechberg might prevail. Vanderville did not voice how faint a chance it represented in his view. As they rehearsed the most efficacious way to disguise and deploy the stratagem, there was a knock at the door, and one of the *auberge* porters appeared, and addressed Vanderville.

'*Cavaliere*, the Baron Pellegrew has called for you. I regret I was unable to prevent him going up to your quarters, which is most irregular, but it is hard to resist the baron.'

'I quite understand,' said Vanderville, 'I often have the same problem.'

—

'I have brought you something that may prove useful in your endeavours tonight,' said Gracchus, as Vanderville entered his chambers. He placed a paper parcel on the bed. Vanderville, whose mind was full of the duel, wondered for a moment if it contained pistols. Seeing his consternation Gracchus added, 'Surely you have not forgotten your promise to secure the bailli's document?'

Vanderville had indeed, in his concern for de Rechberg, quite put from his mind Gracchus's proposed nocturnal breach of the bailli's sanctum. How on earth was he to get any sleep? He must needs postpone one or the other. He searched for a diplomatic way to broach the subject, for he knew that Gracchus disapproved of duelling.

Gracchus opened his parcel triumphantly and displayed the contents. Vanderville saw that it contained a pair of carpet slippers. He gathered them up with scant attempt at gratitude, and with private reflections on their inutility resolved to abandon them at the first opportunity. 'You insist on this impractical enterprise then?' he queried.

'It is essential to my combinations. I regret the attendant peril but were it not vital I would not insist. Still,' he said brightly, 'compared to leaping from a ship under sail this ought to be a mere bagatelle for you.'

'I see.' Vanderville considered reminding Gracchus that the leap had cost Vassallo his life but thought better of it. 'Did you also discover the key to the cabinet?' he asked tartly. 'That might prove rather more useful.'

'Naturally,' said Gracchus, removing the key from his pocket and throwing it over to Vanderville. 'One more thing, Vanderville.'

'Of course – anything,' said Vanderville sullenly, catching the key.

'I believe that *Cavaliere* de Rechberg may be the next victim of the murderer, who has a prejudice against the knights of the Bavarian *langue*. They are being wiped out in descending order of seniority, and de Rechberg is the next most senior.'

'Ah,' said Vanderville.

'We cannot allow that to happen. You must make yourself de Rechberg's guardian and ensure no harm comes to him. You must stick to him like a tick!'

'You want me to bury my head in his body?' asked Vanderville.

'In his arse, if need be.' Gracchus pounded the table enthusiastically with his fist, narrowly missing sending the carpet slippers to the floor. 'I do not much care how you accomplish it, but you must keep him alive!'

'I must suspend my efforts in that direction until after five tomorrow morning,' said Vanderville miserably. He recounted the recent developments to Gracchus who sat with a growing impatience at news of the impending duel.

'If you need to protect the knights, wouldn't it be simpler just to arrest the murderer?' proposed Vanderville pathetically. 'Don't you have some idea? You said you were close to a conclusion.'

It was Gracchus's turn to shift uncomfortably under scrutiny. Under duress, he recounted his own day to a disbelieving Vanderville, and revealed selected details of his interview with Eva. 'The evidence points at her, Vanderville,' he repeated to Vanderville's disbelieving shake of the head.

'When have you cared so much for evidence, or come to that, for preserving the rhythm of the esoteric metronome that is the knight's law? In any case the proof against her is slight. What about the Minerves?' demanded Vanderville. 'What about Haintlet if it comes to that? He has no credible alibi for de Seeau's murder.'

'Haintlet is the type to kill with impunity, it is true,' pondered Gracchus despondently. 'And what happens to him after we leave this place is a matter of indifference to me – but for now we need him alive just as much as de Rechberg. As for the secret society of the Minerves, it's all so much flim-flam. That sniveller Gatt may become tumescent for the Minerves, but he is an inconsiderable specimen.

'I do not believe Carpegna himself is truly convinced of the culpability of the secret societies. It merely serves his purpose to round up a few miscreants to enhance the prospect of being noticed by his superiors in Rome. He knows which way the wind is blowing for Malta and wants to demonstrate a success before Bonaparte arrives and expels the Holy Office.'

'So, you would throw Donna Eva to these wolves? Despite her obvious benevolence?'

'Bestowing charity on a few orphans?' He shook his head sadly. 'It doesn't weigh much in the grand scheme of things.'

'What do you care about the grand scheme of things! You have told me a hundred times you have turned your back on idealistic endeavours. While you have been moaning about the Republic's failings, we have liberated north Italy, and all Batavia from tyranny. The Republic may not be perfect, but it's the future. Who knows where we will be in ten years if we continue as we have started?' He kicked a suit of armour in frustration. 'I wish you would tell me what the blazes you are doing on this rock that you think will save your rotten soul.'

Gracchus spread his hands evenly. 'Look at the facts as they present themselves. Yes, the Bavarian *langue* is crawling with midden-beasts, a nest of corruption. Naturally I sympathise with Eva's brave stand against this foulness. But if she is the murderer, how does she know she is even killing the right knights?'

'How do you know she isn't?' retorted Vanderville. 'I would bury the lot of them except de Rechberg, and possibly von Torring.'

'Our path is indicated. When you have finished railing against the skies, I suggest you direct your energies towards thinking up a way to keep de Rechberg and Haintlet from murdering each other. This duel must be stopped, Vanderville.' Gracchus pushed the slippers back across the table, 'I must take my leave – I have other business tonight.'

'Back to the slave *bagnio*?' jeered Vanderville. 'Thinking of making a purchase?'

But Gracchus was already at the door. He turned and looked sadly back. 'Just stop that duel,' he said, closing the door gently behind him.

Vanderville was left alone with his foreboding. It was a strange, disjointed time. He had been content to pull in harness with Gracchus once more, but whether as a result of his newly acquired wealth, or because he was engaged on some secret theme of his own, he now found him distant. They were at loggerheads once more.

For his part Gracchus also felt regret as he paused uncertainly on the stairs. His familiar reliance on his young companion was strained, and without taking him into his confidence he found himself unable to unburden himself of his affairs. He missed the easy companionship of Mombello, of Rome, that seemed so far away now.

In the meantime, he had to prevent further murders as a priority, his uneasy alliance with Eva must be maintained, until his plans matured, at which point he could leave *her* to be exposed, or perhaps he would be more sporting to give her notice to leave the island before her role came to light – but she would have thought of that, and made her own arrangements… and he had also to ensure the loyalty of the merchant Rais Murad, who was necessary to his evolutions.

Despite his apparent certainty he was troubled by Eva's involvement. When given a chance to bargain for herself, she had not. She asked nothing for herself but had concern only for others.

—

Before the vigil bells had chimed Vanderville was advancing stocking-clad towards the bailli's apartments. He lightly ran up the steps to the great hall, slipped inside, and stood with his back to the wall. He listened. Everything was quiet. The moon dappled floor was cool under his feet, and he thanked the architects of Valletta that the fine broad flagstones were not fashioned of creaking wooden boards to betray him. The centre of the hall was well lit by the silvery lustre of moonlight streaming through the tall, unshuttered windows, and he had the impression that he had strayed between the pages of a Troubadour romance and was stalking the hall of some great baron's castle. It seemed unreal, as if some murder-bent fiend intent on poignard-themed mischief might emerge from behind one of the solemn Gobelin tapestries at any moment. He cursed again Gracchus's latest plot. Having found a refuge in the Bavarians' *auberge*, he was now in greater peril than ever. The ties of the brethren, masonic and professional, would not endure if he was caught as an armed intruder in their leader's chambers at night. He took a deep breath to calm his nerves. Stealth and scrutiny were indicated then, he told himself, and when his eyes had adapted to the light, he scanned the shadows cautiously and left his coign of vantage.

As he traversed the hall the silence was broken by the plaintive cry of a seagull swooping past the windows and he caught himself holding his breath, so loud did it seem to him in the vasty space. He pulled his collar up and pushed his shoulders back. This was the age of oil lights and argon, not that of feudal mayhem, he assured himself. But nonetheless the sword he carried felt inadequate, and he repressed a thought that it might prove fain against a man iron-shod *cap-a-piè*.

There was a profound stillness inside the bailli's private apartment when he reached it. The shutters were closed against the night air, and the puny glimmer of moonlight from the hall cast a paltry glow, so he tiptoed to the solar window to draw the boards back.

He had the intruder's heightened senses and exhilaration, and the view from the window towards the sea struck him afresh. The moon casting its sickly gleam over Valletta made it appear like some city seen in dreams. Behind lay the monotonous grandeur of ocean beyond Fort Sant' Elmo, where all around nothing broke the distant horizon. He paused a moment too long at the window until the chime of a hundred bells from the numberless churches and convents startled him back to his task.

The cabinet was soon opened, and he rifled the papers inside hurriedly, paying scant attention to the numerous engravings of nymphs and satyrs in improbable postures. There were many papers and no sign of Gracchus's quarry. He became increasingly convinced that the envelope wasn't there!

But once he had removed the first stack, at the very back of the cabinet he saw a corner of pale silver ribbon under more papers. As he lifted the documents, he saw they were headed with a mysterious pyramid symbol, and he pulled one out to see more closely. It was in German, and he could make only parts of it out, but as he read with growing astonishment, he concluded that it was part of a correspondence between members of the Minerves secret society. Without thinking he grabbed half a dozen of the letters up and stuffed the lot into his breast pocket. He replaced the other papers, closed the cabinet, locked it, and with the red silk envelope Gracchus sought in his hand, he stealthily withdrew from the solar to retrace his steps.

As soon as he was clear of the great hall, he pulled the door to behind him and slumped back against it in the dark. He rested his chin gratefully on his chest and released a long sigh of relief into the cooler air of the staircase. It was done, and he was home free once he gained the security of his room. No sooner was his breath expelled than his eyes caught a flicker of movement in the darkness of the stairs. Lifting his head apprehensively, he watched in abject horror, as a form detached itself from the shadows below. The obscure shape materialised into a gargantuan figure advancing stealthily towards him. Vanderville pressed his back against the door for security and, as if in response, the gloomy shade multiplied into two, then three enormous armed phantoms who towered over him as they advanced.

The situation was beyond reason, but he responded in the only manner possible. His hand crept down his flank towards the steel hilt of his sword, and it was then that his eyes caught a flicker of candlelight on the stair. The phantoms juddered and dissipated as if they were shades of smoke and were succeeded by the low murmur of conversation rising from below. Here was a more temporal enemy! Armed men were ascending the flight of stairs, and the light they carried had thrown their ominous shadows in grotesque exaggeration against the wall.

He let the hilt of his sword fall back into place and fumbled with the incriminating envelope, attempting to thrust it into his pocket. He succeeded only in spilling it on the floor and was trying to retrieve it when Haintlet and his cronies arrived clattering upwards towards him. They had the flushed faces and damp hair that signaled a recent heavy bout at the wine barrels and looked equal to any mischief.

'What do you have there?' demanded Haintlet, drawing to a halt and holding up the candlestick he carried to peer more closely at Vanderville.

'This?' said Vanderville, tucking the protruding envelope back into his coat. 'It is a… It is nothing. Just a medical preparation efficacious in the treatment of wounds.'

'You needn't bother with that,' murmured one of Haintlet's companions. 'Fra' de Rechberg will leave the field of combat like a needleworker's pad. Even the unparalleled skill of the Order's surgeons will be in vain.'

Haintlet alone was not smiling. 'Difficulty sleeping Tirdflingen?' he asked, pushing his candle into Vanderville's face. In the shadows of the stairwell, his face glistened with malevolent curiosity. 'Or perhaps you have forgotten the way to your chamber?'

'I was on my way to the armoury to set an edge on a sword,' said Vanderville tersely.

'Sharpen one for yourself if you like,' said Haintlet's companion grinning maliciously. 'We could make a mêlée of it tomorrow.' They smirked convivially to one another as they continued up the stairs, only Haintlet allowing his gaze to linger suspiciously on Vanderville as he passed upwards.

Chapter Fourteen

The duellists rose with the Pater Nostra bells at four o'clock in the morning. It was a peaceful hour, and the streets were quiet but for the sounds of creaking wheels and padded mule hoofs. The acrid smell of freshly kindled dung fires drifted on the faint breeze. Arriving in Strada Federico the combatants discarded their mantles, exposing the plain shirts they wore beneath with the right sleeve rolled up to expose the arm. They drew their weapons and handed the scabbards and mantles to their seconds.

There was to be no last-minute reprieve. Haintlet's second had met Vanderville's request for an apology, with an icy refusal. These things, he explained, had to be expunged in the accepted way. His tone had indicated scant regard for the attempted intervention and even a sort of embarrassment that the matter had been raised at all. Vanderville had been forced to defer adroitly to avoid any impugning of de Rechberg's honour. His only idea was to hope that honour would be satisfied with a minimum of blood, which might depend on de Rechberg striking first.

And so now the seconds stood in the alley silently behind their champions, who flexed their weapons and stretched their legs.

'We must be quickly about our business,' whispered Haintlet's second conspiratorially. 'The preparations for the defence of the island mean that we can add militia patrols to those of the *sbirri* and the grandmaster's guard as potential interruptions. Let alone the people who are abroad for blood.'

Vanderville nodded. Suspected collaborators were at grave risk in the days since news of the French fleet's departure from Toulon. He had heard that a lynching had been witnessed from the window of the *Auberge* of Provence the day before. A French merchant had been hacked to death. There was no shriek, no sound of lamentation heard, the deed was done, and the crowd gradually and quietly dispersed. Vanderville had seen such things in Italy, and they had endured in his dreams sporadically since, hovering accusingly at the edges of his waking consciousness. Sometimes at night they made themselves free, drifting out from the cracks in his mind like a sickly yellow mist, and swirling in the mist were the wailing faces of the men he had seen die. He pushed these unwelcome considerations aside, and focused all of his attention on the Strada Federico.

Surprisingly the duel began well for de Rechberg. Whether it was the effects of his debauch, or that the early morning ill-suited him, Haintlet displayed none of the demonic speed for which he was renowned. His footwork was almost indolent, and twice de Rechberg seemed certain to take advantage and spit him. Once he even touched him on the chest, but the thrust was impeded by the buckle of Haintlet's braces and only made him bleed slightly. After a brief inspection Haintlet's second concluded that this was not an adequate wound to satisfy honour and so they would have to continue the fight.

But each time de Rechberg pounced forward, Demon evaded him by the skin of his teeth, and gradually Haintlet's superior sword-wit returned, and with it, Vanderville's dawning comprehension that Haintlet was playing his opponent into over-confidence. This certainty rose as surely as the sun squinting its way into the alley.

It was not long after that revelation that matters took a more ominous turn for de Rechberg. His opponent's inhuman conditioning began to show over de Rechberg's merely mortal fitness. As the crisis approached, Vanderville prepared himself for disaster, and braced himself to intervene. Interference would mean social death for de Rechberg, but quite possibly actual mortal consequences for Gracchus and himself if he did not.

He quavered on the brink of resolution and then, unexpectedly, de Rechberg found an opening. Giving ground with his weight always over the back foot he invited Haintlet to commit and Vanderville realised with a rising thrill that he was preparing his conceit attack. When Haintlet took the bait he would shift his weapon to the off hand, deflect Haintlet's sword with his right hand and have the measure of his opponent allowing him to counterattack. But in the execution, he stumbled badly and Haintlet pounced. Driving forward off his front foot he thrust through the other man's guard and into the flesh of his thigh.

As quickly as he had attacked, he withdrew, and Vanderville started forward, but Haintlet's second compelled him back insistently, making space for the combat to continue. De Rechberg grimly tested the strength of his leg. Blood was oozing darkly into his breeches already. Gingerly he resumed his stance, as Haintlet wiped his blade on the mantle held by his second and then returned to his mark with pursed lips and hard eyes.

And then they were interrupted. Two figures were looming up behind Haintlet, a young woman in her *faldetta* and her plump *duenna* wrapped in a voluminous shawl. The combatants lowered their swords hurriedly and stepped apart. The stamping of the swordsmen's feet had raised the white dust of the street, and with the sun behind the new arrivals, it was hard through the miasma to make their faces out. They tottered oh so slowly up the alley towards the cluster of waiting men and Vanderville's heart lurched as he recognised them. The woman was Eva and as they came closer, he saw that the shambling *duenna* was not a woman, but Gracchus, enveloped in his oriental shawl.

Haintlet turned towards the intruders warily, and observing their lack of menace, threw up his arms in exasperation and took up his stance once more. De Rechberg, who had taken advantage of the respite to bind his bleeding leg with a handkerchief, wearily followed suit.

'Gentlemen, for shame, forbear this outrage!' shouted Gracchus, and Vanderville winced.

Haintlet straightened up and waved dismissively at de Rechberg to lower his blade. He swivelled to address the newcomers. 'Who says so?' he bellowed belligerently. 'I see nothing but an old she-goat, or something very like, and a public woman. You have no place here, Baron Periwinkle.'

'The grandmaster has expressly forbidden duelling in Valletta's streets,' said Gracchus, arriving before Haintlet, and mustering his own full height.

'Custom has long suspended those rulings in this hallowed place,' said Haintlet, gesturing at the alley. He raised his blade to keep Gracchus and Eva at a distance and flicked it from one to the other of them. 'Only a respectable lady or a knight may interrupt us here…' The sword tip wavered a moment before Eva's face, and then flashed to Gracchus's chest, where with an abrupt motion of the blade it cast the shawl aside to expose his breast, 'And I see neither here. Be careful Baron, not all of the island has fallen under your spell.'

Gracchus pushed aside the sword with the back of his hand, and without removing his eyes from Haintlet's face, cautiously reached inside his breast pocket. He drew forth a small object and brandished it before Haintlet's astonished gaze. It was a tiny, gilded cross of the Order. The arms were made of glass and glittered in the morning sun like a thousand tiny crystals. The two seconds stepped forward to see more closely.

'Touché, Baron,' said Eva quietly, and Haintlet flinched, recoiling from the cross as if he really was some demon.

'You have been admitted as a brother of the Order?' enquired Haintlet's second curtly, and Gracchus nodded.

'His Eminence the grandmaster confessed me as a knight of honour last night. A touching piece of magisterial grace that has convinced me that there may be good in honour after all.'

His eyes rested briefly on Vanderville as he spoke, 'I am on my way to breakfast with His Eminence now, and I hope I shall have no cause to report a brawl to him. Neither of you will wish to risk exile just as the great moment of redemption falls upon the Order's shoulders. It would be a shame to miss Bonaparte, even if,' he looked at de Rechberg, 'you have been stupid enough to get yourself wounded.'

Haintlet's second was already draping his mantle round his man's shoulders, and Vanderville offered de Rechberg an arm to lean on. As the defeated swordsmen departed in opposite directions, Gracchus stepped forward to block Haintlet's path.

'I believe you owe the lady an apology, *cavaliere*,' he said with low emphasis.

Haintlet muttered a few words under his breath and was gone in a swirl of dust as his black mantle swept the pavement, his second trailing behind him.

Gracchus shrugged. 'I must speak to you at the first opportunity,' he whispered to Vanderville urgently. 'But for now, I must wait on the grandmaster.' He bowed to Eva, looked once more at de Rechberg, and sighed, then took his leave.

Eva inspected de Rechberg's wound. 'If you can make it down the street a small way, I saw a public *kalesh* waiting for custom, and we can take you to the hospital.'

'Not the Order's hospital,' said de Rechberg, grimacing at her touch. 'Can't you take me to the Maddalene?'

'The women's hospital? I hardly think so,' she answered. 'Yet Don Stecchi might agree to tend to you. Take him to my house, Tirdflingen, I will arrange for him to wait on you there.'

As Vanderville helped de Rechberg into the *kalesh* he said to Eva quietly, 'Thank you for coming. You arrived at an opportune moment.'

'I? I would be pleased to see Haintlet skewered. And as for de Rechberg, well he is a knight too, so must take his chances. You have only the baron to thank.'

'Yet I thank both of you. However curious it is to see the investigator, and his prey proceeding hand in friendly hand.'

'We are hardly friends,' said Eva, shutting the door of the carriage with a bang. 'Travellers of a common road at best.'

When they arrived at Eva's house, they helped de Rechberg up the stairs to the salon where Vanderville laid him on the couch, while Eva despatched Duccio for Don Stecchi. That worthy hurried in soon afterwards with his medical bag.

'He has pinked you,' said Don Stecchi. 'Despite that you should recover in time to resume your post soon, and then Bonaparte can have his turn at making mincemeat of the rest of you. I prescribe plenty of claret, and beef if you can get it, you have lost a little blood.'

There was a clatter on the stairs and Franca bustled in with Granchio hobbling behind her. He had not passed the door before he was gabbling. 'Have you heard the news?' he blurted without preamble at Vanderville, and then, seeing de Rechberg he clammed up. Franca too, shrank back from the knight, drawing her *faldetta* across her face.

'Come up to the terrace,' said Vanderville, 'and tell me there. *Cavaliere* de Rechberg needs to rest before he is carted back to the *auberge*.'

Duccio joined them, bursting with excitement, and they were hardly up the stairs before Granchio burst out with his tale. It appeared that after the duel, Haintlet and his companion had been making their way back to the *auberge* when Franca happened to spot them while she was watering the plant on the windowsill of her little bolthole. As the two knights made their way up the alley, she had taken the opportunity to precipitate the plant pot onto their heads. The projectile had missed Haintlet, but by so little as to shower his breeches with dirt. They were bubbling with joy and excitement at the escapade.

'If you had hit him, you would have been arrested for murder!' expostulated Vanderville, smiling despite himself.

'So much the better,' said Granchio. 'One less of them to oppose the French.'

'*Cavaliere* Haintlet didn't see anything,' said Franca proudly, and Vanderville saw again that in company with her companion from the *Fraternita* she became more childlike. 'He was covered in mud, and hopping from foot to foot as though he were possessed! It was wonderful, you should have seen him.'

'And the other knight? His companion?' asked Vanderville.

'He may have seen something, but he couldn't make out my face at that distance, I was quick to close the window, and anyway, everyone else in the street was opening their own windows to see the fun.'

Vanderville shook his head, he was not so sure; Franca was distinctive, with or without her *faldetta*, and if the knight had recognised her, then her place of refuge was no longer safe. The house would be marked either way, by the address found in von Seeau's effects, but now her window was known, they would identify the door to her apartment soon enough. He gathered them round, suddenly serious, 'You must promise me, all of you, to stop these games. Let Bonaparte take care of the knights when he comes.'

'There are enough for all of us,' Granchio boasted proudly.

'They are still dangerous, and you must avoid them as long as you are able,' warned Vanderville.

—

On arriving at the palace Gracchus was led through a labyrinth of passages, guided by a liveried flunkey, who opened a kind of wicket door and let him into a tiny courtyard garden with as little ceremony as he would have turned a goose adrift on a common. A small figure was hunched over a smaller garden table in the centre of the garden surrounded by espaliered orange trees in tubs that filled the garden with a floating fragrance.

The grandmaster, strangely diminished without his state robes, was huddled in a shawl even older than Gracchus's own. He sniffled into a handkerchief, 'Join me, Pellegrew,' he said, beckoning. 'At breakfast I am a stranger to ceremony.'

Gracchus settled himself into the spare chair and searched the grandmaster's face. It was grey and drawn, he looked as if he had not slept.

'One can change shirts, places and pills, but not bad health once it has set in,' grumbled the grandmaster, sucking at a quartered orange sourly. Gracchus surveyed the table eagerly; the sea breezes had sharpened his temporal appetite. He sat with alacrity and flicked out a napkin of exceedingly fine linen. There were oranges, lemons, dates, figs, almonds, and pomegranates piled up before him, and he draped the napkin around his neck and applied himself steadily.

'There are no oranges in my own garden,' he observed. 'Yesterday morning instead of jigging along Merchant's Street dodging sedan chairs and *kaleshes*, while bowing to *cavaliere* this, and nodding my head to *monsignor* that, I strolled to the market where I obtained a hatful of oranges and a quantity of small land tortoises in exchange for a very few coins.'

'You have plebian tastes for a great man,' observed the grandmaster, watching him. 'I envy you the simplicity of your existence. Great wealth and abundance of leisure make glad bedfellows.'

Gracchus chewed moodily; his present situation felt anything but simple to him.

'Before we talk of matters of moment, may I ask whether you have concluded the puzzle of Bailli von Torring's dead knight?' asked the grandmaster, and Gracchus nodded.

'I anticipate a resolution any day now. The matter is all but settled.'

'That is well,' said von Hompesch. 'In that case, I too have good news. The council has all but agreed to support your project. The funds must be transferred instantly – today you understand. The Order's bankers operate a most arcane process for the transfer of funds, so an arrangement for the money to be temporarily held by an intermediary has been put in place by my man of affairs. By this means you will be able to conclude your business swiftly whereas the funds will be safe until such time as arrangements can be made to transfer them to the Order formally.' He smiled. 'It is irregular, but as I understand it, rapidity is of the essence.'

'I am pleased to hear that,' replied Gracchus, 'because I have finalised my arrangements. The last piece should have fallen into place by now.'

The grandmaster wiped orange juice from his chin with considered thoroughness. 'It would be well if you arranged the details discretely. Time is short if you are to be away before our French guests arrive, and it would be well to pre-empt that event in case of any disruption. I will call my secretary to conclude the necessary paperwork.'

The grandmaster rang a little bell, and as he did so, Gracchus laid his little gilt cross on the table.

'I found this in my residence and thought it might belong to you,' he said.

The grandmaster picked the cross up, and turned it carefully in his hands, peering keenly at the arms and inscription. Finally, he looked up sharply. 'Do you know the significance of this?'

'I know only knights may bear the cross. And that compels me to a minor confession. On the way here I had to expose it as if it belonged to me. I assure you it was a very small sin to avert a greater evil. I beg Your Eminence's indulgence and take consolation in returning it to you.'

Von Hompesch hefted the jewel in his hand, and then slipped it into a fold of his clothes. 'If only we could always tell which is the greater evil,' he contemplated aloud, 'how much lighter these crosses would be.'

—

Vanderville was waiting outside the palace when Gracchus emerged. As Gracchus resumed his tinted spectacles, Vanderville examined him with concern. He seemed awfully pale and tired. Probably been eating too much again and has a touch of liver, he thought. 'Have you really been made a knight?' he wondered aloud.

Gracchus laughed, 'I found the cross in a drawer in my palazzo and thought it might come in handy.' He beamed. 'It was a beautiful thing though, in rock crystal and gilded bronze, I should have liked to retain it as a souvenir. Anyway, I have returned it to its rightful owner. Now,' he said impatiently. 'Did you retrieve the bailli's envelope?'

Vanderville drew the package from his breast and handed it over to Gracchus, who slid it instantly inside his own coat. 'There was something else,' he said hesitantly, and produced the Minerve's letters. Gracchus picked one up, put on his spectacles and read it with increasing interest, it concerned a petty dispute between Bailli von Torring, the head of the Minerves on Malta, and the society's network in Bavaria and was of scant interest. He laid this aside and scanned the next letters with growing enthusiasm.

'This is volatile stuff!' he uttered excitedly. 'Did you not read these? The Minerves have a man in Bonaparte's fleet headquarters, which must be how von Torring came to know of you and your mission here.' He flipped the letter to read the other side, evading Vanderville's attempts to grasp it.

'The agent asserts that Berthier's intelligence bureau has spies on the island of Gozo who communicate by carrier pigeon with Valletta…' He rifled ahead through the remaining letters. 'The last communication from the Valletta spy mentions the finding of Vassallo's body and asserts that the sender is in danger. The Minerve's contact says that attempts should be made by the knights to trace the Valletta spy, whose identity is unknown.'

'That must be Mayflower!' Vanderville tried, and failed again, to seize the letter from Gracchus. 'I confess I read German only with difficulty. But if this was sent when Vassallo washed up, it postdates von Seeau's death. Does it reveal his identity?'

'It does not. The Minervan agent did not learn so much. Yet since his last communication was recent, we may conclude that von Seeau could not have been Mayflower. There is something that will interest you on this last page though. It is an earlier letter concerning Vassallo and the means he was to use to establish communication with Mayflower on their rendezvous. Apparently, it arrived too late to allow the interception of Mayflower, and in any case the place of rendezvous is not named. But a form of code phrases is suggested. Vassallo was to ask, "Are you one of them?" and Mayflower, for surely this is he, would reply, "I am all of them."'

A smile passed across Vanderville's face. 'This is the key then. Now it is just a matter of time before I unveil my agent.'

'You have helped our cause immensely by putting these in my hands, Vanderville, even if there is no immediate clue to the death of the knights. But if the bailli should learn that we have taken possession of this correspondence, we will bring the wrath of the secret society down on our own heads. You have taken a tolerable risk, my friend.'

'I did not take them all,' said Vanderville. 'I doubt he will even notice they are missing unless he was to go through the whole bundle which he cannot do before he returns from the country. There was only one red silk portfolio though that he may miss.'

Chapter Fifteen

Returning to his residence Gracchus was informed that he had a morning caller, who was waiting in the garden. He was disappointed to find the inquisitor waiting there, with all the evidence of having made an assault on the breakfast he had taken the precaution of having ordered in case of meeting with ill fare at the palace.

'I have good news for you, Baron,' said Carpegna, wiping his mouth, 'and as I was in the area on Church business, I thought I would take the liberty of dropping in.'

'What business is that?' asked Gracchus, who disapproved of overmuch conversation before, or indeed at, breakfast, and who was inclined to be curmudgeonly as he regarded the desolate remains of an omelette.

'The Order are making some improvements to Piazza Forbici. About time, too, the ditches are full of the witch's flower, and I have asked them to be cleared on several occasions. In addition, I thought it was a good opportunity to register the children living there for their catechism. My assessor, Canon Gatt is more than capable of supervising, so I thought I would allow myself the pleasure of your company while he gets things in motion.'

How weak-willed to leave the harassing of children to a menial, thought Gracchus, but aloud he said only, 'Delegation is a wonderful tool for the sensitive soul.'

'The soul may be a matter of levity for you, Baron,' said Carpegna, 'but my own will rest easier when those of the children are secured. Do not imagine that this is merely a question of dogma, important as that is. I want those children in the security of the orphan's hospital where they will be safe and educated to lead useful lives to the benefit of themselves and the community. Do you find my motives so unreasonable?'

Gracchus shook his head, slowly, still considering his breakfast table with regret, and pondering the wisdom of simply re-ordering everything so that he could begin from scratch.

'It is not the children's fault that they are astray, and they will not be punished,' continued Carpegna. 'I'm more interested in those who oppose our endeavours. I am inclined to suspect their motives as malign.'

'Yes, well,' said Gracchus, who was keen to resume examining Vanderville's trove of purloined documents. 'If there is nothing else, I had better get on.'

'Before I take my leave, I thought you might be pleased to know that your donation to the church in Vittoriosa was most gratefully received. And I am now in a position to share the list you requested,' said Carpegna. 'The necessary clearance arrived by courier from Rome last night.'

Gracchus yawned, 'I thought the mail ships were all blocked by the French squadron.'

'The Holy Office has its own channels of communication,' said Carpegna. 'Quicker and more discrete than the regular mail.' He proffered a paper file, and Gracchus quickly scanned it. It consisted of a long series of reports on the members of the Order. He flicked through to those concerning the *Auberge* de Bavaria. The content was gossipy and conjectural like so many informer's reports. Eventually he arrived at the part relating to secret societies.

'But if this is accurate, it is the opposite of what we thought!' he queried, looking up startled at Carpegna.

'Yes, curious, is it not?' admitted the inquisitor. 'There is a cell of Minerves embedded in the *Langue* of Bavaria, but those knights killed are not in their number. In fact, only three of the knights are not members of the post-Illumine infection, and two of them have been strangled already.'

Gracchus quickly flicked through the remaining pages, 'And the remaining knight is?'

'Look under Cervantes,' said Carpegna, smiling ominously.

'Abbe Ferdinand Haintlet Cervantes, Commander of Altotting. Known also as Demon Cervantes. The Black Knight. Demone, Demonio,' read Gracchus aloud.

'None other,' smiled Carpegna. 'Corruptor of children, murderer and libertine.'

'Cervantes?' wondered Gracchus, 'A Spanish name it is usually considered...'

'Yes,' said Carpegna, 'he is in fact Spanish, but he didn't choose to join the Spanish *langue*. His mother is half Polish, so he applied to the Bavarian langue and somehow got in. The word is that the Spanish refused to take him.'

'The demon of the Order,' read Gracchus. 'An unschooled judicial murderer. Has a ridiculous wife who adores him, but whom he detests. His inclinations are generally violent; obsessed with duelling because he is lacking in any other competence.' He slammed the file shut. 'This is the man whose life we must preserve? A fine piece of work.'

'Don't you see?' reasoned Carpegna, 'The Minerves are not admitting the deviant knights into their ranks. And it is those knights who are being killed. Is it because they are opposed to the Minerves?'

'No,' said Gracchus. 'It is because they are foul in spirit, and that offends the philosophers. Those of a vulgar or evil mind cannot attain the higher grades.'

'We have a similar system in the Church,' said Carpegna. 'Which is why dear Gatt is a canon still.'

'Well, this is very helpful,' said Gracchus. 'Do please not let me occupy any more of your time.' As he showed the inquisitor out, he whispered to his servant to send a runner for Vanderville.

'The Minerves are cleaning house, or someone else is doing it for them. I am now certain that *Cavaliere* Haintlet will be the next victim of the murderer,' Gracchus said to Vanderville carefully, as he leafed through the documents spread out on the table before him. He held up a hand to stifle Vanderville's burgeoning protest. 'We cannot allow him to be killed, richly though he may deserve strangling down some alleyway. A further casualty among his brethren will surely cause the bailli to withdraw his protection from us both.'

'Ah,' said Vanderville, 'is that why you have summoned me here in this ungodly haste? I had given up on returning to bed and was just about to call on Donna Eva for dancing instruction. So de Rechberg is not in imminent danger, but Haintlet is. What if *Cavaliere* Haintlet meets with an accident anyway?' he suggested hopefully. 'His propensity for mayhem makes it not unlikely.'

Gracchus frowned and hitched his spectacles up his nose. 'That cannot be allowed to happen. No mischief must befall Haintlet, or we are lost. You and I will find ourselves in the prisons of the Order or worse. No,' he continued shaking his head ruefully, 'I can see no alternative.'

'Stick to him like a tick?' suggested Vanderville, taking up his sword and making for the door.

—

'Why are you following me around like a dog, Tirdflingen?' said Haintlet, bouncing down the stairs of the *Auberge* de Bavaria, 'Is this part of your master's investigations?'

'Believe me, I regret the necessity intensely,' said Vanderville, scrambling to keep up. 'I have appointments that merit my attention rather more than you do.'

'Oh, I do not resent it, never fear, I know you have a murderer to catch. And in any case, none of the other knights of the *langue* are talking to me today. As long as you don't intend to trail me to my assignation tonight, I shall be glad of having some company – even yours. But look here, Vanderville; de Seeau and Abbe Alois von Schilternberg were my friends.' He paused at the bottom of the stair, his hand on his sword hilt. 'Do you really think I had anything to do with their deaths?'

'De Rechberg is also your friend,' Vanderville reminded him curtly, pulling up next to him breathlessly.

'I have no intention of fighting other knights. It is unfortunate that it happens that way, and I avoid it whenever possible, but as you saw, de Rechberg challenged *me*.' He stalked out of the *auberge*, glared up at the blinding sun, and adjusting his hat, set off down the street, 'And I did not hurt him much, he will be on duty again in a week,' he said over his shoulder. 'I would suggest another bout when he's better, but the bailli has threatened instant expulsion from the *langue* for anyone who fights during the present troubles.'

Vanderville gave up. 'Are you on duty today, then?'

'It would appear so. I have the honour to command a company of the Regiment of Malta who have been detailed to clear the beggars' market in Piazza Forbici. Their filthy shacks obstruct the field of fire of the guns from fortress Sant' Elmo. Should Valletta fall, as a last resort the grandmaster will take refuge there because Sant' Elmo's guns command the city. There we can hold fast until aid can be sent to the Order. Frankly, if it was up to me, I would use the cannon to clear the lice from the marketplace. In that, at least, your General Bonaparte had the right idea when he cleaned the Parisian streets.' He hitched up his sword belt eagerly, and hastened his pace. Haintlet entered the Piazza Forbici by the market stalls with Vanderville hot on his tail. Near the market traders lurked Canon Gatt, his face much bruised still under the brim of his hat. He stood beside a closed *kalesh* with several *sbirri* lounging nearby. He shot a malicious glance at Vanderville when he saw him in company with Haintlet.

'Good day to you, Canon Gatt,' hailed Haintlet, waving his arm in off-handed salute. 'I am pleased to see your face improved. I warrant you will enjoy watching this morning's work. You may be reminded of Christ clearing the merchants from the temple!' He laid hands on the nearest market stall and wrenched it over. The stallholders scattered, clucking like chickens before a fox in the pen. 'If my day concludes as I hope, in a somewhat less Christian manner, I will have something juicy to confess to you tomorrow. You will enjoy the details I am sure.'

Gatt eyed him sourly and rubbed his jaw without answering, so Haintlet went to muster his company of soldiers, who were trickling in half-heartedly, trailing their muskets. The preparations for defence of the island interested Vanderville professionally, but the clearing of the artillery field of fire before the fortress seemed a spurious waste of time to him. The fortifications of the island were impressively extensive, but it was apparent that Valletta and the Grand Harbour were the keys. If they were taken the rest of the islands would necessarily follow. The Order might cling onto Sant' Elmo for a few weeks, or even months, but their cause was ultimately futile. They were too decayed as a military force to engage a modern army.

Once the company of the Maltese Regiment began to assemble in the piazza those market traders still trading started to dismantle their apparatus in haste. Vanderville watched the regiment form with a trained eye and found them reasonably well trained and drilled. It would make no difference. There were nowhere near enough of them to trouble the French demi-brigades that had embarked with General Bonaparte.

He crossed the piazza to approach the pillory, where the *Fraternita*, overjoyed with the spectacle of the regiment formed up for inspection, were hooting with laughter, and marching up and down the pillory steps in imitation of the soldiers. Franca was at the pillory smiling at the boys' antics, and she was the first to greet Vanderville. She descended the steps with a shy smile and removed some flowers from the basket she carried. 'There,' she said, pinning a spray of blooms to Vanderville's coat. 'Now you have a knight's star like the baron.'

Vanderville thanked her gallantly and inspected the yellow flowers. Among them were small budding fruit which were indeed shaped something like the eight-pointed cross of the Order, but two of its points on one side were slightly tilted at an angle with their opposite points. It was the same flower he had seen cultivated in her flowerpots, and on Eva's terrace.

'It is charming,' he said, aware of Duccio's critical gaze as he admired Franca's smile again. 'What do you call it?'

'Il Warda Tal-Kavalieri, but they also call it the witch's flower. It grows only in the ditch of the fortress and nowhere else. Or it did, before they cleared the ground. The tale says that the flower sprang from the earth watered by the blood of the knights who fell defending their post from the Turk.'

'A good omen then,' said Vanderville.

'I hope so.'

'And where is my star?' asked Duccio, pushing between them.

'Help yourself,' she said, proffering the basket without turning her gaze from Vanderville.

'Crosses for all!' trumpeted Duccio, distributing the flowers among the *Fraternita*.

'Will you help me?' Vanderville asked Franca. 'The *Fraternita* need to leave the piazza. They can shelter at the baron's palazzo for now. I despair of mustering them, but they will follow you.'

'You cannot bottle the wind,' she said, 'but I will try for you.'

She was right. For the *Fraternita*, the day was fast developing into a joyous festival. The market traders were labouring under the abuse of hard-faced soldiers, and a good deal of hard words were being exchanged on each side. As the stalls of the more recalcitrant were upended, the children darted forth to peck up the discarded market produce like a flock of ravenous starlings. Carrying their trophies back to their perch on the pillory they gamboled like bacchantes seized by inebriation and gorged on their booty. All the while, Gatt watched them from the shadows of the portico that lined the market.

Vanderville saw Gracchus wandering haplessly into the piazza with a look of bewilderment, so he went to remove him from the soldiers' path of destruction. Once he had steered him clear, he explained the situation.

'I have told the children they can take refuge at your palazzo; they won't sleep indoors or bother your servants but stay in the garden.'

Gracchus searched his anxious face and nodded. 'Very well. Of course they can go indoors, there is space aplenty. The servants will kick up a fuss, and report it to His Eminence's spies, so perhaps I had better go and prepare the way.'

Vanderville nodded, and cast his eyes back to those henchmen under Gatt's supervision. They had intercepted a stray member of the *Fraternita*, and were clustered around him like crows baiting a fledgling. Following Vanderville's apprehensive glance, Gracchus added, 'I must rest my legs a while first. I shall wait for you at the pillory.'

Vanderville strode towards the *kalesh* waiting near the portico to remonstrate with Gatt. He found him there surrounded by his men. His reddened face was still the worse for wear.

'Is it necessary to be quite so forceful with the children?' Vanderville asked, as civilly as he could manage.

'We have orders to collect them, and that's what we will do. Where they go after that is between them and the inquisitor.'

The soldiers began throwing over what remained of the stalls beside them, and Vanderville cursed them.

'The regiment have their business to conduct, and we of the Holy Office have ours,' said Gatt. 'If you intend to meddle, all sorts of questions of precedence arise, and I'd rather not give the soldiers a headache by having you arrested.' He suddenly stopped and stared at the flower buds in Vanderville's buttonhole. 'Where did you get that witch's flower?' he asked suspiciously.

'They grow in the ditch,' said Vanderville. Gatt's attendants were manhandling the child into the *kalesh*, and he assessed his chances of effecting a release without conviction.

Gracchus dragged a discarded chair from the café to the shade behind the pillory cross from which vantage point he could survey the entire piazza. Haintlet appeared to be enjoying himself enormously, he strode over to the pillory, and turning his back on its hooting inhabitants, planted his feet and threw back his mantle to posture with one hand on his sword hilt. The pose adopted was redolent of the popular engravings of republican battle heroes and behind him Duccio jumped up and imitated his stance, one small hand on his wooden knife hilt.

'Behold,' he crowed. 'The hero of the battle of the marketplace. Have you pen, O nimble Granchio? Then take my likeness down.'

Haintlet took no notice, but one or two of the soldiers of the regiment saw and smiled. Emboldened, Duccio began to strut up and down the top level of the pillory shouting imaginary orders in a fair approximation of Haintlet's nasal voice. Haintlet's men stopped to watch appreciatively and cheered the cavorting boy and his boisterous companions. Eventually, unable to ignore Duccio in the role of gallivanting jester any longer, Haintlet affected to have just noticed him, and addressed him.

'You must leave now with Canon Gatt, all of you, haven't you heard the tale of what happens to disobedient children?'

Franca stood and answered for them, placing herself on the bottom step between him and the *Fraternita*.

'I have another story for you, *cavaliere*. It concerns a man who violated children. For this atrocity God would not pardon him.'

'A heresy,' interjected Granchio morosely, 'but let us hope it is true.'

'He would have been broken on the wheel, but he was a knight…'

'And all know, where the knights go first, God merely follows,' crowed Duccio triumphantly, kissing his yellow flower with mock reverence.

Franca's face was obscured from Gracchus by the hood of her *faldetta*, but he saw Haintlet staring at her with a blank expression. His eyes seemed to be looking straight through her, at a point a hundred yards beyond.

'A decent woman should only appear twice in public; on the day she is married – and buried,' he said to himself finally, as if he had reached some kind of conclusion. And he nodded thoughtfully, and spat on the ground for emphasis. Duccio and Granchio moved protectively to either side of Franca, and Gracchus frowned, reading the mounting tension with concern.

Yet neither the boys, nor Gracchus read the flicker of warning in the knight's eyes until it was too late. He was gazing bovinely at the ground, his lips moving as if he was lost in placid thought or memory, when suddenly from nowhere he struck Franca with his fist on the side of her head, and she crumpled to the ground. In an instant he was straddling her prone form, ripping her *faldetta* free to expose her head. With a merciless absorption, he grasped her hair and slammed her head against the lowest step, pausing only to deal with Duccio, who came up flailing his arms and was dropped by an elbow to the face. The advancing Granchio was immobilised by Haintlet's reptilian glare, and cringed, flinching impotently away from the impact of those cold empty eyes. But his attempted intervention provoked Gracchus, who had been stunned by the speed of the relentless violence, into movement and he sprang to his feet and hobbled down the steps.

Haintlet released his hold of Franca's hair and straightened up slowly, turning the full force of his stare on Gracchus. When Franca moaned, and stirred at his feet, he kicked her limp body without looking at her. His hand on the hilt of his sword, and his eyes never releasing their hold over Gracchus, he backed away into the ranks of his soldiers. Casting upon Gracchus one last look of pure malice, he turned his back, and stalked away across the piazza surrounded by his men.

Gracchus watched him out of the piazza as the *Fraternita* huddled around the forms of Duccio and Franca. When the soldiers were almost gone, Gracchus took a small boy by the elbow and whispered urgently to him to run to Eva's house for assistance. Then he saw that Franca was helped up and checked that Duccio was breathing. Granchio sat alone and desolate on the utmost step of the pillory, his face turned away from his comrades to hide tears of shame, but Gracchus had no words to comfort him, and besides, he had just seen Vanderville striding out from under the portico towards them, dragging a child by the arm. Gatt was huddled with his men around their vehicle heaping imprecations on Vanderville's uncaring shoulders. Gracchus hurried to intercept him.

'Come, come, away with me,' Gracchus murmured urgently to Vanderville, taking his arm insistently. Vanderville frowned as he spotted the distraught knot of children before the pillory, and shaking off Gracchus's hold he covered the ground towards them.

—

Gracchus had been relieved when Eva arrived at the pillory with Don Stecchi narrowly behind her. They recovered Franca into a *kalesh* and took her immediately to the women's hospital to be examined. Vanderville brooded on the pillory steps as Gracchus oversaw this process. His brow was darkened, and the habitual twitch of his brow indicated deep contemplation and imminent violent action. Gracchus's attempts to divert the lieutenant's anger in a practical direction were aided by the need to minister to Duccio's continued groggy infirmity, and they eventually carried him to Gracchus's residence, followed by the entire *Fraternita* staggering in mournful procession, carrying their meagre possessions over their shoulders.

In the garden they laid the injured boy down gently on the garden bench, while Gracchus organised the servants and tried to keep the *Fraternita* from crowding Duccio. The boy's wits were a little disordered, and his face was purpling rapidly, forcing one eye to close, but by the time Don Stecchi knocked gently at the gate, it seemed that the damage was not too grave, and Stecchi conformed that Franca too, was not possessed of any broken bones. Vanderville maintained position at his side until he was sure that the child breathed regularly. Fearing that Vanderville was apt to get out of control, Gracchus tried to maintain a position between him and the garden gate, but the young officer was uncharacteristically silent, and merely busied himself carrying water and linen for Don Stecchi. Gracchus was relieved to see him so biddable, and pushed away the thoughts and plans for dealing with his anger and its consequences that had bubbled to the surface of his fervent mind. There would be time to get Vanderville in hand once the immediate danger had passed.

Granchio had hovered on the fringes of the garden as the patient was administered to, but as Don Stecchi probed in Duccio's mouth for cracked teeth, he inched forward towards his compatriot and stood in silent misery at his side. Finally, as the blood was swabbed from Duccio's face, Granchio found his voice.

'Why isn't Franca here?' he demanded of Don Stecchi in a quavering voice. 'Where have you taken her?'

'She didn't want to join you. She has renounced the *Fraternita delle Forbici*,' said Don Stecchi, wiping his hands on a rag, and not meeting the boy's eye. 'She says she is tired of involvement in your troubles and plots. I have taken her to Donna Mifsud's apartment, and I recommend you stay some distance from those two.'

'She said that?' asked the Granchio, stunned. 'We must go there.'

'I have told you no. She doesn't want to see anyone. And I have given her something to help her sleep.'

There was a gentle clang as the garden gate closed. Gracchus looked up surprised, and then cast his eyes around the garden. Vanderville was nowhere to been seen, and of his coat and sword that had lain on one of the benches there was no sign.

Chapter Sixteen

Gracchus paused at a bollard on the dockside, and Eva waited for him to recover his breath.

'It was good of you to take the children in,' she said. 'I sleep better knowing that they are under your protection, and they are unlikely to get up to more of their mischief under your roof.'

'Mischief? You make them sound like a crew of pirates. I have found them biddable to the point of docility.'

'Speaking of pirates, is that your Rais Murad?' She indicated a colourful figure leaving a ship.

Gracchus peered hopefully at the ship, 'It may be.'

'Does he have Italian?'

'He speaks a little of all languages, and a lot of none I have heard. He is familiar with the *lingua franca* of the slaves though, which is an amalgamation of all the languages of the coasts. He knows Malta well; he says he grew up on the wharves here.'

Eva murmured, 'Valletta is a finishing school for *coglione*, that much is true. Speaking of which, Canon Gatt sent one of his creatures to my house yesterday. He was not admitted, but muttered some nonsense about returning to force entry. I should not have known who sent him if the *Fraternita* had not observed him in council with Gatt and La Baida. This is the second time recently I have had visitors of this nature; I do not know who sent the others. I hope you are keeping our bargain, Baron Pellegrew. Now I have come to know you better I should dislike being forced to expose you.'

Gracchus navigated his way over some ropes lying on the quay, and in the process entangled his stick in their tarry coils.

He regarded its soiled tip ruefully. 'If the inquisitor has taken an interest in your premises, it is through no agency of mine. I note in passing that the surveillance of the grandmaster's men on my own palace has become more pronounced; they no longer bother to conceal their interest and have grown pettily officious and offensive in manner to my staff. It may be that our mutual enemies are preparing to spring a trap. Let us not become divided by forces beyond our control, Donna Eva. As long as my identity remains shrouded, I shall not betray you.'

She nodded. 'For now, our courses seem to be entwined, Baron. Now introduce me to this serpent you have been cultivating, and you will see what manner of ally you have ensnared for yourself.'

As they grew closer to the ship, Gracchus made out Rais Murad more clearly. His shirt was open, under his rich red jacket worn short to the waist, and below this was the extraordinary combination of a puffy yellow kilt twinned with bucket boots straight from the pirate wardrobe of yore. The extraordinary get up, completed by a small delicately curved dirk more akin to an apple knife than a weapon, drew no eyes on the bustling port side. His crew, by contrast, were neatly and unobtrusively equipped, sombre and less drunk than most sailors.

Gracchus was about to hail him in what he considered the approved nautical manner, when the captain turned and, espying them, removed the pipe clenched between his teeth, and beamed a great smile as he stepped forward to embrace Gracchus in the effusive eastern style. Gracchus returned his embrace uncertainly with warmth, while clouds of tobacco smoke enveloped them both.

Breaking the embrace after what seemed an eternity to Gracchus, Murad indicated the moored vessel. 'Behold your *Fortunato*. Fast and equipped to carry six hundred souls.'

'We said nine hundred,' replied Gracchus, his face discarding its assumed congeniality.

'Exactly,' responded the captain, his own smile broad and ingenuous, cracking open his weather tanned face. 'The other ship will arrive today, God willing.'

Gracchus cocked his head critically as he considered this latest form of duplicity. His knowledge of matters nautical was scant, and Murad practiced on him at every turn. He became aware that the captain was leering at him in a peculiar way.

'Ah,' he said, eventually comprehending. 'Rais Murad, may I present Donna Mifsud? Donna Mifsud, this is the captain of my ships.'

There ensued an extraordinary exchange of rehearsed charm that Gracchus bore with fortitude. On Murad's part it was outrageously affected, but Eva played her part perfectly: she was affable without losing an inch of dignity, and somehow delightfully open and charming without the least flirtatiousness. It had been a happy inspiration to invite her. When he saw an opportunity to interrupt these converging flows of courtesies, Gracchus interjected, 'May I leave you both for one moment while I look over the ship?'

Rais Murad shrugged, 'She belongs to you, so if you feel an inspection necessary...' He summoned the ship's master, who took charge of Gracchus, and they commenced a tour above and below decks.

Twenty minutes later, Gracchus came back up the hatch, his face grim, followed by the gesticulating master who appeared upset. Gracchus hauled himself up the ladder to the quarterdeck and bustled up to Murad, who had conducted Eva there, where she was evading his attempts to take her by the hand.

'Rais Murad, this vessel is equipped as a slaver,' he bristled.

'What better for your business, Baron?' replied Murad, and the master beside him turned his face away to stifle a smirk. Murad performed a hugely expansive mannerised gesture, which reflected concern, incredulity, and reassurance in equal measure.

'If you want to transport as many people as possible, as quickly as possible, you choose a vessel equipped to do so.

I don't think they will be so picky as you, they will just be happy to be on their way home.' Then he relented with an appeasing tone, 'Look, I'm sorry Baron, if you think I have erred in judgement in my choice of ships, but think of this, it is only for a short, a very short voyage, that this will endure.'

'The accommodation is completely unacceptable,' insisted Gracchus.

'As for that, we must all suffer our own hardships. Perhaps God sends this travesty of bondage, so that the blessed relief of his mercy may be more profound, after this last reminder of the grief that has been suffered by these poor creatures.'

'It is intolerable,' said Gracchus. 'You must procure more ships.'

Rais Murad removed his pipe from his mouth and sucked his teeth with a smack of his lips. 'It will be expensive, Signore Baron, we have already spoken for two. But if your purse will stand it…'

'Just do it. This vessel is not sufficient in any case, find two more of similar draft.'

Murad turned and barked an order at the master, who disappeared below.

'And Rais…?'

'Signore Baron?'

'It has occurred to me that a man experienced in the trade of humans might consider that greater advantage would accrue to him if he could, instead of transporting his passengers to freedom, submit them to the market.'

Rais Murad nodded slowly, 'Yes, there are those who would do that,' he said, chewing his words thoroughly. 'But not I.'

'I know that I can rely on your integrity,' said Gracchus. 'Because I have obtained a certain document that was in the possession of Bailli von Torring.'

Murad licked his lips, his eyes shining, and his pipe almost forgotten. 'That document would be worth a king's ransom to obtain.'

Gracchus veiled his eyes, and nodded astutely. 'It will be my pleasure to remit it to you, in time,' he said.

'*Usanza*,' replied Murad with a bow. 'I am in your hands *Musaa*. Your turn today, mine, perhaps, tomorrow.'

Afterwards, as they walked along the wharf, Gracchus asked Eva, 'Why does he call me that?'

'It is a joke, I think,' she said thoughtfully. '*Musaa* is the Arabic for Moses, the Hebrew liberator who led his people to freedom out of bondage.'

'You believe he is an Arab then?'

'Oh no. He is a Circassian.'

'Like Franca?'

'Yes. Circassian men are exalted for their beauty. Their imposing bearing, their romantic dress, and their natural dignity of mien, stamp them as very superior. Do you not find him a remarkable-looking man?'

'My perception is somewhat clouded in this respect, I fear. I find him too nearly a true incarnation of perfidy. Do you think Franca, speaking his natural language, might serve me well in negotiations with him?'

Eva shuddered. 'Baron, do not think of it. She told me it was one of her own relations who sold her, and this man is too like her description of those people.'

—

Vanderville had spent most of the day searching for Haintlet without success. Whether it was the warning shadow in his eyes, or simple prejudice, no one would help him to locate the man, and he tramped his way back to the *Auberge* de Bavaria dust covered, frustrated, and footsore in the darkening hour after dusk had fled.

Eva had sent news that she was nursing Franca, and they were not to be disturbed, so on the way to the *auberge* he paused at Gracchus's palazzo to check on the *Fraternita*. The entire assembly of children were squabbling under the bower in the garden where a copper-coloured dog, larger than most of the smaller children, sat solemnly amidst them, regarded by all. Vanderville assessed the dog, and the dog sniffed Vanderville. It was a scrawny beast, as meagre as its new owners.

'Where did you come by him?'

'I traded Granchio's virtue to a knight in exchange for him,' announced Duccio. 'He is coming to collect after the matins bell.' There were jeers from the assembled company, and remarks to the effect that he had been robbed.

'He was outside the church,' declared Granchio, who was sitting a little apart from the others, 'and he followed you because you smell of grease.'

'I had to use the biscuits Barone il Karrakka gave me for the *Fraternita*,' said Duccio, putting a proprietorial arm around the creature. The assembled company groaned as one.

'We can't ask the baron to feed him,' said Granchio. 'You must give him to Franca. He will protect her now that we cannot.'

Duccio cocked his head, the idea of appearing as benefactor and protector seemed to appeal to him, and they agreed that the dog would be delivered as soon as Franca was recovered.

When Vanderville resumed his route to the *auberge*, his intention was to seek out de Rechberg in the refectory, or his apartments if he was not yet able to walk, and ask him to act as his second. De Rechberg would issue the challenge, and set it for the morning, at which time he would meet Haintlet in the Strada San Federico and kill him. Or die trying. But a surprise awaited him at the lobby of the *auberge*.

'The bailli summons you,' said the door porter. Vanderville was about to suggest that he would make an engagement later to see von Torring, but as he opened his mouth to protest, he became aware of two of the porter's subordinates moving into position behind him. He sighed, and followed the grim porter as he led the way to the staircase. The escort melted away as Vanderville was presented at the door of the bailli's apartments.

'I thought the bailli was in the country,' he said to the porter.

'He was,' said the man. 'Until unwelcome events forced him to return.'

Myriad reflections passed through Vanderville's mind. If the bailli had discovered the theft of his documents, he would be in deep water, but he had not been asked for his sword, so he was not under arrest – yet. That made imminent exposure unlikely, so the game was still afoot. The guards were dismissed at the door to von Torring's quarters, and the porter announced him.

'You are aware that practice of duelling is prohibited?' began the bailli with no prelude as Vanderville entered. He made no reply but drew himself up in front of von Torring's desk at attention.

'Even in normal times,' continued the bailli, 'it is wasteful and has dire consequences, but in our present circumstances it threatens the very existence of our order. Fra' Haintlet suffers from duelling mania, but that does not mean you should involve yourself in his brawls.

'The other persons involved have been confined to the *auberge* under arrest while an investigation is launched. Luckily for them their position as officers of the garrison means that an immediate prosecution in unlikely. You, however, are in an anomalous situation. You are not under my orders, but you are a guest. A guest of very doubtful antecedents, I might add. As such, I cannot restrict your movements, although the grandmaster may yet choose to do so. I am however able to withdraw the protection of the *auberge* from you, and I have done so. I ask you to take up your quarters elsewhere from this evening. Before leaving, you will please surrender the arms of the *auberge* that are in your possession to the armoury.'

He looked up sternly. 'And you will be pleased to remove that ridiculous emblem from your coat,' he said, staring at the flowers pinned to Vanderville's breast.

Vanderville was evidently dismissed, and as he left, he reflected that he had best use the evening to clear his own scant possessions out from the *auberge* and take them to the safety of Gracchus's palazzo. If his involvement in de Rechberg's duel had breached bailli's edict and rendered him persona non grata, he shuddered to think what would happen when he embarked on the second duel he so hotly anticipated.

The banishment from the *auberge* would not render his position much less comfortable. He had gleaned all he could of von Seeau's precedents, and indeed was starting to wonder whether that not-much-regretted knight had even been Mayflower. Had he simply jumped to that conclusion because he had expected to find Mayflower in the Maddalene church? Might it not be the case that Mayflower, like himself, had come across the dead knight and departed precipitately in alarm? Or had Mayflower been the agent of von Seeau's destruction?

These disparate reflections were jostling in his mind when a fresh conjecture pushed them aside. If von Seeau was not Mayflower, then the agent might still be present, concealed close by, and all he had to do to complete his mission was discover him and make his own true identity known. The prospect of this revival in his circumstances was a happy one, and he made his way downstairs to the armoury in an improving mood.

The stair was unlit except for a dim light from an oriel window. As he descended, he unbuckled the sword belt that de Rechberg had lent him and bundling the belt about the blade, hung it on a wall hook.

The shadowy *salle d'armes* was deserted, but the door to the armoury stood open, and it was from there that a faint flicker of candlelight shone, announcing the presence of some knight cleaning his arms. He walked in and was greeted by the familiar smell of oiled leather and steel. As he approached the table on which various arms were laid out beside a lamp that held the candle, he heard the door creak and turned to see a form indistinct in the shadows. Vanderville stepped instinctively behind the table and the man stepped forward and his dour face became lit by the glowing light. It was Haintlet, his hateful face sinister in the gloom.

'We will fight if you please,' he said, slapping the blade he carried at his side.

'Certainly,' said Vanderville grimly, struggling to suppress the hatred that threatened to choke off his words. 'Name the place and we will meet in the morning.'

'No,' said the demon. 'Here, now.' He drew his sword and threw the scabbard aside, advancing on Vanderville, the point of his blade flashing in the flickering light.

Vanderville drew back from the table, seizing up the nearest *epée*. The situation was irregular, contrary to all the codes of duelling, and it was unavoidable. This was what he had wanted. Wanted ever since he saw Franca's face, and been preparing himself for, and yet still the knight had caught him off guard and put him at a disadvantage.

He gave more ground in the confined space and then suddenly Haintlet was upon him, navigating the corner of the table with inhuman speed, and forcing Vanderville to react to his initial feint with a clumsy dodge that brought him closer to the table. He grasped the candle lamp and held it upwards and out in his off hand to better see the flicking tip of his opponent's blade. Haintlet's eyes were obscured from him – all the lessons he had suffered emphasized that he must watch the eyes of his opponent rather than the blade, but here there was no choice. The attacks came in from unexpected angles with a rapidity that left him panting as he whirled and leapt to evade the relentless fusillade.

He was losing ground too quickly, and the lamp wasn't helping, serving merely to illuminate his position and unbalance him. Another bewildering flurry of combinations emerging from the shadows stretched his defence, and he realised his only chance was to reduce the angles from which he was exposed. He flung the lamp towards his opponent and had the satisfaction of hearing him grunt. Using the respite bought, he vaulted the table and barged through the door into the *salle d'armes*.

He did not think he could outlive the minute in that black hall, and he continued into the dimly lit corridor leading to the stairs and spun around to take up his guard just in the very nick of time.

Haintlet burst into the passage, his eyes glittering blackly, and advanced with a stamp and a flood of blows. Hopelessly besieged again, Vanderville began to retire with a settled pace towards the staircase, selling each step resolutely. The narrowness of the passage reduced Demon's advantage, and the dark tapestries on the walls muffled the sound of their pants and the clash of steel. But the darkness handicapped him, for although the corridor was lit from the window at the top of the stairs, that served to illuminate Vanderville from behind, leaving his opponent to advance from the dark.

Avoid systemizing, Vanderville reminded himself. His stamp indicates a flare, anticipate it! He began to send forwards the odd reminder of his own angry spirit; but Haintlet pressed so eagerly upon him, that he knew he would soon reach the end of the passage and have nothing but the stair behind him. He might hold him off until then, but he could not touch his superior adversary and the unequal contest would end there with his legs cut out from under him as he was forced to mount the steps backwards.

At last Vanderville's retreating foot nudged the first step, and he uncertainly probed backwards with the other foot, unbalancing himself, and instantaneously Haintlet pounced. Vanderville stumbled backwards, his guard low to protect his legs from the expected thrust, but he had guessed wrong. With a flash of clarity Vanderville knew he was too late to protect himself as Haintlet's advance to lunge took him wide using his speed to render Vanderville's defence inadequate. But the expected blow did not land. In his movement Haintlet's hilt had encountered the tapestry lining the corridor and snagged there. He was slowed enough that Vanderville might take advantage, and abandoning all science, he launched a hurriedly improvised version of De Rechberg's gambit. Swapping his blade between hands he blocked high with his right hand and hurled his lunge at Haintlet's unprotected flank from the steps.

His point ran Haintlet through the belly under his belt, passing so deeply from one side to the other, that the sword was wrenched clean from Vanderville's hand as Haintlet withdrew, staggering a few scant steps before tumbling to his knees with an exasperated grunt. He wrenched out the sword with an irate grimace and clutched at his rent belly with both hands. As it minutely dawned on him that his hurt was mortal, he groaned again, and toppled over to writhe on the floor in a spreading morass of black blood.

Vanderville advanced carefully and retrieved the sword that lay beside the wreck of Haintlet. As his shadow fell over him, Haintlet opened those eyes that had been intent on some private agony and grimaced, his snarl dissolving in a cough.

'Low... low trick you served me,' he panted, 'but you will not have the last word here.'

Vanderville straightened. He felt no compassion for the wounded man; on the contrary, he wished nothing more than for his agony to be prolonged. His only concern was that they would be discovered before Haintlet lost enough blood to make his demise certain.

'The surgeon...' muttered Haintlet. 'There is a surgeon at the hospital. Send for him. And...' he swallowed uncomfortably, seeing the look in Vanderville's eyes. 'A priest then. I must be shrived.'

'You will have neither.'

Haintlet waved the statement away. 'Unlucky...' he murmured indistinctly, 'so damned unlucky, always...' When his hand was removed from his belly, more of his life blood surged forth in an ominous momentum. 'The *meretrice* Donna Mifsud,' he mumbled, blood oozing from his mouth, and his voice growing weaker still. 'Your patron, your mentor – a strange thing for a gentleman to have a whore as a patron – is not what she...'

His spirit and voice were fading fast, and Vanderville knelt in the sordid puddle to catch his whisper. Haintlet suddenly grabbed a handful of Vanderville's shirt front and pulled him close as he tried to form words, but nothing came from his blood-flecked lips, and he failed to utter whatever threat he intended. Vanderville pried loose his red-stained fingers and rose, stepping away adroitly. As he had anticipated, Haintlet's other hand had reached inside his coat and drawn out a long thin knife, which glistened darkly in the gloom. It flopped pathetically over his breast; the strength to brandish it had deserted him. 'Not… like this,' he whispered to himself. 'Not to me. Not like this.'

His strength almost gone, Haintlet's despairing glassy eyes gleamed with the last drops of hate he could muster, and he clasped the knife with both trembling hands.

Vanderville snorted. 'What are you going to do with that now. Throw it?'

As what must surely have been the final convulsion overtook him, Haintlet lashed out with all he could muster of his former vitality and stabbed Vanderville through the foot. The blade passed through his shoe and snapped off on the stone floor. Vanderville yelped in shock and raised his own weapon, but it was too late. The thrashing strike had used the last of Haintlet's spirit, and his head fell back exhausted on the flagstones, his spasming throat issuing the last staccato rattle.

Chapter Seventeen

When the *Fraternita* declared a prejudice against sleeping indoors Gracchus had ordered the disapproving servants to strip the linen cupboards to provide cover for them. The unwelcome sheets and blankets were now bundled in crannies of his garden, while the trees were gaily festooned with the *Fraternita*'s belongings, lending the bower the air of a gypsy encampment.

During the night Gracchus's sleep had been broken by a disturbance in the garden, and he had crept to the window to witness a confrontation between the leaders of the *Fraternita*. The moon illuminated the two sitting by the fountain away from where the others slept in little still bundles. It appeared that Granchio was baiting Duccio who hissed indignantly, 'What would you know of it? What's the use of you being in love with anyone?'

'What is the use of being in love with one of your sisters?' hissed Granchio.

They shoved each other with increasing vigour, and Duccio shook Granchio till his teeth rattled, 'Accursed *karrakka*. You disgusting misbegotten son of a *banavolja*. Dare to repeat that.'

'I repeat – you are in love with Franca, though you pretend not to realise it! You wish to lie with her, just as the knights do, and you are no better than them. Your shame lowers you and dishonours the *Fraternita delle Forbici*.'

They continued wrestling and it ended, naturally, with Granchio's defeat, his physical resources being so much inferior. Duccio hurled him away towards the corner of the fountain.

'You are all talk and noisy clacking claws, but when it comes to the business of war, you are useless. Useless like your precious *Fraternita*. We cannot even protect our friends, what use are the head-woven castles you spend your days on?'

He stalked off, and Granchio waited until his friend was gone, then he crawled under the bushes, took his head in his hands, and wept. Gracchus listened to the deep sobbing, thought better of speaking, and softly closed the pane to.

In the morning he went to wake the children, who had talked late, and slept long. 'Granchio?' he called quietly, but there was no answer. He moved gently to the bushes and peered inside. The child was curled up asleep in a flattened pile of leaves, like a cat in its bower, his deformed hands clutching his waistcoat around him. Gracchus pulled his head away without waking him.

He had spent much of the previous evening escorting the children into the kitchen to be fed, and now the work recommenced afresh for breakfast. Cook had refused admission entirely until threatened by dismissal, and even then, she would only allow two of the children at a time inside under escort. She banged her pans theatrically as she worked and sniffed disapprovingly as Gracchus teased information and stories from the children whilst they sucked noisily at bowls of broth. Each was reticent about their own origins, but less cagey about those of the others and he began to piece their pathetic stories together.

When he woke and presented himself with no trace of his lonely night, Granchio proved informative regarding Duccio's precedents. The boy's father had died when they were plucking figs from a tree. Duccio fell from the ladder and landed on his father, breaking his neck. He was five years old at the time, and his mother could no longer bear to have him around, and so she sold him to the man who came round selling trinkets to the country girls. He was then exchanged for a drinks bill, and that is how he came to Valletta where he escaped his master and took to the piazza.

'What about treating Granchio at the hospital?' Gracchus asked Duccio, as that worthy took his turn in the kitchen. 'It seems to me that of all the things the Knights have accomplished here, the hospital is the greatest. Is there nothing they can do for him there?'

Duccio was looking in the kitchen gutter for scraps. He picked up a dusty apple core and examined it speculatively before answering. 'No boys under the age of seven may be admitted to the Hospital for treatment.' He took a bite of the apple and grimaced, 'Nobody knows how old Granchio is, and since he has not bothered increasing his size in harness with his years, they will not take him.'

'His age is not recorded anywhere?' probed Gracchus. 'Parish records for example?'

'No, he was a foundling. If he were a slave, it would be different, because younger ones are worth more.'

Gracchus watched the boy self-reliantly scavenging through the kitchen bins and considered their future dourly. He looked out of the window at the other children again. Washed clothes hung from the trailing vines. They had discovered the courtyard animals of the cook and two boys had removed some of the rabbits from a hutch and were discussing their qualities.

'Your rabbit is a wizard.'

'Bah, who wants rabbits fouled by black magic, sired by Il Nero.'

'He fires fire-tipped arrows from his *cazzo*.'

Gracchus smiled contentedly. He had found that the children accepted him effortlessly. His clumsiness and ungainly form may have provoked their sympathy, and when he was not close by, they called him *Il Karrakka*, which the cook told him reluctantly meant an unwieldy person. He realised that obsolete, near crippled as he was, they considered him one of their own, except as far as his great wealth indicated that he was *Il-Habba tas-Sultan* – in the grandmaster's pay. He sighed, it was the morning of the grandmaster's poetry party, and he was to depart Valletta in company with the grandmaster that morning, but he had much to accomplish first. He left the garden key with Granchio, ordered him to detain Vanderville should he return, and went out on his business.

—

Vanderville had left the Bavarian *auberge* with an affected nonchalance, made painful by regret, and by the wound in his foot, which he had summarily dealt with by changing his blood-soaked stocking for a handkerchief. His personal effects he had abandoned, wanting to put as much distance between the *auberge* and himself as possible before Haintlet's body was discovered. Passing the door porters with a smiling civility they did not return, he resolved to seek refuge with Donna Eva. He persuaded himself that this stratagem was owed to the relative nearness of Strada della Ficara, but an unwelcome pricking of his conscience suggested that he was not yet prepared to reveal the result of his sanguine evening's work to a doubtless disapproving Gracchus.

As he approached her house, he considered his situation. It was undoubtably grave. To kill a knight in a regular duel was a serious matter, but to do so in a brawl, unwitnessed, and the combat unsanctioned by the presence of seconds to ensure due process, could have no consequence but his immediate arrest. His only recourse was denial, for after all, was it not true that the *Auberge* de Bavaria had been losing knights at an unfortunate rate over the past weeks? And had he not been forbidden the *auberge*? Could he hope that Haintlet's demise might be chalked up to the elusive murderer?

It seemed unlikely that his hopes would prove well-founded. Haintlet's mortal wound was a sword thrust, which was in stark variance to the previous two deaths by strangulation. It seemed inevitable to him that eventually the *auberge* would connect him with the mess in their armoury, and when they did so, he could expect no quarter. Under the circumstances he was grateful that he had not returned his borrowed sword as instructed by the bailli.

He shelved these considerations as he arrived at Donna Eva's door, and remembered after knocking that these premises were also under embargo for the duration of Franca's recovery. In the event, despite his trepidation, on seeing he was wounded Eva did not stand on ceremony, and it transpired that she had dispatched Franca to her bolthole, with strict orders to Stecchi to watch over her. Considering this, Vanderville reflected that she was probably right. With Haintlet out of the way, the apartment was as secure a place as another. The dog would watch her, and it was quieter than Strada della Ficara.

Seeing his limp, she conducted him without fuss to the couch in the window and made him comfortable. It was too late to call again for the ministrations of Don Stecchi, and so his presence and explanations were deferred until the morning. She brought water to wash his foot and departed with his damaged boot allowing herself the mildest comment on his tendency to turn up at strange hours and in parlous condition.

The morning necessarily entailed explanations, and he was relieved to find that Eva's primary concern was to have him conveyed to Gracchus's residence. She proposed that they wait for Duccio's morning call, before despatching him to requisition Gracchus's *kalesh*. The news of his nocturnal combat she met with equanimity, neither exulting, nor regretting in Haintlet's fall. Instead, she restricted herself to observing, 'The baron's concern for the lives of the Bavarians does not seem to have reached your ears. Never mind, since you are forced to stay here until Duccio has breakfasted to his content, we may as well continue your education. He will help Don Stecchi with the pigeons later, so we can arrange with him to call here and look at your foot.' She began examining his wound, which had responded well to the night air.

'Donna Eva, there is something I must ask you.'

'Do concentrate, Vanderville. You must learn to cultivate your conversation better. Direct questioning is obscene.

Approach your subject laterally, apply wit. Do not bleed on the floor if you can possibly help it.'

'You must know my objective in coming here to Valletta.'

'It is not necessary for you to tell me. You may put me and our charges in danger. Perhaps it is better you keep it to yourself. Now, deportment. Do try to stand less like a soldier. A lady does not like to be made to feel like a rampart you are about to storm.'

'I beg your pardon, Donna Eva, my mind is ill-arraigned today. I am thinking of those who oppose the rule of the knights. It seems to me that there are those would welcome the arrival of the French.' He paused significantly, before unfurling Vassallo's code phrase. 'Are you one of them?'

She looked at him peculiarly. 'Oh very well. I am not unaware that you have attempted to approach me on this subject before, and I was reluctant to engage. However, since despite your hot-headed approach, you have after all, done some good, I feel that I can do you some trifling favour in return. Not least because you may be leaving us soon. You seek to advance the cause of your masters in France, I have something that will help you.'

She went to the bureau that stood in her room, and unlocked it with a key she held on a ribbon around her neck. She withdrew a folder with a wry smile, and Vanderville's heart leapt. So here was Mayflower after all. Of course, he thought, it made perfect sense. Her position allowed her extensive social contact with the knights and provided the opportunity to observe and communicate without fear of suspicion being cast on her movements. It was a miracle he had not made the connection earlier. She had been at the Maddalene complex the morning of his arrival assisting in the hospital with Franca and Stecchi, and doubtless had taken a moment to slip into the church by means of the connecting passage to meet Vassallo. It was all so neat, and doubtless Gracchus was correct that, finding von Seeau unexpectedly present in the church, and perhaps offered insult or injury, she had helped him into the next life.

She turned towards him, and he surveyed her closely. Were these hands those of a murderer? It seemed unlikely, and yet she was robust, and ferocious in her defence of her charges. It was possible to imagine her in the pew behind the knight, throwing a cord around his neck. She began to open the folder as she walked towards him and then she paused, and a look of bafflement crossed her face, and she turned it in her hands, and frowned. Vanderville limped across the space between them and peered inside the folder. It was empty.

—

The slave prison was a lofty quadrangular building overlooking the harbour, neatly bracketed by magazines and monastic buildings, the twin emblems of the Order's business. Gracchus looked up at the prison gates with dislike and settled himself down on the hump of the aqueduct that carried water under its walls. He needed to compose his thoughts before entering, for entering the *bagnio* morally exhausted him. The squalor and concentrated misery of the incarcerated people packed together in hammocks like tiers of silkworms waiting to hatch, the fetid atmosphere and casual brutality of the *carcerieri* who guarded the prisoners appalled him. The *carcerieri* on the gate studiously ignored him, they were under orders to do so.

Despite his repeated visits, he felt a certain furtiveness. Today he carried a great deal of coin about him to dispense to the Prodomo, the knight who served as prison governor and he didn't want to be enticed into conversation, befriended, or even observed. Mercifully, the spies of the grandmaster who habitually dogged his movements had departed that morning, doubtless to carry news of the *Fraternita*'s adoption at his place of residence, but they would be back soon enough, carrying fresh trouble with them. He sighed heavily, and settled down to wait for the slaves to leave for the day, so that he might enter unimpeded, and drew his shawl around his head as armour against the curious, and as he did so, the heavy bags concealed in it clinked.

'Good day to you Baron Pellegrew,' came a voice, and he looked up with a jump, into the face and courteous smile of Inquisitor Carpegna. 'I would know you anywhere in your curious disguise,' he said cheerfully. 'Are you here to make a purchase?'

Gracchus turned a baleful eye on him. 'I have yet to grow so degraded as to contribute to the debasement of my fellow beings.'

'Forgive my curiosity – it is a bad habit I know. I'm naturally inquisitive – it goes with the job!' His eyes lit up as he said it, and Gracchus wondered wearily how many times he had made the joke.

'But I am disturbing you. You are waiting for your secretary perhaps?'

'Not at all,' replied Gracchus, making a supreme effort to affect amiability. 'He waits on His Eminence the grandmaster tonight at San Antonio and must prepare his repertoire. I myself am here to dispense alms. The Prodomo expects me.'

Carpegna gave a wry grimace. 'When dispensing charity, it is invariably the case that one must moisten the crown of the tree, when it is the roots that need water. The crown, already sufficiently provided for by the rain, hardly registers the surfeit you provide but absorbs it nonetheless whereas the roots, deprived by the crown from their means of sustenance, wither unhindered.'

'A tragedy for the roots, but also for the tree, I suppose,' offered Gracchus with a touch of sourness. His liking for lengthy metaphors was limited to those of his own invention, and he suspected that Carpegna was about to lecture him.

'Perhaps,' said Carpegna. 'In time.'

'And them?' asked Gracchus, indicating the Muslim slaves in their topknots, who had begun their exodus from the *bagnio*.

'It is the nature of things. We do not deny them the salvation of the Church. And while they consider the nature of their heresy – it isn't really even a heresy, so is outside my ward – we do what we can, or rather His Eminence does, to alleviate their lot. They have a mosque where they can pray according to their creed. Much good may it do them,' he laughed, and allowed himself a benign smile at the dome of St John, which loomed across the roof tops at them.

'The wretched cease to turn towards heaven when they find themselves forsaken upon earth.'

Carpegna sighed, and meditated, 'Such suffering – having the means at one's disposal to end so much misery would be a wonderful thing.'

Gracchus expressed surprise at something that verged on tolerance, 'Do you suggest that the remission of evil is not the business of the Church?'

'You have the prejudices of the benighted north Gracchus. You need to be enlightened if you will forgive me the pun. We are not savages, we men of the inquisition. Nor is this Convent mired in the dark ages despite our feudal splendour. It is just that the abhorrence of slavery is an issue so often revisited and to such trivial effect that it is an injustice generally ignored, like an old family dog to which one accords a perfunctory pat from time to time. Let us consider the pat as given. Now we can talk of something which amuses us both.'

Carpegna's candour and natural likeability won through, and Gracchus almost warmed to him. But one can never trust an inquisitor, he reminded himself, like a Jesuit there was always another level of deceit.

As if to confirm this Carpegna, apparently carelessly, inquired, 'The decision of the Grand Council tomorrow still weighs in the balance I believe?'

Gracchus spread his hands expansively, 'I am afraid the equilibrium has been upset. All of the signs are that Bailli von Torring has withdrawn his support for my project.'

Carpegna bobbed his head sympathetically. 'You must not fret, Gracchus, you have achieved a great deal here. No one has ever pushed the council so far so quickly before. It is unprecedented, and if you have fallen at the ultimate step, you may console yourself that we are in the middle of a great crisis here that draws everyone's attention away from more worthy matters. Do not blame yourself.'

'You called me Gracchus.'

'Did I?' replied Carpegna lightly. 'A slip of the tongue. I must have overheard your secretary calling you that. A nickname perhaps?'

News, thought Gracchus, travels swiftly from Rome. This was a fresh complication, but was it yet another danger?

Carpegna moved blithely on. 'To echo the Bailli von Torring, I don't know why you persist in your project. Bonaparte is in the offing, and when he takes Malta...'

'If,' said Gracchus. 'If he takes Malta.'

'When,' reasserted Carpegna. 'He will abolish the institution of slavery. Is that not the stated intent of the Republic in those territories it appropriates?'

'I believe so,' said Gracchus, 'but two things stand in the way. First, I do not trust Bonaparte. He does not see himself as the blind instrument of the Republic anymore, nor does he bind himself by their designs or laws. And secondly, if these people are freed by the French, what will become of them? In Italy I saw how Bonaparte closed the convents. Everything, the nursing hospitals, the orphanages – the full apparatus of the Church state, was swallowed to support the Republic's expansionism. It will be the same in Malta, the slaves will be set at liberty to starve on the wharves, and the alternative which they will find themselves unable to refuse, will be to enlist in, and be consumed by, General Bonaparte's lumbering military colossus.

'Any true scheme of emancipation, poor though it may be, must include funds to feed and repatriate these unfortunates.' He shook his head with irritation, the inquisitor was drawing him into unwanted confidences. 'Anyway, what about you, Monsignor? What will you do when Bonaparte expels your

Order from the island? The dissolution of the Holy Office has been the unvarying policy of the Republic wherever their forces prevail.'

'That is true alas,' said Carpegna sadly. 'I daresay I will be permitted to depart for the mainland unmolested. It was my intention to go to Rome soon anyway. I will carry with me evidence of a terrible conspiracy hatched on this island. The Holy Father is awaiting my final proofs before he acts against the liberal sect who have infected the Order. I shall not conceal from you that such a spiritual triumph will bring strong temporal rewards. You will take it on trust that I desire these rewards, and my advancement to a post close to the seat of His Holiness, not as an end in themselves, but to strengthen the Church and reinforce its endeavours to sustain the faith.'

'I believe you,' sighed Gracchus. 'I don't know why. But forgive me, do you believe you have time to both collect these proofs, and take ship from Malta before Bonaparte arrives?'

Carpegna smiled. 'All that is necessary to stiffen His Holiness's resolve is a revelation *en flagrante*, that certain members of the conspiracy be surprised at their foul devotions, and you have apprised me that they will be meeting tonight. Now I have only to find out where.'

'I?' said Gracchus astonished.

'I am afraid so. You let slip that your secretary will leave Valletta for San Antonio imminently. The Bailli Torring is also absent from Valletta. His men have been observed preparing his suite for departure. The two men are antithetical in all things except their passion for the fraternal societies. It is necessary that the adepts meet to plot their response to the imminent arrival of Bonaparte's armada. Therefore, the meeting will occur today.'

'I see,' said Gracchus, mulling this fresh anxiety, and discounting it as another of Carpegna's nonsenses. He was about to reveal to the inquisitor that von Hompesch's plans were likely to reveal nothing more sinister than a poetry party. But, he reflected, Carpegna would not be swayed by reason. Charming, capable, and astute as he was, he was blinded by his fanatical belief in his own infallibility, never more so than when directed at his pet fiends, the long-extinguished cult of the Illumines, and their successors, the Minerves. Let him go to the party at San Antonio and receive his rude awakening in the fullness of time, he thought. It served his purposes to have the inquisitor's attention focussed outside of Valletta.

'The grandmaster is aware of the prevalence of fraternal societies on the island. He is allowing them to prosper but denies their existence. The Holy Father has been informed. He is outraged and yet he is willing to forgive the culprits should they repent. As for myself, I have received orders to demand the immediate termination of these abominations. Those who dare resist or hinder the pope's justified demand will be excommunicated.'

'It is necessary for your purposes that the secret societies are all portrayed in the most diabolical manner. Are the accusations not more horrible than the truth, reflecting as they do the twisted, nay perverted imaginations of the accusers? The desperate search for imagined infernal plots and conspiracies is nothing more than a perversion of the eschatological perspective. The desire to seek self-importance and the justification of one's miserable and insignificant existence through the fantasy that one is an instrument of divine retribution and a possessor of arcane knowledge.

'I wonder,' he continued, choosing his words carefully, 'are there not other sins, graver sins, rife among the knights that deserve correction more?'

'It will come as no surprise to you that I am entirely aware of the other activities of certain of the knights, but these gross failures of the flesh I must consider commonplace sins compared to Freemasonry, which is akin to heresy. If I were in the business of hearing and acting on confessions, I would have all the knights in the Convent on their knees doing Hail Marys constantly. But I am not, I am here for a sole purpose – to protect the integrity of the Catholic faith.'

Gracchus bowed his head thoughtfully. Although Carpegna was made sinister by virtue of his position, it seemed he was not interested in Gracchus's own endeavours on the island in a moral sense, nor did he appear concerned by Gracchus's deceptions. He merely wanted to expel the Freemasons and win a promotion from Rome. Could he be trusted as an unlikely ally?

'Don't worry about your young friend, Baron. I know he is innocent of intrigue. Of this one at least,' laughed Carpegna. 'He is safe from me, although the grandmaster will not be best pleased to have been made a fool of by a creature of Bonaparte.'

'He will look after himself,' said Gracchus, with an assurance he did not fully feel. 'But you didn't tell me your own business in the *bagnio*?' said Gracchus, as Carpegna prepared to depart.

'Mine? Just the sordid business of my trade I am afraid,' he smiled wanly. 'The heathen slaves work a fine trade in love potions and spells. We have recently had to clap in irons members of a conspiracy to harvest and sell flowers as love charms. Fortunately for me the dormitories here abound with informers. Nobody inside could claim to have a friend, on the contrary, all are enemies of each other, and traitors each and every one, so it is easy enough to round them up. Their collaborators on the outside are a harder nut to crack.' He shrugged. 'But we'll get them soon, we always do. I think I know now who is at the bottom of it.'

Vanderville found Gracchus walking on the ramparts below Sant' Elmo on the wall known as St Christopher's. He caught him up and hobbled along besides him for a while, until forced to rest. His bandaged foot was painful, but Stecchi had said it would not prove grave unless the blade had been poisoned. He doubtless meant the remark light-heartedly, but Vanderville, whose precipitous escape from the *auberge* had rendered him destitute of his remaining clothes and customary good spirits, had despondently reflected that such malevolence was not beyond *Cavaliere* Haintlet.

It was windy and there were few other promenaders, the only activity being the Order's artillerymen putting their guns in order, and neither spoke until Gracchus halted, returned to where Vanderville sat, and sighed portentously. He leant on the wall and looked out over the harbour.

'Ill news from the *Auberge* de Bavaria, I am told.'

'Ah, Gracchus. You can chalk that one up to me. An affair of honour,' said Vanderville unhappily.

'What? Are you giving me to understand that in addition to the maniac stalking the Knights, you are conducting your own private campaign of genocide? This is scarcely helpful, Vanderville. What was the offence given? No, wait, don't answer that, I can think of half a dozen myself easily.' He laughed bitterly. 'I doubt the Bailli von Torring's mood will be improved by this news. You had better ensnare the grandmaster with your verse or we are finished here. They will dangle us from the ramparts, and you will watch your comrades' ships sail in from the end of the hangman's rope.'

'There is something else,' said Vanderville reluctantly, and Gracchus emitted a long-suffering sigh as the events at Eva's house were related to him. 'The curious thing is,' continued Vanderville, 'it appears that although she had the means to supply the details Mayflower had offered, Donna Eva herself has not been in touch with anyone. She insists, and I believe her, that the identity of Mayflower is unknown to her, and her possession of similar documents must perforce be a coincidence.'

'If she does not know when her documents were lost, then she is of no use in uncovering your mysterious spy. If, indeed, she ever possessed these alleged papers. No, forget Mayflower, Vanderville, that blossom has withered long ago. Your attentions would be better employed in keeping our skins in one piece.

'What is that?' asked Gracchus, peering at Vanderville's lapel.

'Franca gave it to me.'

'Brilliant. If the knights aren't already annoyed enough with you over murdering one of their own, you mock them with this emblem. Where is she now?'

'Donna Eva is keeping her indoors. But look here, Gracchus, you must admit that at least this rock is a better place for one less Haintlet, and I was not seen. There is nothing to directly connect me to the death.' Gracchus ignored him and he tried again. 'They told me at your palace that your spirits were oppressed, and you had come to walk in the salt air.'

Gracchus nodded assent; his gaze was on Vittoriosa.

'Do not think, Vanderville, that I care overmuch about a skewered knight more or less. My spirits are obliged to suffer periodically from the accumulated mass of senseless deaths, rather than any small addition to their number. I still feel the accusing eyes of those who suffered on the guillotine, you know.

'They seem so pointless now; even at the time they seemed superfluous, an indulgence of vengeance on the unthinking rich; those unfortunates born to a life of ridiculous luxury and unfeeling self-indulgence. It was like sending household pets to the abattoir. They were bewildered, and knew nothing, learnt nothing, of the reasons for which they were sacrificed.'

The gunners began noisily chipping rust from their balls with lump hammers and placing them in roses besides the cannon. Others were arranging completed rounds under canvas covers beside each gun, and they moved away from the ringing of the hammers.

'I feel the gaze of the dead on me still,' repeated Gracchus. 'Mutely imploring that their death should have signified something. And you know what? It was nothing, it was meaningless and banal. A commonplace horror, too inconsequent to be considered overmuch, and too grubby to stand long contemplation. And the bill of all that blood, did it achieve anything? Mean anything at all? It just schooled the revolutionaries in how to kill without remorse, a lesson they resolutely applied to their own in an endless eruption of gore. And now they are coming here.'

Vanderville held his peace, finding the waters too deep for him to essay a foot, and followed Gracchus's gaze across the Grand Harbour. His eye was caught by a stern posture amidst the life and colour of the boats plying their ceaseless routes across the main.

'Look, there by the mole,' he said. 'No, the *mole* Gracchus, not the crab buoys.'

Gracchus followed his pointing finger. 'So. Carpegna has come to Valletta. Good, he has taken the bait, and brought his minions too.'

'Gracchus,' said Vanderville gently. 'Don Stecchi said you have been to the slave *bagnio* again – are you planning to break those people out of the prison?'

'Something like that, yes,' answered Gracchus, avoiding Vanderville's eye.

'I am worried for you,' said Vanderville. 'Seriously worried. This is the most powerful fortress, the most secure, in Christendom. Never mind the various police forces and the grandmaster's guard, they also have their own private army, and a navy too!

'Furthermore, they are prepared for an imminent attack, they are at their highest possible level of alertness and preparation for war. What makes you think you can just waltz out of here with nine hundred people? What will you do? Tuck them under your *faldetta*?'

'It's not a bad idea,' mused Gracchus with a wilful grin.

'You are maddening at times, Gracchus. You will get us both killed,' said Vanderville with a shake of his head. 'You forget this is an island surrounded by thousands of leagues of sea. There is no way off.'

'And yet *you* made your way in, no?'

Chapter Eighteen

Finding his wound rendered him equally unsuited to boot or stirrup, Vanderville used the last of the funds he had squeezed from an increasingly parsimonious Gracchus to hire a *kalesh*. It bore him out under the great fortified gates of Valletta, surrounded by an imposing mass of modern and well-constructed ditches, bastions, redoubts, ravelins, and counterscarp galleries. They were impressive, but there were so many fortifications here, and around the grand harbour, that Vanderville assessed bringing them to a proper state of defence would require forty thousand armed men, and he had not seen a tenth of that number under arms. He filed this information mentally, and composed himself as the *kalesh* took the road to the country residence of the grandmaster at San Antonio.

As he rattled along in unaccustomed luxury, he patted the satchel that held his unloved poetry books to reassure himself once more that all was ready for the recital and settled himself down to watch the passing view. Having passed an extent of brown, treeless, rather hilly country intersected by thousands of stone walls which divided and sustained little enclosures formed like terraces, he saw little to justify Gracchus's description of St Antonio as an oasis. The whole country was studded with churches and small windowless dwellings raised on the barren rock, with scarce a tree to enliven the dusky-tinted view, which recalled to him nothing so much as a great cemetery, subdivided into family portions. He decided to take a nap.

Sleep would not come. His mind kept dragging his thoughts back to Mayflower and his conversation with Eva. She had been adamant that she was not Mayflower, and that she had no knowledge of Vassallo or any part in a clandestine communication. Her journals contained notes kept on the inclinations of the various knights she encountered merely as an aide memoir on their tastes and preferences and as kind of insurance should she ever require a favour. She had professed ignorance of when the journals had been abstracted from their hiding place, not having consulted them for, oh, ages. He frowned to himself, who could have taken them? One of the *Fraternita*? Don Stecchi? Or even her rival La Baida? Eva had been evasive, her only suggestion was that she had been visited recently by the inquisitor's men, who interviewed her about the herbal processes she conducted with Don Stecchi. They had warned her about this, and while she had protested the innocence of her activity, one of them had half-heartedly searched the house.

Eventually he must have slept, because the braying of the mule announced his arrival, waking him from slumber. He still felt unequal to company, and on descending from the *kalesh*, his foot had protested most volubly, so he skirted the house and limped into the seclusion of a terraced rose garden adjoined to the imposing residence by a rank of French windows.

Gracchus was there, walking alone, and cradling a small velvet box in his hand.

'What is that?' asked Vanderville, waving his hat in greeting.

Gracchus opened the box to show him. It contained the small crystal and bronze cross he had displayed to such effect in the alleyway to stop the duel.

'A gift from the grandmaster,' he explained. 'I have been informed I shall be admitted to the Order as a lay member, and he returned my cross.'

Vanderville sat on a bench and rubbed his foot dolefully. 'How splendid. Does this entail our deliverance from the noose?'

Gracchus recalled sourly how the grandmaster had concluded the council by saying, 'I would like to do something for you, Pellegrew. There is no time for a proper investiture, but until that can be organised, I would like you to accept this.' It was, he supposed, a recognition that his humane endeavours were worthy of the Hospitaller tradition in its less martial aspect.

'I fear not. If anything, this honour merely places me more firmly at the mercy of von Hompesch's caprice. Your position is unaltered, anything short of a poetic triumph today, and your enemies on the council will be emboldened to move against you.'

Vanderville swallowed awkwardly. The subject of his recital was one he preferred to avoid. His nerves were already invoked in his stomach.

'I should prefer not to be hanged,' he muttered, 'everything is in hand.'

'Seeing you on the gallows would be a minor compensation for this day's ill work,' said Gracchus glumly.

'Trouble in the council?' asked Vanderville sympathetically, sitting on a planter tub to take the weight from his complaining foot.

'There is a squadron of French ships off Gozo. A mere squadron! The French consul was with the grandmaster today, allaying his panic by explaining that the French armada is on its way south, and these few vessels are merely requesting watering privileges. The grandmaster is supposed to permit them to enter one at a time to take on fresh water, but he is prevaricating, afraid of a *coup de main*. There are also some suspicious Greek merchant vessels that moored this morning. You wouldn't know anything about that, would you?'

Vanderville rubbed his chin thoughtfully. 'So, it is to be Egypt then after all.' The prospect excited him immeasurably. The army had been ablaze with rumour for months, and the possibility of seeing the camel and other wonders of a strange distant land appealed to him.

Gracchus nodded thoughtfully. 'The Council discussed the destiny of the Order, and drew up a roster of those knights available for the defence of the island. Three of the baillis spoke in favour of the French for one reason or another. The Portuguese *langue* is as suspect as the Italian – more than half of the council in fact are of dubious loyalty to the Order, but the grandmaster prevailed.'

'The Order will fight, then,' Vanderville said quietly.

'I fear so. The forces for the defence of the islands are to be drawn from the mere two hundred knights present in the Convent, fifty of whom are either too old or too infirm for active service. Responsibility was parcelled out for the various important posts of defence. Naturally, they did not describe the fortifications or their garrisons in detail, but it appears that the forts are modern, strong, and well-armed with deep magazines. The *glacis* are mined by a network of tunnels and should anyone attempt to traverse them they can be blown one by one.'

Vanderville nodded his thanks. If he could join the French fleet, the intelligence would serve him well, and perhaps compensate to some degree for his failure to secure Mayflower's briefing notes.

'There is something else,' Gracchus spread his hands. 'De Rechberg arrived here just before you, looking wretched. He, and the Bavarians have stood aloof from me so far. His manner leads me to suspect that they wish us, or you at least, ill. I have taken steps to prevent their malice, but should I not succeed, you had better prepare for the worst.'

–

The social reception that followed the conclusion of council business was being held in a suite of saloons fitted up in a sparse style. But the ceilings were high, making them cool and agreeable, and servants were constantly employed in sprinkling water on the floors to preserve the air in a temperate state.

The gentlemen present were almost all knights and were lolling upon ponderous armchairs or lounging about the apartments in groups. The Bavarians pointedly ignored Vanderville, and when he limped up to de Rechberg, the knight's manner and reception was cool.

'You have heard the news? Fra' Haintlet will be buried tomorrow,' said de Rechberg.

'I see,' said Vanderville. There was an awkward pause, and Vanderville shifted uncomfortably to his stronger foot.

'What happened to you?' asked de Rechberg, staring pointedly at Vanderville's boot, which bulged where it concealed bandages.

'A turned ankle running for my *kalesh*. Was there anything unusual about his death?'

De Rechberg shook his head. 'Not that I saw. It was violent, a little squalid and meaningless, like so much of his life. Is this connected to the baron's belief that the Bavarians are eliminating their own? If so, I can assure you he is in error.' He sighed and glanced furtively over his shoulder at his bailli.

'The *auberge* are, on the whole, against *you*, whom they suspect of murdering one of our own. Most of them are, as I suspect you know, Minerves, and Haintlet, like von Seeau was excluded from that society on grounds of his foul personal immorality. Yet even without those binding bonds of the brethren, we Bavarians are an unforgiving lot. Fraternity and all that. There will be a meeting held to determine your culpability.'

'You fought him yourself—'

'Yes, Haintlet was an unpleasant excuse for a man, and undeserving of his cowl. Yet as you know, there is a difference between a duel and a brawl. Haintlet was found with a bloody knife in his hand, so they are looking for a wounded man.' He glanced at Vanderville's boots again. 'When they notice *that*, they will be certain, and then they will come for you. So I tell you as a friend that they will decide against you. If you have a place to run to, run. If you can hide, hide. The Convent is about to become very dangerous for you.'

Before Vanderville could do more than gape as he processed this warning, the grandmaster bustled up to them and de Rechberg excused himself with a nod to Vanderville that possessed an ominous finality.

Hompesch was without his robes of state and his meagre frame was draped in a simple frock coat. He noticed Vanderville's anxious air and survey of his person and explained graciously.

'The legend of a lodge meeting means that we can meet here as equals without any ceremonial burden of precedence and so on. No bowing and scraping means we get through business more quickly, and before the poetry party we had a lot to get through upstairs.'

'Is the lodge meeting widely known then?' asked Vanderville with surprise, thinking about Carpegna's obsession with masonic rites.

'Membership in a lodge is not solely concerned with being in the centre of the intellectual avant-garde. It is about developing international channels of communication as much as it is about philosophy or sociological theorising. The Church disapproves, but I am master here.

'In any case, this party is arranged for lovers of avant-garde poetry, and is not a meeting of the Minerves, nor any conspiracy against the Church, although naturally many of the individuals present belong to one or other of the societies. So, as you can see, we are broadminded here, so do not feel you have to omit any of your spicier compositions.' The grandmaster licked his lips encouragingly.

Vanderville nodded approvingly, feeling on firmer ground. He had prepared a rendition of some of Tirdflingen's compatriots' material just in case, yet after de Rechberg's warning his mind was turning away from poetry. His free movement in Valletta was already difficult, how could he survive with the

Bavarians hunting him? At least it appeared that the Bavarians had not shared their misgivings with the rest of the Order. Not yet. It appeared that their attitude to the grandmaster was like that of unruly schoolboys maintaining an omerta against the authority of a headmaster.

'By the way, which lodge admitted you?' the grandmaster asked in a fervent whisper, seizing his hand, and drawing him to one side. 'Are you a Lazarist, perhaps?' Taking the young officer's blank muteness as encouragement he croaked, 'A Philadelphian then, eh?'

While von Hompesch kneaded his pliant hand between his own leathery digits, Vanderville's eyes sought out Gracchus who was watching them closely. In reply to his mute appeal Gracchus extricated him diplomatically by arriving at his side to plead with the grandmaster that Tirdflingen must prepare for his recital.

'How on earth do you deal with him?' asked Vanderville as Gracchus led him away.

'I simply nod enigmatically to all of his suggestions, and let his imagination fill in the fine detail. Brush strokes are all that are required to pose as a member of these stupid fraternities. An occasional reference to the oracle of Delphi, the pyramids, or to the higher grades, with a nod and a wink seems to send them into raptures.

'Pyramids?' said Vanderville. 'I don't think they even exist. I cannot believe in pyramids.'

'Oh, they exist, I assure you, but their size is vastly exaggerated, of that, I am sure. I suppose when you see them you will find they cannot be larger than a Parisian town house.'

'Speaking of houses, I need a place of refuge. The Bavarians have connected me with Haintlet's demise.'

'As long as my person and residence are sacrosanct, I believe I have at least an even chance of keeping you alive in my palazzo. Even the Minerves can scarcely touch you there, without resorting to methods their honour would scorn. No. I am convinced you are safe for now,' said Gracchus too blithely for Vanderville's liking. 'Anyway, the knights go to their posts tonight; the island is being put in a state of defence.'

Vanderville circulated the gathering and became gradually painfully aware that his former allies among the Bavarian knights were avoiding him. One after another, they evaded his gaze or found a reason to refuse his company.

The time to entertain the guests came all too soon for his liking, and as drinks were served by the grandmaster's household in anticipation and one or two amateur poets among the knights sang their own contributions, his stomach began to contract and oppress him. As he took his place centre stage an expectant hush fell upon the room; the ceiling seemed to lower, the walls drew in more closely, and sound altered in his perception as if he had been plunged under water.

He managed to avoid having to begin with his own newest efforts by starting with a ribald favourite by Dfydd ap Gwilym, 'Ode to the Penis'. This was met by robust approval, in fact the bawdy nature of much of this verse appeared to be one good reason why the meetings had a covert nature to them. He followed it up with some readings from Tirdflingen's book.

After he had concluded this opening, the grandmaster stood and cleared his throat abundantly to summon the company's attention. 'I have been looking forward enormously to your newest oration young man,' he said, and addressed the congregation at large. 'Pray quiet for young Tirdflingen, whom I insist is to give us something from his new muse in the style of far-flung Galles.'

Gracchus was in a strange impatient mood, and kept glancing around as if he expected to be collared by one of the guests at any moment. He nudged Vanderville needlessly. 'Got your text?'

Vanderville nodded. He hadn't got on very well with Tirdflingen's oeuvre, but he thought he had absorbed a bit of the style and had smashed off a few lines with help from Don

Stecchi's dusty copy of some wandering Greek pirate. He got to his feet and, tossing his papers on the table before him, he began. His voice was nervous, but grew in strength as the rhythm took hold of him,

> 'On the weed wracked shores,
> Of the ale-dark sea,
> I stood and dreamed of the fog shrouded sarsen stone,
> Where rain-lit wraiths gambol and sparred
> In the darkling dusk of St Swithin's eve,
> Amid the leaden skies of Galles.
> My ale-sick heart accompanied morosely,
> The horse of ap Gwynn through bumbling dale
> Sat by him with windswept soul,
> At flatulent hearths,
> Where the widows spin mute,
> Supped home wrought cawl,
> And suffered with him unspeakable indigestion,
> Of the bit rare bred,
> While he lied of time pass'd tales.'

Vanderville began to relax into his part. It was going well. Apart from the Bailli von Torring who was pointedly ignoring him and talking in a subdued voice with some of the other Grand Crosses, he appeared to be carrying off his impression. The audience was fully attentive, and the grandmaster was nodding happily along, his eyes half closed in avid thrilled concentration. Even the Bavarians had paused to listen, intent on his words and for a few moments Vanderville almost felt pleasure at holding the company's attention rapt in his hands. Buoyed by this sensation he made the mistake of essaying a half-smile at de Rechberg. The knight frowned, and instantly moved closer to the other Bavarians, and as they whispered among themselves their manner grew more agitated. He saw one pointing towards him, and was aware of his own awkward posture, favouring the wounded foot. Desperately trying not to lose track of his recitation, he tore his eyes away from them. But unbidden they drifted back and he saw them muttering ominously, and when they lifted their eyes back to him, their collective gaze was hostile, and their attitude more openly belligerent.

His intention it had been, to satisfy his audience with but a little more verse. In the event, through no fault of his, so it came to pass. For the Bavarians had divided into groups of two or three and while several covered the exits from the room, others were making their way towards him. Casually, as if without intention, they drew through the crowded assembly closer to his post. He felt drops of sweat trickle down his forehead and muster in his eyebrows, and forced himself to focus on the goggling placid face of the grandmaster and concentrate on his lyrics.

Now he sensed two of the Bavarians glide into place behind him. Could they really mean to assassinate him here in front of the grandmaster? It was possible. He had seen worse done in a crowd. A shove, a stab, a flurry of sharp blows and the assembly would part horrified, their gaze held by the dying man while the assassins moved away unhindered and melted back into the throng. Any moment his reservoir of sub-Homeric pastiche would run dry, and he became more and more convinced they would strike as he ceased to speak. When he finished the grandmaster would rise and address him, and as the eyes of the gathering turned to Hompesch it would be done.

His throat became dry, and he stumbled over the last stanza, drawing a frown from Hompesch. Gracchus! He suddenly thought. Where was Gracchus? His eyes flickered urgently across the audience, barely registering de Rechberg's sad concerned face, seeking that bundle of carpet slippers and ill-advised robes that concealed his last hope.

Then, from the corner of one eye he located him. Gracchus was edging mysteriously along the wall towards the French windows that led to the garden. He appeared oblivious to

Vanderville's predicament and intent on some theme of his own, moving fly-wise in little pauses and bursting skips with his back pressed against the wallpaper. The full-length windows were closed, and veiled by light translucent muslin curtains, and at the window closest to Gracchus, Vanderville saw a shadow, as if someone lurked outside. As he entered on his last line, he felt sure that he could feel the breath of a Bavarian on the back of his neck, and he flinched involuntarily. He raised his voice, hoping to draw Gracchus's attention, but instead Gracchus stalked noiselessly to the window and abruptly prodded the handle open with his walking cane.

The window lurched backwards into the saloon, slamming back on its hinges. A sable habited figure fell in through the open portal causing a commotion among the nearest guests, and the entire company's attention was diverted from the nervous bard's faltering oration to the furious figure sprawled on the floor by the entrance.

'Ah, another poetry enthusiast I presume,' said Gracchus blithely, and Vanderville seized the distraction to spring forward towards the grandmaster, traversing the distance and reaching the safety of his side in two capacious bounds he barely believed possible himself.

'My apologies, Monsignor Carpegna,' said the grandmaster acidly, rising from his chair. 'I didn't know you were so fond of versifying. If you wanted an invitation, you had only to ask.'

Carpegna got shakily to his feet. He appeared bewildered to find himself at a poetry reading instead of a bacchanal of the Minerves. Several of his assistants hovered uncertainly on the terrace behind him. 'My apologies for casting gloom upon this occasion, Your Eminence,' he stuttered.

The grandmaster leant shakily on the table before him and roared, 'Gloom? You provoke it Carpegna! You carry it with you, and where you enter, it follows.'

Carpegna bowed drily, and in an instance his customary equanimity was restored. 'If you will permit me – my soul rejoices to know that your imagination has wrapped me in a thicket's shadow: for never is the lightning so glorious as when it flashes from the darkest clouds.'

This nod to the poetic nature of the gathering mollified all with its wit except those Bavarians whom Vanderville had so narrowly escaped. Their faces betrayed a realisation that the opportune moment had passed when, of all people, de Rechberg carried the uncomfortable hiatus to a resolution by clearing his throat and beginning to applaud Vanderville most pointedly. Restored to propriety, the grandmaster, who Vanderville suspected appropriated the applause to himself, said some very fine things in praise of the new verses, and Carpegna exploited the general humour to withdraw discreetly to the terrace where his men waited.

The grandmaster went so far as to embrace Vanderville, and the whole assembly seemed on the verge of gaping, till coffee opportunely appeared. As it was carried around, this magic beverage diffused a temporary animation, and for a moment or two, conversation moved on with a degree of pleasing extravagance; but the flash was soon dissipated, and nothing remained afterwards save cards and stupidity.

In the intervals of shuffling and dealing, some talked over the affairs of the Grand Council with less reserve than Vanderville had expected; and two or three of them asked some feeble questions about the tumults in Paris. As soon as he felt secure enough of his safety, Vanderville stepped outside onto the terrace. The grandmaster's guard were milling there, in uncertain communion with Carpegna's escort, and their presence was for once reassuring.

Gracchus was leaning on his cane in the garden, deep in thought. The main boundary of the terrace looked out over the larger garden and the immediate grounds of the house were abundantly watered and covered with orange and lemon trees.

A real prodigy in a country where so little grew to please the eye. But towards the side of the terrace where he rested in the shade was a different prospect. In contrast to the formal gardens, here there were no elegant thickets of pine. The groves in the immediate vicinity were instead composed of dwarfish scrub trees and cinder-coloured olives. Under their branches reposed whitening sun-bleached bones, scraps of leather, and broken pantiles. A face peered out from among the bushes and scowled at him. He recognised one of Rais Murad's piratical crew, who was beckoning to him urgently.

Gracchus leaned over the balustrade of the terrace and hissed, 'What are you doing approaching me here in public? This is not as was agreed.'

'A message from Rais Murad,' grumbled the pirate. 'He must see you now. Tonight.'

'Impossible,' said Gracchus from the corner of his mouth, 'My business keeps me here.'

'The rais says that he must see that which you have for him. Otherwise, the contract is lost. He will be unable to sail. He must see you tonight.'

'I repeat that I am not at liberty to indulge your master's whims,' snapped Gracchus angrily. Heads turned on the terrace behind him, and he lowered his voice. 'Tell your master that I will see him tomorrow as planned. When he embarks the passengers, he can see that which he seeks at that time. That is my message to him.' The bushes rustled and the man disappeared.

Gracchus turned away back to the company and resumed his bland mien with some difficulty. Damn Rais Murad and his prevaricating duplicity, he thought, leaning heavily on his stick. The audacity of issuing demands and changing the contract at the last minute. He would use the letter from Bailli Torring to enforce compliance and confound the man's damned brinkmanship.

Carpegna appeared on the terrace and prowled up to him. 'You are a devil upon three legs, Baron,' he observed with a half-smile as he arrived. Gracchus waved a self-deprecatory hand, 'I promised you Minerves, and here they all are.' He waved an arm vaguely in the direction of a group of Bavarians at the far end of the terrace. They were being closely observed by the inquisitor's men who stood off at a polite distance while maintaining their surveillance. Gracchus reflected with some satisfaction that no mischief would be enacted upon Vanderville as long as these two groups circled each other warily.

'It amused you to play a trick on me, and I am not insensible to the fun of the occasion,' continued Carpegna, joining him at the balustrade. 'The truth is, I am content to escape the three cities for a few hours. I prefer it here in the countryside. The air is less fetid, if a little thick with conspiracy.' They looked out over the splendid view together.

Gracchus peered at the inquisitor, his head with its thin pale hair was turned to the vista, and his long delicate nose seemed to be sniffing the country air like an eager hound pointing for hares. 'His Eminence the grandmaster was not pleased to see you; I hope that is not an inconvenience.'

Carpegna sighed, his shoulders sagging sadly. 'He won today. It may be my turn tomorrow. Neither priest nor soldier except in name; he has all the cunning of a rat. The sort of particularly stupid rat who puts his head into a trap to see if there is a piece of cheese there. As for me, it is nothing to be made a laughingstock.'

'Although the grandmaster was not as amused as most.'

Carpegna shrugged. 'It is more important that the Bavarian's activities have been disrupted. I have half a mind to put a watch on their *auberge* to frustrate their bailli. It will not hurt the Minerves to know that they are watched.'

'An excellent idea. Why not enlist the *sbirri* to follow them too? They will bear the closest of watches at this dangerous moment for the Order, and it appears you have no shortage of personnel. Did I see your familiar Canon Gatt here earlier?'

'Gatt does not really care for parties. He is livid with rage that his intimate Haintlet has been assassinated, and strongly suspects your secretary. When angry, he is prone to take out his temper on those unfortunates under his charge in the Holy Office's detention chambers, so I diverted him to other duties to keep him out of harm's way. Some fresh air will not hurt his humour.'

'I was not aware that Gatt had acquaintances inside the Bavarian *auberge*. Perhaps it suits your purpose to have him consort with one of those you are investigating though?'

'Haintlet a Minerve? Never.' He laughed dryly. 'His sins were of a different stamp, may God rest his soul.'

That seemed unlikely to Gracchus, whose idea of divine mercy did not conceive of it extending so far as those who corrupted children. He was wondering whether Gatt had also been von Seeau's confessor when Carpegna abruptly changed the subject.

'It appears that the Bailli von Torring removing his support from you has put an end to your design,' said Carpegna. He shrugged his thin shoulders. 'I have a proposal for you. The knights here, their business concluded, and their little war with France arranged, will drink until late in the morning. They will then rattle back to Valletta as if the devil were their coachman. By midday they may be sufficiently restored to resume their robes and wigs, and go to the real council to have their decision confirmed. I also sit on that council.

'I will help you there by raising an emergency motion regarding your business. In exchange I beg only a few letters belonging to the Minerves that are in your possession. You might further add a few remarks on all you have learnt of them, which you could kindly draw up later tonight by the strength of midnight oil. My support will be sufficient to replace that of von Torring, the motion will be carried in your favour, and we will both fulfil our plans before Bonaparte arrives. Do you agree?'

As Carpegna had predicted the party continued into the evening despite many of the knights leaving for Valletta to arrange their business and collect their arms before going to take up their defensive posts. Vanderville was relieved to find many of the Bavarians among this number – frustrated by the close attention of the inquisitor's watchers they were some of the first to leave. As the early drinkers succumbed, their place was filled with new arrivals come to offer their congratulations to the grandmaster, to hear the news, and to gamble. The footmen served ices made with ice imported from Mount Etna on Sicily while the knights toasted the grandmaster's decision for war, and argued, in French, about how best to repulse the French.

Some of the younger knights' high spirits exceeded the bounds of propriety, and later Vanderville had a hazy recollection of dignity forgone. The wretched de Rechberg avoided him assiduously, instead drinking persistently and joylessly with some of the French knights. Eventually de Rechberg leapt from a second storey window defiantly shouting, 'Those who love me, follow me!' and reopened his wound. Von Torring had been at the local rough brandy and at one moment demonstrated a Bavarian jig with abandon, a mistake for a man of his ungainly form, but his liberal consumption made him easy to evade, and Vanderville escaped anything worse than a few baleful glances.

Gracchus was among the early leavers. He pled the pressure of business and departed in his borrowed coach. It was one o'clock in the morning before all the new coming company were assembled, and Vanderville left them there, still dreaming of glory over their coffee and card-tables.

His *kalesh* rattled and lurched back through dry and dusty lanes scented with the night-fragrances but he was grateful for its bone shaking amenity all the same. Army service had habituated Vanderville to moving fast across country and sleeping rough, wrapped in a cloak in a dry ditch or the lee of a wall, sometimes finding shelter, but often without any, in all kinds of weather, so that a carriage, even of the crudest sort, was still a luxury to him.

He allowed the *kalesh* to take him past the sentinels at Valletta's gates, and then abandoned its stifling leather interior to walk off his drunk in the heat of the night air. An ambush outside the Convent where any party of knights was conspicuous had seemed unlikely to him, but inside, where the Bavarians were more sure of their ground, he felt safer travelling quietly and alone. Tension lay over Valletta like the sticky fronds of a spider's web, and gangs of ruffians and militia patrols were vying to dominate the streets, so he kept to the backways, and there he kept a wary eye out for trouble and one hand on his sword hilt.

He was struck by a sudden urge to see Franca, who had been isolated from him since the fracas in Piazza Forbici. He arrived in her street with the inebriate's confidence that despite the late hour, he would be welcome. He could hear the dog howling incessantly upstairs, but her door was not locked. He went up. The apartment was empty but for the forlorn hound. The devotional image and her flowers were gone.

When he descended, Duccio was at the door, cringing and shifting his feet miserably. Vanderville resisted an urge to take him by the shirtfront and asked as patiently as he could manage, 'Where is she? Is she safe? Did you watch, as I told you?'

'I must tell you something. She's gone. I talked to the neighbours and they say the inquisitor's men were here with Canon Gatt. They searched the apartment and arrested her for witchcraft. Gatt came down with a bundle of things, carrying a plant pot triumphantly, and when he came out, Franca was with him, still groggy on one of Don Stecchi's sleeping draughts. They took her.'

'Took her? Where?'

'I followed them to the harbour. They took a barca for Vittoriosa, where the inquisitor's palace lies,' he shuddered.

Vanderville clapped his hands to his head. This final unforeseen calamity had destroyed his equanimity. It was some moments before his head cleared, and helped by the hand of the concerned Duccio on his shoulder, he felt equal to meeting the new contingency.

—

Duccio took him to the rampart overlooking the Grand Harbour to show him where the *Taz al Inquisitore* lay, and presently Granchio joined them there. Vanderville's mantle offered him some protection from identification when drawn up over his head, and from under its heavy hood, he surveyed the moonlit serenity of the grand harbour. In the three urban areas beyond the harbour's water Vittoriosa lay centrally, with Fort St Angelo on its tip. 'The inquisitor's palace is there,' said Duccio. 'Behind the fort.'

Vanderville sucked his breath in. The great fort was the twin of Sant' Elmo and its hundred eyes and uncountable gun ports guarded Vittoriosa as Sant' Elmo guarded Valletta.

'We have friends there,' said Duccio. 'It is not hopeless. If we surprise them, we have one chance. They will not expect us so quickly, or so directly.'

'The thing is not possible,' said Granchio quietly. 'The dungeons of the *Taz al Inquisitore* are too tough a nut for the *Fraternita*. We may as well hope to peel the cheese of the moon.'

'It is inconceivable that we should abandon her,' protested Duccio. 'It betrays all our principles. She is one of us!'

'She left the *Fraternita*,' said Granchio sadly.

'You are right,' said Duccio, crestfallen. 'I have not forgotten.'

Vanderville cast his professional eye over the endless sweep of bastion piled upon bastion, curtains and fosse, cavalier, and counter fosse like a tower of children's blocks that stood between him and that place. They loomed in unsurmountable oppressive crests between the harbour and the inquisitor's stronghold. His gaze travelled past the maze of streets and forts and rested on the low hills a great distance away, purpled by the dawn's rising light.

'Cities are all very fine, but sometimes I wish for the open country,' he said.

'Its lure is obscure to me,' said Granchio. 'I have scarce passed the gates of Valletta since I came here.'

'You will today,' said Vanderville, 'we are going to Vittoriosa.'

Chapter Nineteen

Down by the merchant wharves at the far end of the harbour Vanderville was slip-slopping in coffee booths and staring at a few dull-painted boards, searching for a likely-looking boatman. He had been up all-night planning and preparing as he marshalled the forces of the *Fraternita*, and it was hard to work out which was hurting him more: his shoulder or his foot. The sea everywhere was covered with fishing boats, and such a stillness prevailed that the voices of the fishermen could be clearly heard across the shining plain of the harbour. The mole was quiet, instead of ten ranks of vessels, there were only three.

'The glass is sinking. They won't be in before tomorrow,' opined one salty lounger sewing nets on the quay. The Greek merchant ships that had arrived the day before were the sole hub of activity. Among the rough sailors drinking by the new arrivals Vanderville heard a strange *lingua franca* composed of three or four different tongues spoken by swaggering Levant skippers and mongrel smugglers. The atmosphere was permeated with the eyewatering fumes of cheap tobacco and burning goat effluent, and their smoke softly wafted over the upended wine barrels set with planks that served as tables, where sailors yawned dismally, their breath redolent of garlic and exhaustion, as they breakfasted on milk bread rolls.

As Vanderville stalked past a noisy group he had dismissed on sight as too piratical, he found himself suddenly sprawled on his hands and knees, and he felt the hood that had concealed his identity flung back upon his shoulders. Had he…? Yes, he had been tripped. Deliberately tripped by a man sat upon one of the barrels that served as chairs. He raised himself cautiously, his hand sliding methodically backwards to expose the sword hilt, beneath his mantle.

'We are some ways from the shades of Mombello,' said a voice from over his shoulder. Vanderville hesitated and resisted by a whisker the urge to spin and draw. Instead, he composed himself before turning to find an open, cheerful, and welcome face grinning at him from amid the cover of a barbarous set of Greek whiskers winding out from the familiar curly head of hair. A bright sailor's kerchief over shirt sleeves, short and wide gun-mouth slop trousers of slop stuff, and silver-buckled shoes providing a sparkle of brilliance against the black unstockinged legs completed the un-soldierlike ensemble of his old friend Lieutenant Hercule.

Hercule cast a curious appraising eye over the gaping Vanderville, and one great foot slid out a chair. 'Well met, my dirt eating friend,' he railed good-humouredly, and leaning in close as Vanderville took the chair, he whispered in a lower register. 'We are here on the same business, I'll warrant, though my disguise is more effective than yours.'

Vanderville stifled his surprise and nodded a kind of assent. 'You came in on the Greek merchantmen last night?'

Hercule nodded. 'Those two ships contain the advance guard. The local contacts are supposed to be arranging everything for us, but they are standing back a bit. Until they decide on the arrangements, we are confined to the docks and the fish market, and they are keeping watchmen over us.' He nodded at several points around the quay where individuals of the Valletta militia in their colourful sashes were conspicuously posted.

Vanderville smiled. 'Yes, I usually have a couple of those dogging my shadow too, you get used to it. It is not them that I am worried about.' He stole a glance around their buccaneering table fellows, and pulled his mantle back up to shroud his face. 'Are all these Greeks with you?'

'They are as Greek as I am,' said Hercule, grinning. 'And the smuggling holes in the ships are stuffed full of Maltese patriots, and the tools we will need to arm more of the locals.' He winked broadly. 'We are standing by until the General arrives, and then things will get very exciting, very quickly.'

Vanderville exhaled in astonishment. After days of solo peril, the comfort of sitting in company with a comrade was welcome, and deliciously reassuring. They stared at the sea companionably in silence for a while. Hercule's perch was a well-chosen vantage point, from which they could watch the comings and goings on the waterfront and keep an eye on the ships. Eventually Vanderville broke the silence. He wrinkled his nose and sniffed suspiciously. 'Have you oiled your hair?' he accused.

'The pomade is part of my disguise.' Hercule smoothed his glistening locks complacently with one hand. 'Murad gave me the recipe.'

Vanderville took in another cautious waft from his side of the table and failed to suppress a frown. 'It is certainly nautical,' he opined.

'I think that's the barrel you are sitting on,' offered Hercule with a hearty chuckle. He slapped the table, 'The pomade is called Ottoman Nights. It costs a pretty penny, but what price to evoke the mystery of the sea and the turbulent passions of the East?'

'The turbot passions more like...' Vanderville began but abandoned the line of repartee, as they were distracted by two of the militia who were remonstrating with the crew of one of the Greek ships.

'Excuse me a moment,' Hercule said, shoving off from the barrel, and he went to head off the trouble.

Vanderville sighed and turned his attention to the rest of the quay while he pondered the news of Bonaparte's imminent arrival. The long-awaited moment had come upon him at the worst possible time. He was unable to deliver Mayflower's intelligence to the fleet, and utterly focussed on the *Fraternita*'s strategy to deliver their comrade. His sharp gaze ranged over the harbour, but always returned to the heights of Vittoriosa, the old citadel of the knights on the opposite side of the Grand Harbour.

Hercule soon returned, and Vanderville surveyed him thoughtfully, sensing an opportunity. Joseph Domingue Hercule was a fine man with an extremely powerful physique and a good large-nosed black face. His family was originally from Africa, but he was born in Cuba, and had since served in every country Vanderville could think of, finally winning his officer's epaulettes in Italy as a member of Bonaparte's coveted personal bodyguard, the Guides. His intrepidity and courage were a byword, even in a squadron composed exclusively of heroes.

'It may be that you can help me with something while you wait for the big plan to develop,' began Vanderville cautiously and he began to outline his plans for the evening.

Hercule let out a low whistle. 'I knew you would be in it up to your teeth,' he smirked gleefully. 'We are supposed to be incognito, and not drawing attention to ourselves. Nor can I stray too far from the ship, but if we can exert ourselves discreetly, I am your man.'

'I can't promise there won't be a noise,' said Vanderville. 'Some heads may have to be knocked in.'

'So much the better,' said Hercule. He nodded at his crew, 'These fellows are a dull lot until the cannons start belching. You had better tell me what is afoot.' He flashed another grin, and lent in conspiratorially, his buccaneering earrings glinting in the sunlight as he waited for Vanderville to explain the details of his plot.

—

The two friends were soon embarked in a small barca, whose even motion as it carried them across the Grand Harbour was very agreeable to Vanderville after the jolting of Valletta's mule *kaleshes*. The air was calm, the sky cloudless, a faint breeze just breathing on the deep lightly bore the boat across the water, and they soon drew near to the old city. Hercule was at the prow, craning his neck towards the heights of Fort Sant' Angelo that dominated the harbourside.

'I am the bearer of a message from Italy for you,' said Hercule, over his shoulder. 'A certain person close to the General has been delivered of a boy.'

Vanderville dipped his head in mute acknowledgement. There was nothing to say. He had heard that the newly married Paolette Bonaparte had been expecting a happy event, and that she was ensconced in a luxurious new house near Milan, from which post her husband, General Leclerc, was enjoying the post of Chief of Staff of the Army of Italy, a present from his brother-in-law. He neither knew, nor wanted to learn anything more. That chapter was closed to him.

'The child is named Dermide,' said Hercule. 'Dermide Louis Napoleon.'

Vanderville shrugged absently. One of the appealing things about his present situation was that it left him no time to contemplate Paolette Bonaparte and the conflicting emotions she aroused in him. He was recovered from these reflections by the confused hum that had begun to pervade the evening stillness as they approached the shore. Barcas were constantly passing and repassing, and their own boatman turned with much address through a crowd of small boats and barges that blocked up the way and moored smoothly beside a broad pavement, covered with people in all dresses, and of all nations.

'Tonight, we will use one of the ship's boats,' said Hercule quietly, leaping ashore. 'How many will we carry?'

'Ten, plus you and I,' said Vanderville. 'But the others are small.'

He led the short way through the back streets to the palazzo of the Holy Office, the infamous Palazz tal-Inkwizitur. On the way he explained that the pertinent area was in one of the narrow torturous alleys bordering that palazzo. There was nowhere to linger inconspicuously, so he suggested they circle the area once to make their reconnaissance, and then return to the quay.

'The street urchins of Vittoriosa are allied to the *Fraternita delle Forbici*, and their local knowledge has proved invaluable,' Vanderville told Hercule as they walked. 'Prisoners who have been confined in the Palazz tal-Inkwizitur are sworn to secrecy regarding the conditions and places of confinement. Since on the whole they prove unkeen to revisit those memories, a veil of secrecy reigns over the depths of the palazzo, so, it has been difficult to locate Franca's place of imprisonment. There have, however, been opportunities to bribe some of the staff of the upper levels of the palace thanks to a liberal application from Gracchus's bottomless coffers, and from them we learnt that the dungeons housed only one prisoner who required those articles peculiar to her sex. The cell containing that prisoner adjoins the street outside with which it communicates by a small grill for air. This opens at ground level outside, in the plinth footing that compensates for the steep slope of the street.'

Their destination was a squalid alley, infested by lame dogs, voracious mosquitoes, and beggars reeking of urine and loneliness. Shambolic arches spanned the gap between the Palazz tal-Inkwizitur and its near neighbours, as if to buttress the whole tottering mass from tumbling down into the harbour, and the shade they cast kept the lane in shadow even now as midday approached.

Halfway down there was a dogleg in the alley, where a frightful beggar was seated in a basket balanced on a wooden crate. The rags which served him for clothing were fastened around him by a cord, while the torments he had undergone had, as it appeared, deprived him of the use of his legs. He presided over a shoal of children with distorted countenances among whom the art of producing sores, ulcers, and scabby pates in the most loathsome perfection had been perfected.

As for the beggar king himself, as they approached closer, they saw that around his shoulders he bore a cloak like that of a pilgrim. The monogram of Christ was plainly distinguished on his chest, meant either as a consolation for his own sufferings or to exhort his brethren to bear with patience the pain and mortification of a state of perpetual undernourishment.

'Heaven prosper their noble excellencies, long may they be blessed with the use of their limbs,' he croaked as they drew nearer, and his cohorts of the lame, the maimed, the scabby and greasy, came railing and bawling about their feet. Hercule, who was susceptible, drew back in disgust and made haste to throw down a plentiful shower of tinkling copper coins. Vanderville stopped his hand and removed a single copper.

Approaching the beggar king, he stooped low to drop the offering into the outstretched claw. But, ignoring the proffered coin, the hand grasped him by the wrist and pulled him closer. Hercule reached out, alarmed for the security of his friend's wallet. But the loathsome beggar was whispering urgently into Vanderville's ear. With a mumbled blessing the creature released his grip, and to Hercule's relief they continued up the alleyway and away from the low and miserable place.

They completed their circumnavigation of the palazzo without further incident and returned to the boat by a different route without speaking to a soul.

'When do we meet this *Fraternita* of yours?' asked a bewildered Hercule.

'You just did,' said Vanderville wryly. 'We return at the sound of the compline bell. All will be ready then.'

—

From his vantage point on Donna Eva's rooftop terrace Gracchus looked out over the roofs of Valletta. They were laid out like a patchwork petrified thicket under the bright sun. Scarce a tree was visible among the stony channels, but here and there the small craggy pinnacles of bell towers announced the conventual churches, and St John's dome was a granite tor bulging forth from its lesser cluster. Behind him the raised voices continued to squabble relentlessly. A hurried council of war had been summoned and was proceeding as such councils must, with excessive cavilling and meaningless expressions of caution.

'Let us not dwell on the dangers, for the love of Our Lady,' said Gracchus, elevating his voice above the babble. 'As for the grandmaster's wrath, the Maltese call him a sultan you know, and with good reason. His avarice will outweigh his honour. The mechanisms of ransom are arcane, but I have cut the Gordian knot with my golden razor. All will go smoothly.'

It was true, he reflected. The difficulty of negotiating with multiple owners had prolonged discussions for weeks, and at one point it had seemed that the grandmaster was wont to sell only the order's own slaves. However, with the advent of the French fleet, the value of human misery had begun to plummet, and Gracchus had consequently forced rapid compromises on price. Eventually he had secured the release of more people than he hoped for even in his most sanguine dreams, and they were ready to be released from the *bagnio* at his word.

'There must be none of those celebrations customary on manumission,' he reminded the others. 'The departure must be discreet, stealthy, and unobtrusive, the people must not know that Christian ships are to be used.'

'We must move quickly, but with stealth,' Eva said in the pause that ensued. 'We must take the tunnels in the grottos.'

'There is no other way?' questioned Gracchus, his voice strangely constrained. Subterranean passages had become anathema to him after his experiences with Vanderville at Villa Mombello the preceding summer.

'There are the roof tops if you have an aversion to confined spaces,' she added cautiously. 'It is how the children get around when they want to be unnoticed,' and to Vanderville she explained, 'I thought after your precipitate entry into our world you would prefer another route. The caverns are damned cramped and confine strange creatures of course. But they are more unpleasant to the eye than dangerous, and the way is swift.'

Vanderville shaded his brow with a hand as if suddenly weary. His shoulder twinged sharply. He had seen enough of Maltese roof tops to last him this lifetime 'The roof tops will not bear the weight,' he muttered casting a judicious eye over Gracchus and Stecchi.

'What will it be?' insisted Eva. 'Time presses, there is much to be organised, and I must have your answer, the tunnels or the roof tops?'

'The roof tops,' Gracchus asserted.

'The tunnels,' countermanded Vanderville.

'I confess,' said Don Stecchi, 'to a mortal fear of heights, but forget this talk of tunnels and rooftop flitting. I am on the verge of an idea if you will permit time to deliberate. When do we leave?'

'We can set out as soon as I return from Vittoriosa,' suggested Vanderville. 'I hope by midnight.'

'I must take my people to the ships *tonight*, not tomorrow morning,' insisted Gracchus.

'Very grand Moses, but we must recover Franca from the Palazz al Inquistore *now*!' fumed Vanderville.

'We will divide our forces,' announced Donna Eva, smoothly. 'The *Fraternita* are with Vanderville of course, with his friend Hercule.'

Hercule twirled his moustaches at her with a twinkling eye. Nor did he prevent his great shoulder muscles from flexing impulsively.

'While the baron and I will go to conduct the slaves to the boats,' she continued imperviously.

'Ships,' interrupted Hercule.

'Oh, for the love of God,' moaned Don Stecchi. 'Let her finish, and be still.'

'Thank you,' she said. 'You will come with us, Don Stecchi.'

'With pleasure, and I believe I can summon more help if needed, or at least persuade people to look the other way as our caravan passes. Next week is the feast of St Anthony of Padua, patron saint of the enslaved, no less. I believe we can pre-empt the liturgical calendar for a worthy cause, and we shall pass through the streets themselves as a procession of the devout hooded, the slaves will be less conspicuous.

'We shall begin tonight for the evenings belong to the Maltese. No knight rises from the gaming table 'til the early hours, and most of the priests are at their compline prayers. But those who work, the sinews of the island, are about and see everything. They watch, but they do not tell, or if they do, nothing reaches ears that are not ours. In this way we need scale neither the heights, nor the depths.'

Gracchus nodded. 'It is well-conceived. The governor of the *bagnio* has been handsomely paid off; he will create no problems. The militia patrols we must risk, and trust to the power of deception. Can you arrange the appropriate mummery at such short notice?'

Stecchi assumed a hurt expression. 'Yes, it can be done from the church's magazine, if you are willing to pay for the candles.'

—

Duccio was on his hands and knees in the alley mud, his body concealed under the box that Granchio's basket rested upon, so that only his feet were exposed. His head was thrust through the tiny window of the Inquisition's prison, whose bars had been so laboriously sawed through. 'Franca,' he hissed. 'Are you there?' A soft answering call came, and his head popped back up again. 'She is there. She sounds a long way away. She says her hands are tied, I will have to go down there, and release her.'

Vanderville nodded urgently. Hercule was wearing a silk rope slung over his shoulders, and his practised hands knotted the loose end into a loop that he passed between Duccio's legs. The boy carefully paid the rope out into the cavity. Just as all was ready, a whistle came from the mouth of the alley and the beggar children balked in trepidation – it was the warning signal!

Holding one finger to his lips, Vanderville swiftly slipped the rope from Hercule's shoulders to release him, and, in one smooth movement he pushed him into the dark recess behind one of the arches that spanned the dogleg. They were pressed face to face, with Hercule's body braced against the back of the arch, and Vanderville crushed in as far as possible to expose no part of himself. He drew his mantle over both their faces. The urgency in his face and tenseness of his body communicated the need for silence to Hercule, who unavoidably enfolded him in a stifling embrace. Through a gap in the mantle, Vanderville watched Duccio slide back out of the hole, sliding the front of the crate back into place before clambering onto it, drawing his knees up to his chin protectively.

'What is this!' came a familiar voice. 'You may not raise your hovels here.' A figure wearing a clerical cowl stamped into Vanderville's line of sight. He could not see the face, but the sneering voice was sufficient to identify its owner.

'Clear this alley instantly, before I call the guard.' Gatt pointed a quivering finger at the beggars, and Vanderville saw that his hand was heavily bandaged. Perhaps the dog that guarded Franca had not been so toothless after all. The children shrank back, cowering, and their sentries parted like waves before his wrath. Only Duccio, with a desperate resignation on his face, clung to the crate as the priest went to grasp him.

Vanderville squeezed the only part of Hercule he could reach in warning. He closed his eyes to focus and allowed the blackness that permitted violence to surge up inside him. Images of himself forcing Gatt backwards into the shadows, his thumbs crushing those protruding eyes to pulp, his teeth tearing the man's face, flitted across his vision. He shuddered, tensing himself to spring upon the priest.

Then a quavering voice spoke. 'Father, for the love of the Virgin, give me a silver coin.'

Vanderville allowed his screwed-up eyes to ease open. Where the mantle did not obscure his vision, he saw the tiny figure of Granchio appear from the gloom of the alley and hold up a warped arm to tug at the priest's cloak.

'Certainly not,' said Gatt, recoiling in disgust and sweeping his cape shy of Granchio's grasping fingers.

'Then give me sixpence at least,' the voice was cool now.

'Not one penny.'

'A farthing?'

'Nothing.'

The pauper Granchio fell back on one last plea. 'Then give me a blessing.'

'That I will gladly give you. Much good it will do you. Kneel, cripple.'

Granchio rolled his eyes, 'On second thoughts, if your blessing is worth less than a farthing, I don't think I shall bother – you may keep it.'

The priest went to strike him, but an angry hissing rose from the shadows and the Fraternity materialised as one. Suddenly the priest was no longer a heron stamping on mice, but a lingerer on the sands sensing the rip tide rise swarming about his feet. He un-balled his raised fist and dropped it to his side. Then gathering up the folds of his cloak he spun on his heel, swallowed his words brusquely, and he was gone.

Vanderville exhaled, unaware until then that he had been holding his breath. As he watched the shadowy form of the priest appear silhouetted in the faint light at the far end of the alley, he straightened up, releasing Hercule, whose lapel he found he had clenched in one hand.

'You need a new toothbrush,' said Hercule, grimacing.

'You need to change your hair oil,' retorted Vanderville.

It was the work of a moment to open the crate again and reattach the rope around Hercule. Once more Duccio thrust his head and shoulders into the gap between the bars of the casement, and then he pulled it out again.

'It's no use,' he spluttered brusquely, 'I can't see anything.'

Vanderville had a sense of time flooding by, and himself powerless to halt the flow. 'Hercule, strike a light, quickly!' he uttered.

'Make way,' he told the boy. 'Let me look.'

The opening was narrow. His own shoulders would never pass the gaps in the bars, but a slimmer figure might. The walls were thick, and as the casement sloped downwards steeply inside the wall, he could see no more. Hercule passed Duccio a burning wick and Vanderville adjusted the rope under the boy's arms. 'Go backwards,' he whispered.

As the boy set off on his descent, Vanderville paid out the rope, his shoulders braced against the grill. The wick held warily away from the silk cord began to illuminate the scene with its guttering light and then Duccio froze as a deep clang like a door being slammed echoed somewhere in the dungeons below.

'Go on!' Vanderville whispered urgently, and Duccio slipped off the casement ledge and disappeared from view. The rope went slack as the boy arrived on the floor of the cell and released himself from it. Vanderville had paid out some five metres but ample remained. By Duccio's light Vanderville could make out the distant end of the cell's graffitied walls, and part of a simple wooden bedstead. Standing in the only free space, near the door opposite the window aperture, was Franca. She squinted up at him. Then the light died.

'It's gone out,' murmured the urgent voice of Duccio below.

Vanderville felt something squirming past him, and Granchio twisted in adroitly under his elbow, clutching Hercule's flint and steel in his hand.

'I'm going down,' he announced.

With a sigh, Vanderville raised the loose rope, bound him to it, and helped him through the hole, onto the ledge.

Someone touched Vanderville's shoulder gently. 'This is taking too long!' hissed Hercule. 'What if the priest has roused the guard?'

'Hold them off,' said Vanderville grimly over his shoulder.

The procession set off as the sun sank. Before them passed Don Stecchi exposing the holy wafer; and whilst half a dozen squeaking fiddles fugued and flourished away barbarously behind him, a whole battalion of candle-bearing devotees, sweltering in long white hoods and flannels, under which they bore every rag they possessed, gabbled away in their heathen tongues despite Gracchus's admonition of silence.

This papal piety, in warm weather, was no very fragrant circumstance, and against his own counsel Gracchus had been persuaded by Don Stecchi to adopt the hooded robe of the faithful. He had resisted this imposition to the last extremity until word came from his palace that armed men had been at his palazzo seeking him. Whether they were from the knights, the Holy Office, or the cut-throats of Rais Murad, he did not know, but it was apparent that his shroud of disguise had grown a little tattered, and that his personal notoriety was a greater danger to the proposed caravan's passing than the curiosity of the patrols. He was inclined to blame Vanderville for the collapse of his cover identity, for it had been sturdy enough before the lieutenant's arrival in Valletta. Now, with his legend fuller of holes than a sieve, he was arrayed in a soiled canvas cloak that was unfortunately redolent of its previous wearer's exertions.

He sought the open air of the side streets as soon as he was able. His eye met nothing out of the ordinary, but he imagined round unfeeling faces at every door and harmless curiosity gazing from every window. Behind the shutters of the balcony grazed the proprietors as unfeeling as their beasts, with nothing but a rustling and hum of conversation to reveal their presence, and the occasional titter of mirth or mockery as the procession passed below. Occasionally one or two women in long cloaks and mantles glided by at a distance; but their dress was so shroud-like and their whole appearance so ghostly, that he would have been afraid to accost them, and they took no notice of him.

The caravan processed sedately enough at first, and if the locals were baffled by this nocturnal alteration of the ecclesiastic almanac, those few who witnessed it's passing bore the novelty stoically enough. The long-suffering Maltese apparently had graver matters to occupy their attention than a religious procession conducted to an awry calendar. Gracchus was relieved, Stecchi sombrely staid, and Eva almost exultant at the success of their gambit. It was not until they were almost at the dock that things fell apart.

Before the descent to the water, there was a small, unlit piazza to cross, and Don Stecchi paused the head of the caravan, and whispered an injunction that they must pass quietly, for one side of the piazza housed a notorious gambling casino, sure to be full of knights at play at the card tables, even in these perilous times. The hooded slaves passed the message back through their ranks by touch and gesture, and finally the low hum of guttural Arabic ceased.

Along the route, they had been gradually joined by a number of locals who clearly viewed the opportunity to join the devout as too good to pass up. They apparently thought the procession a spontaneous reaction to the threats hanging over the Convent, and wished to add their support to the prayers the faithful would no doubt offer up at the conclusion of their passage through the city. Excluded from the tight-packed ranks of the liberated people, they marched alongside, rather than among the cavalcade, following two parallel routes either side, and it was these people who ignored the injunction for silence as they crossed the piazza. Don Stecchi had led the column down past the piazza, and Gracchus and Eva, who were posted on the flanks as they crossed, were ready to regain their positions at the head when it happened.

It was early for any knight to depart his nocturnal lair of debauchery, and their departure had been based on the calculation that the lure of the gaming tables would provide them with a window of opportunity. Should they be stopped in the street by a knight, numerous as they were, the band would be at a great moral disadvantage, and time was too short to begin explaining that the departure had been sanctioned by the grandmaster himself. He had stopped short of providing Gracchus with true bona fides, merely observing that he would do everything in his power to ease the passage and prevent the unauthorised intervention of the arrogant young nobles under his command. And yet that was what occurred.

The doors of the casino suddenly swung open, releasing shafts of light into the piazza that illuminated the shrouded hoods of the passing procession. Into the beams of light lurched three stumbling figures, whose hazy bonhomie came to an abrupt halt as, blinking incredulously, they came to a stop at the bottom of the casino steps. One of them took a swig from a bottle in his hand, and leaned heavily on one of his companions, but the third, who appeared to have maintained a tighter grip on his faculties, strode confidently forward to where Eva stood, and as Gracchus moved in her direction, he demanded loudly that she halt and remove her hood.

The head coverings of those garments supplied by Don Stecchi were a familiar sight, and ubiquitously donned during the frequent religious processions of Malta, as in every city in the south, yet even so, the lack of any facial features except the eyes peering from twin ragged holes in the white mask was a discomforting vision, and the spectacle of hundreds of such eyeholes turned on him, dented even the carapace of confidence that enveloped the knight. When Eva failed to respond to his demand, his hand first reached out to take her hood, and then paused, wavering, and it was Gracchus who broke the deadlock by arriving next to her, his own discarded hood held respectfully in his hands, his eyes blinking in the bright light that silhouetted the knight.

'Baron Pellegrew,' said von Torring. 'What a surprise.' Hearing his tone, the two other knights closed up to him, their figures instantly recognisable in the gloom by the swords they carried. The authority of von Torring thus bolstered, he appeared to grow in stature, and the Maltese people who had joined the procession stood respectfully back, forming a circle around them. Von Torring sneered at Gracchus, 'I think I know what is going on here under this subterfuge.' He pointed at Eva, 'Your secretary – the Frenchman?'

'Is not with us,' replied Gracchus, calmly. He observed that one of those accompanying the bailli was the young de Rechberg who looked distinctly uncomfortable. He felt Eva tremble besides him, and knew that the moment was critical, with the outcome swaying nebulously in the balance. He took her hand, squeezed it, and said, 'Continue the procession – get them moving again.'

'One moment,' said von Torring stepping forward, and Eva froze. The slaves drew back from him, and Gracchus became acutely aware of the expectant faces of the Maltese around them. 'I shall satisfy myself of your identity first. And these people,' he indicated the halted shrouded forms of the procession, 'are going nowhere.'

Eva released Gracchus's hand, and as von Torring motioned to de Rechberg to remove her mask, she raised her hands to her face and pulled it over her head. De Rechberg paused as she was revealed, but although his face was white, he did not remove his hand from the hilt of his sword on which it rested.

Eva took a step forward towards the bailli, and Gracchus was surprised to discover for the first time that she was taller by some inches than him. A figure detached itself from the townsfolk and stood beside her, and he was astonished to see that it was La Baida, her rival and fellow public woman.

'The time when you give orders on this island has come to an end Fra' von Torring,' she said, and Gracchus saw a peculiar rictus pass across the bailli's face. De Rechberg stepped back towards his master, and as he did so there was a reflex among the crowd surrounding them, and the circle of space around the knights tightened. The third knight gingerly placed his bottle on the ground, almost overbalancing in doing so. The bottle teetered and then rolled over. The sound as it toppled over was unusually sharp in the expectant hush of the crowd thronging the piazza. Gracchus was suddenly conscious of the great mass of hooded figures at his back, and he knew then what was about to happen.

Von Torring may have suspected too, but the habit of command was too engrained in the salt-etched lines of his face. He opened his mouth to reiterate his order, but as he did so, the Maltese began to sing. There were only one two voices at first, beginning one of those devotional songs that accompanied the display of the sacrament on Saints' days. La Baida was perhaps the next to take up the lilting chant. They sang not in the language of the Church, the French of the nobles, nor even the Italian that passed as the *lingua franca* of the disparate groups that cohabited the islands, but in Maltese. It was a graceless guttural tongue to Gracchus's discerning ear, but that night it sounded beautiful to him, expressing the deep religious spirit, and sense of community that bound the people to each other. It was a tongue that excluded the seven *langues* of the Order, and as the crowd took up the song, the circle around the knights pushed forward, forming a barrier between the discomforted knights and the procession, which started to move forwards again, slowly at first, and then with growing confidence. Over the heads of the islanders, Gracchus saw the face of the bailli purpling, as his two cohorts pulled him back to the casino steps and the security of the light, but their swords remained sheathed. Was it only his imagination that told him that de Rechberg's face shared neither the outrage of von Torring, nor the apprehension of his comrade. He would not know, because Eva took his arm and pulled him away, and then they were on the ramp down to the docks where the ship was waiting.

'Well Baron,' murmured Eva, 'you have pulled off your masterstroke. How does it feel to liberate a nation?'

Gracchus was on the verge of allowing himself the merest kernel of pride. This he stifled as he replied, 'For the love of all that is good under this cobalt sky, do not provoke the clouds to lower.' He looked anxiously ahead towards the ships. 'We must hope that Vanderville and Hercule have succeeded in rescuing your charge, and tomorrow we can add her to the number embarked.'

Eva slowed to a halt. 'Embark Franca on the ships? That is hardly necessary. She shall return to me.' Then meeting Gracchus's unyielding gaze, she became almost flustered for the first time since he had known her.

'She is your property after all. You can insist if you like, but I aver that she will be safer off the island.'

Eva turned her face away from him. 'You do not cease to astonish me Gracchus,' she said, using his name for the first time. 'When she is of age, she will decide for herself. Until then, she, and you, must trust me better.'

'Are you not coming to see the loading?'

'I shall not. There are many things still to arrange. We will meet in the morning.'

Watching her *faldetta* disappear up the quay steps, Gracchus felt a twinge of doubt. From behind she could have been anyone, and the garment made her a stranger to him again.

At the dock well-greased palms ensured a rapid loading as Don Stecchi chivvied the unwilling passengers into divesting themselves of his store of hoods before boarding. The crew had formed a human chain from the quay to the hold and were passing the human bundles swiftly below. Gracchus came down the gang plank with that strange agility of his and walked extremely fast up the dock, like someone with urgent news on his mind. He accosted Rais Murad.

'I will meet you here at the Lauds bell tomorrow when the sun rises,' he said to Murad, as they watched the loading.

Murad shook his head emphatically, 'We must finish loading tonight. The other ships are late, and there will be no time to load them now. We must slip away before the light comes.'

'I am not ready, there is still work to do.'

'Tonight, or you will not save anyone,' said Rais Murad flatly, not looking at him. 'The French fleet is in the offing, and we must leave as soon as the breeze permits.'

'You leave when the other ships are fully loaded. In the morning,' stated Gracchus.

Murad shook his head wearily, then nodded. 'Don't forget the document,' he replied curtly, and he marched up the gang plank onto the *Fortunato*.

—

Duccio had just managed to untie Franca's hands when there came the ominous sound of a key creaking in the door lock. Vanderville saw a strange glance of complicity flash between the faces of the children, and then Granchio and Duccio posted themselves silently on either side of the door. Granchio snuffed the wick in his fingers as the door groaned open on tired hinges.

In the doorway was outlined the figure of Canon Gatt, divested of coat, waistcoat, and neck stock. He used the fingers of one large hand to smooth his hair, in the other he held an oil lamp high. 'Time for your catechism my dear,' he croaked as he came through the door, and Franca shrank away from the priest until Vanderville lost sight of her under the aperture ledge.

What happened next made sense to Vanderville only later. He saw two shadows advance on the canon from behind. From the hands of one of them swung a weighted cord. The smaller figure rolled to the ground behind Gatt's feet, and the other boy leapt onto the back of the smaller. In a smooth motion, he whirled the cord around the man's neck, caught the weighted end in his free hand and hurled himself backwards. Obstructed by the crouching figure behind him, the canon overbalanced, and went over backwards at full tilt, dropping his lamp. In an instant, he was prostrate on the floor, his legs kicking feebly, and his hands scrabbling frantically for the cord embedded in the fleshy folds of his throat. The burning oil spattered across the floor from his dropped lamp lit the grisly scene. Granchio had wrapped his arms around the man's legs and clung against their kicking desperately. Duccio meanwhile was braced against the back of the canon's shoulders, heaving on the cord with every sinew of his strength.

Vanderville had watched the dreadful spectacle unfold in spellbound horror, and only a furious tug at the rope reminded him that Franca had attached herself and was demanding extraction. After she had wriggled through the aperture and been enfolded in Hercule's arms and Vanderville's mantle it was the turn of Duccio. Vanderville forced himself to concentrate on hauling the boy up and spared the prostrate figure on the cell floor only the briefest of thoughts. Duccio was heavier than either of the others, and by the time he had negotiated the ascent and was out, the light from the spilt oil was dying fast. The boy's eyes locked defiantly with Vanderville's as he wriggled past him, as if to say, 'and now you know how it was done.' Vandeville set his mouth resolutely closed, and pushed past Duccio back into the aperture.

Granchio was hopping from foot to foot in impatience as the rope was thrown down for the last time. Intent on his climb, he did not see the still figure on the floor stir and rise behind him. Vanderville's shouted warning came too late, or was misheard, lost in the growl with which Gatt threw himself upon the boy. Vanderville's last glimpse was of Granchio's face, his eyes shining in the dying glow of the light as he grappled hopelessly, and then their stamping feet extinguished the light and all was black, and dreadful. Vanderville stayed at the aperture as long as he dared until the tension on the rope snapped, and it came loose snaking free up the aperture's slope towards him.

Vanderville's appalled face told his companions all they needed to know. Franca dragged Duccio struggling away from the bars, and Hercule clapped a hand on Vanderville's shoulder, for there was the beginning of a commotion to be heard in the palace. 'To the boats – now, or they will take us all,' he urged.

Chapter Twenty

Punctual as a zealous official the sun rose, tweaking cupola and campanile out of the morning mist, gilding balconies, and galvanising statues. Complacently it looked down on some of man's loveliest creations, the dome of the cathedral, the clock of the grandmaster's palace, and the predatory, hawklike silhouette of the Sant' Elmo lighthouse. Regretting his breakfast, which would await him in vain, Gracchus set out once more for the docks. As he left his residence, his porter handed him a letter, which he stuffed impatiently into his pocket as he hurried off down the lane.

As soon as the ships were despatched, he thought, he must pay a call on the worthy Donna Eva. Vanderville's revelation on returning from Vittoriosa had finally cleared her of the suspicion of murder. It was all so clear to him now. The *Fraternita*, preyed upon by the outcast deviant circle composed of the errant Bavarian knights and Canon Gatt, had ceased to acquiesce in their exploitation. Abandoned by all, they had sought strength in each other, and become the predators themselves. Using the scant talents and resources at their disposal, the children had used Franca to lure the unsuspecting knights to their doom, and combined, had achieved what they could not alone.

He could not approve of their methods, and their souls were as undoubtably damned as they themselves suspected, and yet were not their achievements aligned with his own? He smoothed down his waistcoat, which had grown tight during his sojourn as a rich man, and felt himself as close to satisfaction as he dared approach. Well – he was no longer rich, that was at an end, and the future was still fraught with peril, but at the end of that morning's work would he not have achieved something if not great, then at least worth the stakes?

He was looking forward to basking in the admiration of Vanderville for once, and perhaps even a small part of him hoped for Eva's approbation.

He wanted to know if she had known of the children's crusade. He felt sure she must have suspected it and possibly connived but was not sure that she would reveal her hand. There were still unanswered questions to be pondered and explored at leisure with her, should the uncertain days ahead afford him any. Her cherished ward, Franca – how far had she gone to inveigle the knights into peril? Undoubtably, she had been the bait used by the *Fraternita* to reach their ends, and had passed about the streets concealed in Eva's borrowed *faldetta*. Yet surely Eva would never permit Franca's guilt to be confirmed.

Before, when he had thought her a murderer, he had not particularly cared what happened to Donna' Eva after he had left the island, but with the approach of that moment, his doubts had crystallised. I have done her an injustice, he told himself. Her motives were sound, her instincts good. She protected the children against all the world offered them, even to the point of assuming the burden of their guilt, rather than let them face the consequences of their murderous excursions.

The evening before, a despondent Vanderville had arrived with the exhausted *Fraternita* at his palazzo. Hercule had carried Franca to her apartment and stood guard there. When Vanderville related the events of the night before to Gracchus he had listened with increasing understanding. The servants were earwigging, and they had talked low and late in the garden without reaching resolution. In the end they had decided to rest and revisit the subject in the morning.

Vanderville left Gracchus watching the sun come up, exhausted but his work done. He had gone to take over from Hercule guarding Franca. There was trouble at the Greek ships, and a messenger had implored Hercule's instant return. His return to duty was a loss for the conspirators. Fearing strong-arm tactics by Murad, Gracchus had entrusted the bailli's red silk envelope to Vanderville for safety, the plan being that they would carry it to the docks in the morning, Hercule and Vanderville providing security against the rais' crew and ill intentions. Vanderville would have to suffice. Despite his unwillingness to accept the essential illegality of the *Fraternita*'s murderous excursions, and in spite of his culpable guilelessness in failing to observe that the very gang who had rescued him after his fall from the roof tops had been perfectly placed to murder von Seeau, Gracchus was confident that Vanderville's arm would not fail him against Rais Murad. The young man was, after all, not without his uses – endearing fool though he was.

Ships were forbidden to enter or exit the harbour by night, so Murad should have spent all morning warping the other ships to the quay to embark the freed people. There was no sign of Vanderville on the dock, and as he pulled out his watch to check the time, the letter his porter had thrust at him fell out. Gracchus picked it up and turned it over curiously in his hands. The exterior was unmarked. He slipped it open as he walked towards the *Fortunato*, and pushing his spectacles up his nose, he read.

Baron Pellegrew,

By the time you have read this I will have crossed the harbour and delivered myself into the hands of Il-Palazz tal-Inkwizitur. I will carry with me such ample and spurious proofs of my own deep involvement in witchcraft as will enable me to offer Carpegna my person, in exchange for which I shall negotiate the release of that unfortunate child.

Although I find myself a prisoner, despite my own efforts and yours, I trust I shall not remain one for long. The material on Bailli Torring's activities in the Minerves that our long acquaintance has provided me with makes my position not powerless, and I will relate this to the inquisitor at a moment when sufficient time under examination has passed as I judge sufficient to enable you to have the children removed away from this place, where God has forsaken them.

Do not be concerned on my behalf, my proofs are artfully arranged to collapse upon closer enquiry and lead to my exculpation. I foresee nothing worse for me than humiliation and indignity to no effect. Should my plans go awry, and despite my precautions I should remain in the hands of the Holy office, be content, as I shall, to know that it is as good a thing I have done, as I have ever done. But let us not dwell on the dangers!

You will forgive me also, Baron, for wishing you farewell by this means rather than conveying in person my deep respect and tender affection. I have been up all night preparing and found that I could not wait any longer. I am exhausted, and I am not used to it. I have never been an old woman before.

Your affectionate friend, Eva Mifsud.

PS I have sent instructions to my man of affairs to make Franca the heir of that portion of my property not bound to the Maddalene, and it is to that institution that I intend to retire, all being well, to pass my remaining days in the retired life of a lay nursing sister.

Foolish and precipitate! Gracchus cursed, crumpling the letter back into his pocket. How proud of her to place a noble gesture above practical considerations, and he had just been considering her a paragon of sense and perception. Well, it was out of his hands now, Carpegna would jump at the chance to exchange a street urchin for evidence of actual organised witchcraft. Having failed to extirpate the Minerves, he would have at least something to demonstrate his fervour and competency to his masters in Rome when he reached them.

He resolved that after the ships were despatched, he would send Vanderville to Vittoriosa to intercept Eva if there was still time. After weeks of enforced leisure in Malta as his negotiations wended their torturous way to fruition, everything was coming down to a last few frenzied hours, and he could not allow even concern for Eva to capsize his plans now.

Murad spotted him besides the ship and leant from the taffrail of the quarterdeck to hail him. 'We are ready to sail, the morning breeze favours us, but in half an hour it will be too late. Do you have it?'

'My man is bringing the document, he should be here even now,' cavilled Gracchus, struggling to rid his voice of nerves. He hustled to the foot of the gang plank, and Murad met him there. Glancing anxiously down the wharf he saw a figure in a green *faldetta* approach a group of the crew who were unmooring the ship's hawser at a bollard, and for one hope-filled moment he thought he knew Eva there. But it was not, it was Franca, her protégé, and now heir. She was talking and gesticulating angrily with one of the crew. As they turned her away, with ribald shouts and angry gestures, she forced a small oilskin packet into the hands of one of them, and retreated a short distance with a scowl.

'What is she doing here?' he asked Rais Murad.

'Manumission,' grunted Rais Murad, and he spat. 'Everyone who can afford to leave wants a passage off the island. We have been turning them away all morning.'

Gracchus checked his watch again. He squinted up and down the dock, and his heart leapt as he saw someone hurrying towards them. But it was not Vanderville, but Don Stecchi who arrived, his cassock flapping as he lumbered breathlessly up. Gracchus turned back to Murad.

'I see the *Fortunato*,' he snapped. 'Where are the other promised ships?'

'*Todo mangiado*, Signore Baron,' drawled Murad, reverting to the slave's *lingua franca*.

'Eaten? What do you mean?'

'Gone, lost, beyond recall. Seized by the fleet of Rais Bonaparte on their way here and pressed into his service.' He spat over his shoulder. 'But do not worry, we can still embark six hundred on the *Fortunato*, as I told you.'

'And the others?'

'God willing, we will return for them. They have gone to the old *bagnio* for now.'

'The *old bagnio*?'

'Si Signore. The one they used before the new *bagnio* was built. It is closer, much better for us.' He whistled. 'Not so comfortable, you understand, because it is nothing but an abandoned grain warehouse on the wharves.'

'I know of this place,' said Don Stecchi, shuddering. 'An underground dungeon, entered by rope ladder through a tiny hole in the roof, closed by an iron grate. Children throw muck and stones through the grate to taunt the prisoners who are forced to huddle in their own filth.'

'Just so,' protested Murad with a pacifying gesture. 'But closer, Signore, more convenient. And safe for now. We will return for them as soon as Rais Bonaparte has passed through,' he said as if that concluded the matter.

Seeing Gracchus turning puce with rage Don Stecchi took his arm and led him aside. He allowed the priest to calm him as they walked on the dock, while Murad shrugged and went back to ordering the master to prepare the ship for departure.

'Baron,' Stecchi whispered urgently. 'Listen to me. I will go to this place and make arrangements for the comfort of the people.' Gracchus was staring back at the ship darkly, and Stecchi shook his arm again. 'Do you hear me? You have saved them – they are free now, even if they must stay here a little longer. Go back to Rais Murad now, stay calm, and let him leave. I will arrange everything and meet you here later. Now go!'

Gracchus did as he said, he stared up and down the wharf again as Don Stecchi left. Where was Vanderville? Murad was gesticulating angrily at him from the quarterdeck. He pointed to the sails of the ship, where sailors swarmed, unfurling the canvas, and then to the harbour mouth. The flag of the *Fortunato* fluttered in the breeze. The import of his gestures was clear, it was time to leave. Gracchus trudged back to the ship, and Murad clattered down the gang plank to meet him on the dock.

'We sail,' he said bluntly. 'Do you have it?'

Gracchus considered. Murad had said he would not sail without seeing the document. But it appeared he had every intention of doing so. Did he intend to re-enslave the released prisoners once he cleared Malta? It was possible, but as long as he possessed the document, Murad was in his power. He would have to arrange to have it sent on to him. This would take careful handling. He adopted an appeasing smile, and opened his mouth to propose a bargain, but they were interrupted.

Three of Murad's pirates stalked up to them and one handed him something. 'A package for you, Rais, delivered by that girl,' he muttered, knuckling his forehead, and pointing to where Franca lingered. Murad frowned and took the packet. With a knife he slit it open and pulled out a red silk envelope. He beamed as he read it, mouthing the words to himself. He held it up by its silver ribbon, so it dangled in front of Gracchus's face.

'What is the meaning of this?' spluttered Gracchus as the two other pirates stationed behind him took hold of his arms.

Murad's face creaked into a cruel grin, and his earrings twitched and sparkled. 'It means terms have changed.'

'We have been on too long a journey together. Do not do this Murad.'

'Your journey is just beginning, *Musaa*,' said Murad with a sneer, and he cleared his throat exultantly on the ground.

Chapter Twenty-one

Vanderville was startled awake by two paws landing on the end of the blanket he had laid out on the floor, and a wet panting announced the arrival of the dog. Vanderville eyed the beast unenthusiastically. 'Franca...' he called, but there was no answer from the bed. The dog commenced licking his feet devotedly. His head was pounding now, and he had the nagging feeling that he was supposed to be somewhere else.

He surveyed the crumpled sheets on the empty bed. He could remember nothing beyond their last conversation. He grudgingly summoned his recollections of the night before. Necessity as well as security had prescribed that Vanderville should sojourn at Franca's apartment. He found that Eva was less worried about the agents of the Holy Office or the Bavarian knights than she was of the *sbirri* belonging to the grandmaster. They had prepared for sleep in awkward proximity. While Vanderville faced the wall and tugged at his boots, he became aware that she was struggling free of her corset. Eventually she called on him for help with the lacing.

'Vanderville, is it true that French women have abandoned their stays?'

'The collapse from grace of the corset is as overemphasised as the fall of the Bastille prison. Like the Bastille, the corset has its equivalent under the Republic. It is no more likely to disappear than the great whales from whose bones it is constructed.' He finished loosening her strings and turned with relief back to his boots. The injured foot had swelled, making the operation of removing that boot slow and agonising.

'I see. Vanderville, will the baron expose the *Fraternita*?'

'I don't know,' he finally eased off his boot and examined the bandages. Blood had seeped through, and where it had dried, it was the colour of charcoal. 'But the truth has a habit of getting out, and if we managed to put the pieces together, others will eventually too. I don't know what Gracchus will do. He is unpredictable in his approach to everything but a buffet table. We can talk to him after he rescues his people. And you had better leave the island as soon as you can, too. French ships are coming…'

'What people?' she asked, and Vanderville remembered that she had been incarcerated when Gracchus had revealed his grand project.

'The slaves from the *bagnio*.'

'They are really leaving then?'

'Yes. It is strange, in Rome I accused Gracchus of not caring about people, and yet here he is, spending vast quantities of cash to remit the slaves. A remission of evil, he calls it. I think it is some sort of penance he has imposed on himself. He even called the ship he bought after an ex-slave we met in Rome. One thing is certain, afterwards he will be as poor as a church mouse again. And Bonaparte will not be pleased with him taking matters into his own hands. I am not sure where that leaves me. If I had only found out who Mayflower is, I would have a triumph of my own to present to my superiors.' He opened the last layer of bandages on his foot and surveyed his wound. It was better than he had expected. Although sore, it was tolerably clean, and he resolved to ask Stecchi for more of the balm he had applied.

'Mayflower? What do you mean?' She poured him a glass of wine. 'Drink this, it will help you sleep. You will need all the help you can get sleeping there,' she pointed at the floor. 'I have no mat for you, I am afraid.'

Vanderville yawned, he did not expect to struggle to sleep, even with the dull ache in his exposed foot. He was accustomed to lower billets than this.

'Mayflower was a French agent, or someone who opposed the knights anyway. It was the reason I came here. Mayflower had arranged to meet a Maltese patriot called Vassallo, and I was supposed to persuade him to help the French army by passing his information to them. I don't know what happened to him. Perhaps when Vassallo was lost he simply faded back into the shadows. Perhaps he realised that Vassallo was working with us and didn't like the Republic any more than he did the knights. Either way, the information he could have provided is lost to me.'

'Would it be worth so very much to you?'

'Donna Eva had some documents along the same lines that would have helped me, and they might have done the trick. I suppose she compiled them herself, but she claims she is not Mayflower, and had no contact with the French, nor even knew how to reach them until she decided to trust me. She was keeping them as her own insurance policy I suppose, to ingratiate herself with the invaders if she could find a way. Perhaps Don Stecchi is Mayflower; he would have known where to find her scribblings, and he has pigeons too. Possibly some are trained as carrier pigeons to carry messages to the island of Gozo.'

He had turned to face her as he spoke, hoping to find some clue in her eyes, but finding her undressed, he turned away again in embarrassment.

'Carrier pigeons?' she said, not unpleased at his discomfiture. 'The only use he has for pigeons is to eat them, and Donna Eva never goes near a live pigeon – they make her sneeze. Stop thinking about it now. You can find your Mayflower in the morning when we have slept. I promise I will help you then, but I am exhausted now.'

Later, in the dark when they were both drifting off, he had asked her the question that had kept him awake.

'How did it begin?'

'Von Schiltenberg crushed a child's spine under the wheels of his *kalesh*. There was an inquiry, but he was found not culpable by his peers. The lives of the *Fraternita* are apparently worthless in the eyes of the law. We knew then that if we did not take steps to protect ourselves, we would all fall victim eventually.'

'Did Donna Eva know?'

'She had no idea! That's how careful we were. We had to keep her outside, because she could not be involved – it would have been dangerous for her. I suspect that she has guessed now, thanks to the baron's prying. But she helped without knowing, even before he interfered, because she always kept notes on the knights she saw privately, and those she met socially, and her kind talk among themselves about the bad ones, and those with particularly sordid or obscene tastes in amusement. She keeps a journal, and since she taught me to read… I found out who the guilty knights were, and who posed us the greatest danger.'

'So that was your part in it?'

'At first yes. Granchio lured the first one, and we took him outside La Baida's. That was a risk, but Schilternberg liked Granchio, and it was the only way. We became more cautious after that. After Schiltenberg the knights were becoming more suspicious.'

'And you decided that by wearing Donna Eva's *faldetta* you could become the bait?'

'Yes, no one notices the street children as they go about their business. We are beneath notice, and if they see us, it is only with contempt, or avarice for what they can take from us. In a woman's clothes I became powerful – it was my idea.'

'Would you ever have stopped?'

'When we had finished, I suppose so, but the list kept growing. There was Haintlet of course, but he scared us, so we were leaving him to last. Then there was Gatt, who was the worst of those we knew about. But in Vittoriosa he was untouchable. We knew we had to lure him to Valletta, and that was when La Baida accusing Donna Eva of witchcraft gave me the idea. If we could get him to my apartment, alone, we might have a chance. Unfortunately he came at the wrong time and with others.'

'You took unconscionable risks, all of you.'

'Von Seeau and Schiltenberg were bad men. Gatt, the Bavarian knights, we only took those who were bad. But I know we did wrong. That is why the *Fraternita* are petrified of completing their catechism. They know they will have to be confessed. Do you go to hell for killing people Dermide, even if they truly deserve it?'

'I devoutly hope not,' murmured Vanderville, 'but I am no expert. You might ask Don Stecchi.'

'Franca,' he remembered saying earnestly. 'Why don't you come away with me? I could get you, and Donna Eva too if you like, onto a French ship. In France, or any of the new republics, you would be free of these feudal predators. You could start a new life.'

'So instead of living in a knight's gilded cage, we could become the mistresses of French officers and traipse after the army?'

Vanderville had blanched. 'In France, you could at least choose to marry who you wanted to.'

'You think I ought to marry a minister? Or one of the Directors even? How is that different from the trap Eva has set for me?' She had sat up and pulled her bedjacket around her. 'Or perhaps you think I should become Donna Dermide Vanderville? What makes you think I want to get married at all? If I want to escape this rock, I'm sure I can find a better way than that.'

She had slept then, and eventually so did he, in the only way he was comfortable, on his side, with his sword laid out close enough that he could touch it. That the morning would bring new dangers, he was sure, for the Convent would grow only more dangerous as Bonaparte's fleet arrived, and he knew what happened to a city under siege, with loyalties dissolving as the old certainties dissolved, and scores being settled among the inhabitants. But that was for the morrow.

Now, in the morning, there was no sign or sound of Franca. Vanderville, perplexed, stood up and started to sluice himself at the washstand that stood behind a battered screen. He had slept deeply – a soundless, senseless oblivion. Although his head was heavy from too much sleep he was grateful not to remember any dreams – since the brutal struggle with Haintlet his nightmares had started to return, and with them the memories of the bloody carnage of the Verona Pasqua.

Vanderville had deliberately forgotten as much as he could of the terrible scenes he had witnessed at that time, but at night his mind continued to slip the restraints he had placed upon it. He shook his head angrily to clear the unhelpful and insistent memories.

He peered out of the small window, rubbing the stubble on his chin speculatively. The sun was higher in the sky than the day before... or he was late. Christ! Gracchus was waiting for him at the docks! He whirled around gathering his clothes haphazardly. He needed to be at the dock with the letter, or there would be hell to pay. He looked regretfully at the wine bottle on the table, how had he overslept so badly?

He sniffed the wine bottle cautiously, and then again with growing conviction. 'Franca!' he shouted, dashing to the door, and flinging it open, but there was no answer. Well, he couldn't wait, he must get to the docks. Gracchus would be furious at having to wait for him.

The descent through the streets took him longer than he had anticipated. The wound in his foot had not been rested sufficiently and now there was hell to pay. He gritted his teeth and pushed on, limping his way through the pain. There would be time enough to rest up when he went into hiding, and perhaps Eva and Don Stecchi would experiment on him further with their apothecaries' potions and salves.

The prime bells rang just as he clattered down the steps to the quay where Gracchus had been loading the evening before with

Rais Murad. He winced as he reached the pavement, increasingly sure he could not walk another step without removing his boot. Six o'clock already! He was a full hour late. The quay seemed infinitely long as he hobbled down it, and he was so intent on the fiery agony pulsing through his leg that only a litany of continually repeated oaths prevented him from collapsing. He pulled up, clutching his thigh and stifled a moan. In his fervour he must have overshot the ship. He turned to look back the way he had come. Intent on his foot, he had passed the berth where Gracchus's vessel had been moored. But the berth was empty. The ship gone. Bewildered, he accosted an idling dockhand.

'You would be looking for *The Fortunato*?' the man asked slowly in broken Italian, chewing tobacco off-handedly as he spoke.

'The ship of Rais Murad, yes,' blurted Vanderville, nodding fervently.

The dockhand removed his chewing quid and spat on the floor. 'Sailed this morning. Last one out, I rekkin. You've missed her.'

'Have you seen a stout man, rather taller than my height, dressed strangely, walks with a limp, and wearing green spectacles?'

'The fat Baron made of gold? Yes. I seen him.' He scratched his head. 'He went onboard and left with the others. Didn't look much like he wanted to,' the man opined.

'What do you mean, man?' snapped Vanderville.

'Which he was carried onboard a-wailing and a-grinding of his teeth. If he wasn't the owner of the ship, I woulda opined that he was pressed against his will.'

Vanderville stared at him in mute horror.

'Not every soul is born to the sea. Some don't take to sailing much. Happen he was feared of the gripe, mebbe.' The man grimaced, spat again, resumed his quid, and ambled off down the quay.

'Wait!' Vanderville called after him. 'I need a ship. Who sails next? I can pay,' he put his hand in his pocket for his wallet and found nothing. It was gone, and with it all his money. And Gracchus's document too, he suddenly realised.

'The Order's galleys came in this morning, but they won't be leaving today, maybe not ever. You're too late for sailing out of here,' the dockhand laughed bleakly, and turning nimbly, disappeared into the morass of dockyard debris.

Vanderville spun furiously on his heel. Some ship must be putting to sea, he thought, and he needed to be on that ship. Hercule! He squinted across the harbour to the place where the Greek ships had lain. Gone, their berths empty.

As he gazed across the harbour one or two churches began pealing their bells once more. He turned to look at the city in bewilderment, had they missed the hour? He reached for von Seeau's watch, but that too was gone. Furious, he commenced a search of his pockets, and it was in the tail pocket of his coat that he found it. A bundle of documents tied together with string. The merest scan confirmed his suspicions. Here, at last, were the elusive Mayflower documents: names, motivations, reports of clandestine plans and proposals for the surrender of the island to the French. All written up in a tiny, crabbed hand. And delivered to him by Franca while he slept the sleep of the drugged. He marvelled at her ingenuity.

The resonance of further bells came from the far heights of the city. Gradually the sound was picked up by other towers and repeated until every cupola, every campanile in the city was clamouring. The sonorous, the bass, the trilling, all calling in unison. The effect was magnificent, and not to be outdone, the bells of the other cities around the harbour responded, the sound leaping across the water and arriving in great deafening waves against the harbour side on which he stood.

He looked around expectantly, and realised that the Grand Harbour, normally so busy was strangely still. One or two small boats were adrift in the great basin, but their crews were inactive. There was none of the bustling activity common to sailors or fishermen going about their tasks. Those onboard were all gazing out to sea, towards the mouth of the great harbour. He took off his hat and used it to shade his eyes as he followed their gaze. Beyond the walls of Sant' Elmo an extraordinary sight awaited him.

The sea, as far as his eyes could reach, was covered with the masts of innumerable ships, like a great floating forest. The fleet stretched from horizon to horizon, and before it, one or two fishing smacks were racing for the shelter of harbour. The great guns of the knight's fortress began to boom out the alarm and Vanderville sat down despairing on a bollard and put his head in his hands.

Historical notes

This story contains a hearty mixture of real and invented characters. On the whole, the knights belong to the former category and the Maltese to the latter, although in the case of the Bavarian knights I have borrowed little from history but their names. The name Vassallo is purloined from a real Maltese patriot, who was more fortunate than his fictional counterpart, and survived the events of 1798.

Vanderville's leap is of course, a fictional event. As noted in the text, the account of a previous leap during the great siege was impossible, as the outer curtain fortifications present in 1797 had yet to be constructed and the topography of the shoreline was altered during building work. However, based on the channel's proximity to the ramparts today, and the distances involved, it is just possible that Vanderville's story is true...

The institution of slavery in Malta, along with much of the Mediterranean territory, was much as described here. The French Republic, after five shameful years of prevarication, had abolished the trade in enslaved people in 1794, and those slaves found on Malta after the French descent were liberated as a consequence of the island becoming French territory. A great number of these liberated individuals found themselves conscripted into the ranks of the French army and carried to north Africa: the very secondary evil that Gracchus sought to prevent.

The tangled and tightly interwoven networks of secret societies in eighteenth-century civil life are represented accurately. Despite the Church's disapproval, Freemasonry was so ubiquitous among the aristocratic classes as to be no more socially notorious than any of the other minor sins the nobility indulged in. However, the brethren were still considered by many in authority to be a threat to the social order and suspected of having been instrumental in both the American and the French revolutions. Correspondingly, they periodically suffered persecution and surveillance in many states.

The decayed situation and lack of purpose of the Order of the Knights of Malta in the final period of their stewardship of Malta is well documented. Their glory days were well past, and the institution was struggling to find a relevant role in the new Europe. The French Revolution had struck a body blow to their sources of funding, and while they were reeling, Bonaparte finished them off and brought their tenure as masters of Malta to an end. He was merely the first in a pack of vultures waiting to descend on the island, jealous of its strategic location, natural beauty, famous fortifications, and human resources. The Maltese would have to wait another century and a half for independence.

The author may appear on occasion in these pages to have dealt with the Order of St John a little roughly. The year of 1797 found an organisation that had been the wonder of Europe two hundred years earlier at a particularly low ebb. It bore little resemblance to that militant marvel led through the Great Siege by heroes, or indeed to the reformed Order of our own times. The Maltese people, on the other hand, are depicted here much as they are today: hardy, dogmatic, endlessly resourceful and proudly independent.

Acknowledgements

I am particularly grateful to Nicki Bianchi and Annabelle Malia for their hospitality and guidance on Maltese matters. If any errors remain in the manuscript, the fault lies entirely on my side.